Year of Wonders

Geraldine Brooks is the author of two acclaimed works of non-fiction, *Nine Parts of Desire* and *Foreign Correspondence*. She is also a former war correspondent whose writing has appeared in publications such as the *Wall Street Journal*, the *New York Times* and the *Guardian*. *Year of Wonders* is her first novel.

'Geraldine Brooks's *Year of Wonders* is a wonder indeed: a marriage of language and story unlike anything I have ever read. Read it for the inventiveness of the language alone – a real treat.' Anita Shreve

'*Year of Wonders* is a staggering fictional debut that matches journalistic accumulation of detail to natural narrative flair. Brooks has been posted to some of the most hellish combat zones of the modern world; but her most harrowing assignment has been the interior world of her historical imagination.' *Guardian*

'Very well-written, atmospheric . . . The plot is gripping, I like the psychological subtlety of characters struggling with a shifting world, and it's packed with historical detail.' *Daily Mail*

'With an intensely observant eye, a rigorous regard for period detail, and assured, elegant prose, Brooks re-creates a year in the life of a remote British village decimated by the Bubonic plague . . . Brooks keeps readers glued through starkly dramatic episodes and a haunting story of flawed, despairing human beings. This poignant and powerful account carries the pulsing beat of a sensitive imagination and the challenge of moral complexity.' *Publishers Weekly*

'An evocative historical novel . . . Geraldine Brooks displays a natural gift for characterisation and narrative, with the result that *Year of Wonders* is a riveting read.' *Scotland on Sunday*

Also by Geraldine Brooks

NON-FICTION

Foreign Correspondence:
A Pen Pal's Journey from Down Under
to All Over

Nine Parts of Desire:
The Hidden World of Islamic Women

Year of Wonders

a novel of the Plague

GERALDINE BROOKS

●
HARPER PERENNIAL
London, New York, Toronto and Sydney

This paperback edition first published in 2002
First published in Great Britain in 2001 by Fourth Estate
A Division of HarperCollins*Publishers*
77–85 Fulham Palace Road,
London w6 8jb
www.4thestate.com

7

A catalogue record for this book is available from the
British Library.

ISBN 1-84115-458-X

Typeset by Palimpsest Book Production Limited,
Polmont, Stirlingshire
Printed and bound in Great Britain by
Clays Ltd, St Ives plc

For Tony.
Without you, I never would
have gone there.

O let it be enough what thou hast done,
When spotted deaths ran arm'd through every street,
With poison'd darts, which not the good could shun,
The speedy could outfly, or valiant meet.

The living few, and frequent funerals then,
Proclaim'd thy wrath on this forsaken place:
And now those few who are return'd agen
Thy searching judgments to their dwellings trace.

From *Annus Mirabilis, The Year of Wonders,
1666*, by John Dryden

Leaf-Fall,
1666

Apple-picking Time

I used to love this season. The wood stacked by the door, the tang of its sap still speaking of forest. The hay made, all golden in the low afternoon light. The rumble of the apples tumbling into the cellar bins. Smells and sights and sounds that said this year it would be all right: there'd be food and warmth for the babies by the time the snows came. I used to love to walk in the apple orchard at this time of the year, to feel the soft give underfoot when I trod on a fallen fruit. Thick, sweet scents of rotting apple and wet wood. This year, the hay stooks are few and the woodpile scant, and neither matters much to me.

They brought the apples yesterday, a cartload for the rectory cellar. Late pickings, of course: I saw brown spots on more than a few. I had words with the carter over it, but he told me we were lucky to get as good as we got, and I suppose it's true enough. There are so few people to do the picking. So few people to do anything. And those of us who are left walk around as if we're half asleep. We are all so tired.

I took an apple that was crisp and good and sliced it, thin as paper, and carried it into that dim room where he sits, still and silent. His hand is on the Bible, but he never opens it. Not anymore. I asked him if he'd like me to read it to him. He turned his head to look at me, and I started. It was the first time he'd looked at me in days. I'd forgotten what his eyes could do – what they could make us do – when he stared down from the pulpit and held us, one by one, in his gaze. His eyes are the same, but his face has altered so, drawn and haggard, each line etched deep. When he came here, just three years since, the whole village made a jest of his youthful looks and laughed at the idea of being preached at by such a pup. If they saw him now, they would not laugh, even if they could remember how to do so.

'You cannot read, Anna.'

'To be sure, I can, Rector. Mrs. Mompellion taught me.'

He winced and turned away as I mentioned her, and instantly I regretted it. He does not trouble to bind his hair these days, and from where I stood the long, dark fall of it hid his face, so that I could not read his expression. But his voice, when he spoke again, was composed enough. 'Did she so? Did she so?' he muttered. 'Well, then, perhaps one day I'll hear you and see what kind of a job she made of it. But not today, thank you, Anna. Not today. That will be all.'

A servant has no right to stay, once she's dismissed. But I did stay, plumping the cushion, placing a shawl. He won't let me lay a fire. He won't let me give him even that little bit of comfort. Finally, when I'd run out of things to pretend to do, I left him.

In the kitchen, I chose a couple of the spotted apples I'd culled from the buckets and walked out to the stables. The courtyard hadn't been swept in a sennight. It smelled of rotting straw and horse piss. I had to hitch up my skirt to keep it off the muck. Before I was halfway across, I could hear the thud of his horse's rump as he turned and strutted in his confinement, gouging clefts into the floor of the stall. There's no one strong or skilled enough now to handle him.

The stable boy, whose job it was to keep the courtyard raked, was asleep on the floor of the tack room. He jumped when he saw me, making a great show of searching for the snath that had slipped from his hand when he'd dozed off. The sight of the scythe blade still upon his workbench vexed me, for I'd asked him to mend it long since, and the timothy now was naught but blown seed head and no longer worth the cutting. I was set to scold him about this, and about the filth outside, but his poor face, so pinched and exhausted, made me swallow the words.

Dust motes sparkled in the sudden shaft of sunlight as I opened the stable door. The horse stopped his pawing, holding one hoof aloft and blinking in the unfamiliar glare. Then he reared up on his muscled haunches and punched the air, saying, as plainly as he could, 'If you aren't him, get out of here.' Although I don't know when a brush was last laid on him, his coat still gleamed like bronze where the light touched it. When Mr. Mompellion had arrived here on this horse, the common talk had been that such a fine stallion was no fit steed for a priest. And people liked not to hear the rector calling him Anteros, after one of the old Puritans told them it was the name of a pagan idol. When I made so bold as to ask Mr. Mompellion about it, he had only laughed and said that even Puritans should recall that pagans, too, are children of God and their stories part of His creation.

I stood with my back pressed against the stall, talking gently to the great horse. 'Ah, I'm so sorry you're cramped up in here all day. I brought you a small something.' Slowly, I reached into the pocket of my pinafore and held out an apple. He turned his massive head a little, showing me the white of one liquid eye. I kept prattling, softly, as I used to with the children when they were scared or hurt. 'You like apples. I know you do. Go on, then, and have it.' He pawed the ground again, but with less conviction. Slowly, his nostrils flaring as he studied the scent of the apple, and of me, he stretched his broad neck toward me. His mouth was soft as a glove, and warm, as it brushed my hand, taking the apple in a single bite. As I reached into my pocket for the second one, he tossed his head and the apple juice sprayed. He was up now, angrily boxing the air, and I knew I'd lost the moment. I dropped the other apple on the floor of the stall and slid out quickly, resting my back against the closed door, wiping a string of horse spittle from my face. The stable boy slid his eyes at me and went silently on with his mending.

Well, I thought, it's easier to bring a small comfort to that poor beast than it is to his master. When I came back into the house, I could hear the rector out of his chair, pacing. The rectory floors are old and thin, and I could follow his steps by the creak of the boards. Up and back he walked, up and back, up and back. If only I could get him downstairs, to do his pacing in the garden. But once, when I suggested it, he looked as if I'd proposed something as ambitious as a trek up the White Peak. When I went to fetch his plate, the apple slices were all there, untouched, turning brown. Tomorrow, I'll start to work with the cider press. He'll take a drink without noticing sometimes, even when I can't get him to eat anything. And it's no use letting a cellar full of fruit go bad. If there's one thing I can't stand anymore, it's the scent of a rotting apple.

At day's end, when I leave the rectory for home, I prefer to walk through the orchard on the hill rather than go by the road and risk meeting people. After all we've been through together, it's just not possible to pass with a polite, 'Good night t'ye.' And yet I haven't the strength for more. Sometimes, not often, the orchard can bring back better times to me. These memories of happiness are fleeting things, reflections in a stream, glimpsed all broken for a second and then swept away in the current of grief that is our life now. I can't say that I ever feel what it felt like then, when I was happy. But sometimes something will touch the place where that feeling was, a touch as slight and swift as the brush of a moth's wing in the dark.

In the orchard of a summer night, if I close my eyes, I can hear the small voices of children: whispers and laughter, running feet and rustling leaves. Come this time of year, it's Sam that I think of – strong Sam Frith grabbing me around the waist and lifting me into the low, curved branch of a gnarly, old tree. I was just fifteen. 'Marry me,' he said. And why wouldn't I? My father's croft had ever been a joyless place. My father loved a pot better than he loved his children, though he kept on getting them, year passing year. To my stepmother, Aphra, I was always a pair of hands before I was a person, someone to toil after her babies. Yet it was she who spoke up for me, and it was her words that swayed my father to give his assent. In his eyes I was but a child still, too young to be handfasted. 'Open your eyes, husband, and look at her,' said Aphra. 'You're the only man in the village who doesn't. Better she be wedded early to Frith than bedded untimely by some youth with a prick more upright than his morals.'

Sam Frith was a miner with his own good lead seam to work. He had a fine small cottage and no children from a first wife who'd died. It did not take him long to give me children. Two sons in three years. Three good years. I should say, for there are many now too young to remember it, that it was not a time when we were raised up thinking to be happy. The Puritans, who are few amongst us now, and sorely pressed, had the running of this village then. It was their sermons we grew up listening to in a church bare of adornment, their notions of what was heathenish that hushed the Sabbath and quieted the church bells, that took the ale from the tavern and the lace from the dresses, the ribands from the Maypole and the laughter out of the public lanes. So the happiness I got from my sons, and from the life that Sam provided, burst on me as sudden as the first spring thaw.

When it all turned to hardship and bleakness again, I was not surprised. I went calmly to the door that terrible night with the torches smoking and the voices yelling and the men with their faces all black so that they looked headless in the dark. The orchard can bring back that night, too, if I let my mind linger there. I stood in the doorway with the baby in my arms, watching the torches bobbing and weaving crazy lines of light through the trees. 'Walk slow,' I whispered. 'Walk slow, because it won't be true until I hear the words.' And they did walk slow, trudging up that little hill as if it were a mountain. But slow as they came, in the end they arrived, jostling and shuffling. They pushed the biggest one, Sam's friend, out in front. There was a mush of rotten apple on his boot. Funny thing to notice, but I suppose I was looking down so that I wouldn't have to look into his face.

They were four days digging out Sam's body. They took it straight to the sexton's instead of bringing it home to me. They tried to keep me from it, but I wouldn't be kept. I would do that last thing for him. She knew. 'Tell them to let her go to him,' Elinor Mompellion said to the rector in that gentle voice of hers. Once she spoke, it was over. She so rarely asked anything of him. And once Michael Mompellion nodded, they parted, those big men, moving aside and letting me through.

To be sure, there wasn't much there that was him. But what there was, I tended. That was two years ago. Since then, I've tended so many bodies, people I loved and people I barely knew. But Sam's was the first. I bathed him with the soap he liked, because he said it smelled of the children. Poor slow Sam. He never quite realized that it was the children who smelled of the soap. I washed them in it every night before he came home. I made it with heather blooms, a much gentler soap than the one I made for him. His soap was almost all grit and lye. It had to be, to scrape that paste of sweat and soil

8

from his skin. He would bury his poor tired face in the babies' hair and breathe the fresh scent of them. It was the closest he got to the airy hillsides. Down in the mine at daybreak, out again after sundown. A life in the dark. And a death there, too.

And now it is Elinor Mompellion's Michael who sits all day in the dark, with the shutters closed. And I try to serve him, although sometimes I feel that I'm tending just another in that long procession of dead. But I do it. I do it for her. I tell myself I do it for her. Why else would I do it, after all?

I open the door to my cottage these evenings on a silence so thick it falls upon me like a blanket. Of all the lonely moments of my day, this one is always the loneliest. I confess I have sometimes been reduced to muttering my thoughts aloud like a madwoman when the need for a human voice becomes too strong. I mislike this, for I fear the line between myself and madness is as fine these days as a cobweb, and I have seen what it means when a soul crosses over into that dim and wretched place. But I, who always prided myself on grace, now allow myself a deliberate clumsiness. I let my feet land heavily. I clatter the hearth tools. And when I draw water, I let the bucket chain grind on the stone, just to hear ragged noise instead of the smothering silence.

When I have a tallow stub, I read until it gutters. Mrs. Mompellion always allowed me to take the stubs from the rectory, and although there are very few nowadays, I do not know how I would manage without. For the hour in which I am able to lose myself in someone else's thoughts is the greatest relief I can find from the burden of my own memories. The volumes, too, I bring from the rectory, as Mrs. Mompellion bade me borrow any book I chose. When the light is gone, the nights are long, for I sleep badly, my arms reaching in slumber for my babies' small, warm bodies, jolting suddenly wakeful when I do not find them.

Mornings are generally much kinder to me than evenings, full as they are of birds' songs and fowls' clucking and the ordinary promise that comes with any sunrise. I keep a cow now, a boon that I was not in purse to have in the days when Jamie or Tom could have benefited from the milk. I found her last winter, wandering gaunt in the middle of the road, her hide draped loose upon her bony nethers. Her big eyes looked at me with such a vacant, hopeless stare that I felt I was gazing into a mirror. My neighbours' cottage was empty, the ivy already creeping across the windows and the grey lichens crusting the sills. So I drove her inside and fitted it up as her boose, fattening her through the cold months with their oats – abundant food of which the dead had no need. She had her calf alone there, without complaint. By the time I found him I guess he had been born two hours, his back and sides dried out but still wet behind the ears. I helped him get his first drink, putting my fingers in his mouth and squirting her teat between them onto his slippery tongue. In return, the next night I stole a bit of her rich, yellow birth milk to make a beastings pie, baked with egg and sugar, and took it to Mr. Mompellion, rejoicing when he ate it as if he were my child, thinking how Elinor would be glad of it. The little bull calf is sleek now, and his mother's brown eyes regard me with a kindly patience. I love to lean my head against her warm flank and breathe the scent of her hide as the steaming milk foams into my bucket. I carry it to the rectory to make a posset or churn sweet butter or skim the cream to serve with a dish of blackberries – whatever I think will best tempt Mr. Mompellion. When I have enough in the pail for our small needs, I turn her out to graze. She has fattened so since last winter that every day now I fear she will lodge halfway through the doorway.

Apple-picking Time

Bucket in hand, I leave the cottage by the front door, for in the mornings I feel more able to meet whomever might be abroad. We live all aslant here, on this steep flank of the great White Peak. We are always tilting forwards to toil uphill, or bracing backwards on our heels to slow a swift descent. Sometimes, I wonder what it would be like to live in a place where the land did not angle so, and people could walk upright with their eyes on a straight horizon. Even the main street of our town has a camber to it, so that the people on the uphill side stand higher than those on the downhill.

Our village is a thin thread of dwellings, unspooling east and west of the church. The main road frays here and there into a few narrower paths that lead to the mill, to Bradford Hall, the larger farms, and the lonelier crofts. We have always built here with what we have to hand, so our walls are hewn of the common grey stone and the roofs thatched with heather. Behind the cottages on either side of the road lie tilled fields and grazing commons, but these end abruptly in a sudden rise or fall of ground: the looming Edge to the north of us, its sheer stone face sharply marking the end of settled land and the beginning of the moors, and to the south, the swift, deep dip of the Dale.

It is a strange prospect, our main street these days. I used to rue its dustiness in summer and muddiness in winter, the rain all rizen in the wheel ruts making glassy hazards for the unwary stepper. But now there is neither ice nor mud nor dust, for the road is grassed over, with just a cow-track down the centre where the slight use of a few passing feet has worn the weeds down. For hundreds of years, the people of this village pushed Nature back from its precincts. It has taken less than a year to begin to reclaim its place. In the very middle of the street, a walnut shell lies broken, and from it, already, sprouts a sapling that wants to grow up to block our way entire. I have watched it from its first seed leaves, wondering when someone would pull it out. No one has yet done so, and now it stands already a yard high. Footprints testify that we are all walking round it. I wonder if it is indifference, or whether, like me, others are so brimful of endings that they cannot bear to wrench even a scrawny sapling from its tenuous grip on life.

I made my way to the rectory gate without meeting any soul. So my guard was down and I was unready to face the person who, in all the world, I least wished to see. I had entered the gate and had my back turned to the house, refastening the latch, when I heard the rustle of silk behind me. I turned suddenly, slopping milk from my bucket as I did so. Elizabeth Bradford scowled as a droplet landed on the aubergine hem of her gown. 'Clumsy!' she hissed. And so I reencountered her much as I had last seen her more than one year earlier; sour-faced and spoiled. But the habits of a lifetime are hard-shed, and I had dropped into a curtsy without willing it, my body acting despite the firm resolve of my mind to show this woman no such deference.

Typically, she did not even bother with a greeting. 'Where is Mompellion?' she demanded. 'I have been rapping upon that door for a good quarter hour. Surely he cannot be so early abroad?'

I made my voice unctuously polite. 'Miss Bradford,' I said, ignoring her question, 'it is a great surprise, and an honour unlooked for, to see you here in our village. You left us in such haste, and so long since, that we had despaired of ever more being graced by your presence.'

Elizabeth Bradford's pride was so overweening and her understanding so limited that she heard only the words and missed the tone. 'Indeed.' She nodded. 'My parents were well aware that our departure would leave an unfillable gap here. They have always felt their obligations most keenly. It was, as you know, that sense of obligation that caused them to remove us all from Bradford Hall, to preserve the health of our family so that we could continue to fulfil our responsibilities. Surely Mompellion read my father's letter to the parish?'

'He did,' I replied. I did not add that he had used it as an occasion to preach one of the most incendiary sermons we ever had from him.

'So, where is he? I have been kept waiting long enough already, and my business is urgent.'

'Miss Bradford, I must tell you that the rector sees no one at present. The late events in this place, and his own grievous loss, have left him exhausted and quite unequal to shouldering the burdens of the parish at this time.'

'Well, that may be, insofar as the normal run of parishioners is concerned. But he does not know that my family is returned here. Be so good as to inform him that I require to speak with him at once.'

I saw no purpose in further discourse with this woman. And I have to own that I was consumed with curiosity to see if the news of the Bradfords' return would rouse Mr. Mompellion, or draw forth any sign of feeling. Perhaps wrath could rouse him where charity had not. Perhaps he needed to be singed by just such a brand.

I swept by her and walked on ahead to open the rectory's great door. She pinched her face at this; she was not accustomed to sharing a doorway with servants, and I could see she had expected me to pass to the kitchen garth and then come and let her in with accustomed ceremony. Well, times had changed in the Bradfords' absence, and the sooner she accustomed herself to the inconveniences of the new era the better.

She pushed past me and found her own way to the parlour, pulling off her gloves and flicking them impatiently against the palm of her hand. I saw the surprise in her face as she registered the bareness of the room, stripped as it was of all its former comforts. I went on to the kitchen. No matter how urgent her business, she would have to wait until Mr. Mompellion broke his fast, since that scant serving of oatcake and brawn was the only meal I knew with any certainty that he would take. She was pacing, barely able to contain herself, as I passed by some minutes later with the laden tray. I glimpsed her through the open door. Her brow was drawn so low, her scowl so deep, that she looked as if someone had grabbed her face from beneath and dragged it groundwards. Upstairs, I took a minute to compose myself before I knocked on the door. I did not want to say, or look, more than I should when I announced to the rector his caller.

'Come,' he said. He was standing by the window when I entered, and the shutters, for once, were opened. His back was to me as he spoke. 'Elinor would be sorry to see what has become of her garden,' he said.

I did not know at first how to answer that. To speak the evident truth – yes, indeed, she would – seemed likely only to feed his gloom. To deny his proposition would be a falsehood.

'I expect she would understand why it is so,' I said, bending to set out the dishes from his tray. 'And even if we had hands enough to do the ordinary tasks – to pull the weeds and prune the dead-wood – yet it would not be her garden. We would lack her eye. What made it her garden was the way she could look at a handful of tiny seeds in the bareness of winter and imagine how they would be, months later, sunlit and in flower. It was as if she painted with blooms.'

When I straightened, he had turned and was staring at me. The shock of it went through me once again.

'You *knew* her!' He said it as if it had only just come to him.

To cover my confusion, I blurted out what I had hoped to convey with care. 'Miss Bradford is in the parlour. The family is returned to the Hall. She says she needs to speak with you urgently.'

What happened next astonished me so much that I almost dropped the tray. He laughed. A rich, amused laugh the like of which I hadn't heard for so long I'd forgotten the sound of it.

'I know. I saw her. Banging on my door like a siege engine. Truly, I thought she meant to break it down.'

'What answer should I give her, Rector?'

'Tell her to go to Hell.'

When he saw my face, he laughed again. My eyes must have been wide as chargers. Wiping a tear of mirth from his own, he struggled for composure. 'No, I see. You can barely be expected to carry such a message. Put it into whatever words you like, but convey to Miss Bradford that I will not see her, and get her from this house.'

It was as if there were two of me, walking down those stairs. One of them was the timid girl who had worked for the Bradfords in a state of dread, fearing their hard looks and harsh words. The other was Anna Frith, a woman who had faced more terrors than many warriors. Elizabeth Bradford was a coward. She was the daughter of cowards. As I entered the parlour and faced her thunderous countenance, I knew I had nothing more to fear from her.

'I am sorry, Miss Bradford, but the rector is unable to see you at present.' I kept my voice as level as I could, but as her jaw worked in that angry face, I found myself thinking of my cow worrying at her cud, and I felt the contagion of Mr. Mompellion's strange fit of mirth. It was all I could do then to keep my composure and continue. 'He is, as I said, not currently performing any pastoral duties, nor does he go into society or receive any person.'

'How dare you smirk at me, you insolent slattern!' she cried. 'He will not refuse me, he dare not. Out of my way!' She moved for the door, but I was quicker, blocking her path like a collie facing down an unruly tup. We stared at each other for a long moment. 'Oh, very well,' she said, picking up her gloves from the mantel as if purposing to leave. I stood aside then, meaning to show her to the front door, but instead, she pushed past me and was upon the steps to Mr. Mompellion's room when the rector himself appeared on the landing.

'Miss Bradford,' he said, 'do me the kindness of remaining where you are.' His voice was low but its jussive tone stopped her. He had shed the hunched posture of the past months and stood tall and straight. He had lost flesh, but now, as he stood there, animated at last, I could see that gauntness had not ravaged him but rather given his face a kind of distinction. There had been a time when, if you looked at him when he was not speaking, you might have called his a plain face, save for the deep-set grey eyes that were striking, always, for their expressiveness. Now, the hollowness of his cheeks called attention to those eyes, so that you could not take your gaze from them.

'I would be obliged if you would refrain from insulting members of my household whilst they are carrying out my instructions,' he said. 'Please be good enough to allow Mrs. Frith to show you to the door.'

'You can't do this!' Miss Bradford replied, but this time in the tone of a very young child who has been thwarted in its pursuit of a plaything. The rector was standing half a flight of stairs above her, so that she had to gaze up at him like a supplicant. 'My mother has need of you . . .'

'My dear Miss Bradford,' he interrupted coldly. 'There were many people here with needs this past year, needs that you and your family were in a position to have satisfied. And yet you were not . . . here. Kindly ask your mother to do me the honour of advancing the same tolerance for my absence now that your family arrogated for so long in regard to its own.'

She was flushed now, her face a blotchy patchwork. Suddenly, surprisingly, she began to cry. 'My father is not any longer . . . my father does not . . . It is my mother. My mother is very ill. She fears . . . she believes she will die of it. The Oxford surgeon swore it was a tumour but there is no question now . . . Please, Reverend Mompellion, her mind is much disordered; she will take no rest and speaks of nothing but seeing you. That is why we are come back here, that you may console her and help her face her death.'

He was silent for a long moment, and I felt sure that his next words would be a request to me to look out his coat and hat so that he could go to the Hall. His face, when he spoke, was sad, as I had so often seen it. But his voice was strange and rough.

'If your mother seeks me out to give her absolution like a Papist, then she has made a long and uncomfortable journey to no end. Let her speak direct to God to ask forgiveness for her conduct. But I fear she may find Him a poor listener, as many of us here have done.' And with that he turned his back and climbed the stairs to his room, closing the door behind him.

Elizabeth Bradford threw out a hand to steady herself and gripped the banister until bone of her knuckles showed through the skin. She was trembling, her shoulders shaking with sobs that she struggled to suppress. Instinctively, I went to her. Despite my years of aversion for her, and hers of contempt for me, she folded up into my arms like a child. I had meant to help her to the door, but she was in such a state that I could not bring myself to shove her out, though it was clearly the rector's wish that she be gone. Instead, I found myself shepherding her to the kitchen and easing her down upon the bucket bench. There, she gave herself up so completely to sobbing that the little piece of lace she used as a handkin was soaked through. I held out a dishclout, and to my astonishment she took it and blew her nose as indelicately and unselfconsciously as an urchin. I offered her a mug of water and she drank it thirstily. 'I said the family was back, but in truth it is just my mother and me and our own servants. I do not know how I can help her, she grieves so. My father will have none of her ever since he learned the truth of her condition. My mother has no tumour. But what she has, at her age, may surely kill her just the same. And my father says he cares not. He has ever been cruel to her, but now he excels himself in his wretchedness. He is saying the most terrible things . . . He has called his own wife whore . . .' And there she finally stopped herself. She had said more than she intended. Far more than she should. Rising from the bench as if it had suddenly turned to a hob that was blistering her noble backside, she squared her shoulders and handed me the soiled dish-clout and the empty mug without a thank you. 'I can find my own way out,' she said, brushing past me without a glance. I did not follow her, but I knew she was gone by the slam of the great oaken door.

It was only with her going that I gave myself pause to be aston-ished by what Mr. Mompellion had said to her. His mind had become even darker than I had thought. I was concerned for him. I did not know what I could do to bring him comfort. Nevertheless, I climbed the stairs to his room as quietly as I could and listened outside his door. Inside there was silence. I knocked gently, and when he did not answer I opened the door. He was seated with his head in his hands. The Bible, as always, was beside him, unopened. I had a sudden, keen memory of him, sitting just so, at the end of one of the darkest days of the past winter. The difference was that Elinor had been seated beside him, her gentle voice reading from the Psalms. It was as if I heard it still, a low hum, so soothing, broken only by the soft rustle as she turned the pages. Without asking his leave, I picked up the Bible and turned to a passage I knew well:

'Bless the Lord, O my soul;
And forget not all his benefits,
Who forgives all your iniquity,
Who heals all your diseases,
Who redeems your life from the Pit . . .'

He rose from his chair and took the book from my hand. His voice was low, but brittle. 'Very well read, Anna. I see my Elinor may add a credential as a fine teacher to her catalogue of excellent qualities. But why did you not choose this one?' He flipped a few pages, and began to declaim:

'Your wife will be like a fruitful vine
Within your house;
Your children will be like olive shoots
Around your table . . .'

He raised his eyes and glared at me. Then slowly, deliberately, he opened his hand. The book slipped from his fingers. Instinctively, I leapt forward to catch it, but he grabbed my arm, and the Bible hit the floor with a dull thump.

We stood there, face-to-face, his hand tightening on my forearm until I thought he might break it. 'Rector,' I said, struggling to control my voice. At that, he dropped my arm as if it were a burning brand and raked his hand through his hair. The pressure of his grip had left a welt, throbbing. I could feel the tears welling in my eyes, and I turned away so that he would not see them. I did not ask his leave to go.

Spring,
1665

Ring of Roses

T he winter that followed Sam's death in the mine was the hardest season I had ever known. So, in the following spring, when George Viccars came banging on my door looking for lodging, I thought God had sent him. Later, there were those who would say it had been the Devil.

Little Jamie came running to tell me, all flushed and excited, tripping over his feet and his words. 'There a man, mummy. There a man at the door.'

George Viccars swept his hat from his head as I came from the garth, and he kept his gaze down on the floor, respectfully. Different from all those men who look you over like a beef at saleyard. When you're a widow at eighteen, you grow used to those looks and hard towards the men who give them.

'If you please, Mistress Frith, they told me at the rectory you might have a room to let.'

He was a journeyman tailor, he said, and his own good, plain clothes told that he was a competent one. He was clean and neat even though he'd been on the road all the long way from Canterbury, and I suppose that impressed me. He had just secured a post with my neighbour, Alexander Hadfield, who presently had a surfeit of orders to fill. He seemed a modest man, and quiet-spoken, although when he told me he was prepared to pay sixpence a week for the attic space in my eaves, I'd have taken him if he was loud as a drunkard and muddy as a sow. I sorely missed the income from Sam's mine, for I was still nursing Tom, and my small earnings from the flock were only a little augmented by my mornings' work at the rectory and occasional service at the Hall, when they needed extra hands. Mr. Viccars's sixpence would mean a lot in our cottage. But by the end of the week, it was me who was ready to pay him. George Viccars brought laughter back into the house. And later, when I could think at all, I was glad that I could think about those days in the spring and the summer when Jamie was laughing.

The young Martin girl minded the baby and Jamie for me while I worked. She was a decent girl and watchful with the children but Puritan in her ways, thinking that laughter and fun are ungodly. Jamie misliked her sternness and was always so glad when he'd see me coming home that he'd rush to the door and grab me around the knees. But the day after Mr. Viccars arrived, Jamie wasn't at the door. I could hear his high little laugh coming from the hearth, and I remember wondering what had come over Jane Martin that she'd actually brought herself to play with him. When I got to the door, Jane was stirring the soup with her usual thin-lipped glare. It was Mr. Viccars who was on the floor, on all fours, with Jamie on his back, riding around the room, squealing with delight.

'Jamie! Get off poor Mr. Viccars!' I exclaimed. But Mr. Viccars just laughed, threw back his blond head, and neighed. 'I'm his horse, Mrs. Frith, if you've no objection. He's a very fine rider, and he rarely beats me with the whip.' The day after that, I came home and found Jamie decked out like a Harlequin in all the fabric scraps from Mr. Viccars's whisket. And the day after, the two of them were at work slinging oat sacks from the chairs to make a hiding house.

I tried to let George Viccars know how much I valued his kindness, but he brushed my thanks away. 'Ah, he's a fine little boy. His father must have been more than proud of him.' So I tried to repay him by making a better table than we might otherwise have had, and his praise for my cooking was generous. The neighbour towns at that time had no tailor, so Mr. Hadfield had work to spare for his new assistant. Mr. Viccars would sew long into the evening, burning down a whole rushlight as he sat late by the fire plying his needle. Sometimes, when I was not too tired, I would set myself some chore near the hearth to keep him company awhile, and he would reward me with many tales of the places he'd sojourned. He had seen much for a young man, and his powers of description were good. Like most in this village, I had no occasion to travel farther than the market town seven miles distant. Our closest city, Chesterfield, lies twice as far, and I never had cause to journey there. Mr. Viccars knew the great cities of London and York, the bustling port life of Plymouth, and the everchanging pilgrim trade at Canterbury. I was pleased to hear his stories of these places and the manner of life of the people biding there.

These were a kind of evening I'd never had with Sam, who looked to me for all his information of the tiny world for which he cared. He liked to hear only of the villagers he'd known since childhood, the small doings that defined their days. And so I gave him such news as the arrival of Martin Highfield's new bull calf and the expectation of Widow Hamilton for her wool-clip. He was content just to sit, exhausted, his big frame spilling from the chair that seemed so small when he was in it. I would prattle of what I'd heard of the villagers and the children's doings and he would let the words wash over him, gazing at me with a half smile no matter what I said. When I ran out of talk, his smile would widen and he'd reach for me. His hands were big, cracked things with broken, blackened nails, and his idea of lovemaking was a swift and sweaty tumble, a spasm and then sleep. Afterward, I would lie awake under the weight of his arm and try to imagine the dim recesses of his mind. Sam's world was a dark, damp maze of rakes and scrins thirty feet under the ground. He knew how to crack limestone with water and with fire; he knew the going rate for a dish of lead; he knew whose seams were likely to be Old Man before the year turned, and who had nicked whose claim up along the Edge. Inasmuch as he knew what love meant, he knew he loved me, and all the more so when I gave him the boys. His whole life was confined by these things.

Mr. Viccars seemed never to have been confined at all. When he entered our cottage, he brought the wide world with him. He had been born a Peakrill lad in a village near to Kinder Scout but had been sent off to Plymouth to take up tailoring, and in that port town had seen silk traders who traversed the Orient and had befriended lace makers even from among our enemies the Dutch. He could tell such tales: of Barbary seamen who wrapped their copper-coloured faces in turbans of rich indigo; of a Musalman merchant who kept four wives all veiled so that each moved about with just one eye peeking from her shroud. He had gone to London at the end of his apprenticeship, for the return and restoration of King Charles II had created prosperity among all manner of trades. There, he had enjoyed much work sewing liveries for courtiers' servants. But the city had tired him.

'London is for the very young and the very rich,' he said. 'Others cannot long thrive there.' I smiled and said that since he had yet to pass his middle twenties he seemed young enough to me to be able to dodge footpads and withstand late nights in alehouses.

'Maybe so, Mistress,' he replied. 'But I grew tired of seeing no farther than the blackened wall at the opposite side of the street and hearing nothing but the racket of carriage wheels. I longed for space and for good air. You cannot believe that what men breathe in London really is air at all, for the coal fires send soot and sulphur everywhere, fouling the water and turning even the palaces into grimy, black hulks. The city is like a corpulent man trying to fit himself into the jerkin he wore as a boy. So many have moved there looking for work that souls are heaped up to live ten and twelve to a room no larger than the one we sit in. Poor souls have tried to add on to their dwellings and garner space as they can, so that misshapen parts of buildings lean out across the alleyways and teeter high atop decaying roofs that you wonder can hold the weight. The gutters and spouts are fixed on any how, so that even long after rain has passed, the wet drips down upon you to leave you always clammy damp.'

He had also grown weary, he said, of gentlemen who bespoke a household's liveries and then left him to wait a year or more for the settlement of his accounts. 'And I can tell you that by then I felt myself lucky to be paid at all,' he added, for he had had colleagues driven destitute by lordly defaulters.

When he had ascertained I was not by any means of a Puritan bent, he shared with me some tales of the bawdiness and carousing he had witnessed in the city after the king sailed home from exile. At first I felt sure he embroidered these as skilfully as the fabrics under his hand, and so I challenged him one evening, as we sat companionably, he on the floor, long legs crossed and draped with the linen piece he was stitching, me at the table, my fingers greasy as I patted out the oatcakes and slung them up on a string before the fire to dry.

'No, Mistress. If anything, I am exaggerating in the contrariwise direction, for I have no wish to offend you.'

I laughed at this and told him I was not too nice to hear the truth and wished to know how things stood in the world. I may have urged him too much in this way, or perhaps it was the second mug of my own good ale that I poured for him, for he launched then into some tales of the king travelling in disguise to a whorehouse and having his pockets thoroughly picked there. Mr. Viccars was surprised when I laughed at this and told him I hoped the lady in question made off with a king's ransom, for certainly she had earned it in servicing such a one and many worse.

'You don't blame her for choosing a living of lustfulness and debauchery?' he enquired, his eyebrow raised in mock severity.

'May be I might,' I replied. 'But before I blamed, I would like to know the extent of her choices in the hard world that you have described to me. If you are drowning in a sewer, your first concern might be that you are drowning, not how vile you smell.' Perhaps I spoke too frankly at this, for his next revelation about the works of the king's favourite poet, the Earl of Rochester, did shock me, so much so that I remember yet the main part of the lines he declaimed. Mr. Viccars was a fine mimic. Before he gave me the verses, he fixed his frank, open countenance into a parody of a foppish sneer and turned his own gentle voice into a lordly bray:

> 'I rise at eleven, I dine at two,
> I get drunk before seven, and the next thing I do
> I send for my whore when, for fear of the clap,
> I come in her hand and I spew in her lap . . .'

I didn't let him get any further in his recitation, stopping my ears with my hands and excusing myself directly, for truly although I am loath to judge others, I can scarce credit that the nobles and gentry who so stand upon their superiority to such as we can yet be so base as to make the worst of us seem like angels. Later, lying in my room with my babies curled on the pallet beside me, I was sorry I had acted so. I longed to learn about the places and the people that I could never hope to see, and now I feared I would appear such a prude to Mr. Viccars that he would no longer speak freely with me.

And surely the poor man looked mortified the next day, afraid that he had irrevocably offended me. I told him then that I had had it directly from our rector that knowledge is not itself evil, it is only the use to which one puts it that may imperil the soul. I said I was grateful for the insight into the state of our country's highest councils and would be more grateful still to hear other such poems, for are not all His Majesty's loyal subjects bound to strive to emulate their king? And so we made a jest of it, and as spring softened into summer, so we became more easy with each other.

Mr. Hadfield had ordered a box of cloth from London and there was great excitement when the parcel arrived, as there always is at the coming of goods from the city, with many in the village interested to see what manner of colour and figure might now be worn in town. Because the parcel arrived damp, having travelled the last of its journey in an open cart unprotected from rain, Mr. Hadfield asked Mr. Viccars to see to its drying, and so he contrived lines in the garth of our cottage and slung the fabrics out to air, thus giving everyone ample chance to look and comment. Jamie made a game of it, of course, running up and down between the flapping fabrics, pretending he was a knight at a joust.

Mr. Viccars was so well fixed with orders that I was surprised indeed when, just a few days after the London fabrics arrived, I returned from my work to find a dress of finespun wool lying folded on the pallet in my room. It was a golden green, the colour of sunlight-dappled leaves, of modest style, but well cut and flattering, its whisk and hands trimmed in Genoa lace. I'd never had so fine a thing – even for my handfast I'd worn the borrowed dress of a friend. And since Sam had died I'd been in the one shapeless smock of rough serge, Puritan black, innocent of any adornment. I expected to go on so, for neither my means nor my inclination had led me to look to bedecking myself. And yet I held the soft gown up to me and walked by the window, thrilled as a girl, trying to catch a glimpse of my reflection in the pane. It was in the glass I saw Mr. Viccars standing behind me, and I dropped the dress, embarrassed to be caught so immodestly preening. But he was smiling his big open smile, and he looked down deferentially when he grasped my mortified state.

'Forgive me, but I thought of you directly I sighted that cloth, for the green is exactly the colour of your eyes.'

I felt my face flush, and my vexation at blushing just made my cheeks and throat burn all the hotter. 'Good sir, you are kind, but I cannot accept this dress from you. You are here as my lodger, and glad I am to have such a one as you. But you must know that to be man and woman under one roof is a perilous matter. I fear that we approach too near to terms of friendship . . .'

'I would we may,' he interrupted quietly, his expression now serious and his eyes on mine. At that I blushed scarlet all over again and knew not how to answer him. His face also was rather flushed, and I wondered if he, too, was blushing. But then, as he took a step towards me, he staggered a little and had to fling a hand against the wall to steady himself. At this I felt a small surge of anger, thinking that he had been helping himself to the ale jar and preparing myself in case his behaviour began to resemble the grog-swilling oafs I had sometimes had to deal with since Sam died. But Mr. Viccars kept his hands to himself, raising them to his brow and rubbing at it, as if it pained him. 'Have the dress in any wise,' he said quietly. 'For I mean only to thank you for keeping a comfortable house and welcoming a stranger.'

'Sir, I thank you, but I cannot think it right,' I said, folding the gown and holding it out to him.

'Why do you not seek advice on the morrow when you are at the rectory?' he said. 'Surely if your pastor sees no harm in it, there may be found none?'

I saw some wisdom in what he proposed and assented to it. If not the rector – for I could not see opening my heart on such a matter to him – I knew that Mrs. Mompellion would know how to advise me. And there was still, I was surprised to discover, woman enough alive within me to want to wear that dress.

'Will you not at least try it upon yourself? For a workman likes to know where he stands in the mastery of his craft, and if you learn on the morrow that you mayn't accept this gift in all propriety, at least you will have rewarded my pains and gratified my pride of workmanship by letting me see how I have done.'

Did I do right, I wonder, in so readily agreeing to his suggestion? I stood there in the doorway, fingering the fine stuff, and my curiosity to have the dress upon my body overbore my sense of what was or was not fit to do. I waved Mr. Viccars down the stairs to await me and shrugged myself out of my rough tunic. For the first time in months, I noticed how dingy were the linens I wore beneath, blotched with sweat and stained by leaking milk. It seemed improper to put the new dress over these unclean things, so I slipped them off as well and stood for a moment, regarding my own body. Hard work and a lean winter had robbed me of the softness left behind after Tom's birth. Sam had liked me fleshy. I wondered what Mr. Viccars liked. The thought stirred me, so that my skin flushed and my throat tightened. I gathered up the green dress. It slid softly over my bare flesh. My body felt alive as it hadn't in a long time, and I knew quite well that only part of the reason was the feel of the dress. As I moved, the skirt swayed, and I felt an urge to move with it, to dance again like a girl.

Mr. Viccars had his back to me, warming his hands at the fire. When he heard my tread on the stair, he turned and caught his breath, and his face brightened in a smile of appreciation. I twirled, making the skirt swirl around me. He clapped his hands and then held them wide. 'Mistress, I would make you a dozen such gowns to display your beauty!' Then, the playful tone left his voice and it dropped, becoming husky. 'I would you might think me worthy to provide for you in all matters.' He crossed the room and placed his hands on my waist, drew me gently towards him, and kissed me. I will not say I know what would have happened then if his skin, when it brushed mine, had not been so hot that I pulled back.

'But you are fevered!' I exclaimed, reaching, as mothers will, to lay a hand on his forehead. Thus was a moment lost, for better or worse.

'It is true,' he said, releasing me and once again rubbing at his temples. 'All this day I have felt a grudging of ague, and now it rises and my head pounds, and I do feel a most dreadful ache probing at my bones.'

'Get you to your bed,' I said gently. 'I will give you a cooling draught to take up with you. We will speak again of these things on the morrow, when you are restored.'

I do not know how Mr. Viccars slept that night, but I rested ill, confused by a tumble of thoughts and reawakened feelings that were not entirely welcome to me. I lay a long time in the dark, listening to the babies breathe their slight, soft, animal breaths beside me. I closed my eyes and conjured the feel of Mr. Viccars's hands landing gently on my waist and tightening their grip there. I was like one who forgets all day to eat until the scent from some other's roasting pan reminds her she is ravenous. My hand reached in the darkness and closed around Tom's tiny, budlike fist, and I realized that though I loved the touch of my children's little hands, there was another kind of touch – hard and insistent – for which my body hungered.

In the morning, I rose before cock crow so as to accomplish my household chores before Mr. Viccars descended from his garret. I did not wish to encounter him until I had had more space to examine my desires. I left the children in their sleepy tangle, tiny Tom curled up like a nutmeat in its shell, Jamie's slender little arms flung wide across the pallet. They both smelled so sweet, lying there in their night-warmth. Their heads, covered in their father's fine, fair down, gleamed bright in the dimness. My heavy, dark hair could not have been more unlike their pale curls, but their small faces, insofar as you can discern such things in features so unformed, were said by everyone to favour my own looks more than their father's. I put my face to their necks and breathed the yeasty scent of them. God warns us not to love any earthly thing above Himself, and yet He sets in a mother's heart such a fierce passion for her babes that I do not comprehend how He can test us so.

Downstairs, I fanned the embers and relaid the fire and then went out to the well to draw the day's water, setting a big kettle to heat and drawing a basinful to wash myself as soon as the ground-chill had gone from it. Drawing more, I scrubbed the gritstone flags, and while they dried I drew my shawl around me and took my broth and bread out into the brightening garth, watching the sky's edge turn rosy and the mists rise from the two streams that bracket our hamlet. Our village has a fair prospect, and that morn the air was rich with summer's loamy fragrance. It was a morning fit for the contemplation of new beginnings, and as I watched a whinchat trailing a worm to feed his young, I wondered if I, too, should look for a helper in the rearing of my boys.

Sam had left me the cottage and the sheepfold behind, but they had nicked his stowe the day they brought his body out of the mine. I told them that day that they need not wait to nick it again, for three weeks, six weeks, or nine, I could neither shore the fallen walls nor was I in purse to have another do it. Jonas Howe has the seam now, and being a good man, and a friend of Sam's, he feels he has choused me, although why he should I know not, as it can hardly be a swindle when the law here time out of mind has made it plain that those who cannot pull a dish of lead from a mine within three nicks may not keep it. He said he would make miners of my boys alongside his own when they were of age. Though I thanked him for his promise, I was not sincere when I did so, for I firmly hoped not to see them in that rodent life, gnawing at rock, fearing flood and fire and crushing fall. But the tailoring trade was another gate's business, and I would be pleased to have them learn it. Beside, George Viccars was a good man with a quick understanding. I enjoyed his company. Certainly, I had not shrunk from his touch. I had married Sam for far less cause. But then again, I was not fifteen anymore, and choices no longer had that same clear, bright edge to them.

When I'd broken my fast I searched the bushes for a brace of eggs for Mr. Viccars and another for Jamie. My fowl are unruly and never will lay in their roost. Then I returned inside to knead the dough for the morrow's bread and covered it to rise in a bowl near to the fire. I decided to leave the remaining chores for the afternoon and returned upstairs to set Tom to my breast so that Jane Martin would find him with full belly when she arrived shortly to watch over him. As I hoped, he barely stirred as I lifted him, greeting me only with a single long stare before closing his eyes and commencing his contented suckling.

As a result of my early rising, I was at the rectory well before seven, and yet Elinor Mompellion was already in her garden, a pile of prunings rising high beside her. Unlike most ladies, Mrs. Mompellion did not scruple to toil with her hands. Especially she loved to work in her garden, and it was not uncommon to see her face as streaked with dirt as a charwoman's from carelessly pushing back wisps of hair that loosened as she dug and weeded.

At five and twenty, Elinor Mompellion had the fragile beauty of a child. She was all pale and pearly, her hair a fine, fair nimbus around skin so sheer that you could see the veins pulsing at her temples. Even her eyes were pale, a white-washed blue like a winter sky. When I'd first met her, she reminded me of the blow-ball of a dandelion, so insubstantial that a breath might carry her away. But that was before I knew her. The frail body was paired with a sinewy mind, capable of violent enthusiasms and possessed of a driving energy to make and do. Sometimes, it seemed as if the wrong soul had been placed inside that slight body, for she pushed herself to her limits and beyond, and was often ill as a result. There was something in her that could not, or would not, see the distinctions that the world wished to make between weak and strong, between women and men, labourer and lord.

The garden was fragrant that morning with the sharp tang of lavender. It seemed that the colours and patterns of the plantings changed by the day under her skilled hands, the misty blues of forget-me-nots ceding to the rich midnight larkspurs, then easing to the soft pinks of the mallow flowers. Under every window she had set bowpots of jessamine and gilly flowers so that the scents wafted sweetly through the house. Mrs. Mompellion called the garden her little Eden, and I believe God did not mislike her claim, for all manner of flowers flourished there, far beyond what are commonly expected to grow and thrive through the hard winters on this mountainside.

That morning I found her on her knees, deadheading the daisies. 'Good morning, Anna,' she said as she saw me. 'Did you know that the tea made of this unassuming little flower serves to cool a fever?

As a mother you'd do well to add some herb lore to your store of knowledge, for you never can be sure when your children's well-being might depend upon it.' Mrs. Mompellion never let a minute pass without trying to better me, and for the most part I was a willing pupil. When she had discovered that I hungered to learn, she commenced to shovel knowledge my way as vigorously as she spaded the cowpats into her beloved flower beds.

I was ready to take what she gave. I had always loved high language. My chief joy as a child had been to go to church, not because I was uncommonly good, but because I longed to listen to the fine words of the prayers. *Lamb of God, Man of Sorrows, Word made Flesh.* I would lose myself in the cadence of the phrases. Even as our pastor then, the old Puritan Stanley, denounced the litanies of the saints and the idolatrous prayers of the Papists for Mary, I clung to the words he decried. *Lily of the Valley, Mystic Rose, Star of the Sea. Behold the Handmaid of the Lord. Let it be done unto me according to Thy Word.* Once I realized that I could memorize bright snatches of the liturgy, I set myself to do it every Sunday, adding to my harvest like a farmer building his stook. Sometimes, if I could escape from under my stepmother's eye, I would linger in the churchyard, trying to copy the forms of the letters inscribed upon the tombstones. When I knew the names of the dead, I could match the shapes engraved there with the sounds I reasoned they must stand for. I used a sharpened stick for my pen and a patch of smoothed earth as my tablet.

Once, my father, carting a load of firewood to the rectory, came upon me so. I started when I saw him, so that the stick snapped in my hand and drove a splinter into my palm. Josiah Bont was a man of few words, and those mostly curses. I did not expect him to understand my strong longing towards what to him must surely seem a useless skill. I have said that he loved a pot. I should add that the pot did not love him, and made of him a sour and menacing creature.

I cringed from him that day, waiting for his fist to fall. He was a big man, ever quick with a blow – and often for less cause. And yet he did not strike me for shirking my chores, but only looked down at the letters I had attempted, rubbed a grimy fist across his stubbled chin, and walked on.

Later, when several of the other village children taunted me about it, I learned that my father had actually been crowing about me at the Miner's Tavern that day, saying that he wished he had the means to have me schooled. It was an easy boast, one he would never have to make good upon, for there were no schools, even for boys, in villages such as ours. But the news of this warmed me and made the children's teasing a small matter, for I had never had a word of praise from my father's lips, and to learn that he thought me clever made me begin to think that perhaps I might be so. After this, I became more open and would go about my work muttering snatches of Psalms or sentences from the Sunday sermon, meaning purely to pleasure my ear but earning an undeserved name for religious devotion. It was just such a reputation that led to my recommendation for employment at the rectory, and thus opened the door to the real learning that I craved.

Within a year of her coming, Elinor Mompellion had taught me my letters so well that, though my hand remained unlovely, I could read with only some small difficulties from almost any volume in her library. She would come by my cottage most afternoons, while Tom slept, and set me a lesson to work upon while she went on the remainder of her pastoral visits. She would call in again on her way home to see how I had managed and help me over any hurdles. Often, I would stop in the midst of our lessons and laugh for the sheer joy of it. And she would smile with me, for as I loved to learn, so she loved to teach.

Sometimes, I would feel some guilt in my pleasure, for I believed

I gained all this attention because of her failure to conceive a child. When she and Michael Mompellion arrived here, so young and newly wedded, the entire village watched and waited. Months passed, and then seasons, but Mrs. Mompellion's waist stayed slim as a girl's. And we all – the whole parish – benefited from her barrenness, as she mothered the children who weren't mothered enough in their own crowded crofts, took interest in promising youths who lacked preferment, counselled the troubled, and visited the sick, making herself indispensable in any number of ways to all kinds and classes of people.

But of her herb knowledge I wanted none; it is one thing for a pastor's wife to have such learning and another thing again for a widow woman of my sort. I knew how easy it is for widow to be turned witch in the common mind, and the first cause generally is that she meddles somehow in medicinals. We had had a witch scare in the village when I was but a girl, and the one who had stood accused, Mem Gowdie, was the cunning woman to whom all looked for remedies and poultices and help with confinements. It had been a cruel year of scant harvest, and many women miscarried. When one strange pair of twins was stillborn, fused together at the breast-bone, many had begun muttering of Devilment, and their eyes turned to Widow Gowdie, clamouring upon her as a witch. Mr. Stanley took it upon himself to test the accusations, taking Mem Gowdie with him alone into a field and spending many hours there, dealing with her solemnly. I do not know by what tests he tried her, but after, he declared that he conceived her entirely innocent as to that evil and upbraided the men and women who had accused her. But he also had harsh words for Mem, saying she defied God's will in telling folk that they could prevent illness with her teas and sachets and simples. Mr. Stanley believed that sickness was sent by God to test and chastise those souls He would save. If we sought to evade such, we would miss the lessons God willed us to learn, at the cost of worse torments after our death.

Though none now dared whisper witch against old Mem, there were some who still looked aslant at her young niece, Anys, who lived with her and assisted at confinements and in the growing and drying and mixing of her brews. My stepmother was one of these. Aphra harboured a wealth of superstitions in her simple mind and was ever ready to believe in sky-signs or charms or philtres. She approached Anys with a mixture of fear and awe, and perhaps some envy. I had been at my father's croft when Anys had come with a salve for the sticky-eye, which all the young ones were catching at the time. I had been surprised to see Aphra stealthily hiding a scissors, spread full open like a cross, under a bit of blanket upon the chair upon which she invited Anys to sit. I chided her for it, after Anys was gone. But she waved off my disapproval, showing me then the hag-stone she'd draped over her children's pallet and the phial of salt she'd tucked into the doorpost.

'Say what you will, Anna. That girl walks with too much pride in her step for a poor orphan,' my stepmother opined. 'She carries herself like one who knows summat more than we do.' Well, I said, and so she did. Was she not well skilled in physick, and weren't we all the better off on account of it? Had Anys not just brought us a salve for the sticky-eye that would soothe the children's pains far quicker than Aphra or I had means to do it? Aphra simply made a face.

'You've seen the way the men, old and young, sniff around her as if she were a bitch in heat. You can call it physick all you like, but I think she's brewing up more than cordials in that croft of her'n.' I pointed out that when a young woman was as fine figured and fair of face as Anys, men hardly had to be bewitched into interest in her, especially if that young woman had no father or brothers to remind them where to keep their eyes. Aphra scowled as I said this, and I felt I probed near the place where her ill will to Anys resided.

Aphra, neither handsome nor quick-witted, had settled for marriage with my dissolute father when she had passed six and twenty years with no better man making her an offer. They did well enough together since neither expected much. Aphra enjoyed a pot almost as much as my father, and the two of them spent half their lives in drunken rutting. But I think that in her heart Aphra had never ceased to pine for the kind of power a woman like Anys might wield. How else to account for her ill thoughts towards one who did only good by her and her children? It was true enough that Anys was refractory and cared not for the conventions of this small and watchful town, yet there were others less upright who did not draw such disapproval as she. Aphra's superstitious mutterings found many willing ears amongst the villagers, and sometimes I worried for Anys on account of it.

I let Mrs. Mompellion wax on about the efficacy of rue and chamomile and busied myself rooting out the thistleweeds, as it is labour that requires hard pulling and can tend to make Mrs. Mompellion very faint if she stoops over it too long. Presently, I went to the kitchen to begin the day's real labour and in the scrubbing of deal and sanding of pewter consumed the morning hours. There are some who imagine that the work of a housemaid is the dullest of drudgery, but I have never found it so. At the rectory and at the Bradfords' great Hall, I found much enjoyment in the tending of fine things. When you have been raised in a bare croft, eating with wooden spoons from crude platters, there are a hundred small and subtle pleasures to be garnered in the smooth slipperiness of a fine porcelain cup under your hands in a tub of soapsuds or the leathery scent of a book as you work the beeswax into its binding. As well, these simple tasks engaged only the hands and left the mind free to wander unfettered down all manner of interesting pathways. Sometimes, as

I polished the Mompellions' damascene chest, I would study its delicate inlays and wonder about the faraway craftsman who had fashioned it, trying to imagine the manner of his life, under a hot sun and a strange God. Mr. Viccars had a rich and lovely fabric that he called damask, and I fell to wondering if that bolt of cloth had stood in the same bazaar as the chest and made the same long journey from desert to this damp mountainside. Thinking of Mr. Viccars broke my reverie and reminded me that I had not raised the problem of the dress with Mrs. Mompellion. But then I realized it was nigh to noon and Tom would be fair-clemmed and mewling for his milk. So I left the rectory in haste, thinking that the matter of the dress and its propriety could be raised with Mrs. Mompellion at some later time.

But that later time never came. For when I arrived at the cottage, the quiet inside was of the old kind in the days before Mr. Viccars joined our household. There was not laughter or merry shouting from within, and indeed, in the kitchen I found only a sullen Jane Martin distracting Tom with a finger of arrowroot and water, while Jamie, all subdued, played alone by the hearth, making towers from the bavins and thus strewing bits of broken kindling everywhere. Mr. Viccars's sewing corner was as I'd left it that morning, with the threads and patterns piled neat and untouched from the night before. The eggs I'd left for him lay still in their whisket. Tom, seeing me, squirmed in Jane Martin's arms and opened his wide, gummy mouth like a baby bird. I reached for him and set him to nurse before I enquired about Mr. Viccars.

'Indeed, I have not seen him. I believed him to be gone out early to the Hadfields',' she said.

'But his breakfast is uneaten,' I replied. Jane Martin shrugged. She had made it plain by her manner that she misliked the presence of a male lodger in the house, although since Rector Mompellion had sent us Mr. Viccars she had had to hold her peace about it.

'He a bed, Mummy,' said Jamie forlornly. 'I goed up to find him but he yelled me, "Go 'way."'

Mr. Viccars must be ill indeed, I reasoned. Anxious as I was to attend to him, I had to complete Tom's feeding first. Once he was satisfied, I drew a pitcher of fresh water, cut a slice of bread, and climbed to Mr. Viccars's garret. I could hear the moans as soon as I set a foot on the attic ladder. Alarmed, I failed to knock, simply opening the hatch into the low-ceilinged space.

I almost dropped the pitcher in my shock. The fair young face of the evening before was gone from the pallet in front of me. George Viccars lay with his head pushed to the side by a lump the size of a newborn piglet, a great, shiny, yellow-purple knob of pulsing flesh. His face, half turned away from me because of the excrescence, was flushed scarlet, or rather, blotched, with shapes like rings of rose petals blooming under his skin. His blond hair was a dark, wet mess upon his head, and his pillow was drenched with sweat. There was a sweet, pungent smell in the garret. A smell like rotting apples.

'Please, water,' he whispered. I held the cup to his parched mouth, and he drank greedily, his face distorted from the grief of the effort. He paused from his drinking only as a spasm of shivering and sneezing racked his body. I poured, and poured again until the pitcher was drained. 'Thank you,' he gasped. 'And now I pray you be gone from here lest this foul contagion touch you.'

'Nay,' I said, 'I must see you comfortable.'

'Mistress, none may do that now except the priest. Pray fetch Mompellion, if he will dare to come to me.'

'Say not so!' I scolded him. 'This fever will break, and you will be well enough presently.'

'Nay, Mistress, I know the signs of this wretched illness. Just get you gone from here, for the love of your babes.'

I did go at that, but only to my own room to fetch my blanket and pillow – the one to warm his shivers and the other to replace the drenched thing beneath his horrible head. He moaned as I reentered the garret. As I attempted to lift him to place the pillow, he cried out piteously, for the pain from that massive boil was intense. Then the purple thing burst all of a sudden open, slitting like a pea pod and issuing forth creamy pus all spotted through with shreds of dead flesh. The sickly sweet smell of apples was gone, replaced by a stench of week-old fish. I gagged as I made haste to swab the mess from the poor man's face and shoulder and stanch his seeping wound.

'For the love of God, Anna' – he was straining his hoarse throat, his voice breaking like a boy, summoning I don't know what strength to speak above a whisper – 'Get thee gone from here! Thou can't help me! Look to thyself!'

I feared that this agitation would kill him in his weakened state, and so I picked up the ruined bedding and left him. Downstairs, two horrified faces greeted me, Jamie's wide-eyed with incomprehension, and Jane's pale with knowing dread. She had already shed her pinafore in preparation to leave us for the day, and her hand was upon the door bar as I appeared. 'I pray you, stay with the children while I fetch the rector, for I fear Mr. Viccars's state is grave,' I said. At that, she wrung her hands, and I could see that her girlish heart was at war with her Puritan spine. I didn't wait to see who would win the battle but simply swept by her, dumping the bedding in the door-yard as I went.

I was running, my eyes down and fixed on the path, so I did not see the rector astride Anteros, on his way from an errand in nearby Hathersage. But he saw me, turned and wheeled that great horse, and cantered to my side.

'Good heavens, Anna, whatever is amiss?' he cried, sliding from the saddle and offering a hand to steady me as I gasped to catch my breath. Through ragged gulps, I conveyed the gravity of Mr. Viccars's condition. 'Indeed, I am sorry for it,' the rector said, his face clouded with concern. Without wasting any more words, he handed me up onto the horse and remounted.

It is so vivid to me, the man he was that day. I can recall how naturally he took charge, calming me and then poor Mr. Viccars; how he stayed tirelessly at his bedside all through that afternoon and then again the next, fighting first for the man's body and then, when that cause was clearly lost, for his soul. Mr. Viccars muttered and raved, ranted, cursed, and cried out in pain. Much of what he said was incomprehensible. But from time to time he would cease tossing on the pallet and open his eyes wide, rasping 'Burn it all! Burn it all! For the love of God, burn it!' By the second night, he had ceased his thrashing and simply lay staring, locked in a kind of silent struggle. His mouth was all crusted with sordes, and hourly I would dribble a little water on his lips and wipe them; he would look at me, his brow creasing with effort as he tried to express his thanks. As the night wore on, it was clear that he was failing, and Mr. Mompellion would not leave him, even when, towards morning, Mr. Viccars passed into a fitful kind of sleep, his breath shallow and uneven. The light through the attic window was violet and the larks were singing. I like to think that, somewhere through his delirium, the sweet sound might have brought him some small measure of relief.

He died clutching the bedsheet. Gently, I untangled each hand, straightening his long, limp fingers. They were beautiful hands, soft save for the one callused place toughened by a lifetime of needle pricks. Remembering the deft way they'd moved in the fire glow, the tears spilled from my eyes. I told myself I was crying for the waste of it; that those fingers that had acquired so much skill would never fashion another lovely thing. In truth, I think I was crying for a different kind of waste; wondering why I had waited until so near this death to feel the touch of those hands.

I folded them on George Viccars's breast, and Mr. Mompellion laid his own hand atop them, offering a final prayer. I remember being struck then by how much larger the rector's hand was – the hard hand of a labouring man rather than the limp, white paw of a priest. I could not think why it should be so, for he came, as I gathered, from a family of clergy and had but recently been at his books in Cambridge. There was not much between Mr. Mompellion and Mr. Viccars in age, for the reverend was but eight and twenty. And yet his young man's face, if you looked at it closely, was scored with furrows at the brow and starbursts of crows' feet beside the eyes – the marks of a mobile face that has frowned much in contemplation and laughed much in company. I have said that it could seem a plain face, but I think that what I mean to say is that it was his voice, and not his face, that you noticed. Once he began to speak, the sound of it was so compelling that you focused all your thoughts upon the words, and not upon the man who uttered them. It was a voice full of light and dark. Light not only as it glimmers, but also as it glares. Dark not only as it brings cold and fear, but also as it gives rest and shade.

He turned his eyes on me then, and spoke to me in a silken whisper that seemed to fall upon my grief like a comforting shawl. He thanked me for my assistance through the night. I had done what I could; bringing cold and hot compresses to ease the fevers and the shivering; making infusions to purify the air in that small, ill-smelling sickroom; carrying away the pans of bile and piss and sweat-drenched rags.

'It is a hard thing,' I said, 'for a man to die amongst strangers, with no family to mourn him.'

'Death is always hard, wheresoever it finds a man. And untimely death harder than most.' He began to chant, slowly, as if he were groping in his memory for the words:

'My wounds stink and are corrupt,
My loins are filled with a loathsome disease and there is
    no soundness in my flesh.
My lovers and my friends stand aloof from my sore,
My kinsmen stand far off . . .'

'Do you know that Psalm, Anna?' I shook my head. 'No; it is unlovely and not much sung. But you did not stand aloof from Mr. Viccars; you did not stand far off. I think that George Viccars passed his last weeks happily in your family. You should console yourself in the joy that you and your sons were able to give to him, and the mercy that you, especially, have shown.'

He said he would carry the body downstairs where the sexton, who was elderly, might more easily retrieve it. George Viccars was a tall man and must have weighed near to fourteen stone, but Mr. Mompellion lifted that dead weight as if it were nothing and descended the loft ladder with the limp body slung across his shoulder. Downstairs, he laid George Viccars gently upon a sheet as tenderly as a father setting down a sleeping babe.

The Thunder of His Voice

The sexton came early for George Viccars's body. Since there were no kin, his funeral rites would be simple and swift. 'Sooner the better, eh, Mistress,' the old man said as he hauled the corpse to his cart. 'He's nowt to linger 'ere for. Too late to stitch hissef a shroud.'

Because of the long night's labour, Mr. Mompellion had bidden me not to come to the rectory that morning. 'Rest instead,' he said, pausing at the doorway in the early light. Anteros had been tethered all night in the garth and had trod the soil there into grassless craters. I nodded, but anticipated little rest. I had been commanded to serve at dinner at the Hall that afternoon, and before that I would have to scour the house from bottom to top and then figure on the disposition of Mr. Viccars's effects. As if he'd caught my thought, the rector paused as he raised his foot to the stirrup, patted the horse, and turned back to me, coming close and dropping his voice. 'You would do well to follow Mr. Viccars's instructions as to his things,' he said. I must have looked baffled, for I wasn't sure for the moment to what he was referring. 'He said to burn everything, and that may be good advice.'

I was still on my hands and knees in the attic, scrubbing the worn floorboards, when the first of Mr. Viccars's customers came rapping on the door. Before I opened it, I knew the caller was Anys Gowdie.

Anys was so skilled with plants and balms that she knew how to extract their fragrant oils, and these she wore on her person so that a light, pleasant scent, like summer fruits and flowers, always preceded her. Despite the common opinion of her in the village, I had always had admiration for Anys. She was quick of mind and swift of tongue, always ready to answer a set down with the kind of witty rebuke most of us can think of only long after the moment of insult has passed. No matter how freely they might besmear her character, and no matter how many charms they might dangle about themselves in her presence, there were few women who would do without her in the birthing room. She brought a calm kindness with her there, very different from her sharp manner in the streets. And she had a deft-handedness in difficult deliveries that her aunt had come to rely upon. I liked her, too, because it takes a kind of courage to care so little for what people whisper, especially in a place as small as this.

She had come looking for Mr. Viccars, to collect a dress he had made for her. When I told her what had befallen him, her face clouded with sorrow. And then, typically, she upbraided me. 'Why did you not call on my aunt and me, instead of Mompellion? A good infusion would have served George better than the empty mutterings of a priest.'

I was used to being shocked by Anys, but this time she had managed to outdo even herself, delivering two scandalizing thoughts in a single utterance. The first shock was her frank blasphemy. The second was the familiarity with which she referred to Mr. Viccars, whom I had never yet called by his first name. On what terms of intimacy had they been, that she should call him so? My suspicions were only heightened when, after rummaging through the whisket in which he kept his work, we found the dress that he had made for her. For all the years of my childhood, when the Puritans held sway here, we wore for our outer garments only what they called the Sadd

48

Colours – black for preference, or the dark brown called Dying Leaf. Since the return of the king, brighter hues had crept back to most wardrobes, but long habit still constrained the choices of most of us. Not Anys. She had bespoke a gown of a scarlet so vivid it almost hurt my eyes. I had never seen Mr. Viccars at work on it, and I wondered if he had contrived to keep it from me, in case I remarked upon it. The gown was finished all but for the hem, which Anys said she had come that morning to have him adjust for her at a final fitting. When she held the dress up, I saw that the neckline was cut low as a doxy's, and I could not discipline my thoughts. I imagined her, tall and splendid, her honey-gold hair tumbling loose, her amber eyes half closed, and Mr. Viccars kneeling at her feet, letting his long fingers drift from the hem to caress her ankle and then travelling under the soft fabric, skilled hands on fragrant skin, upward and slowly upward ... Within seconds, I was flushed as scarlet as that damnable dress.

'Mr. Viccars told me to burn his work for fear of spreading his contagion,' I said, swallowing hard to ease the tightness in my throat.

'You shall do no such thing!' she exclaimed, and I foresaw in her dismay the difficulty I would have with all his clients. If Anys Gowdie, familiar as she was with the face of illness, felt so on the matter, it was unlikely any others would be persuadable. Few of us here live in ample circumstances, and none loves waste. Anyone who had placed a deposit on work from Mr. Viccars would want whatever of that work he had accomplished, and notwithstanding Mr. Mompellion's injunction, I had no right to withhold it from them. Anys Gowdie left with her harlot's gown folded under her arm, and as the day wore on and the news of Mr. Viccars's death spread, as news does here, I was interrupted again and again by his clients claiming pieces of his work. All I could do was to pass on what he had said in his delirium. Not a one of them consented to having his or her garment – even were it only a pile of cut-out fabric pieces – consigned to the fire. In the end, I burned only his own clothes. And then, finally, as the coals fell and galled themselves, I at last found the will to toss the dress he had made for me into the grate, golden-green gashed by flames of bright vermillion.

It was a long walk, and all uphill, to Bradford Hall, and I was as tired as I've ever been as I set out that afternoon for my employment there. And yet I did not go direct, but rather headed east, towards the Gowdie cottage. I could not get Anys's 'George,' or her scarlet gown, out of my mind. Generally, I am not a gossip. I care not who tumbles whom in what warm boose. And now that Mr. Viccars was dead, it hardly mattered, to me or any person, where he might have put his prick. And yet, even so, I had a month's mind to know how matters had stood between him and Anys Gowdie, if only to take the measure of his true regard for me.

The Gowdies' cottage was set off at the eastern edge of town, after the smithy, a lonely dwelling at the edge of the big Riley farm. It was a tiny place, just one room propped upon another, so ill-built that the thatch sat rakishly atop the whole like a cap pulled crooked across a brow. The cottage was set hard into the side of the hill, crouching before the winter winds that roared across the moors. It announced itself by smell long before you could catch sight of it. Sometimes sickly sweet, sometimes astringent, the scents of herbal brews and cordials wafted powerfully from the precincts of the little home. Inside, the tiny room had a low-beamed ceiling. The light was always dim, to protect the virtue of the drying plants. At this time of year, when the Gowdies were cutting their summer herbs, the bunches hung from the beams in such profusion that you had to bend almost double when you entered the door. Always when I visited, I wondered that tall Anys contrived to live in such a place, for surely she could not stand upright. The Gowdies always had a fire going for the making of their draughts, and since the flue of the ancient chimney drew poorly, the air was smoky and the walls black with soot. Still, at least the smoke was sweet-scented, for the Gowdies always burned rosemary, which they said purified the air of any sickness that ailing villagers might unwittingly carry when coming there for help.

There was no answer when I knocked upon the door, so I walked round to the stone wall that sheltered the Gowdies' physick garden. The garden had been part of our village for as long as I could remember. I had always assumed that Mem planted it, but once, when I had said something about that to Anys, she had mocked me for my ignorance.

'This garden, as any fool could see, was old before Mem Gowdie was even thought of.' She had run her hand along the bough of an espaliered plum, and I saw that, of course, the tree, with its gnarled and knotty trunk, was ancient. 'We do not even know the name of the wise woman who first laid out these beds, but the garden thrived here long before we came to tend it, and it will go on long after we depart. My aunt and I are just the latest in a long line of women who have been charged with its care.'

The stone walls sheltered a profusion of plants. I knew by name less than a tenth part of what grew there. Many of the herbs had already been harvested, revealing the careful regularity of the stone-edged beds, sown to a plan that only Anys and her aunt understood. Anys knelt now amidst a clump of glossy green stems. Each tall stalk held a cluster of buds opening into blooms of midnight-blue. She was digging at the roots and rose as I came down the straw-strewn path, dusting the soil from her hands.

'It is a handsome plant,' I said.

'Handsome – and potent,' she replied. 'They call it wolf's bane, but it is bane to more than those poor creatures. Eat a small piece of this root and you will be dead by nightfall.'

'Why do you have it here, then?' I must have looked stricken, for she laughed at me.

'Not to serve you for your supper! The wort, ground and mixed with oils, makes a very good rub for aching joints, and we will have many of those in this village as the winter hardens. But I do not think you came here to admire my blue flowers,' she said. 'Come inside and take a drink with me.'

We entered the cottage, and she set the bunch of roots upon a crowded workbench and washed her hands in a bucket. 'Be kind enough to sit, Anna Frith,' she said, 'for I must needs sit, too, or crick my neck standing here.' She shooed a grey gib-cat off a rickety chair and pulled up a stool for herself. I was grateful to have found Anys alone. I would have been pressed to account for my visit had it been old Mem working solitary in the garden, and I would have been ill-set to raise the matter on my mind if her aunt were sitting at our elbow. As it was, I hardly knew how to begin upon such a delicate subject. Although we were of an age, Anys and I had not grown up together. She had been raised in a village closer to the Dark Peak, and had been sent to her aunt when her mother died untimely. She had been about ten years old. I remember the day she arrived, sitting straight and tall in an open cart while all the village came out to peer at her. I remember it so vividly because she returned every stare and never flinched from the pointed fingers. I was a shy child then, and I remember thinking that if I had been her, I would have been hiding under the burlaps, wailing my heart out.

She handed me a glass of strong-smelling brew and poured herself one, also. I inspected the contents of my cup. It was an unappealing shade of pale green, with an even paler froth atop it. 'Nettle beer. It will strengthen your blood,' Anys said. 'All women should drink it daily.'

As I lifted the cup, I remembered, with embarrassment, how as a child I had joined with others to mock Anys Gowdie, who would stop by the path or in the midst of a field and pluck fresh leaves, then eat them where she stood. It shamed me to recall how we had taunted her, crying out, 'Cow! Cow! Grass-eater!' Anys had only laughed and looked us over, one by one. 'At least my nose isn't stuffed with snot, like yours, Meg Bailey. And my skin isn't bubbling with blebs, like yours, Geoffry Bain.' And she listed all our defects to us, standing there taller than any other child her age and glowing with good health, all the way from the top of her glossy head to the tips of her fine, strong fingernails. Not so very much later, when I was first with child, I had gone to her, humbled, and asked her to guide me in what greens I could gather and eat to strengthen myself and the babe I carried. It had been an odd thing, at first, the taste of such stuff, but I had soon felt the benefit of it.

The nettle beer, however, was new to me. The flavour, as I sipped, was mild and not unpleasant, while the effect on my tired body was refreshing. I held the cup to my lips longer than I needed, so as to postpone launching myself upon my awkward subject. I need not have troubled. 'And so I suppose you need to know whether I lay with George,' Anys declared, in the same uninflected tone that might have said, 'And so I suppose you need some yarrow leaves.' The cup trembled in my hand, and the green stuff sloshed onto the swept-earth floor. Anys gave a short laugh. 'Of course I did. He was too young and handsome to have to slake his fires with his fist.' I hardly know how I looked at that, but Anys's eyes as she regarded me were lit with amusement. 'Drink up. You'll feel better. It was naught more to either of us than a meal to a hungry traveller.'

She leaned forwards to stir some leaves steeping in a big black kettle near the fire. 'His intentions to you were otherwise. If that's what's worrying you, set your mind easy. He wanted you to wife, Anna Frith, and I told him he'd do well with you, if he could talk you round to it. For I see that you've changed somewhat since Sam Frith passed. I think you like to go and come without a man's say-so. I told him your boys were his best chance to win you. For, unlike me, you have them to look to, so you can never live just for yourself.'

I tried to imagine the two of them lying together discussing such things. 'But why,' I blurted, 'if you were on such terms, did you not marry him yourself?'

'Oh, Anna, Anna!' She shook her head at me and smiled as one does at a slow-witted child. I felt my colour rise. I was confounded as to what I had said that had amused her so. She must have sensed my vexation, for she stopped smiling, took the cup from my hand, and looked at me with seriousness.

'Why would I marry? I'm not made to be any man's chattel. I have my work, which I love. I have my home – it is not much, I grant, yet sufficient for my shelter. But more than these, I have something very few women can claim: my freedom. I will not lightly surrender it. And besides,' she said, shooting me a sly sideways glance from under her long lashes, 'sometimes a woman needs a draught of nettle beer to wake her up, and sometimes she needs a dish of valerian tea to calm her down. Why cultivate a garden with only one plant in it?'

I smiled hesitantly, as if to show that I could see the jest, for it fell into my heart that I wanted her good opinion and would not have her think me a dim and simple girl. She rose then to be about her work, and so I left her, more confused than when I'd arrived. She was a rare creature, Anys Gowdie, and I had to own that I admired her for listening to her own heart rather than having her life ruled by others' conventions. I, meanwhile, was on my way to be ruled for the afternoon by people I loathed. I trudged on towards Bradford Hall, passing through the edge of the Riley woods. The sun was bright that day, and strong shadows from the trees fell in bands across the path. Dark and light, dark and light, dark and light. That was how I had been taught to view the world. The Puritans who had ministered to us here had held that all actions and thoughts could be only one of two natures: godly and right, or Satanic and evil. But Anys Gowdie confounded such thinking. There was no doubt that she did good: in many ways, the well-being of our village rested more on her works, and those of her aunt, than on the works of the rectory's occupant. And yet her fornication and her blasphemy branded her a sinner in the reckoning of our religion.

I was still puzzling over this as I reached the wood's abrupt edge and began skirting the golden fields of the Riley farm. They had been all day scything there – twenty men for twenty acres. The Hancocks, who farmed the Riley land, had six strong sons of their own and so needed far less help than others at their harvest. Mrs. Hancock and her daughters-in-law wearily followed behind their husbands, tying up the last of the loose stalks into sheaves burnished by the sunlight. I saw them that afternoon through Anys's eyes: shackled to their menfolk as surely as the plough-horse to the shares.

Lib Hancock, the eldest brother's wife, had been a friend to me since childhood, and as she straightened for a moment to ease her back, she raised a hand to shade her eyes and perceived that it was I, walking at the field's edge. She waved to me, then turned for a word to her mother-in-law before leaving her work and crossing the field towards me.

'Sit with me for a short while, Anna!' she called. 'For I am in need of a rest.'

I was in no hurry to get to the Bradfords', so I walked with her to a grassy bank. She dropped down on it gratefully and closed her eyes for a moment. I rubbed at her shoulders and she purred with the ease my kneading hands brought her.

'A sorry business about your lodger,' she said. 'He seemed a good man.'

'He was that,' I said. 'He was uncommonly kind to my boys.' Lib tilted her head back and gave me an odd look. 'And to me, of course,' I added. 'As to everyone.'

'I believe my mother-in-law had him in mind for Nell,' she said. Nell, the only girl in the Hancock family, was so strictly kept by her many brothers that we often jested that she'd never get wedded, since no man could venture near enough to see what she looked like. Knowing what I now knew of Mr. Viccars, I laughed despite my sadness.

'Was any woman in this village *not* considering the bedding of that man?'

I have said that Lib and I were close – we had ever exchanged girlish confidences. It was this habit, I suppose, that led me into the account I made her then, a bawdy confession of my own lust, which I had the right to confide to her, and then that which I did not: the news I'd just learned of Anys's sport with my lodger.

'Now, Lib,' I said at last, rising reluctantly to continue on my way, 'mind you do not prate my news all around the Hancock house this night.'

She laughed at that, and pushed me playfully on the shoulder. 'Oh, and as if I'd be talking of tumblings in front of Mother Hancock and that houseful of men! You've got a peculiar view of our household, you have. The only mating fit for remark at the Hancock table is when the tups get put to the ewes!' We both laughed then, kissed each other, and parted to our diverse toils.

At the edge of the field, the hedgerows were deep green in their glossy leaves and the blackberries beginning to plump and redden. Fat lambs, their fleeces gilded by sunlight, grazed in lush grasses. But for all its loveliness, the last half mile of this walk was always unpleasant to me, even when I wasn't so fatigued. I disliked all of the Bradford family, and I especially feared the colonel. And I misliked myself for giving way to that fear.

Colonel Henry Bradford was said by all to have been an intelligent soldier who had led his men with uncommon valour. Perhaps his military success had made him arrogant, or perhaps such a man should never have retired to the quiet life of a country gentleman. In any case, there was no sign of wise leadership in the way he conducted his household. He seemed to take a perverse amusement in belittling his wife. She was the daughter of a wealthy but ill-connected family, a vapid beauty whose looks had stirred a brief infatuation in the colonel that lasted just until he pocketed her marriage portion. Since then, he had never let pass an opportunity to disparage her connections or slight her understanding. She, though still quite beautiful, had become brittle after long years of such treatment. Cowed and nervous, she fretted constantly over where next her husband would find fault, and so kept her staff on constant edge, always reordering the household routine so that the simplest tasks became effortful. The Bradfords' son was a rake-shamed, drunken fanfarroon who fortunately stayed mostly in London. On the rare occasions he was at the Hall, I tried to find excuses for declining work there, and when I could not afford to do so, endeavoured to stay out of his line of sight and made sure I could never be entrapped into being alone with him. Miss Bradford was, as I have said, a proud and sour young woman, whose only glimmer of goodness seemed to come from a real solicitude for her unhappy mother. When her father was away, she seemed able to quiet her mother's nerves and soothe her fretfulness, and one could work there without fear of tirades. But when the colonel returned, everyone, from Mrs. Bradford and her daughter down to the lowliest scullery maid, tensed like a cur waiting for the boot.

Since Bradford Hall had a moderately large staff, I was only required to serve at table for parties of some size or importance. The Hall had a great room that looked very well when arranged for dining. The two big bacon settles were pulled out from the walls, their dark oak polished to a rich, black gleam. At leaf-fall, just after the hogs were slaughtered, the scent of the new-cured flitches hanging inside could be overpowering. But by late summer, the bacon was long eaten and only a faint and pleasant smoky aroma remained beneath the fresher scents of beeswax and lavender. Silver shone in the low light and the canary, glowing in large goblets, warmed even the cold faces of the Bradfords. No one, of course, ever thought to tell me who the guests were that I would be waiting upon, and so I was pleased to see at least the friendly faces of the Mompellions among the dozen at that day's dinner.

The colonel's pride was gratified by the presence of Elinor Mompellion at his table. For one thing, she looked exquisite that afternoon in a simple gown of creamy silk. A few fine pearls gleamed in her pale hair. But more than her delicate beauty, Colonel Bradford appreciated her substantial connections. She had been a member of one of the oldest and most extensively landed families in the shire. It was noised about that in choosing Mompellion, she had spurned another suitor who might have made her a duchess. Colonel Bradford would never be able to fathom such a choice. But then, there was so much about her that eluded him. All he grasped was that a connection with her enhanced his own standing, and to him that was all that mattered. As I dipped to take away her soup plate, Elinor Mompellion, seated to the colonel's left, placed a hand lightly on the forearm of the London gentleman to her right, interrupting the flow of his prattle. She turned to me with a grave smile. 'I hope you are feeling quite well after your dreadful night, Anna.' I heard the ring of the colonel's butter knife dropping onto his plate and the hiss of his indrawn breath. I kept my eyes on the dishes in my hand, afraid to risk a glance in his direction. 'Quite. Thank you, ma'am,' I murmured quickly and slid on to clear the next plate. I feared if I gave her a second's chance she would continue to converse with me, causing Colonel Bradford to expire from shock.

At the Hall, I had learned to keep my mind on my duties and let the talk, which was mostly trivial, wash over me like the twittering of birds in a distant thicket. At that large table, little of the conversation was general. Most people exchanged empty pleasantries with those seated next to them, and the result was a low buzz of mingled voices, broken occasionally by Miss Bradford's affected, mirthless laugh. When I left the room with the meat platters, that was the state of things. But by the time I returned, carrying desserts, all the candles had been lit against the gathering dark and only the young Londoner next to Mrs. Mompellion was speaking. He was a style of gentleman we did not much see in our small village, his periwig so large and elaborate that his rather pinched, white-powdered face seemed lost beneath its mass of tumbling curls. He wore a patch on his right cheek. I expect that whichever of the Bradfords' servants attended his toilet had been unfamiliar with how to affix such fashionable spots, for it flapped distractingly as the young man chewed his food. I had thought him rather absurd on first glimpse, but now he looked grave, and as he spoke, his hands fluttered from lace cuffs like white moths, throwing long shadows across the table. The faces turned towards him were pale and alarmed.

'You have never seen anything like it on the roads. Innumerable men on horseback, wagons, and carts bulging with baggage. I tell you, everyone capable of leaving the city is doing so or plans to do it. The poor meantimes are pitching up tents out on Hampstead Heath. One walks, if one must walk, in the very centre of the roadway to avoid the contagion seeping from dwellings. Those who must move through the poorer parishes cover their faces in herb-stuffed masks contrived like the beaks of great birds. People go through the streets like drunkards, weaving from this side to that so as to avoid passing too close to any other pedestrian. And yet one cannot take a hackney, for the last person inside may have breathed contagion.' He dropped his voice then and looked all around, seeming to enjoy the attention his words were garnering. 'They say you can hear the screams of the dying, locked up all alone in the houses marked with the red crosses. The Great Orbs are all on the move, I tell you: there is talk that the king plans to remove his court to Oxford. For myself, I saw no reason to tarry. The city is emptying so fast that there is little worthwhile society to be had. One rarely sees a wigg'd gallant or a powdered lady, for wealth and connection are no shield against Plague.'

The word dropped like an anvil among the tinkling silverware. The bright room dimmed for me as if someone had snuffed every candle all at once. I clutched the platter I carried so that I would not drop it and stood stock-still until I was sure of my balance. I gathered myself and tried to steady my breath. I had seen enough people carried off by illness in my life. There are many fevers that can kill a man other than the Plague. And George Viccars hadn't been near London in more than a year. So how could he have been touched by the city's pestilence?

Colonel Bradford cleared his throat. 'Come now, Robert! Do not alarm the ladies. The next thing they will be shunning your company for fear of infection!'

'Do not joke, sir, for on the turnpike north of London, I encountered an angry mob, brandishing hoes and pitchforks, denying entry to their village inn to any who were travelling from London. It was a low place, in any wise, nowhere I would have sought shelter even on the filthiest of nights, so I rode onwards unmolested. But before long, to be a Londoner will not be a credential worth owning to. It will be surprising how many of us will invent rusticated histories for ourselves, mind me well. You'll soon learn that my chief abode these last years was Wetwang, not Westminster.'

There was a little stir at this, for the town the young man was mocking was a good deal bigger than the one in which he was presently being entertained. 'Well, good thing you got out, eh?' said the colonel, to cover the lapse. 'Clean air up here, no putrid fevers.'

Down the table, I noticed the Mompellions exchanging meaning looks. Trying to still my shaking hands, I set down the dessert I carried and stepped back into the shadows against the wall. 'It's hard to believe,' the young man continued, 'but some few are staying in town who have the easy means to go. Lord Radisson – I believe you are acquainted with his lordship – has been bruiting it about that he feels it his duty to stay and "set an example." Example of what? A wretched death, I warrant.'

'Think of what you are saying,' Mr. Mompellion interrupted. His voice – rich, loud, grave – cut off the Bradfords' airy laughter. Colonel Bradford turned to him with a raised eyebrow, as if to censure rudeness. Mrs. Bradford tried to turn her titter to a cough. Mr. Mompellion continued, 'If all who have the means run each time this disease appears, then the seeds of the Plague will go with them and be sown far and wide throughout the land until the clean places are infected and the contagion is magnified a thousandfold. If God saw fit to send this scourge, I believe it would be His will that one face it where one was, with courage, and thus contain its evil.'

'Oh?' said the colonel superciliously. 'And if God sends a lion to rip your flesh, will you stand steadfastly then, too? I think not. I think you will run from the danger, as any sensible man would.'

'Your analogy is excellent, sir,' said Mr. Mompellion; his voice had the commanding timbre that he used in the pulpit. 'Let us explore it. For I will certainly stand and face the lion if, by running, I would cause the beast to follow me, and thus draw him closer to the dwelling places of innocents who demand my protection.'

At the mention of innocents, Jamie's little face flashed before me. What if the young Londoner were correct? Jamie had lived in George Viccars's pocket. All that day before the illness first rose in him, Jamie had been climbing on his back, prancing by his side.

The young man broke into the silence that greeted Mr. Mompellion's speech. 'Well, sir, very bravely stated. But I must tell you that those who know this disease best – and that would be the physicians and the barber-surgeons – have been the fleetest of foot in leaving town. One cannot get cupped for a cough or bled for the gout, no matter if you have a sovereign to give in fee. Which leads me to conclude that the physicians have written us a clear prescription, and that is this: the best physick against the Plague is to run far away from it. And I, for one, intend to follow that prescription religiously.'

'You say "religiously," but I think your choice of word is poor,' said Mr. Mompellion. 'For if one speaks "religiously," then one must recall that God has the power to keep you safe in peril, or to bring peril to overtake you, no matter how far or fast you run.'

'Indeed, sir. And many who believed that now are rotting corpses passing through the streets in cartloads, on their way to the great pits.' Miss Bradford raised a hand to her brow, ostentatiously feigning a faintness that her avid eyes belied. The young man turned to her, reading her desire for morbid detail, and continued, 'I have had it from one whose man had need to go there in fruitless search of a kinsman. He reported that the corpses are tipped in, afforded no more respect than one would give a dead dog. A layer of bodies, a few spades of soil, and then more bodies tumbled in atop. They lie there so, just like yonder dessert.' He pointed at the layered cake, which I had set down upon the table. I saw the Mompellions wince, but the young man smirked at his own wit and then turned pointedly towards the rector.

'And do you know who were the fastest to follow the physicians out of the city, sir? Why, it were the Anglican ministers, just such as yourself. There's many a London pulpit being filled by a nonconformist on account of it.'

Michael Mompellion looked down then and studied his hands. 'If what you say is true, sir, then I am indeed sorry for it. I will say that if it be the case, then my brothers in faith are the lesser men.' He sighed then and looked at his wife. 'Perhaps they might believe that God now is preaching to the city, and what needs add their small utterance to the thunder of His voice?'

There was a full moon that night, which was fortunate, for otherwise I'm sure I would have fallen into a ditch as I stumbled home, almost running despite my exhaustion, as the thistles tore at my ankles and the briars caught at my skirt. I could barely speak to the Martin girl as she roused herself heavily from her fireside slumber. I threw off my cloak and rushed up the stairs. A square of silvery light bathed the two little bodies. Both breathed easily. Jamie had an arm round his brother. I stretched out a hand to his forehead, terrified of what I might feel. My fingers brushed his soft skin. It was blessedly cool.

'Thank you,' I said. 'Oh, thank you, God.'

Rat-fall

The weeks that followed George Viccars's death ushered in the loveliest September weather I ever recall. There are some who deem this mountainside bleak country, and I can see how it might seem so: the land all chewed up by the miners, their stowes like scaffolds upon the moors, and their bings like weedy molehills interrupting the pale mauve tide of the heather. This is not a vivid place. Our only strong hue is green, and this we have in every shade: the emerald velvet mosses, the glossy, tangled ivies, and in spring, the gold-greens of tender new grasses. For the rest, we move through a patchwork of greys. The limestone outcrops are a whitish-grey, the millstone grit from which we build our cottages a warmer greyish-yellow. Grey is the sky colour here, the dove-breast clouds louring so upon the hilltops that sometimes you feel you could just reach up and bury your hands in their softness.

But those autumn weeks were flooded with an unaccustomed surfeit of sunlight. The sky was clear blue almost every day, and the air, instead of hinting frost, remained warm and dry. I was so relieved that Jamie and Tom were not ill, I lived in those days as at a fair. Jamie himself was downcast, having lost his dear friend Mr. Viccars. In truth, the death of his father had been easier for him to bear, because with Sam down the mine for most of Jamie's waking hours, the two had spent little time in each other's company. In the few short months he had lived with us, Mr. Viccars had become an indispensable companion. His death left an emptiness that I resolved to fill, taking time to make our simple chores into something of a game so that Jamie would not feel the loss so keenly.

At day's end I liked to know that the ewes were each with their lambs and none had caught themselves up in briars or burrows. So in the afternoons, when I went to check the flock, I would take Jamie and Tom with me, and we would dawdle along our way, stopping to find what story each clump of stones or hollow tree might yield us. A line of fungus marching up a fallen branch might become, in our tale, the stairway to a faery's bower, while an acorn cap might be the cup left behind by a party of feasting wood mice.

Our flock is small, just one and twenty ewes. From the time I married Sam, my rule has been to make mutton of any who proves an inept mother, and the result is an easy lambing when the weather is with us. We had had a good lambing back in the spring, so the last thing I was looking for that day was a ewe in labour. But we found her, and fortunate, for she was lying upon her side, panting in the shade of a rowan whose redding leaves also seemed quite out of season in that heat. Her tongue was out, and she was straining. I unslung Tom and laid him on a patch of clover. Jamie stood behind me as I knelt down and ran my hands inside the ewe, trying to stretch her. I could feel the nub of a nose and the hardness of one hoof, but I could barely get all my fingers in to grasp it.

'Mummy, may I help?' said Jamie, and looking at his tiny fingers I said yes, sitting him down in front of me with the ewe's rear open before us like a big, glistening blossom. He slid his little hands easily up into that slippery wetness and exclaimed as he felt the nobbly knees of her backward baby. I braced against the ewe with my heels and together we tugged, he gripping the knees with his small strength while I strained at the hoofs. Suddenly a bundle of wet wool flew out with a big, sucking slosh, and the two of us fell backwards on the grass. It was a fine lamb, small but strong, an unexpected gift. The ewe was a young one that had not lambed before, and I was pleased to see her set straight to work cleaning the caul from her babe's face; presently the lamb rewarded her with an enormous sneeze. We laughed, Jamie's eyes round and proud and happy.

We left them, the mother licking the remains of the yellow sac off her baby's fleece, and wandered from the field and into the copse where the stream runs, to wash the blood and muck from our own hands and clothes. The water bubbled and sang over the layers of shale. Because the day was warm and we were hot from our efforts, I stripped Jamie down to his skin and let him splash naked while I rinsed his smock and my pinafore and flung them over a bush to dry. I had unpinned my whisk, untied my cap, and pulled off my hose. My skirt tucked up, I found a flat rock and sat down to feed Tom, letting the rills run over my toes while Jamie paddled. I stroked the fine, downy hair on Tom's head and watched Jamie splashing in the cool water. He had lately reached that age when a mother looks at her babe and finds him a babe no longer, but a child full formed. The curves have turned into long, graceful lines: the fat and folded legs stretched out into lithe limbs; the rounded belly slimmed to a straight-standing body. A face, suddenly capable of the full range of expression, has smoothed its way out of all those crinkled chins and plumped-out cheeks. I loved to look at Jamie's new self, the smoothness of his skin, the curve of his neck, and the tilt of his golden head, always gazing curiously at some new wonder in his world.

He was springing from stone to stone, waving his arms wildly to keep his footing as he chased the darting, blue-bodied dragonflies. As I watched, one alit on a branch near my hand. The glassy panes of her wings caught the light in rainbow colours, like the stained windows in our church. I laid a finger softly on the twig and could feel the swift shivering and hear the faint hum from her vibrating wings. Then she took off, swooping down upon a passing wasp. Her legs had seemed flimsy as threads, but they snapped around the wasp like an iron trap. Still in flight, her powerful jaws closed on the insect and devoured it. So it goes, I thought idly. A birth and a death, each unlooked for.

I leant back against the stream's bank and closed my eyes. I must have dozed for a moment, or otherwise I surely would have heard the tread of boots coming through the trees. As it was, he was almost upon me when I opened my eyes and met his, lifted from the open book he carried. I jumped up, fumbling and tugging at my bodice. Tom opened his pink mouth and howled indignantly at the interruption to his feeding.

The rector raised a hand and smiled kindly. 'He is quite just to protest my intrusion. Do not discompose yourself, Anna. I'm sorry to have startled you, but I was so lost in my book, and in the loveliness of this day, that I was not aware there was anyone else in the copse.'

I was too surprised and mortified by the rector's sudden appearance to make any civil reply to him. To my further astonishment, he did not walk on then, but sat down upon a neighbouring rock and pulled off his own boots so that his feet, too, could dandle in the rills. He reached down into the clear water and cupped his hands, splashing the coolness onto his face and then running his fingers through his long, black hair. He lifted his face up to the dappled sunlight and closed his eyes.

'How easy it is to feel the goodness of God on such a day!' he whispered. 'Sometimes I wonder why we shut ourselves up in churches. What can man make, after all, that evokes the Divine as a place such as this?'

I maintained my stupid silence, unable to quiet my mind to think of any answer. Tom continued to cry loudly. Mr. Mompellion looked at him, squirming in my arms, and then reached across to take him from me. Surprised, I gave him over, and then was even more surprised at the practised way that Mr. Mompellion held him, up against his shoulder, firmly patting him on the back. Tom stopped crying almost at once and let forth a huge, wet belch. The rector laughed. 'I learned from caring for my little sisters that one who is neither mother nor wet nurse must hold a babe so, upright, so that it ceases to search for the teat.' I must have looked amazed at this, for Mr. Mompellion glanced at me and laughed again. 'You must not think that a minister's life is lived entirely among lofty words spoken from high pulpits.' He inclined his head to where Jamie, downstream from us, was so engrossed in building his stick dams across the stream that he had barely raised his head to register the rector's presence. 'We all begin as naked children, playing in the mud.'

At that, he handed Tom back to me, rose, and made his way downstream towards Jamie. Halfway there, he set his foot on a moss-slicked stone. His arms fanned in crazy circles as he tried to regain his balance, and Jamie jumped up in the water, laughing with the wild, uncouth mirth of a three-year-old. I frowned and glared at Jamie, but Mr. Mompellion threw back his head and laughed along with him, splashing the few yards left between them with his hands outstretched to grab my squealing little boy and toss him high into the air. The two of them played so for a time, and then Mr. Mompellion turned back towards me and Tom and settled himself once more on the bank near us. He sighed, and closed his eyes again, his lips curved in a slight smile.

'I pity those who live in towns and do not learn to love all this – the sweet scent of wet weeds and the ordinary, daily miracles of creation. It was of these I was reading when I interrupted you. Would you like to hear some words from my text?'

I nodded, and he reached for his book. 'These are the writings of Augustine of Hippo, a monk who grew great in his theology long ago on Africa's Barbary Coast. Here he asks himself what we mean when we talk of miracles.'

I can recall only snatches of what he read. But I do remember how his voice seemed to blend with the cadences of the stream and give the words an enduring music. 'Consider changes of day and night . . . the fall of leaves and their return to the trees the following spring, the infinite power in seeds . . . and then give me a man who sees and experiences these things for the first time, with whom we can still talk – he is amazed and overwhelmed at these miracles.'

I was sorry when he ceased reading, and would have asked him to go on, if I had not been struck silent by awe of him. For though I worked every day in his house, it was only with his wife that I had easy communication. It was not that he was harsh in manner by any means, but he often seemed so lost in large matters that he did not notice the small doings of his household. I tried my best to come and go and do my tasks without distracting him, and I can say with some pride that there were very few times that he had had cause to notice me. And so I sat there, mute and meditating, and he must have taken my distant look for vacancy or boredom, for he stood up all of a sudden and reached for his boots, saying that he had imposed upon me quite enough and must be about his business.

At that, I did find a small voice in which to thank him most sincerely for his consideration in sharing these great thoughts with me. 'For it is wonderful to me that a lofty thinker such as this should have so close a communion with the ordinary things of the soil and of the seasons.'

He smiled kindly. 'Mrs. Mompellion has spoken to me of your

understanding. She believes it is superior, and I see it may be so.' He took his leave then and turned back towards the rectory. I lingered there with the children for a while, thinking that what was true of Augustine was true also of our minister, and what a strange thing it was to have such a man, so open and so kindly, in our pulpit.

At last, I called to Jamie and we, too, set our feet on the path for home. All along the way, Jamie kept darting off like a swallow, swooping down to pluck the blowsy, late-blooming dog roses. When we neared the cottage, he made me wait by the door while he ran on inside. 'Close your eyes, Mummy,' he cried excitedly. Obediently, I waited, my face buried in my hands, wondering what game he was devising. I heard him thump up the stairs, scrambling, as he did when he was in a hurry, on all fours like a puppy. A few moments passed, and then I heard the upstairs casement creak open.

'All right, Mummy. Now! Look up!' I tilted my face and opened my eyes to find myself in a velvet rain of rose petals. The soft, sweet-scented shower brushed my cheeks. I pulled off my cap and shook out my long hair and let the petals land in its tangles. Little Tom gurgled with joy, his fat fists batting at the bright cascade of pink and creamy yellow. Jamie leant out over the sill above me, shaking the last few petals from a corner of sheet.

'This,' I thought, smiling gratefully up at him, 'this moment is my miracle.'

And thus we passed the wondrous days of our reprieve, and I busied myself in preparation for a winter that was hard to conceive of on those heavy afternoons, when the bees buzzed into hives that brimmed with the heather-scented honey. There were apple ladders poking through the trees and tripods going up all around, waiting for a day cool enough for the hog butchering. Though we had none of our own swine, I always helped my neighbours the Hadfields in return for a portion of bacon. Alexander Hadfield was a fastidious man who preferred cutting cloth to hacking at flesh and bone and would not soil even his second-best suit of clothes in any manner of outdoor work. So Mary's eldest by her first husband would do the slaughter and the butchery. Jonathan Cooper was a big lad like his late father and made short work of it, while his little brother Edward ran about with Jamie, finding ways to shirk the small chores we laid on them. Every time we sent them to fetch a bavin to keep the cauldron boiling, the two of them would disappear behind the woodpile, howling with delight over some new game they'd invented. Finally, Mary left off washing the guts for the sausage casings and went to see what manner of mischief they'd devised themselves. She came back with one hand occupied in holding Edward by the ear and the other extended as far in front of her as possible, dangling something, glossy and black, tied to the end of a string. As she drew closer I could see it was a dead rat, a sorry little corpse, all wet and rheumy-eyed with a smear of bright blood about its muzzle. Behind her, Jamie walked sheepishly, dragging another such. Mary flung the one she carried into the fire, and at her prompting, Jamie reluctantly did the same.

'Can you believe it, Anna, the two of them were playing with these loathsome pests as if they were poppets. The woodpile's full of them, seemingly. All dead, thanks be for small mercies.' Since we couldn't halt our work, Mary called Alexander to deal with the rat-fall, and the two of us shared a quiet laugh as her man, too nice to give a hand with the hog butchery, dispatched bloody rodent corpses instead. Somehow, the sight of him at his task eased our load a little bit as we toiled on, competing against the fading light to get the fat rendered and the sides salted. It was, as ever, hard and hateful work, but I kept my mind fixed on the smell of the bacon sizzling in my skimmer and thought how Jamie would enjoy it a few weeks hence.

W hen at last the skies clouded it was almost a relief. The misty rains seemed restful to the eyes, rinsing the landscape. But the damp after the heat brought fleas beyond any infestation I remember. It is an odd thing, how biting pests of all kinds will find one person flavoursome and another not to their liking at all. In my house, the fleas feasted on my tender children, leaving them covered in madding welts. I burned all our bedstraw before I went to see the Gowdies for a balm. I was half hoping to find Anys by herself again, for I longed to talk more with her, to learn how she had come to understand the world as she did. I thought that she could teach me much about how to manage alone as a woman in the world, how to embrace my state and even exalt in it, as she seemed to. She had hinted frankly enough about her many lovers, and I found myself consumed to know how she managed them, and the nature of her own feelings towards them.

And so I was disappointed when it was old Mem who met me on the step, her shawl saying she was on her way out, and her hasty manner making me think she was due at some confinement, though whose it might be I could not think, for none that I knew who were with child were yet within a month of their time.

'Ah, I could have saved you the walk, Anna, as I'm on my way to the Hadfields. Young Edward Cooper is burning up with fever, so I'm bringing him a draught.' I turned to walk back with her, fretful at this news. Although she was very aged, her hair thin and silvery where it escaped her fraying cap, Mem was straight and lithe as a green cornstalk, and she moved with the vigour of a man. As we hurried to the Hadfields, I had to lengthen my own stride to keep up with her. When we got to the cottage, a strange pied horse was tethered to the post by the watering trough. Mary met us at the door, flustered with anxiety and, it seemed, embarrassment. 'Thank you, thank you indeed for coming, Mem, but Mr. Hadfield sent to Bakewell for the barber-surgeon, and he is with Edward now. I am sure we are all grateful for your wisdom in these matters, but Mr. Hadfield said we must not stint here, and surely Edward's father, God rest him, did leave me in purse to handle the expense.'

Mem made a sour face. She did not think any more of barbersurgeons than they were wont to think of cunning women such as she. And yet Mem helped us as she could for pence or payment in kind as each of us was set to manage it, while the surgeons would not stir without the clank of shillings to line their pockets. Bowing coldly, Mem turned and walked away. But I was curious, and so I lingered until Mary signalled me to follow her. The barber-surgeon had asked to have the child brought downstairs, as I expect he would not deign to work in the crowded upper room. Mr. Hadfield had cleared his tailor's bench and little Edward was laid naked upon it. At first, I could not see the child for the surgeon's dark bulk was in my way, but as he stepped aside to reach into his bag, I winced. The poor little soul was covered in squirming leeches, their sucking parts embedded in his tender arms and neck, and their round, slimy nethers flicking and twitching as they feasted. I supposed it was fortunate that Edward was too far gone in his feverish delirium to understand what had befallen him. Mary's face creased with concern as she held the child's limp hand. Mr. Hadfield stood beside the surgeon, nodding deferentially at his every utterance.

'He is a small child, so we need not draw overmuch to restore the balance of his humours,' the surgeon said to Mr. Hadfield, who was holding Edward's shoulders. When the time had elapsed to his satisfaction, he called for vinegar and applied it to the engorged creatures so that they twitched all the harder, their jaws relaxing as they sought to escape the irritant. With a series of deft tugs, he pinched them off, a spurt of bright blood following, which he stanched with linen scraps that Mr. Hadfield provided him. He rinsed each leech in a cup of water and dropped it into a leather pouch alive with writhing lobes. 'If the child is not improved by nightfall, then you must purge and fast him. I will give you a receipt for a tincture that will open his bowels.' The man was packing his bag as Mary and her husband thanked him. I followed him into the street and, when the Hadfields were out of hearing, made bold with the question that was tormenting me.

'If you please, sir – the child's fever – could it be the Plague?'

The man waved a gloved hand dismissively and did not even turn to look at me. 'No chance of it,' he said. 'The Plague, by God's grace, has not been in our shire these score years. And the child has no Plague tokens on his body. It is a putrid fever merely, and if the parents follow my instructions, he will live.'

His foot was in the stirrup, such was his impatience to be gone. The saddle leather creaked as he settled his ample rump. 'But, sir,' I continued, hardly crediting my own forwardness, 'if there has been no Plague here these twenty years, then perhaps you have seen no cases against which to rightly judge the child's condition.'

'Ignorant woman!' he said, wheeling his horse carelessly so that a damp clod from the late rains flew up and struck me, splattering my skirt. 'Are you saying I don't know my profession?' He flicked the reins and would have been away had I not grasped the horse's bridle. 'Are lumps at the neck and rosy rings on the body not Plague tokens?' I cried.

He pulled up sharply and looked me in the face for the first time. 'Where have you seen these things?' he demanded.

'On the body of my lodger, buried at last full-moon,' I replied.

'And you bide near the Hadfields?'

'The next door.'

At this, he crossed himself. 'Then God save you and this village,' he said. 'And tell your neighbours to call upon me no more.' Then he was off, heading down the road at such a gallop that he almost collided with Martin Miller's haywain as it turned the sharp bend by the Miner's Tavern.

L ittle Edward Cooper was dead before sunset. His brother, Jonathan, lay ill a day later, and Alexander Hadfield but two days after that. At the end of a sennight, Mary Hadfield was widow for a second time in her life, and her two sons lay in the churchyard beside their dead father. I was not there to see them buried, for by then I had mourning of my own to do.

My Tom died as babies do, gently and without complaint. Because they have been such a little time with us, they seem to hold to life but weakly. I used to wonder if it was so because the memory of Heaven still lived within them, so that in leaving here they do not fear death as we do, who no longer know with certainty where it is our spirits go. This, I thought, must be the kindness that God does for them and for us, since He gives so many infants such a little while to bide with us.

The fever rose in him suddenly, before noon, while I was working at the rectory. Jane Martin sent for me straightaway, for which I was grateful. She took Jamie with her to her mother's house, so that I could focus all my thoughts and care on Tom. He cried for a while, when he tried to suckle and couldn't find the strength for it. Then he just lay in my arms, staring at me wide-eyed and whimpering now and then. Soon, his stare became unfixed and distant, and finally he simply closed his eyes and panted. I sat by the hearth and held him, amazed that I hadn't noticed how long his little body had grown, spilling out of my arms now, when once he'd fit in the crook of my elbow. 'Soon you will be with your father,' I whispered. 'He'll still be able to hold you like that. You'll be so comfortable in his strong arms.' Lib Hancock came, carrying fresh farm cheese, which I could not eat, and saying words of comfort that blurred into nonsense in my head. In the afternoon, my stepmother came to take her place. Her words I do remember, for they seared me so.

'Anna, you are a fool.'

I looked up in astonishment, dragging my eyes off Tom's little face for the first time that day. Her plain, pasty features came into focus through my tears, and I saw that her expression was one of exasperation.

'Why do you let yourself love an infant so? I warned you, did I not, to school your heart against this?' It was true. Aphra had seen three of her own babies into the ground before their first year, one through fever, one through flux, and one, a lusty boy, who had just stopped breathing in his bed, with nary a mark upon him. I had stood with her through all these deaths, marvelling at her dry eyes.

'It is folly and ill fortune to love a child until it walks and is well grown. As you now see, as you now see . . .'

Her voice lost its hectoring tone as she saw my eyes filling up. She reached a hand to pat me on the shoulder, but I shrugged her off. 'God made your heart hard, Stepmother,' I said. 'You may thank Him for it. He did not do me such a kindness. For I loved Tom from the moment I first reached down and touched the crown of his head, all wet and bloody as it was . . .'

I was weeping then and could not continue. But even as I spoke so, I knew that it was true that fear of losing him had marched beside that love, every moment of the short time I had him with me. Aphra handed me a hag-stone and mumbled some strange words over it. 'You must hang it over him to keep evil spirits from snatching away his soul.' I took the hag-stone from her and held it in my hand till she left the cottage. Then I flung it into the fire.

When I heard footsteps in the dooryard soon after, I cursed silently, for I knew in my heart that my time with Tom was slipping speedily away, and I did not want to share it. But the gentle knock and the quiet greeting told me it was Elinor Mompellion. I called to her to enter, and with a few soft footsteps she was kneeling beside us, enfolding us in her arms. She did not upbraid me for my grieving but shared in it with me, and so calmed my weeping and my rage. Afterwards, she drew a chair near to the window and read to me from Our Lord's words of love for little children until the light became too dim. I listened to her as an infant to a lullaby, not marking the meaning but taking ease from the sound. I believe she would have stayed all night had I not told her that I would take Tom up to my bed.

I crooned to him as I climbed the stairs and laid him down upon our pallet. He lay just as I placed him, his arms splayed limply. I lay down beside him and drew him close. I pretended to myself that he would wake in the wee hours with his usual lusty cry for milk. For a time his little pulse beat fast, his tiny heart pounding. But towards midnight the rhythms became broken and weak and finally fluttered and faded away. I told him I loved him and would never forget him, and then I folded my body round my dead baby and wept until finally, for the last time, I fell asleep with him in my arms.

When I woke, the light was streaming through the window. The bed was wet, and there was a wild voice howling. Tom's little body had leaked its life's blood from his throat and bowels. My own gown was drenched where I'd clutched him to me. I gathered him up off the gory pallet and ran into the street. My neighbours were all standing there, their faces turned to me, full of grief and fear. Some had tears in their eyes. But the howling voice was mine.

Sign of a Witch

W hen I was a child, my father would talk sometimes of his boyhood as a prentice seaman. Usually, he told us these tales when we had misbehaved, to scare us into better comportment. He spoke of the lash and the pickling that followed, where a man freshly scourged was untied from the mast and dunked into a barrel of stinging brine. He said the cruellest of the boatswains would lay on the whip so that the blows fell time and again on the same place, where the skin had already been peeled in long strips. The most skilful, he said, could land the lash so exactly as to work right through the muscle until the very bone lay bare.

The Plague is cruel in the same way. Its blows fall and fall again upon raw sorrow, so that before you have mourned one person that you love, another is ill in your arms. Jamie was crying bitterly for his brother when his tears turned into the fevered whimpering of the ill. My merry little boy loved his life, and he fought hard to hold on to it. Elinor Mompellion was at my side from the first, and her gentle voice is what I remember best from those dim, woeful days and nights.

'Anna, I must tell you that my Michael suspected Plague from the moment he attended Mr. Viccars's sickbed. You know that he was but lately a student at the University at Cambridge, and he sent at once to his friends, asking them to enquire of the great physicians who are teachers there, to find out what could be known of the latest preventives and remedies. This very day he has had some answer back.' She unfurled the letter from her pocket and scanned it. I peered over her shoulder, trying to make out the sense of it as best I could, for I have had but little experience with handwriting, and though this was written very fair, the reading of it was difficult for me. 'The writer is a dear friend of Mr. Mompellion's, and so you see he spends much time upon salutations and expressions of concern and hopes that Mr. Mompellion may yet be mistaken in his suspicions of the nature of the disease amongst us. But here, finally, he comes to the point and declares that the learned doctors place great faith in these new means of combating the Plague.' And so it was that on the very best authority, and with the best of intentions, my poor boy suffered through some treatments that in the end maybe only prolonged his pain.

Where Mr. Viccars's sore had erupted near his neck, Jamie's rose in his armpit, and he cried piteously from the agony of it, holding his slender little arm far out to his side so as not to hurt himself by the pressure of his own flesh. I had already tried cataplasms of Bay salt and rye meal, made into a paste with egg yolk and strapped across the sore with a piece of soft leather. But the tumour just continued to grow from walnut-size to the dimensions of a goose egg, yet resisted to burst. Mr. Mompellion's friend had written out in detail a receipt from the College of Physicians, and with Mrs. Mompellion's help I tried this next. It called for the roasting in embers of a great onion, hollowed out and filled with a fig, chopped rue, and a dram of Venice treacle. Lucky for us, as I then thought, Mem Gowdie had both the dried figs and the treacle, which is honey mixed with a great number of rare ingredients, its making long and exacting.

I roasted those onions, one after the other, even though the discomfort of their pressure on the swollen place made my child scream and toss and run damp with pain-sweat. It is the hardest thing in the world to inflict hurt on your own child, even if you believe you act for his salvation. I cried as I bound on the hated poultices, then I held him and rocked him and tried to comfort him as best I could, distracting him with all his favourite songs and stories, as many as I could rack my brain to invent.

'Long ago and far away, there lived a little boy,' I whispered to him in the wee hours of the night. I felt the need of fending off the silent dark with a constant stream of chatter. 'He was a good little boy, but very poor, and he lived all his life in a dark room where he had to work long and hard, toiling all day and all night until he was very tired. And that room had just one door, yet the little boy had never passed through it and didn't know what was beyond. And because he didn't know, he was afraid of the door, and though he longed to know what there was outside his room, he never had the heart to lift his hand and lift the latch and see. But one day a bright angel appeared to the little boy, and she said to him, "It's time. You've been very good, and you've done your work well. Now you can set it aside and come with me." She opened the door, and beyond was the most beautiful, sunny garden the boy had ever seen. There were children there, laughing and playing. And they took the little boy by the hand and showed him all the wonders of his new home. And so he lived and played in that golden light for ever and ever, and nothing ever hurt him again.' His eyelids flickered and he gave me a wan smile. I kissed him and whispered, 'Don't be afraid, my darling, don't be afraid.'

In the morning, Anys Gowdie brought a cordial that she said was decocted from the tops of feverfew with a little wormwood in sugared sack. As she and her aunt always did when they brought their remedies, she laid her hands gently on Jamie before she gave him the draught and murmured softly: 'May the seven directions guide this work. May it be pleasing to my grandmothers, the ancient ones. So mote it be.' She had also brought a cooling salve, fragrant of mint, and she asked me if she might apply it to the child to lower his fever. She sat upon the floor with her back to the wall and her knees raised and laid his little body along her thighs, so that his head rested on her knees and his feet at her hips. Her touch was tender and rhythmical, as she brought her hands in long strokes across his brow and down body and limbs. As she stroked him, she sang softly: 'Two angels came from the East. One brought fire, one brought frost. Out, fire! In, frost! By all the Mothers' gentle ghosts.' Jamie had been restless and whimpering, but he calmed as she crooned to him. His eyes fixed on hers with an intent stare, and he grew quiet under her touch.

Anys stroked Jamie and hummed to him until he fell into a blessed sleep. When I lifted him from her lap and laid him upon the pallet, his skin had lost its livid colour and felt cool to my touch. I thanked her from my heart for the relief she had brought to him. Generally, it was her way to shrug off thanks or praise with a gruff set-down, but that morning she was tender with me and took my outstretched hand. 'You are a good mother, Anna Frith.' She regarded me gravely. 'Your arms will not be empty forever. Remember that when the way looks bleak to you.'

Anys, I now see, knew well enough that her care would bring my boy but a brief respite. Hour by hour, as the good effects of the draught and the salve wore off, the fever rose again, and by afternoon he had become delirious. 'Mummy, Tom's calling you!' he whispered urgently in his tiny, cracked voice, flailing his good arm as if to summon me.

'I'm here, my darling. Tell Tommy I'm right here.' I tried to keep the tears out of my voice, but at the mention of Tom my aching breasts began to seep milk until it soaked in great dark patches right through my bodice.

Elinor Mompellion brought a little silk bag for Jamie, through which she had run a soft riband. 'It contains a palliative sent by one of the rector's acquaintances in Cambridge,' she said. 'He directed that it be hung so as to fall over the sufferer's left pap – that would be over his heart, you see.'

'But what is within it?' I asked hopefully.

'Well, ah, I did enquire as to the contents, and I was not persuaded of any great good to come therefrom ... but the man who sent it is a well-esteemed physician, and he says it is a remedy much thought of among the Florentine doctors who have had a large experience with Plague.'

'But what is it?' I asked again.

'It contains a dried toad,' she said. I wept then, even though I knew her intentions were all of the best. I could not help myself.

Mrs. Mompellion also brought food, though I could eat none of it. She sat by me and held my hand and whispered whatever words she thought I could bear to hear. I learned only later, for my thoughts were bent then entirely on my own griefs, that when she left after long hours with me she would go next door to Mary Hadfield, whose mother, having come to comfort her in her great loss, now lay ill herself. And thence across the street to the Sydells, who had three lying sick, and from there on to the Hawksworths' where Jane, who was pregnant, lay ill alongside her husband, Michael.

Jamie suffered for five days before God finally saw fit to take him. The day of his death, the strange circles bloomed on him: vivid crimson welts rising in rings just beneath the topmost layer of his skin. As the hours passed, these turned violet and then purple-black, hardening into crusts. It seemed as if the flesh inside of him was dying while he yet breathed, the putrefying meat pushing and bursting its way out of his failing body. Both of the Mompellions came when word reached them that these new Plague tokens had appeared. Jamie lay on a makeshift pallet before the hearth, where I had lit a low fire against the evening chill. I sat at the head of the pallet, pillowing Jamie's head in my lap and stroking his brow. The reverend knelt down upon the hard gritstone floor and commenced to pray. His wife slid silently from the chair and knelt beside him. I heard the words as if they came from far away.

'Omnipotent God, and most merciful Father, bow down Thine ear to our request, and let Thine eye look upon the miseries of Thy people. Behold, we cry unto Thee for mercy. Stay therefore Thine arm, and loose not the arrow of death to strike this young child into his grave. Call home Thy Angel of Wrath and let not this child perish under the heavy stroke of this dreadful Plague, which is now a dweller amongst us . . .' The fire in the hearth threw a warm glow on the kneeling pair, their heads, dark and fair, bent close together. It was only at the end of the prayer that Elinor Mompellion raised her eyes and looked at me. I shook my head as the tears ran down my face, and she knew her husband's pleas had been in vain.

I cannot recount the days that followed. I know I fought the sexton when he came to take Jamie's body away, crying out in my disordered state and trying to claw off the linen piece wound round him because I feared he could not breathe through it. I know I walked to the church many times. I saw Jamie laid in the ground there beside Tom, and then Mary Hadfield's mother, and three of the Sydell children and Jane Hawksworth's husband and after that her son, born too soon and dead a day later. I stood with Lib Hancock while her husband was buried, and the two of us clung to each other in our grief. But I cannot tell you what was said, in the church or at the graveside, save for the line 'In the midst of life, we are in Death,' which did indeed seem to me to be the whole description of our plight then.

Within a day or two, I found a way to trudge once again through my work, though my hands functioned separate from my mind, and I could not tell you a single task I did during that fortnight, as the days and nights slid by. It was as if a deep fog had settled on me and everything around me, and I groped my way from one chore to the next without really seeing anything clearly. When I had no toil to set my hands to, I spent much time in the churchyard. Not, as you would think, at the graves of my boys. I could not yet bring myself to be among the beloved dead. Instead, I lingered in the quiet grove behind the church, where the old graves are. It is a lumpy place, where the ground has heaved and sighed into grassy mounds and the briar roses tumbled in a bright profusion of ruddied hips over graves whose markings are weathered and barely legible. These I could abide to be among. They marked the losses and sufferings of people I did not know, whose pain I did not share. And from there I could not hear the rhythmic swish and thump of the sexton's shovelling or see the raw sillion laid open to receive the body of another neighbour.

There is, among these old graves, a great soaring stone cross, carved cunningly in the ancient ways of the people who walked these hills beyond the reach of memory. They say that it was brought here from the lonely track that wends near to the summit of the White Peak, and now it looms above the little monuments of our making like some uneasy foreign visitor. I would lean against the cross, resting my forehead against the rough grit of its wind-pitted surface. Remembered prayer-fragments formed and then dissolved, interrupted by the confusion of my thoughts. *Behold the Handmaid of the Lord.* Why was I not one of the many in the chamber of Death? My husband dead, and yet not me. My lodger gone, and yet not me. My neighbours, and yet not me. My babies – my babies! My eyes stung. I pressed my face against the stone and breathed the scent of it, cool and mossy and calming. *Let it be done unto me according to Thy Word.* My fingers traced the twining curves that ran up either side, and I imagined the skilled hands that had carved them. I wished I could talk to that long-ago craftsman. I wanted to know how his people had coped with what God had sent them. There were angels carved into the cross, but also strange creatures whose nature I did not know. Mrs. Mompellion had told me once that the cross came from a time when the Christian faith was new to Britain and had to vie with the old ways of the standing stones and the bloody sacrifices. I wondered dully if the craftsman who made it was thinking to outdo those other, older stone monuments. Had he fashioned it out of a faith that was hard and certain? Or had it been the gesture of a man seeking to appease a God who seemed to want not the love and awe that the Scriptures asked of us, but an endless surfeit of our suffering. *According to Thy Word.* Why were God's words always so harsh?

I believe I might have gone on so, given up to grief and confusion, if it had not been for a hirsel from my flock losing itself upon the moors. It was the third sennight after Jamie's death. I had been negligent of the sheep, and some of them had moved off on their own, searching for the better grass I should have shepherded them to long since. The sky was pewter that afternoon, and the air had the metallic taste of an early snowfall, so I had no choice but to seek them out, even though the task of placing one foot before the other on the uphill walk seemed an effort far beyond me. I was following what I hoped was the trail of their scat along a clough at the edge of the moors, praying to find them and bring them safely down before the light failed, when I heard a horrible yelling coming from near a mine that had been made Old Man by flooding some half dozen years earlier.

There were ten or twelve people in a rough circle, jostling and staggering, their loud voices slurring as if they'd come straight from the Miner's Tavern. Lib Hancock was among them, stumbling from the effects of drink, which I knew well she was not used to. In the centre, upon the ground, was Mem Gowdie, her frail old arms bound before her with a length of fraying rope. Brad Hamilton knelt across her chest as his daughter, Faith, grasped a fistful of the old woman's sparse silver hair and raked at her cheek with a hawthorn prick. 'I'll have it yet, witch!' she cried, as Mem moaned and tried to raise her bound hands to her face to fend off the blows. 'Your blood will drive this sickness from my mother's body.' In the circle, Hamilton's oldest boy, Jude, held his mother in his arms. Rubbing her hand over Mem's scratched and bleeding cheek, Faith stood up unsteadily and smeared the blood on her mother's neck, where the Plague sore rose throbbing.

I was running towards them, skidding and sliding down the steep side of the clough, the loose stones clattering around me, when Mary Hadfield broke from the throng and flung herself down beside poor Mem, pushing her face, all twisted with rage, within inches of the old woman's. 'You killed my family, hag!' Mem writhed, trying to shake her head in denial. 'I heard you curse us for bringing the physician to Edward! I heard you as you left my door! Your malice has brought Plague on my man and my mother and my boys!'

'Mary Hadfield!' I yelled, struggling to be heard over the drunken din. A few faces turned round as I pushed my way, panting, into the circle. 'Mem Gowdie did no such thing! Why are you saying this? I was on your very doorstep with her when that quack physician was in your house. She left your door with her lips sealed. Say rather that the physician hastened your Edward's death with his leeches and purges, before you slander this good soul!'

'Why do you defend her, Anna Frith? Do not your own babies lie rotting in the ground from her cursing? You should be helping us here. Get you gone if you have nowt to do but hinder.'

'Let's swim her!' yelled an ale-soused voice. 'Then we'll see if she's witch or no!'

'Aye!' yelled another, and soon they were dragging Mem, who seemed near insensible from beatings, towards the adit of the flooded mine. Her old, much-mended bodice had given way with the tugging, exposing one withered pap, purple from bruising. The mine was a wide one, and I could see the slick stones descending into darkness.

'You throw her down there, and you'll be murderers!' I yelled, trying to get in front of Brad Hamilton, who seemed the most sensible man amongst them. But when I grabbed his arm I saw that his face was distorted by drink and grief, and then I remembered he'd buried his son John that day. He flung me aside, and I missed my footing and fell hard, my head hitting a cropt of limestone. When I tried to raise it, the earth spun and turned dark.

When I came to myself, Mary Hadfield was wailing, 'She's sinking! She's sinking! She's no witch! God forgive us, we've killed her!' She was tugging first one of the men and then the other, trying to pull them to the adit. Jude held the end of the frayed old rope that had been tied to Mem, staring at it as if he expected to find some answer in its torn strands. I struggled to my feet and peered down into the dark, but I could see nothing but the distorted reflection of my own bloodied, anguished face peering back at me from the surface of the water. When I saw that no one was going to do anything, I pushed them aside and flung myself over the lip of the adit, feeling for the first stemple. But as I put my boot upon it, the rotted wood crumbled and fell away, and I dangled for a moment over the pit before someone, I did not at first see who, reached out an arm and pulled me back.

It was Anys Gowdie. Breathing hard from running all the way up hill from the village, she wasted no words. Someone clearly had brought news to her of what was afoot, for she had a fresh rope tied ready around her waist. She slung it over the old turn-tree and secured it to the stowes, then she slid straight down into that slimy dark. The others had fallen back from her, but now they surged forward, peering down into the mine. One of them staggered into me, the weight of his drunken body pushing me down onto my knees against the rock. With all my force I drove an elbow into his side and shoved him back, and then, wiping the blood from my eyes, I, too, strained to see into the adit. I could just make out Anys's hair, bright against the black water. There was a great deal of splashing, and then she began to climb, the limp body of her aunt lashed to her back. Luckily, many of the stemples were still sound enough to hold such a weight, and as she neared the top, Mary Hadfield and I reached down to grasp her arms and pull her up the last few feet.

Mary and I laid Mem upon the ground and Anys pressed again on her chest as the abusers had done not so many minutes earlier. Dark water spewed from her mouth. The old woman wasn't breathing. 'She's dead!' wailed Mary, and that disordered group took up the keening. Anys paid them no mind but knelt beside the body, covered her aunt's mouth with her own, and breathed into it. Kneeling beside her, I counted out the breaths. After the third, Anys paused. Mem Gowdie's chest rose by itself. She sputtered, groaned, and opened her eyes. The relief I felt lasted only an instant, for Lib, in a crazed voice, began crying: 'Anys Gowdie's raised the dead! It's her that's the witch! Seize her!'

'Lib!' I cried, rising dizzily up off the ground beside Mem and grasping her by both arms. 'Don't be a fool! Who amongst us here hasn't put their mouth to a lamb born unbreathing?'

'Shut *your* mouth, Anna Frith!' Lib Hancock yelled, throwing off my hands and at the same time stepping towards me, bringing her face inches from mine. 'For you yourself told me that this witch consorted with the Devil's spawn who brought the Plague here!

Know you not that Viccars was a manwitch? And she was his vessel!'

'Lib!' I shouted, seizing her by the shoulders and shaking her. 'Don't speak so of the blameless dead! Is not poor Mr. Viccars in his grave as surely as your dear husband?' Her eyes, glazed and strange, regarded me with hatred.

Cries of 'whore' and 'jade' and 'fornicator' were coming now from every twisted mouth, as the mob surged at Anys where she knelt beside her aunt, leaping upon her and clawing at her flesh. Only Mary Hadfield stood back, her face stricken. I pushed Lib out of my way and tried to get to Anys. A wind had whipped around from the north, the maddening, deafening wind we call Gabriel's Hounds. Anys was strong and fought them, and I tried to help her, grasping at one and then another, trying to pull them off her until my head began again to spin. Then Urith Gordon screamed.

'I can't see my reflection in her eyes! Sign of a witch! Sign of a witch! She witched my husband into lying with her!' At that, John Gordon began laying on to Anys like a man possessed. I grabbed at his forearm, trying to pull him back from her, but by then I was covered in blood from the gash on my temple, and I felt the beating in my head and I knew my strength was insufficient to his frenzy. 'Must get Mompellion' was my last thought; as I turned to run, someone struck me a blow that sent me sprawling.

I groaned and tried again to rise, but my limbs would not obey me. I saw the noose go around Anys's neck and knew they planned to hang her with her own rope, using the stowes as the scaffold. What I did not foresee was what happened next, for Anys Gowdie ceased her struggling then and drew herself up to her full, impressive height. Her cap had fallen off and the tendrils of her wet hair fell about her like strange golden snakes. A trickle of bright blood ran from her mouth.

'Yes,' she said, her voice deep and uncanny, 'I am the Devil's creature, and, mark me, he will be revenged for my life!' The men who held her stepped back a piece, making the sign of the cross and the other, older sign, against strong magic.

'Anys!' I groaned. 'Don't say these things! You know they are not so!'

She looked at me where I lay on the ground and gave a ghostly smile. But in her eyes, I read judgment: my loose tongue had helped betray her. Then she looked away and stared all round her at her persecutors. The sun, slipping below the horizon, found a narrow slit in the louring clouds. Through it, sudden and swift, beamed a lonely finger of light. It sped over the hillsides, touching each tree and stone until it reached Anys and lit her up as if she were on fire. Her amber eyes glinted yellow as a cat's.

'I have lain with him. Yes! I have lain with the Devil, and he is mighty and cold as ice to the touch. His seed, too, is cold and abundant as a river running between our thighs. For I have not lain with him alone! No! I tell you now, I have seen your wives lie with him! Yours, Brad Hamilton, and yours, John Gordon, and yours, too, Martin Highfield!' The women moaned or screamed their outrage, but their men were transfixed by Anys and did not look at them.

'We rejoice to do it, all of us together and without shame, many times, one after another, and sometimes two or more at once, sucking him and taking him howsoever he desires to go into us. No man's yard is as great as his. He is as a stallion amongst geldings compared to you.' Here she fixed her glare on the men she had named, and I saw them flinching. 'Every wife has said that her pleasure is extreme, far greater than with any of you!' And she laughed as she said this last, laughed as if she could not control herself. The men bellowed like oxen then and tugged as one upon the rope. It snapped tight and silenced her laughter. Her long legs kicked as they pushed her into the adit.

They were still kicking when John Gordon let go of the rope and looked wildly around for his wife. She saw his crazed eyes and began to run, her moan of fear a gargling bray. John Gordon reached her and brought her down with a blow. He grasped her hair and pulled her face up from the ground, rolling her over like a meal sack. 'Is it true?' he yelled, his knuckles bunched tight and poised above her. 'Did you lay with Satan?' Before she could answer, he smashed his fist into her face. Blood streamed from her nose. He raised his arm to strike her again.

Michael Mompellion's voice, when it came thundering down the clough, was louder and fiercer even than the wind.

'What in the name of God have you done here?'

John Gordon's arm dropped to his side. He turned to stare at the rector. None of us had ever seen such a look upon him. He had a torch in his hand, and it lit his face from beneath so that his eyes were bright, fierce orbs. I thought, as I lay there in my dull pain, that this is how an owl must look to a mouse in that last second before the talons sink into the flesh. And he did swoop then, plunging Anteros down the steep slope, sending the stones flying from beneath his hoofs. I saw that Mary Hadfield was cowering behind him in the saddle and realized she'd had the wit to go and fetch him here. He bore down first upon Brad Hamilton, who was closest to the stowes. Hamilton raised both arms as if to defend himself, but Anteros reared like a battle charger, driving him back. The rector turned the horse and slid from the saddle, throwing down the torch so that it hissed in the mud. He pulled a knife from his belt. Reaching up, he cradled Anys in one arm, slashing the rope with the other. Her beautiful face was unrecognizable, purple and bloated, with the tongue hanging out like a cur's. He drew his cloak up so that it covered her.

Someone – I think it was Martin Highfield – was still drunk or crazed enough to try to defend what had been done.

'She . . . she admitted it,' he slurred dully. 'She confessed she lay with the Devil . . .'

Mompellion raised his voice to a roar. 'Oh, yes, the Devil has been here this night! But not in Anys Gowdie! Fools! Ignorant wretches! Anys Gowdie fought you with the only weapon she had to hand – your own ugly thoughts and evil doubting of one another! Fall on your knees, now!'

And they did, dropping as one to the ground. 'Pray to God that in His infinite mercy He will save your miserable souls.' He drew a breath then and sighed. When he spoke again, the rage was gone from his voice, but each word carried clearly, even over the whine and groan of the wind. 'Do we not have suffering enough in this village? Is there not Death enough here for you all that you bring the crime of murder amongst us as well? Gird yourselves, and pray that God does not exact from you the price that this day's deeds deserve.'

All at once, the voices began: some in slurred murmurs, some crying out loudly upon the Lord, others weeping and beating their breasts. At that time, you see, we all of us believed that God listened to such prayers.

Venom in the Blood

The snow that blew in on that night's wind blanketed the village and brought a deep silence upon us. People crept through the white streets to their business, hunched over and muffled in their shawls as if in hiding. Bad news passed in whispers. Witch's blood did nothing to aid Grace Hamilton, who died of Plague that week, leaving her children Jude and Faith sickening. The storm buried my lost sheep and reduced my flock by a third. I was blurred and vacant from the blow to my head and slept for nigh on a whole day and night before I was steady enough to resume my search for them. By the time I found the poor beasts, huddled together in the ley of a rock outcropt, the snow had covered them in a high white drift and froze them near solid. At the time I was so disordered that my first thought was to be grateful that fewer living things now depended on my care.

Michael Mompellion held a funeral for Anys but Mem Gowdie was not there to witness it. She had got the coughing sickness from her near-drowning and lay insensible in the rectory, where Elinor Mompellion had insisted she be brought. Together, we tended her, which very soon came to nothing much more than sitting by her bed and listening to the rattle of her breath. She had asked, when she was still able to speak, for a comfrey salve on her wounded face. We bound it there with fresh linen, but the bandage would hardly stay upon her sunken cheek. Her skin, friable as a dry winter leaf, bloomed purple and yellow with bruises from the blows she had received. When Mem had delivered both my boys, her strong, skilled hands had soothed my terrors and made my labours easy. Now, her fingers looked as frail as finch's bones, and when I held them in mine I feared that the slightest pressure would snap them.

Her last day was the hardest for me. Towards the end, her breathing would cease entirely for many minutes, and I would think she was at last at peace. But then her throat would give a wet gurgle, straining for air, and her chest would rise and fall in a series of swift, shallow pants. After a moment or two, these would slow and diminish, until she again stopped breathing. This happened more times than I could credit. Each time, the pauses in which she did not breathe grew ever longer. The waiting became unbearable. When the end came, at last, I did not recognize it, but sat there, expecting the greedy rasp that would again begin the cycle. It was not until I heard the rectory clock chime the quarter hour, and then the half, without any breath between them, that I finally called the Mompellions to acknowledge Mem's passing. She died just five days after Anys. With the two of them went the main part of the physick we relied upon, along with the best chance our women had of living through their confinements with healthy infants in their arms.

Neither did the Law of the Land do anything about the killings: the justice of the peace from Bakewell refused to come near our village or accept from us any persons for arrest, saying that no gaol in the parish would consent to hold them until the next assizes. Instead, those few from the mob who were not struck down with the Plague skulked amongst us, gaunt and haunted and awaiting God's judgment. By the following Sunday a mere five of the dozen who'd been at the clough that night were well enough to put on the penitents' garb and go barefoot to church to make their prayers for forgiveness.

When Sunday morning dawned, white and windless, we all trudged thither, the ice-crusted snow crunching beneath our feet. John Gordon was one of those who slipped into the corner of contrition, meeting no one's eyes but bending solicitously over Urith, who clung to his arm, the whiteness of her penitent's robe showing up the purple bruising all round her swollen, broken nose. Lib Hancock, too, was there. She walked past me as I stood in my pew and did not meet my eyes.

Pale and hushed, we took our appointed places, the grieving and the guilty. We were, in this village, some three hundred and three score souls. Less the babes, the frail elderly, those few who must needs labour even on the Lord's Day, and the handful of Quakers and nonconformists who bide up on the high farms, the number who gather each week in our church is a firm two hundred and one score worshippers. Since our places are set from long tradition, an absence is as obvious as a missing tooth. That Sunday, the growing roll of dead and ailing left many empty spaces.

Michael Mompellion did not use his pulpit that Sunday as I had expected. All week, throughout the funeral for Anys, and later, when he had looked in almost hourly on Mem, he had been thin-lipped and taut as a bowstring, as if struggling to contain a terrible rage. For most of that week, he had not taken his customary, companionable dinner with Elinor but worked instead alone in his library composing, as I thought, a sermon that would lacerate. One night, late in the week, as I was making my way bent double under a load of hay for the sheep, I caught sight of him, walking in the storm-stripped orchard with a stooped figure beside him. It was bitter cold, for the snow clouds had blown away, and the stars seemed mirrored in the icy glitter of the white-crusted fields. It was strange to me that the rector should choose such a night for an outdoor audience. But then I recognized the figure at his side and understood why he would not want to announce such a meeting.

Mr. Mompellion was conferring with Thomas Stanley, the Puritan who had quit our parish more than three years since, on Saint Bartholomew's Day, in the Year of Our Lord 1662. Parson Stanley had told us then that he could not in conscience accept the order to use the Book of Common Prayer, and that he was but one of hundreds of priests who were resigning his pulpit on that day. It had been a strange thing for us, to have our small village suddenly thrust into the high matters of king and parliament. It may seem odd that one like me, who grew up in the shadow of such large matters as the execution of one king and the exile and return of another, had stayed so ignorant of her own times. But our village was far from any important road or vital strong point, and our men were valued more for the delving of lead than the firing of it. So all these great events barely lapped at the foot of our mountain and never caught any of us in their flow, until the matter of how and with whom we prayed.

Mr. Stanley was a sincere man, uncommonly gentle for a Puritan and no fanatic, but still his Sunday had been a severe Sabbath and his church had been a cheerless place, innocent of lace or polished brass and stinting even in the beauty of its prayers. Not long after his protest, a law was passed saying that dissenting clergy should keep at least five miles from their old parishes, so that they might not stir up differences. Another law prescribed harsh penalties – fines and prison and even transportation – for all meetings of more than five persons for any worship save that of Common Prayer. Accordingly, Mr. Stanley moved from the rectory and left the village, and we were without a resident priest for almost two years, until the Mompellions came. By then, Mr. Stanley's wife had died, leaving him alone among strangers. It was not in the Mompellions' nature to turn the old man away from the place and people he best knew. I do not know what words were said or what pacts made, but one day he was amongst us again, having slipped quietly back into a croft on the high farm of the Billings, a nonconformist family. By the time the Plague arrived amongst us, he had been returned here for almost a year, an old man who kept his own counsel, lived very private and stayed well clear of village affairs. And if two or even three times five souls gathered from time to time in the Billings' parlour, none of us were inclined to enquire the purpose for it.

But now, it seemed, Mr. Mompellion had sought out Mr. Stanley. It was not until Sunday that I was able finally to know why. Mr. Mompellion climbed the pulpit steps, and instead of the frown that had creased his brow all week, his face that morning looked serene. And so he launched into the sermon that sealed our fates, and yet he was more than halfway into it before anyone in the church realized where he was leading us.

'"Greater love no man hath than this, that he lay down his life for a friend."' He said the familiar words and then dropped his head, letting the fragment of text hover in a silence so lengthy that I worried he had forgot what next he purposed to say. But when he looked up, his face was alight and wreathed in such a smile that the church felt suddenly warmer. His words flowed then, cadenced as a poem. He spoke with passion about God's love and the sufferings His son had endured for our sake, and he held every single one of us in his gaze, making us feel the power of that love and reminding us of how it had fallen, in our time, upon each of us. He intoxicated us with his words, lifting and carrying us away into a strange ecstasy, taking each of us to that place where we kept our sweetest memories.

And then, finally, he approached his point. Were we not bound to return this love to our fellow humans? Even to lay down our own lives, if that was what God asked of us? He had not, until then, mentioned the Plague, and I realized with a surprise that for the half hour he'd been speaking, I had not thought of it, who had thought of nothing else in many weeks.

'Dear brothers and sisters,' he said then, his voice bathing us in affection, 'we know that God sometimes has spoken to His people in a terrible voice, by visiting dread things upon them. And of these things, Plague – this venom in the blood – is one of the most terrible. Who would not fear it? Its boils and its blains and its great carbuncles. Grim Death, the King of Terrors, that marches at its heels.

'Yet God in His infinite and unknowable wisdom has singled us out, alone amongst all the villages in our shire, to receive this Plague. It is a trial for us, I am sure of it. Because of His great love for us, He is giving us here an opportunity that He offers to very few upon this Earth. Here, we poor souls of this village may emulate Our Blessed Lord. Who amongst us would not seize such a chance? Dear friends, I believe we must accept this gift. It is a casket of gold! Let us plunge in our hands to the elbows and carry away these riches!'

He dropped his voice then, as if to let us in on a great secret. 'There are some who would say that God sends us this thing not in love, but in rage. They will say Plague is here because we have earned it in our sinning. For is not the first Plague in all of human history the one that God sent to smite Egypt? Did not Pharaoh disobey God, and was his mighty kingdom not laid waste for it? And in the dark of night, when our firstborn is snatched from us' – here, he paused, his gaze moving across the many pews between us until his eyes, bright and glistening, looked straight into mine – 'at such a time, it is easier to believe in God's vengeance than His mercy.

'But I do not think God sends us this Plague in anger. I do not think we here in this village are Pharaoh in His eyes. Oh, yes, surely we have sinned in our lives, each one of us, and many times. Do we not find Satan like a lapwing crying before us with enticement and vainglory, to draw our mind far away from the God of our salvation?

Friends, all of us, in our time, have listened to the false music of those cries. There is none here who has not followed them – and fallen. None whose mind has not been tossed with corrupt fancies.

'But I think our God does not send this Plague as a punishment for our sins. No!' His eyes travelled across the congregation, searching out the miners and their families, and addressing himself to them, particularly. 'Like the ore that must be melted all to liquid to find the pure metal, so must we be rendered in the fiery furnace of this disease. And as the smith tends his furnace, all through the night if need be, to secure the valuable ore within, so is God here, near to us, nearer perhaps than He has ever come, or ever will come, in all our lives.' Five pews in front of me, I saw the white head of Alun Houghton, Barmester to our miners, coming slowly erect on his massive shoulders as the rector's words penetrated his understanding. The rector seized the moment and stretched out his hand towards him. 'Therefore, let us not flinch, let us not fail! Let us choose *not* the dull lustre of our base state when God would have us shine!'

'Amen!' Houghton's gravelly voice rumbled. A scattering of 'Amens' followed from the other miners.

The rector turned his eyes then to where the Hancocks, the Merrills, the Highfields, and the other farming families sat. 'My friends, the plough that now runs deep in your furrows did not always do so. You know that many backs broke to wrest that soil from clutching root and stubborn stump; you know that hands bled, dragging forth the rocks that sit arrayed now as the fences that mark out worked land from wilderness. Good yield does not come without suffering, it does not come without struggle, and toil, and, yes, loss. Each one of you has cried for the crop blighted by drought or pest. Cried, as you did what you knew you must, and ploughed each plant under, so that the soil could be renewed in the hope of the better season coming. Cry now, my friends, but hope, also! For a better season will follow this time of Plague, if only we trust in God to perform His wonders!'

He looked down then and wiped his hand across his brow. The church was utterly still. We were all of us entirely concentrated on the pulpit and the tall man who stood there, his head bent as if gathering the strength to go on.

'Friends,' he said at last, 'some of us have the means to flee. Some of us have relatives nearby who would gladly shelter us. Others have connections upon whom we could prevail. Some few of us have means to go far from here — anywhere we choose.'

My concentration broke as the Bradfords shifted in the foremost pew. 'But how would we repay the kindness of those who received us, if we carried the seeds of the Plague to them? What burden would we bear if, because of us, hundreds die who might have lived? No! Let us accept this Cross. Let us carry it in God's Holy Name!' The rector's voice had been gaining in power till it rang like a bell. But now he dropped back into a tone of intimacy, like a lover addressing his beloved. 'Dear friends, here we are, and here we *must* stay. Let the boundaries of this village become our whole world. Let none enter and none leave while this Plague lasts.'

He turned then to the material particulars of his scheme for our voluntary besiegement, to which it seemed he had already given much thought. He said he had written to the earl at Chatsworth House not so many miles distant, setting out his proposal and asking aid. The earl had undertaken that if we sealed ourselves off he would provision us all from his own purse with our basic needs in food, fuel, and medicines. These would be left at the Boundary Stone at the southeastern edge of the village, to be collected only when the carters who had carried them were well clear. Those who wished to purchase other items would leave payment either in a shallow, spring-fed well to the north of Wright's Wood, where the flow of the water would carry away any Plague seeds, or in holes gouged into the Boundary Stone that would be kept filled with vinegar, which was said to kill contagion.

'Beloved, remember the words of the Prophet Isaiah: "In returning and rest you shall be saved; in quietness and trust shall be your strength."' He paused and repeated the phrase: 'In quietness and trust,' letting the words sink to a whisper, and from the whisper into silence. 'In quietness and trust . . . Is that not how we should all wish to be?' Yes, we nodded, of course it was. But then, his voice came back, ringing into the very silence he had created. 'But the Israelites did *not* trust, they were *not* quiet. Isaiah tells us this. He says: "And you would not, but you said: No! We will speed upon horses . . . we will ride upon swift steeds . . . A thousand shall flee at the threat of one, at the threat of five you shall flee, till you are left like a flag staff on the top of a mountain, like a signal on a hill." Well, my beloved, I say we shall not flee like the faithless Israelites! No, not at the threat of five, or of ten, or even of a score of deaths. For loneliness awaits those who flee. Loneliness – like a flag staff on a mountain. Loneliness and shunning. The shunning that has ever been the leper's lot. Loneliness, shunning, and fear. Fear will be your only faithful companion, and it will be with you day and night.

'Beloved, I hear you in your hearts, saying that we already fear. We fear this disease and the death it brings. But you will not leave this fear behind you. It will travel with you wheresoever you fly. And on your way, it will gather to itself a host of greater fears. For if you sicken in a stranger's house, they may turn you out, they may abandon you, they may lock you up to die in dreadful solitude. You will thirst, and none shall quench you. You will cry out, and your cries will fade into empty air. For in that stranger's house, all you will receive is blame. For surely they will blame you, for bringing this thing to them. And they will blame you justly! And they will heap their hatred upon you, in the hour when your greatest need is love!'

The voice eased now, and soothed: 'Stay here, in the place that you know, and in the place where you are known. Stay here, upon that piece of Earth whose golden grain and gleaming ore has ever nourished you. Stay here, and here we will be for one another. Stay here, and the Lord's love will be here for us. Stay here, my dearest friends. And I promise you this: while I am spared no one in this village will face their death alone.'

He advised us then to reflect and pray and said that shortly he would ask us for our decision. He came down from the pulpit and went amongst us with Elinor beside him, radiant and kindly, speaking quietly to any who would have words with him. Some families stayed in their pews, their heads bent in prayerful reflection. Others rose and wandered restlessly, forming into clusters here and there, seeking advice from friends and loved ones. It was only then that I noticed that Thomas Stanley had entered the church and taken a place in the very last pew. Now, he came forward, speaking softly to all those who had been, or secretly still were, of a precisian leaning and who perhaps had difficulty in trusting Mr. Mompellion. Quietly, the old man was making clear his full support of the younger.

Sometimes, from amidst the hushed hum of discussion, a voice rose excitedly, and I saw to my shame that my father and Aphra were among a small group whose gestures and head-shakes indicated that they did not agree with the rector's scheme. Mr. Mompellion moved towards these unconvinced, and before long, Mr. Stanley joined them. My father and his wife had drawn a little away, and I came near to them to try to overhear what it was they were saying to each other.

'Think of our bread, husband! If we take to the road, who will feed us? Like as not, we will starve there. Here, he says we will have it surely.'

'Aye, "he says." Well, *I* say that you cannot eat "he says." Fine words make piss-poor fodder. Oh, aye, I'm sure he and his lady wife will get their bread from his friend the earl, but when have the likes of them ever given a ha'penny for the likes of us?'

'Husband, where are your wits? It's nowt love of us will keep them to their word, but love of their own fine skins. It's a surety that the earl wants his estate kept free from Plague, and how better to do that than give us cause to bide here? A few penneth-worth of bread each day would look like a good bargain to him, I'll be bound.' She was a shrewd woman, my stepmother, in spite of all her superstitious fancies.

She saw me then and seemed about to beckon me over to help her plead her case. But I wanted no part of responsibility for any person's decision other than my own, and I turned my face away.

When the Mompellions came to where I stood, Elinor Mompellion held out both her hands and took mine tenderly as the rector spoke to me. 'And you, Anna?' he said. The intensity of his gaze was such that I had to look away from him. 'Tell us you will stay with us, for without you, Mrs. Mompellion and I would be ill set. Indeed, I do not know what we would do without you.' There was no turmoil within me, for I had made my decision. Still, I could not command my voice to give him a reply. When I nodded, Elinor Mompellion embraced me and held me to her for a long moment. The rector moved on, whispering quietly to Mary Hadfield, who was weeping and wringing her hands most piteously. By the time he mounted the steps again and faced us, he and Mr. Stanley between them had shored up every doubter. All of us in the church that day gave their oath to God that we would stay, and not flee, whatever might befall us.

All of us, that is, except the Bradfords. They had slipped out of the church unnoticed and were already at the Hall, packing for their flight to Oxfordshire.

Wide Green Prison

I left the church that morning borne aloft by a strange bliss. It seemed we all partook of it: the faces that had been so gaunt and careworn now seemed warm and alive, and we smiled as we caught one another's eyes, aware of the common grace our decision had brought upon us. And so I was not prepared for the harried look of Maggie Cantwell, pacing by my gate. Maggie was the Bradfords' cook, and as a consequence of her employment had not been in church that morning. She still had on the large white pinafore she wore in the kitchen of Bradford Hall, and her big ruddy face was puce with exertion. A bundle of belongings lay in the snow at her feet.

'Anna, they have turned me off! Eighteen years, and ordered out on a second's notice!' Maggie had family in Bakewell, but whether she would go to them, or if they would receive her, I did not know. Still, I wondered that she had come to me for shelter, for my house and the Hadfields' and the Sydells' were notorious now as the Plague cottages. I motioned her to come inside, but she shook her head. 'Thank you, Anna, and I mean no disrespect. But I am afraid to venture into your cottage, and I know you will understand me. I have come to ask your help to gather my few poor possessions from the Hall, for the Bradfords mean to leave this hour, and they have told us all that after their departure the Hall will be locked and guarded and none of us may enter in it. Only think, it has been our home, too, for all these years, and now they put us out without a roof or a way to earn our bread!' She had been nervously wringing a corner of her pinafore in her fleshy hands, and now she raised it to her cheek to catch her tears.

'Come, Maggie, we don't have time for this now,' I said. 'Your goods will be safe here. I will fetch a handcart and we will go directly for the rest of your things.' And so we set off, Maggie, who was above forty years old and very stout from the enjoyment of her own fine cooking, labouring for breath as we toiled through the snowdrifts back up the hill to the Hall.

'Think of it, Anna,' she panted. 'There I was, basting the joint for the Sunday dinner, when they all storm in from church, early like, and I'm thinking, Ooh, there'll be what for if the meal's not on the table when the colonel looks for it, and I'm rushing meself and worrying at Brand, me pantry boy, when in comes the colonel hisself, who, I don't have to tell *you*, I'm sure, never set foot in the kitchen until this very day, and it's turned off, we all are, just like that, and no thank you or how'll ye do, just put the food on the table and clear out.'

While still far from the Hall, it was possible to perceive the uproar underway there. This was no stealthy retreat. The Hall hummed like a struck hive. Horses stamped in the drive as maids and footmen staggered in and out, bent under the weight of boxes. We entered through the kitchen and could hear the scurrying feet above us, punctuated by the high, imperious voices of the Bradford ladies giving their commands. Not particularly wanting to be noticed by the Bradfords, I crept behind Maggie up the narrow backstairs to the attic she shared with the maidservants. The little room had a steeply sloping roof and a high, square window through which the cold snow-light poured. There were three cots crammed in the tiny space, and by one of them crouched a pale, wide-eyed girl named Jenny, who was breathing hard, trying to tie her spare smock and few small possessions into a bundle and fumbling the knot in her hurry.

'Lordy, Cook, she says we are to be out of here this hour, yet she gives us no time to tend to our own going. I'm off my feet fetching and carting her things, and no sooner have I packed a sash than she says, no, take it out, this one rather. They are taking none of us, not even Mrs. Bradford's maid, Jane, who you know has been with her since a girl. Jane cried and begged her, but she just shook her head and said no, that she and all of us have been too much about the village and might already have Plague in us, so they just mean to leave us here to die, and in the streets, for none of us has a place to go to!'

'No one is going to die, and certainly not in the streets,' I said as calmly as I could. Maggie had a small oak coffer wedged tight beneath her bed, but her girth was such that she couldn't bend down low enough to get it. I dragged at it while she folded the quilt her sister had made for her. Such, with the small sack of clothing she'd left on my step, was the sum of her life's goods. With a little care, we managed to work the coffer down the narrow stairs, she taking most of the weight while I steered from above as best I could. In the kitchen, she paused, as I thought, for breath. But then I saw that her eyes were filling again. She ran her big red hands over the scored and scorched deal table. 'My life, this is,' she said. 'I know every mark on this and how it came there. I know the heft of every blessed knife in here. And now I'm to turn me back and walk away with nothing.' Her head drooped and a tear hung suspended on her fleshy cheek for a moment, then splashed onto the table.

Just then, there was a commotion from the courtyard. I glanced out the kitchen door in time to see Michael Mompellion pulling up Anteros in a scatter of stones. He was off the horse and upon the steps before the startled groom had gathered up his dropped reins. He did not wait to be announced.

'Colonel Bradford!' His voice in the entrance hall was so loud that all the clatter quieted at once. The dust sheets were already upon the large furnishings in the Hall. I crept behind the bulk of a shrouded settle, and from the cover of a fold of sheet I could see the colonel appear at the door to his library. He had a volume he'd evidently been considering for packing in one hand and a letter in the other. Miss Bradford and her mother appeared at the top of the stairs, hesitating there, as if unsure of the etiquette of this encounter.

'Rector Mompellion?' said the colonel. He kept his voice low, in deliberate contrast to the rector's, and affected a quizzical tone. 'You should not have troubled yourself to ride here to fare us well, so hard and in such haste. I had planned to make my adieus to you and your fair wife in this letter.'

He extended his hand with the letter. Mompellion took it absently but didn't look at it. 'I do not want your good-byes. I am here to urge you to reconsider your departure. Your family is first here. The villagers look to you. If you quail, how may I ask them to be brave?'

'I do *not* quail!' the colonel replied coldly. 'I am merely doing what any man of means and sense must do: safeguarding what is mine.'

Mompellion took a step towards him, his broad hands outstretched. 'But think of those you are putting at risk . . .'

The colonel stepped back, keeping his distance from the rector. His voice became a slow, soft drawl, as if to mock the urgency of the rector's. 'I believe, sir, that we have had this conversation, here in this very Hall, albeit then in a hypothetical context. Well, now the hypothesis is proven, and I mean to do as I said I would. I said then, and I say now, that my life and the lives of my family are of more consequence to me than some possible risk to strangers.'

The rector was not to be gainsaid. He moved towards the colonel and clutched him by the arm. 'Well, if the plight of strangers cannot move you, think of the good you might yet do here, among the villagers that know you and look to you. There will be much to be managed in this time of peril. Your courage has long been celebrated. Why not add a new chapter? You have led men to war. You have the skills to command all of us through this crisis. I do not have such skills. Furthermore, I am a newcomer to this place; I do not know these people as you and your family know them, who have been here for many generations. I could learn much from your counsel as to how best go on as events unfold here. And while I am pledged to do my utmost to bring these people comfort, from you and your wife, and from Miss Bradford, the smallest gesture would mean so much more.'

On the landing, Elizabeth Bradford stifled a snort. Her father glanced up at her, his eyes sharing her amusement. 'How flattering!' he exclaimed with a sneer. 'Really, you do us too much honour. Dear sir, I did not raise my daughter to have her play wet nurse to a rabble. And if I desired to succour the afflicted I would have joined you in Holy Orders.'

Mompellion dropped the colonel's arm as if he had just become aware that he had picked up something foul. 'One does not have to be a priest to be a man!' he cried.

He turned and strode towards the hearth. Colonel Bradford's ceremonial swords hung crossed above the mantel in a pair of gleaming arcs. The rector held the colonel's letter still but seemed to have forgotten that he did so. The parchment crumpled under his hand as he reached out for the mantel and leant against it, heavily. He was struggling for command of himself. From where I crouched, I could glimpse his face. He breathed in, deeply, and as he breathed out it seemed that he willed away the deep lines drawn all about his brow and jaw. It was like watching someone don a mask. His expression was still and calm when he turned his back to the hearth and again faced the colonel.

'If you must send your wife and daughter away, then I pray you, stay here yourself and do your duty.'

'Do not presume to tell me my duty! I do not tell you yours, although I might say that you would do well to look to that delicate bride of yours.'

Mompellion coloured a little at this. 'My wife, sir, I will admit I implored to leave this place when I first suspected what now we know in fact. But she refused, saying that her duty was to stay, and now she says I must rejoice in it, for I could hardly ask of others what I had not lain upon the nearest to me.'

'So. Your wife, it seems, is expert at making poor choices. She certainly has had some practice.'

The insult was so broad that I had to swallow a gasp. Mompellion's fists clenched, but he managed to maintain his level tone. 'You may be right. But equally do I believe that the choice you make today is wrong, terribly wrong. If you do this thing, your family's name will be a hissing in the laneways and the cottages. The people will not forgive you for abandoning them.'

'And you think I care for the opinion of a few sweaty miners and their snotty-nosed brats?'

Mompellion drew a sharp breath at that and took a step forwards. The colonel was a masty man, but Mr. Mompellion was a full head taller, and though I could no longer see his face from where I crouched, I imagine his look must have been the same fierce thing I had seen up at the clough on the night of Anys's murder. The colonel raised his hand in a conciliating gesture.

'Look, man, do not think I disparage your efforts this day. A very pretty sermon. You are to be complimented upon it. I do not say that you do ill in making your congregation feel righteous in staying here. On the contrary, I think it was very well done of you. They may as well have some comfort, since they have no choice.'

Since they have no choice. I felt myself tumbling from the high plain onto which Mr. Mompellion's sermon that morning had lofted me. What choice had we, after all? Perhaps, if my children yet lived, there might have been some decision to make; perhaps I would have been driven to consider a desperate flight to some uncertain destination. But I doubted it. For as Aphra had said to my father, it is not easy to surrender the safety of a roof and the certainty of bread for the perils of an open road, with winter setting in and no clear destination at its end. Villages in these parts did not love vagrants at any time, and whipped them on their way. How much less welcome would we be once the word went out of whence we came? Fleeing one danger would have exposed my children to many more. And, as it was, with my boys both lying in the churchyard, I had less than no reason to leave. The Plague already had taken from me the greatest part of what I had to lose; what was left of my life seemed to me, at that moment, barely worth the effort of saving. I realized then that I deserved no great credit for swearing I would stay. I would stay because I had small will to live – and nowhere else to go.

The colonel had turned away from the rector, back towards his library, and now he let his eyes travel over his bookshelves with feigned indifference as he continued to speak. 'But I, as you yourself so astutely perceived, do have a choice. And I propose to exercise it. Now, if you will excuse me, I have, as you will appreciate, a great many other choices to make in consequence, such as, for instance, whether to pack the Dryden or the Milton. Perhaps the Milton? Dryden's themes are ambitious, but his rhymes grow rather tedious, do you not think?'

'Colonel Bradford!' Mompellion's voice rang through the Hall.

'Enjoy your books. Enjoy them now! For there are no pockets in a shroud! Perhaps you do not care for the judgment of this village, but if you do not value these people, there is one who does. He loves them dearly. And be sure, He is the one to whom you will have to answer. I do not lightly speak of God's judgment, but on you I say the vials of His wrath will be opened, and a terrible vengeance poured down! Fear it, Colonel Bradford! Fear a far worse punishment than Plague!'

And at that, he turned, strode back into the courtyard, leapt upon Anteros, and cantered away.

There was no hissing in the street as the Bradfords' carriage passed out of the village on its way to the Oxford road. Men doffed their caps and women curtsied, just as we had always done, simply because that was what we had always done. With the exception of the coachman, who was to be turned off when they reached Oxford, the Bradfords had not retained a single one of their servants. In fact, Colonel Bradford had that morning hired two of the Hancock boys, who never had worked for him, to stand guard at the shuttered and bolted Hall. He told them he was doing so because he did not trust any of his own people to keep their fellows locked out of their longtime home. There were tearful scenes at the last when those who had nowhere to go fell on their knees by the Bradford carriage, grabbing at the hems of the ladies' travelling mantles and kissing the toe of the colonel's boot. Mrs. Bradford and her daughter seemed about to relent in the case of their maids, and enquired of the colonel whether two or three of the young women might not take shelter in the stables or the well house, but Colonel Bradford refused them even that.

And so, as generally happens, those who have most give least, and those with less somehow make shift to share. By nightfall, all the Bradfords' servants had been taken in by one or other village family – all but Maggie and Brand, the pantry boy, who each came from Bakewell and, not being bound by what we now called the Sunday Oath, decided to journey on there and see if their own blood kin would take them in. The rector had charged them with carrying letters he had written to all of the surrounding villages, so that everyone would know as soon as possible exactly how we purposed to go on. And that was almost all they carried. After all the rush to gather her coffer, Maggie decided to leave it behind in the end lest her kin in Bakewell fear that Plague seeds were secreted within it. Maggie and Brand left on foot, the stout woman on the arm of the slender boy, and I suspect not a few in the village envied them as they turned and waved at the Boundary Stone.

And so the rest of us set about learning to live in the wide green prison of our own election. The weather warmed that week, and the snow melted into sticky slush. Generally, the day after such a thaw would have brought a clatter of traffic to the streets, as carters held back by the snow made up on late deliveries and travellers needing to be somewhere took to the roadway. But this time the thaw brought no such busy movements, and so the consequences of our oath began to come clear to us.

It is hard to say why the oath weighed upon me, for it was perhaps only a half dozen times a year that I ventured beyond the limits in which we had now confined ourselves. And yet I found myself walking that Monday morning in the direction of the Boundary Stone, which sat at the edge of a high meadow, just at the point where a spur of land plunged suddenly away down the hill to the village of Stoney Middleton. The path there was well worn from much traffic. As children we had loved to run down, headlong and heedless, often losing our footing in the rush of our own momentum and ending up at the bottom in a muddy tangle of skinny arms and grazed knees. Oftentimes I had made the long, hard climb back up the hill knowing I faced a thrashing for my stained and wrinkled smock.

Now, I just stood and looked longingly at that forbidden path. The storm had stripped the leaves from the bronzed beeches and the yellow-splashed birch. They lay, slicked with snowmelt, darkened and mouldering in deep wind drifts at the path's edges. At the stone, the mason, Martin Milne, was at work drilling out holes for the conducting of our strange new way of commerce. It was a still morning and the ringing of sledge on graver carried like a bell, all the way back to the village. Several folk, drawn by the sound, came to watch the work. Far down the dell we could see the carter waiting, his mule's head down and grazing. The rector's letters apparently had done their work, for the carter would not approach until he received the signal. Mr. Mompellion, too, was there, directing Mr. Milne, and when he deemed the holes sufficiently deep he filled each with vinegar and placed the coins inside. That first delivery was of standard stuffs; flour and salt and such staple goods. The next would add those items especially requested by villagers and written down by the rector upon a list to be placed beside the stone. There was to be a separate list, also: a list that named those who had died. For the nearby villages held many who were friends and kin and ached for news of how we did. There were three names on that first day's list: Martha Bandy, the innkeeper's daughter, and Jude and Faith Hamilton, brother and sister, the latest of the Gowdies' tormentors to be placed alongside them in the ground.

When all was accomplished, Mr. Mompellion waved down to the carter and then we all backed off to a safe distance as the man led his pack mule up the slope. He unloaded as swiftly as he might, took the money and the lists, and then waved back to us. 'Our prayers and our blessings be upon all of ye!' he shouted. 'God have mercy on your goodness!' And then he turned the mule's head down the slope and mounted. We stood and watched as the beast trod a careful path out to where the spur dipped suddenly. The clink of harness grew fainter, until the beast reached the place where the way flattens and becomes easy. There, he picked up his pace and trotted on, until the grey buildings of Stoney Middleton rose up and hid him from our sight.

Beside me, Michael Mompellion sighed. Then, noticing that we all around him looked downcast, he rallied himself, smiled, and raised his voice so that all might hear. 'You see? That simple man gave us his blessing and you may be sure that like prayers are on the lips of all those in our surrounding towns. You are becoming a byword for goodness, dear friends! And with all these prayers, surely God will hear, and grant us His mercy!' The faces that turned to him all looked pinched and serious. For all of us had had the time to reflect on the gravity of our decision, and we well knew what it might bode for us. Mr. Mompellion, to give him credit, was quite aware of this. As we each made our way back along the path to the village, to the various tasks that beckoned us, he moved from one small group of persons to the next, offering words of support. Most seemed to pick up their spirits a little as they spoke with him.

And so we reached the village's main street, and I saw that some of those who had been at the Boundary Stone had paused for speech with those who had not, relating the way in which we would now conduct our dealings with the world. I was due to begin my morning's work at the rectory, so I walked on with Mr. Mompellion. He had retreated into his own thoughts, and I kept my peace so as not to trouble him.

Elinor Mompellion greeted us at the door, her shawl upon her, anxious to be out. She had, she said, been waiting for me, because she had a task elsewhere that would require my help. She took my arm impatiently and almost pushed me down the path before the rector could gather himself to ask what it was or where we were going.

Mrs. Mompellion always walked with a brisk step, but today she was almost running. 'Randoll Daniel was here this morning,' she said. 'His wife is in labour and, with the Gowdies gone, he knew not where to look for help for her. I told him we would be there directly.'

I turned pale at this. My own mother died in her childbed when I was four years old. The baby lay crosswise and she laboured four days as Mem Gowdie tried in vain to manipulate its position. In the end, with my mother unconscious from exhaustion, my father had ridden to Sheffield and returned at last with a barber-surgeon he'd shipped with as a boy. The man, wind-burned and salt-scoured, looked terrifying to me, and I could not believe that his hard hands were to be allowed near the tender body of my mother.

He used a thatcher's hook. My father had taken so much grog to damp his own fear that he did not have the wit to keep me from the room. I ran in there as my mother came to consciousness, bellowing. Mem grabbed me up and carried me away. But not before I saw the tiny, torn-off arm of my stillborn sister. I see it yet: the pale, folded flesh, the tiny, perfect fingers open like a little flower, reaching out to me. Even now I can smell the blood and shit that stained that terrible bed, and the terror of it was with me at my own confinements.

I started to tell Mrs. Mompellion that I could not go with her, that I knew nothing of midwifery, but she cut me off. 'However little you know, it's more than I do, who never has laboured myself nor even birthed any livestock. But you have, Anna. You will know what to do, and I will assist you as best I can.'

'Mrs. Mompellion! Giving birth is one thing! Midwifing is

altogether another gate's business. And neither is a lamb a living human soul. You do not know what you are asking me. Poor Mary Daniel deserves better than us!'

'That is no doubt true, Anna, but we are all she has. Oh, perhaps Mrs. Hancock with seven lying-ins behind her might know a thing or two more, but yesterday the second of her sons sickened and I do not think that she can be asked to leave off tending him, nor do I think it wise to risk carrying fresh Plague seeds into the room of a confinement. So we will do the best we can by Mary Daniel, who is a young fit woman and by the grace of God will have an easy time of it.' She patted the whisket at her side. 'I have here some poppy if her pain is great.'

I shook my head at that. 'Mrs. Mompellion, I do not think we should give her poppy, for labour is not called labour by chance. A woman must do much real work to get her baby born. We would be sore pressed if she were fallen into a poppy stupor.'

'See, Anna! You have already helped me, and Mrs. Daniels. You know a very great deal more than you think you do.' We were approaching the Daniels' cottage. Randoll Daniel, anxious for our arrival, opened the door before we had even knocked upon it. Mary was alone on a pallet that had been brought down from their sleeping loft. The shutters were closed and a blanket had been hung over the entryway, so that the room was very dim. It took a few moments for my eyes to adjust, before I could see that Mary was sitting on the pallet with her back braced against the wall and her knees drawn up to her chest. She was very quiet, but the beads of sweat that stood out on her brow and the veins roping in her young neck made me realize that we had found her in the midst of a strong surge.

Randoll had laid a good fire, the day being chill, and Mrs. Mompellion asked him to set some water to heat on it. I asked him, also, for some fresh, churned butter. I remembered the smell of the butter from my own first confinement. The second time, when we had none, Mem Gowdie had called for some rendered chicken fat. After Tom's birth, both he and I reeked of chicken for a week, for she used the grease to massage and soften my opening and ease his large head through without tearing me. I hoped that in the dim light Mary would not see that my hands were trembling, but as I approached her she closed her eyes and turned even more inwards. Elinor Mompellion did note my fear, and she laid a reassuring hand on my shoulder as I knelt down and lifted the sheet from Mary's knees. Very gently I laid a palm on each one, and Mary, sensing my aim, let them fall open. I muttered Anys's chant, even though I didn't understand it. 'May the seven directions guide this work.' Elinor Mompellion shot me a strange look, but I ignored it. 'May it be pleasing to my grandmothers, the ancient ones. So mote it be.'

Mary Daniel was a small, vigorous woman of about twenty, and her flesh felt firm and healthful under my hands. It is, as I have said, one thing to reach inside a birthing ewe and quite another to invade the body of a living woman. But I tried to quiet that part of my mind hammering away about modesty and violation. I breathed deeply and thought instead how thankful I'd been for the touch of women's hands in my own birthing room, and how important it had been to me then that Mem and Anys seemed so calm and certain of their own skill. I was not calm, nor certain, and I had no skill, but as my fingers reached inside Mary, it seemed that her flesh felt as familiar to me as my own. Mrs. Mompellion held a candle for me, but it was by feel, not sight, that I was working. The news my fingers brought me was first good, and then bad. I could feel but a tiny edge of the rigid door to the womb at the top of Mary's passage, and I cooed to her happily that the worst of her work was behind her. At that, she moaned, the first sound we had heard from her, and a slow smile lightened her face, then immediately turned to a frown as the next surge gathered. I stilled my hands then, and Elinor Mompellion stroked her until it passed.

It was what lay beyond the lip of contracting flesh that troubled me, for I knew that I should be able to feel the hardness of skull there. Instead, the part of the baby presenting itself for birth was soft flesh, and I knew not at first if I felt a buttock or a back or part of a face. I withdrew my hands and spoke softly to Mary, encouraging her to try to walk, if she could. I thought if we could get her moving, then the baby might move, too, into a better lie. Mrs. Mompellion became the prop for her right side, while I took the left, and as we walked up and down that little room, Mrs. Mompellion began to croon a rhythmic song in a language I did not know. 'It's Cornish,' she said. 'My nurse was a Cornishwoman, and she always sang to me when I was a child.'

Time passed. An hour, maybe two or three. In that dim room there was no sense of noontime brightness or morning easing gently into afternoon. The only time that mattered was measured in Mary's ever-increasing intervals of pain. When she finally sank back, exhausted, upon the pallet, I waited for a surge to pass. As soon as it did I insinuated my fingers quickly inside her. The lip was gone. The womb stood wide. There was no doubt now; the baby lay cross-wise. A black panic started to rise in me. I remembered the bloody thatcher's hook.

But then a strange thing happened. It was as if truculent Anys was beside me, whispering impatiently in my ear. 'That man was a ship's barber; he pulled teeth and amputated limbs. He knew nothing of women's bodies. But you *do* know. You can do this, Anna. Use your mother-hands.'

Gently then, so gently, I explored the tiny body of that unborn baby, fingering the knobs and curves to see if I could make sense of them. It seemed to me that what I needed was a foot. If I could manipulate the feet, surely the buttocks would slip into place, and on buttocks one could get a good grip. I found something that felt like a foot, but I worried that it might be a hand instead. A hand was the last thing I wanted. If I pulled a hand by mistake, the shoulder would never be delivered unless it was shattered, the bones sliding broken across one another. I couldn't bear the thought of that. But how could I be sure that what I felt was a foot? There's not much difference between a newborn's stubby little fingers and the flesh buds of its tiny toes. Elinor Mompellion could see my frown and sensed my hesitation.

'What is it, Anna?' she asked in a low voice. I explained my dilemma. 'What you have under your hand – feel for the fifth digit,' she said. 'Now, try to flex it. Does it oppose, like a thumb, or no?'

'No!' I said, almost shouting. 'It's a toe!' Confident now, I pulled. The baby moved, a little. Slowly, working with the surges of Mary's body, I eased and tugged, eased and tugged. Mary was strong and stood up well to the pain that came at her now unrelentingly. When the little feet dangled at last through the womb opening, the pace changed, and everything became urgent. I knew that the pulsing cord must on no account get crushed, and so with the greatest difficulty, I forced a hand past the buttocks and pushed it back. Mary screamed and shook with the agony, and I felt scalding sweat running down my own back. The baby would be born within the next few minutes, I felt sure of it. I was terrified that the head would tilt backwards and be trapped inside, so I felt for the tiny mouth and gently forced a finger inside, to hold the chin down and the head flexed for the next surge. Mary writhed and yelled. I yelled back at her, urging her to push, and push harder, desperate when she surrendered just short of the ultimate effort, and I felt the baby slip back again. Finally, in a slick of blood and brown matter, there he was – a small, slippery boy. And a moment later, he was yelling, too.

Randoll burst through the blanket-door when he heard his lusty son, and his big miner's hand fluttered like a moth from the damp head of the babe to his wife's flushed cheek and back again, as if he didn't know which of them he most wanted to touch. Elinor threw open the shutters as I gathered up the stained cloths, and it was only as the fading light entered the room that I realized we hadn't cut the navel cord. We sent Randoll for a knife and a piece of thread while Mary expelled the glistening afterbirth. Mrs. Mompellion made the cut and bound it up. I looked at her, all dishevelled, spattered with blood, and imagined myself looking worse. We laughed. And, for an hour, in that season of death, we celebrated a life.

But even in the midst of that joy, I knew that I would have to leave the babe nursing at his mother's breast and return to my own cottage, silent and empty, where the only sound that would greet me would be the phantom echoes of my own boys' infant cries. And so, before we took our leave of the Daniels, I found the phial of poppy in Mrs. Mompellion's whisket. I closed my hand upon it, stealthy as a practised thief, and plunged it, deep, into the sleeve of my dress.

So Soon to Be Dust

Maggie Cantwell came back to us in a handcart. It was a chill morning, and a moist fog hung low in the valley, so it was difficult to descry exactly what was in the cart edging its slow way up the hill, with a slight figure behind, bent double, toiling under the load.

Jakob Merrill, the widower who lived nearest the Boundary Stone, ran out of his dwelling to wave the carter away, thinking that perchance he was some peddler, a poor soul from a far town who had blundered towards us ignorant of the perils of this place. But the boy trudged on, and eventually Jakob saw that the bundle in the cart was a human form, all slumped, and finally he recognized the carter. It was hard to make out his features, even as he drew clear of the fog, for he was spattered from head to foot with the damp brown debris of rotten fruit. But as he toiled closer, Jakob recognized him as young Brand, the pantry boy from Bradford Hall.

Brand all but collapsed when he reached the stone, his legs folding up under him. Jakob, quickly comprehending the extremity of their state, dispatched his boy, Seth, to carry the news to the rector, while he set a cauldron of water to heat and told his elder daughter to bring cloths so Brand could clean himself. I was at the rectory when the child arrived with the news. As I helped the rector with his hat and coat, I asked if I might ride back with him to see if I could comfort poor Maggie. When we drew up, Maggie still lay in the cart, it being beyond Jakob Merrill's strength to remove her. He had thrown a horse blanket across her, to give her warmth, but when he removed it, my first thought was that it had but covered a corpse, so blue was she with the cold, and so odd was the arrangement of her limbs. The small cart was insufficient to contain her big body, so her beefy calves and heavy arms spilled out over the sideboards. One of her stockings had a large rip, and the flesh had rushed to the hole, pushing out like sausage meat from a split casing. But it was her face that was most shocking.

When I was a girl, it had pleased me to make poppets for Aphra's little ones. I would form the bodies of plaited grainstalks and then fashion faces from the yellow clay that lay at the base of the sillions. Sometimes, if my effort did not satisfy me, I would drag my hand across the face and begin again, trying for a more humanlike effect. The right side of Maggie Cantwell's face looked like a smear of clay that an impatient potter had likewise disfigured. While the left side, under the mess of dried-on fruit pulp, looked as vivid as ever, the right was a blur, the eye all but closed and seeping, the cheek drooped and the mouth a drooling sneer. Maggie strained to turn her head to take us in with her one good eye, and when she recognized me she gave a sound that was half moan, half shudder and reached for me with a flailing left arm. I clasped her hand, kissed it, and told her all would be well, although I knew that very likely it would not.

Mr. Mompellion did not waste time on words but went quickly to work with Jakob Merrill to get poor Maggie from the cart into the cottage. It took all their strength to accomplish this in a seemly way, for though Maggie was conscious, she was barely so, nor did she have command of her limbs. Mr. Mompellion squatted down behind and wrapped his arms around her chest while Jakob gripped her fleshy legs. The rector did speak then, soothingly, to poor Maggie, to try to blunt the indignity as he and Merrill heaved her into the croft. Inside, young Brand, clean now, sat wrapped in a rough blanket before the fire. Jakob Merrill's daughter, Charity, handed him a steaming mug of mutton broth, and he gripped it so tightly in his two hands that I thought the thing might shatter. Charity held up a blanket for a screen as I stripped off Maggie's befouled garments and bathed her, while Mr. Mompellion crouched beside Brand and enquired gently as to what had happened.

It seemed they had had an uneventful journey through Stoney Middleton; the people there, while keeping a distance, had called out their good wishes as they passed through and had left a parcel of oatcake and a flask of ale for them at the milestone. Farther along the road, a farmer had allowed them to sleep the night amongst his cows in their warm shippon. The trouble had come in the larger town of Bakewell. It was market day when they arrived there nigh on noon, and the streets were crowded. Suddenly, someone had recognized Maggie and raised a shout: 'A woman from the Plague village! Beware! Beware!'

Brand shuddered then. 'Lord forgive me, I ran off and left her. I been gone out from Bakewell since I was a small boy, and I be changed so much since then that no one now would know me. So I thought if I were not with Maggie, happen I might get to my kin in safety.' But Brand had not gone far when his own goodness drew him back. 'I could hear the yelling, see, and I needed to know if she were safe. She'd been good to me in that hard house – oh, time or two she whipped me with a wooden spoon if she didn't like my way of working, but many a time she stood for me, too. So I crept back again and came up behind a vegetable-seller's stall. Then I seen what were happening. They'd taken all the bad apples cast into the pig trough and were hurling them at Maggie. They'd started yelling, chanting: "Out! Out! Out!" And believe me, she were trying to get out of there as fast as she might, but you know she don't move swift, and with all the yelling she were getting confused and staggering first one way, then t'other. I went to her then and grabbed her arm, and we made a run for it as they kept pelting us. And that's when she were planet-struck. She just gave way, folded up, like her right leg suddenly were made of string. "Lord help me," she said, "I feel like a lead pig is tied to me foot." And 'twere the last words I had from her. She crumbled up right there in the middle of the roadway. And that set the mob off into an even bigger to-do. One or two of the children started hurling stones, and I thought if they all took that up it'd be the finish of us.

'You're not going to like it too well, Rector Mompellion, when I tell what I did then. I stole the barrow from the nearest stall and somehow I found the strength to pile her in it. The barrow man cursed me to Hell, but he didn't give chase. Perhaps he reckoned I'd Plagued the cart by touching it. We been on the way here ever since. Scared to stop, I was, lessen another mob formed to get us.' He shivered then in his exhaustion and began to sob.

Michael Mompellion reached an arm around the boy's heaving shoulders and held him tightly. 'You did very well, Brand, even to taking the cart. Set your heart at rest over it. One day, after this travail is passed, you may return it. But think no more on it until that day comes. Be sure that you did right. You could have run and sought your own safety, and yet your loyal heart taught you to do otherwise.' He sighed then. 'This Plague will make heroes of us all, whether we will or no. But you are the first of them.'

Charity had brought a mug of the mutton broth for Maggie, and the two of us tried to prop her up and spoon a little into the good side of her mouth. But it proved futile; her tongue, it seemed, could not lift itself to steer the liquid down her throat. Broth came dribbling out and down her chin. I tried sopping a little piece of oatcake in the broth, but that worked no better, for the poor woman couldn't chew. A fat tear formed itself in her good eye and ran down to join the strings of drool on her chin. Poor Maggie! Food had been her livelihood and her life. What would become of her if she couldn't eat?

'God damn the Bradfords!' The words slipped out of my mouth before I knew I'd uttered them. Rector Mompellion looked at me, but not with the rebuke I'd expected.

'Don't trouble yourself, Anna,' he said. 'I believe He already has.'

The care of Maggie Cantwell seemed too big a burden for poor Jakob Merrill, struggling as he was in that one-room croft to rear a girl of ten and a boy not yet six. But he did say he would give Brand a roof until the youth was able to find a better. Mr. Mompellion said he would bring Maggie to the rectory, but I thought that Mrs. Mompellion would exhaust herself if the load of nursing so complete an invalid now were laid upon all the other heavy tasks she had accepted. I said I would have Maggie at my cottage if I could bespeak some more suitable conveyance to bring her there. I did not think that in her present state and circumstance she would be too nice to lie where the Plague had passed by. We aimed to leave her at the Merrills' till the next morning, so that she could benefit from a full night's rest and warmth.

As Mr. Mompellion mounted Anteros to return to the rectory, I set off on foot in the other direction, to the Miner's Tavern, to see if their horse-trap might be had for her conveyance the next day. It was so cold on the walk that my breath formed little clouds before my face, and I found myself trotting to warm my blood. The Miner's

Tavern stands in a very old building, perhaps the oldest in our village save the church. But where the church is square and proud, the tavern is a strange, bulbous thing, squatting low under its thatch. It is the only building of any size here that is not made of stone but of lathe laid on timber, rendered all over with horse-haired mortar. Over the years, the timbers have buckled and bowed, so that the front of the building protrudes now like the rounded bellies of the men who take too much ale there. Like the church, the tavern is a gathering place, and an important one, for as well as sheltering the pleasures of those who like a pot, it also hosts the gatherings of the Body of the Mine and the miners' Barmote Court, where all matters vital to the delving and marketing of our ore are decided.

The tavern has both a large court and a taproom, ample in area and yet so low of ceiling that most of the miners have to bend their heads to enter it. On such a bitter day it was to the taproom that I hurried. Inside, a good fire toasted the air. There was a fair crowd for a weekday morning, and amongst them was my father. It appeared that he had been at the pot for some time.

'Here, daughter, you look colder than a witch's tit! Let me buy you an ale to put some colour in your cheeks. Ale is the warmest lining of a naked man's coat, eh?'

I shook my head, saying I yet had much work to do at the rectory. I did not ask why he was not about his own work, who had four mouths depending on his earning.

'Ahh, God's blood, girl! It's your father who invites you. And you can take back some wisdom to that prating priest of your'n. You tell him you learned this day that there's more good in a cask of ale than in the four Gospels. You tell him that malt does more to justify God's ways to man than the Bible! Aye, you tell him that. You tell him you stayed to learn a thing or two at the knee of your father!'

Why I said this next I do not know. I have said that I am not a prude, and even if I were, my life with my father should have taught me better than to upbraid him before his friends. But my mind, as I have said, was brimful of Scripture, and some lines from Ephesians just then seemed to issue of their own accord in response to his blasphemy. ' "Let no corrupt communication proceed out of your mouth, but that which is good to the use of edifying." ' I had learned this off many years earlier, long before I knew what 'edifying' meant.

The men around him had had a good guffaw at his utterance, but at my stony response, they turned their laughter on him.

'Eh, Joss Bont, your whelp knows how to nip!' said one, and when I saw the look on my father's face I wanted to hush them all. My father is a roguing knave, even sober. But with the drink in him he becomes dangerous. I could see we were approaching that stage as his colour rose and his mouth turned from grin to snarl.

'Don't think you're too good now, with your fancy quothings, just o' cause that priest and his missus make much o'ye,' and at that he grabbed me by the shoulders and forced me down to kneel in front of him. The filth of his fingers left smears of grime on my whisk. I stared at my father's breeches and noted that they smelled unclean.

'See? I said you'd learn at me knee, and you'll damn well do as I tell ye. Someone fetch me a branks to muzzle this scold!'

The men laughed drunkenly, and the fear rose in me. I saw my mother's face framed in the iron bars, the desperate look in her wild eyes, the inhuman sounds that came from her throat as the iron bit pressed hard against her tongue. He had clapped the branks on her after she cursed him in public for his constant drunkenness. She had worn the helmet a night and a day as my father led her around, taunting her, yanking hard on the chain so that the iron sliced her tongue. The sight of her with her head in that fearful cage had terrified me, tiny child that I was, and I'd run off and hidden myself. When my father finally drank himself into insensibility, some kindly person cut the leather strap that bound the thing to her jaws. By then her tongue was raw, and it swelled so that it was days before she got her speech back.

The pressure of my father's hands weighed on my shoulders, but somehow I felt as if they were at my neck, choking me. The back of my throat tightened, and I wanted to retch. There was a gob of spittle forming in my mouth, and my impulse was to heave it all over him. But I knew him well enough to reason that if I did so in the sight of his tavern friends, he would beat me senseless. One reason that I do not warm to Aphra as I should is that she merely stood by and allowed it to happen, time after time, when I was a child. The only succour she would offer would be to raise her voice if he struck me on the face, 'For we'll never marry her off if you mar her there.'

Years later, when Sam Frith had taken me out of that unhappy croft, his hands, caressing me, found the nobbly place near my right shoulder where the bones at the base of my neck had knit awry. I made the mistake of confiding to him how my father, in a drunken rage, had flung me against the wall when I was about six years old. Sam was slow in everything, even to anger. He made me tell him then of all the other beatings, and as I went on, I could feel him, lying in the dark beside me, growing rigid with rage. He got up off the pallet when I had done recounting the last of it, and he did not even tarry to put on his boots, but walked out the door barefoot with the boots dangling from his hand. He had gone directly to my father. 'This is from a child who was too small to do it for herself,' he said, and he placed his big fist in my father's face, knocking him flat in a blow.

But I had no Sam now. I felt a sudden hot gush down my thigh. Fear had made my body betray me, just as when I was a child. Mortified, I crumpled at my father's feet and, in a tiny voice, begged his pardon. He laughed then, his pride saved by my perfect humiliation. The pressure of his hands eased, and he landed the toe of his boot into my side, just hard enough to push me over into my own mess. I pulled off my pinafore and sopped up as much of the puddle as I could, and then I rushed from the room, too abashed to seek out the innkeeper to arrange for his trap. I ran to my home, weeping and shaking, and as soon as I had the door closed behind me, I stripped every soiled garment and commenced to scrub at myself so roughly that the skin of my thighs turned livid. I was still tearful and trembling when little Seth arrived at my door to fetch me back to Maggie.

As soon as I saw her, the contemplation of her predicament shamed me out of my self-pity. Maggie Cantwell would need no cart in the morning. While I was at the Tavern, she had been struck by another spasm that had turned her good side useless. She lay now in a deep, unnatural-seeming sleep from which no word or touch could rouse her. I reached for her hand, where it lay on the coverlet all twisted in upon itself, shapeless, as if it had been boned. I straightened her fingers – strong from the kneading of dough and the lifting of heavy pans, scarred here and there with the white marks of old knife-nicks or the pink pucker of a healed burn. As I had at George Viccars's bedside, and again at Mem Gowdie's, I thought of all the varied skills that reposed in Maggie Cantwell. This big woman knew how to hack a haunch out of a side of venison but also how to fashion fancies of the finest spun sugar. She was an economical cook who never wasted so much as a pea pod but boiled it in the stockpot to extract whatever nourishment it might yet contain. Why, I wondered, was God so much more prodigal with his Creation? Why did He raise us up out of the clay, to acquire good and expedient skills, and then send us back so soon to be dust when we yet had useful years before us? And why should this good woman lie here, in such extremity, when a man like my father lived to waste his reason in drunkenness?

This time, I did not have many hours to dwell on these troubling questions. Maggie Cantwell was gone before midnight.

The Poppies of Lethe

How do we tumble down a hill? A foot placed incautiously on an unsteady rock or loosened turf, an ankle twisted or a knee buckled, and of a sudden we are gone, our body lost to our own control until we find ourselves sprawled in indignity at the bottom. So it seems apt indeed to speak of the Fall. For sin, too, must always start with but a single misstep, and suddenly we are hurtling towards some uncertain stopping point. All that is sure in the descent is that we will arrive sullied and bruised and unable to regain our former place without hard effort.

Like most miners, Sam had many accidents before the one that took his life. Once, widening a scrin, he dropped a great toadstone that near to crushed his ankle. Mem Gowdie had set the shattered bone with such skill that all who'd seen the fracture were amazed that afterwards he walked without a limp. But the setting had been difficult and she'd had to gouge many bone splinters in the doing, so she had sent Anys to fetch a poppy tincture that he might better bear her probing. She told me then that the poppy she used had been steeping six weeks in grog, and Sam, who did not like to drink but a little ale, winced as he swilled down the five spoonfuls she deemed he needed. Later, he said the dreams he had were the sweetest of his lifetime.

The day after Elinor Mompellion and I delivered the Daniels' baby, I had repented of my theft and taken the stolen phial of poppy to the rectory, meaning to somehow slip it back into Mrs. Mompellion's whisket before its loss was noticed. But every time I had the opportunity, I lacked the will. In the end, I brought it home again and placed it guiltily in a pipkin. I did not have six weeks, nor any grog to make a tincture, but on the night that Maggie Cantwell died I stared at the small plug of tawny resin and wondered what dose it would take to secure a few sweet dreams. I pinched off a sticky morsel of the stuff and put it to my mouth, only to wince at the bitterness. In the end, I cut the plug in half, formed a piece into a lozenge and coated it all over with honey. I swallowed the whole with a swill of ale. Then I stoked the fire and sat staring into its meagre wedge of light.

Time turned into a rope that unravelled as a languid spiral. One strand widened into a broad, swooping curve on which I could glide, drifting easily like a breeze-borne leaf. The zephyr that carried me was mild and warm, even as I soared in its currents high over the White Peak, breaking through the grey clouds and into a place where the sun so dazzled that I had to close my eyes. Somewhere, an owl hooted, and the note seemed to be pulled and stretched, endless, rich, like the rising call of a hunter's horn, and then a score of horns, sounding all at once and in the sweetest harmony. The sun glinted off the serried instruments and then I could see the notes of music, molten, dripping like golden rain. Where they touched the ground, they did not scatter but gathered, leaping up again each upon the other. Walls rose, and soaring arches, building a shining city of fantastic towers, one growing out of the next like tight buds unfurling from a thousand various stems. The city was all white and gold, curving in a wide arc round a sea of sapphire. I looked down and saw myself drifting through the winding streets, a cloak billowing behind me. My children were cloaked also, and they gambolled on either side of me, merry little figures, clinging to my hands. On the high, white walls the sun blazed, beating and throbbing like the blows of a bell-clapper.

I woke to the slow tolling of our church bell, ringing once again for the dead. A pale finger of winter light streamed through a frosty pane and full into my face, which lay pressed against the grit stone floor. I'd lain all night just as I'd landed when I slid from the stool, and my bones, aching from the cold, were so stiff I could barely ease myself upright. My mouth was dry as ashes and tasted as if I'd sucked a gall. I crept round, making up the fire and warming a posset with the slow, crabbed gestures of a crone.

But my mind was more serene than it had been since that warm day – oh! so far away it now seemed – when I had sat nursing Tom with my toes in the brook and Jamie laughing beside me. By the slant of the light, I could tell I'd slept ten hours – the first unbroken sleep I could remember in an age. I scanned the shelf for the remaining piece of poppy resin and felt panic rise when I could not immediately find it. Stiff as I was, I fell to my hands and knees, desperately groping between the gritstones to see where it might have fallen. When my hand closed upon it, I felt the relief of the acquitted. Carefully, I placed it back into the phial and hid it again into the pipkin. The thought that it was there, waiting for me, warmed my mind as the posset and the fire were just now beginning to warm my bones.

When the water lost its chill, I washed my face and raked the tangles from my hair. I could not do much about the rumpled state of my tunic, but I pinned on a clean whisk and hands. The side of my face was still pocked from the imprint of the stone, so I rubbed both cheeks hard and hoped that the cold air would put some roses into them by the time I reached the rectory. As I stepped out into the street, I was clinging to the last wisps of my drugged serenity, as a man fallen into a well might hold fast to the few final threads of a fraying rope. I had not gone but six steps when I dropped again into the dark place of our new reality.

Sally Maston, my neighbour's girl of but five years, was standing in the doorway of her cottage, wide-eyed and silent, clutching her bloody groin. She was wearing a flimsy nightdress, the front of which bloomed like a rose from the blood of her burst Plague sore. I ran to her and gathered her up into my arms.

'There, there,' I cried, 'where is your mummy?'

She gave no answer but fell limp against me. I carried her through the doorway and back into the dim cottage. The fire had guttered in the night, and the room was frigid. Sally's mother lay upon a pallet, pale and cold and many hours dead. Her father sprawled on the floor beside his wife, one hand twined in hers where it had fallen limply off the pallet. He was fevered, his mouth caked with sordes, and struggling for breath. In a wooden crib by the hearth, a baby mewled faintly.

Could a day contain two occasions of such utter misery? That day did, and more than two. Before sunset, no less than four families were visited so, by deaths that reached across generations, snatching children and parents with the same dread hand. The Mompellions reeled from one grievous scene to the next; while the rector prayed with the dying, wrote out their wills and consoled where he could, I helped Mrs. Mompellion with the tending and feeding and finding of kinfolk willing to care for the newly orphaned or soon-to-be so – no easy matter, especially if the child was already sick. We had fallen naturally into this way of dividing our toil; the rector would deal with the business that accompanied dying, while his wife and I managed the matters of those left alive.

My work that day was to make the Maston children as comfortable as I might. Their mother's body I readied for the sexton. For the father I could do little. He lay insensible, barely breathing. When poor old Jon Millstone arrived with his cart and found that the man was not yet dead, though near as good as, I heard him cursing under his breath. I must have looked sternly at him, for he swept his soiled cap from his head and wiped a hand across his brow.

'Ah, forgive me, Mistress, but these times, they do make monsters of us all. It's just that I'm so very tired, I can nay bear the thought of harnessing the cart horse twice when once might've served.' I bade him sit then and went to my cottage for a mug of broth, for the old man was working far beyond his strength. By the time I returned, had warmed the broth, and he had sipped it down, there were two corpses for his cart after all.

I listened to him go and settled to what would surely be a desolate night, a deathwatch merely. The infant was barely clinging to life. Sally tossed and sneezed, restless in her fever. In the early evening, Mrs. Mompellion appeared at the door, her face so pale it looked transparent as a frosted pane. 'Anna,' she said. 'I am just come from the Hancock farm. It is a death house this night. Swithin, the youngest son, is dead, and Lib lies very grave. Anna, I know she was dear to you once. If you wish, I will bide here while you go to her.'

I would not have left the children's side, nor laid extra toil upon Mrs. Mompellion, for any less cause. But the rift with Lib was like an ache, and I longed to ease it. By the time I toiled to the Hancock farm, my old friend was too far gone for speech. I sat with her and stroked her face, willing her to waken for just a word, that I might say something to mend the breach between us. Even such small relief was not granted to me. And so this silent leave-taking with my oldest friend was but another sadness heaped upon the weight of grief I carried.

It was very late when I returned to relieve Mrs. Mompellion at the Maston cottage, but it was a good thing I got there when I did, for it snowed not long after, just enough time, as I judged, as it would take her to have hastened safe inside the rectory's warm walls. It was a wild snow, the kind that blew hard against the cottage and chinked every crevice in the stone. I built the fire up and laid every piece of cloth I could find upon the children. Most winters, we feared storms such as this one. We would watch and wait to see how heavy the falls would lie and how deep would rise the drifts in our narrow lanes and wonder if the snow would close our roads. But now the white banks might grow as high as they would; our roads were as good as closed in any wise.

This storm swiftly spent its fury. The wind dropped not long after midnight, and the baby died in the deep silence that followed. Little Sally lasted into the afternoon of the following day but passed with the early fading of the light. Having bathed her thin body and wrapped her in clean linen, I left her, lying alone, until Jon Millstone found the time to take her. 'Sorry, little one,' I whispered. 'I should sit up with you this night. But I must save my strength for the living. Lie peaceful, my lamb.'

And so I trudged home in the near-dark, stopping at the sheep-fold only long enough to fling some hay to my diminished flock. For myself, I did not bother to eat. Instead, I poured boiling water over the remaining poppy resin, stirring in a half cup of heather-scented honey to mask the bitterness, and carried the mug up to my bed. In my dreams that night, the mountains breathed like sleeping beasts and the wind cast a rich blue shadow. A winged horse flew me through a sky of black velvet, over shimmering deserts of golden glass, through fields of falling stars.

Once again, I awoke in the morning blissfully rested. And once again, the poppy-induced serenity did not last long. This time, it was no outward horror that plunged me back into our hard reality, but my own realization, lying warm in my bed, that I had no further means to secure such oblivion. I lay there, staring up at the beams of my own ceiling, and remembered my last visit to the Gowdies –

how the bunches of drying herbs had brushed against Anys's honey-gold hair. Surely there must have been some poppy fruits hanging there among the goldenseal and the burdock? Perhaps there were already carefully prepared tinctures, put up in cupboards? Or resin in phials such as I had stolen from Mrs. Mompellion? I determined to go straight there and see what I might be able to secure for myself.

The snow had rizen onto the windward side of rocks and trees, where it gleamed like lacquer. My hens huddled in a frost-free corner of the garth, their feathers fluffed against the cold, each standing on one leg while warming the other in its down. I grabbed up some handfuls of hay and stuffed them into my boots to keep my feet dry and warm on the long, damp walk. The sky hung low, deep grey and threatening further snowfall. The pastures were a mottle of yellow and white: thawed patches of cropped stubble laid against bright swathes where snow lay unmelted in furrows. From the high point I could see down to the Riley farm, where the stooks from the harvest still stood in the field, mildewed now and useless. Our custom says the church bells must ring over the stooks for three Sundays before the bringing of the harvest home. But it was the death knell that had tolled over these stooks, and more than thrice. Since the scything of this field, Mrs. Hancock had buried her husband, three of her sons, and one daughter-in-law. This day she would lay Swithin and Lib into the ground. I could not bear to think of her suffering, and so I trudged on, picking my way across frozen turves and trying to avoid the sticky patches of thawing mud. Then I noticed something else amiss. By this hour, the oily black smoke of the Talbot smithy should have been pouring from the new-fired forge. In that still, cold air the smoke should have been drifting and rolling like a dark mist into the valley. But it was the forge itself that was cold, and the Talbot cottage silent. Heavily, I set my feet on the track up to the smith's house, knowing well enough what I would find when I got there.

Kate Talbot opened the door, her fist pressed hard into the small of her aching back. She was round-bellied with her first child, due at Shrovetide. As I had expected, the smell of rotten apples filled the house. That scent, once beloved, now was so married in my mind with sickrooms that it made me gag. But there was another smell, also, in the Talbot house: the odour of burned meat left to rot. Richard Talbot, the strongest man in our village, lay wasted and whimpering upon his bed like an infant, the flesh of his groin singed black as a roasted beef. The place where the iron had seared was laid open to the muscle, seeping pus and green with putrefaction.

I could not take my eyes from this terrible wound. Kate saw me staring and wrung her hands. 'He demanded I do it,' she said in a hoarse whisper. 'Two nights ago, he bade me fire up the forge and heat the poker till it glowed red. I could not bring myself to lay it on him, Anna, so he grabbed it from my hand, feeble as he was, and buried the brand in his own flesh. I can still hear his screaming. Anna, my Richard is a man who has been kicked by horses and smashed by hammers and burned a score of times by hot irons and falling coals. But this pain he gave himself must have been the agony of Hellfire. Afterwards, he lay in a cold sweat, trembling for an hour. He said if we burned the Plague sore away then the disease would surely follow. But he has only worsened since that night, and I do not know how to help him.' I muttered some empty words of comfort, knowing that Richard Talbot would be dead of the rot, if not the Plague, likely before nightfall.

Because I lacked words, I looked around for tasks. The room was chill, for Kate said her back pain was so sharp that she had not been able to bring in more than one log at a time, and the fire had burned down to mere embers. I went out to haul in a bushel-skep of wood, and as I reentered the room I saw Kate bending over Richard, closing her hand on the small triangle of parchment she'd laid nearby his wound. But as quick as she was, I saw plainly what she tried to hide. It was a spell, inscribed thus:

A B R A C A D A B R A
B R A C A D A B R
R A C A D A B
A C A D A
C A D
A

'Kate Talbot!' I chided. 'Surely you know better than these wicked follies!' Her tired face fell, and the tears started. 'No,' I said, instantly regretting my harshness and reaching out to embrace her. 'I'm sorry I spoke so. I know you turn to this because you do not know what else to do.'

'Oh, Anna,' she sobbed. 'I do not, in my heart, believe in it, and yet I bought this charm because that which I do believe has failed me. Richard has ever been a good man. Why does God rack him so? Our prayers in the church bring no relief. So the voice of the Devil whispers to me, "If God will not help you," he says, "mayhap I might . . ."'

At first, she would not say how she had come by the charm, for the charlatan who had choused her out of a shilling for it had also told her that a death curse would come upon her if she told. But I pressed her, trying to make her see that all of it was a malign trick to take her money. Finally, she swallowed hard.

'No, Anna, it were no trick. Wicked, yes, and vain, maybe, but magic, in truth. For the charm were given me by the ghost of Anys Gowdie.'

'Nonsense!' I blurted. But she was pale as the drifting snow outside. More gently, I pressed her: 'Why say you so?'

'I heard her voice in the wind last night when I went out to fetch in a log. She said to place a shilling on the lintel and in the morning a potent charm would lie there in its stead.'

'Kate,' I said, as gently as I could. 'Anys Gowdie is dead and gone. And if she were alive, as I devoutly wish she were, and able to help us, she would not come with worthless charms, for you know her cures were always practical things, made of common earthly weeds and worts, that she in her wisdom knew the health-giving use for. Throw that paper away, Kate,' I said, 'and put aside these foolish, poisonous thoughts. For I am sure we will find that someone of this village – corrupt and greedy, but very much alive – was the voice you heard in the windy night.'

Reluctantly, she opened her hand and let the parchment flutter down on to the bavins. As I blew on the embers, a bright flame leapt up and seized it. 'Take your ease now,' I said, 'and I will tend to your chores here. With rest you might find the world a small bit brighter.'

She lowered her swollen body down upon the bed beside her husband's. I went out to fetch in more wood and heard a piteous mooing from the byre. The cow's bag was hard as stone for want of milking. When the beast felt my fingers bringing her relief, she turned and gazed at me with gratitude. Afterwards, I gathered a few eggs from the garth and baked them with the fresh milk into a curd that Kate could sup on when she wakened.

Having done what I could, I continued on my own errand. While I had been with the Talbots a stiff wind had blown up, cracking the ice on the black branches in a series of sudden, sharp reports. At the Gowdies' cottage, the snow lay in unswept drifts, and I moved through them knee-deep, like wading a river. At the door, I paused, fighting down the guilt I felt at invading the property of the dead. As I stood there, trying to find courage, snowmelt dripped down the thatch and landed upon my neck like icy fingers. I began to wrestle with the damp-swollen door, but my hands, cluzened from the cold, were clumsy. Finally, I dragged it open a crack. Something shot by me in a grey blur, so sudden and swift that I flinched and flattened myself against the wet wood. It was only the Gowdies' gib-cat, who leapt onto the roof, spitting and yowling against my intrusion. I shoved and pushed until the door finally budged enough to admit me. I sidled my way into the dark. Something brushed my face and I gasped, but it was just a frond of meadowsweet that had loosed itself from a bunch hanging by the door.

The wind whipped around the house, its sighs and whispers like a hundred haunting voices. I felt myself trembling and told myself it was the cold, merely. Since the Gowdies were too poor for glazing, the cottage had but a wind-eye up under the eaves, and this they had stuffed with rushes since the first cool days of leaf-fall. I was damp through and needed to kindle a fire for light as well as warmth, but it was so dim in the soot-stained room that I had to feel all around the hearth for the flint and tinder. When I found them, my hands shook so that as many times as I tried, I could not strike a spark.

A sudden light blazed behind me.

'Stand back from the hearth, Anna.'

I jumped up, dropped the flint, caught my foot in a loose hearth-stone, and slipped, facedown onto the earthen floor. Terrified, I raised my head and turned, blinded by the light emanating from the ghost of Anys Gowdie. She hovered in the air above me, white-gowned and brilliant.

'Are you all right?' Elinor Mompellion asked, climbing down the loft ladder with a candle held high in front of her.

Shock, relief, and mortification all descended upon me at once, and with such force that I burst into tears. 'Have you injured yourself?' Mrs. Mompellion said, bending over me, her face, in the circle of candle glow, creased with concern. She raised a corner of her white pinafore to wipe the place where my forehead had struck the floor.

'No, no,' I said, struggling for command of myself. 'I landed hard on my wrist, merely. I – I did not expect to find anyone else here this day, and I was startled.'

'It seems we shared the same idea,' she said, and I, in my confusion, thought she meant that she had come searching for the poppy also. Before I gave voice to my misunderstanding, she continued: 'I came here late yesterday, for it seems evident to me, as I see it must have also to you, that we must take stock of these herbs and such remedies as the Gowdies may have left here. The key to defeating this Plague, I am convinced, must lie here, in the virtue of such plants as can be used to nourish those who remain in health. We must strengthen our bodies that we may continue to resist contagion.' She had taken my place at the hearth now, and by dribbling a little candle wax on a bavin had kindled a promising flame.

'I became so engrossed in sorting and naming the plants that I barely noticed the light fading, and by the time I realized I must needs set out for home, it had begun to snow. I decided it was best to sleep the night here rather than toil the long way to the rectory in such weather. Mr. Mompellion, I knew, would reason I was needed for the night at someone's sickbed. And indeed, I slept so well in this quiet place that I believe I would be sleeping still if your struggles with the door had not waked me. And now we must set to work, for Anna, there are riches here indeed!' And she launched then on a catalogue of what she had so far identified and the virtues of the tonics we could make and distribute.

As I listened to her plans, so selfless and suffused with hope, I felt the wretchedness of my own selfish scheme for escape into a false oblivion.

'Mrs. Mompellion, I –'

'Elinor,' she said, interrupting, 'you and I cannot work on such terms as we now are and continue with the old forms. You must call me Elinor.'

'Elinor . . . I have something to confess to you. I came here not seeking herbs to help others. Only myself.'

'Ah, yes,' she said, quietly. 'You came for these.' From the ceiling rafter, she reached up and effortlessly unstrung a bunch of pregnant seedpods. 'The Greeks called them the Poppies of Lethe. Do you remember? We read about it together. Lethe – the Greeks' river of forgetfulness. Once the souls of the dead tasted its waters they forgot their past lives. It is natural to want to forget, Anna, when every day is a brimful of sadness. But those souls also forgot those that they had loved. You do not want that, surely? I have heard some preach that God wants us to forget the dead, but I cannot believe so. I think He gives us precious recollections so that we may not be parted entirely from those He has given us to love. You must cherish your memories of your babes, Anna, until you see them again in Heaven.'

'I took the poppy from your whisket at the Daniels' cottage.'

'I know it,' she said. 'And did it bring you sweet dreams?'

'Yes,' I whispered. 'The sweetest I have ever known.'

She nodded, her fine hair lit like a halo in the firelight. 'Yes,' she said. 'I remember well.'

'You?' I said, startled. 'You have used this thing?'

'Yes, Anna, even I. For there was a time when I had much that I, too, wanted to forget. That poppy you took from me – it was a relict from that time. I had kept it, you see, even though it is some years since I have resorted to it. But it is a jealous friend and will not lightly loosen its embrace.' She stood up then, reached into a pipkin in the corner, and measured a quantity of crumbled chamomile into a pot. The kettle hanging in the hearth had begun to steam. From it, she poured just enough water to make a pungent tea.

'Do you remember on the way to the Daniels', Anna, that I said to you that I had never birthed a child?'

I nodded dumbly. I could not think where this was leading.

'I did not say I had never been *with* child.'

I must have looked confused at this, for I had worked for Mrs. Mompellion, laundering her clothes and changing her linens, since the day she arrived in our village, still a new bride. If she had been with child I would have known it almost as soon as she herself did. Indeed, I had been watching for her terms, as I wished it for her so.

She reached out a hand then and turned my face to look full into hers. 'Anna, the child I carried was not Mr. Mompellion's.' She read the shock in my face, and her soft fingers, warm from holding her steaming mug, fluttered on my cheek, as if to soothe me. Then her hand dropped and sought mine, as it lay in my lap, and she laced her slender fingers into my chapped and callused ones. 'It is a story full of pain, but I tell it to you now because I want you to know me. I have already asked much of you, Anna, and before this terrible time passes I may ask a great deal more. I want you to know who it is that lays these burdens upon you.'

She turned her face to the fire then, and as she spoke we looked at the flames, rather than at each other. The story she unfolded began on a vast and beautiful Derbyshire estate, in rooms warmed by richly woven carpets and watched over by the pensive eyes of ancestral portraits. She had been the beloved only daughter of a gentleman of great wealth. She was indulged – spoiled, she said – especially after her mother died. Her father and her older brother had been loving but often absent, entrusting her care to a governess who was more learned than she was wise.

Elinor's childhood was filled with pleasure and with the acquisition of knowledge, which to her meant very much the same thing. 'I blush, Anna, to say this to you, knowing what you have made of yourself from such scant stuffs as your life has provided. For myself, any fancy I had to know a thing – Greek or Latin, history, music, art and natural philosophy – all I had to do was express a wish, and these treasures would be laid out before me. And I learned these things. But of life, Anna, and of human nature – of those I did not learn.' Her father thought to keep her sheltered from the world, and so she did not leave the estate nor enter into any but a most restricted society. She had been just fourteen when a neighbour, a young man of twenty and the heir to a dukedom, had begun pursuit of her.

'When my father returned from an absence and found that the two of us had been riding out alone almost daily, he told me that it must cease at once. Oh, he was not stern with me – perhaps had he been sterner I would have heeded him more readily. But perhaps it would have made no difference: For Anna, I was thrilled with this young man and his attentions. He flattered me in every conceivable way. He made me laugh, and he would interrogate everyone in the household about what I liked and did not like and cut the cloth of his behaviour to suit that intelligence. My father told me only that I was far too young for any such intense friendships. He told me he had many plans for me – a presentation at Court, a trip at his side to the great cities of the ancient world. But as he said these things, I could only think, guiltily, how much more I would enjoy them on the arm of Charles – my young man. My father did not tell me that he had doubts about Charles himself, grave doubts about his character, that subsequent events proved well-founded. Perhaps he did not wish to be confronted by the sorts of queries that I would have raised in response to such information. For we lived very quiet, and I had been entirely sheltered from the world that my father and my brother – and Charles – knew all too well.'

Elinor, who loved her father, had obeyed his wishes at first. But when his affairs took him from the estate again a month later, the young man renewed and redoubled his pursuit. 'He begged me to elope with him, and afterwards, he promised, he would make it up with my father, who would not stand against the match once he saw the brilliance of my new state. My governess uncovered the scheme and could have thwarted it. But I begged her, and Charles charmed her and finally bribed her into silence with the gift of a ruby pendant that we later learned he had pilfered from his mother's box. And so she abetted our scheme and kept my father ignorant much longer than would otherwise have been possible.

'With her help, we stole away at dead of night. How can I tell you now why it was that I would do such a thing? I was like the Starlover in Sidney's poem: "My young mind marred, whom love doth windlass so." We planned, as I thought, to make for the Fleet, where marriages could be bought at any hour without licence. But I had never seen London, and so when Charles proposed that we first try this or that entertainment or excursion, I did not hesitate to say, yes, yes, let us do it all.

'You will have guessed what I will next tell you, that the union was consummated before it was consecrated.' Elinor said this in a small voice. 'And then it gradually became clear even to me that he did not intend to have it consecrated at all. I mean to tell you everything, Anna, so hear this: I was so lost in the fires of my own lusts that I did not greatly care.'

Elinor was weeping now, soundlessly, the tears pooling in her pale eyes. I reached up a hand. I wanted to touch her, to wipe them away, but deference, instilled in me since birth, stayed my hand. Elinor looked at me then, and her gaze told me that my touch was welcome. So with the tips of my fingers I brushed the tears from her cheek. Then she grasped my hand and held it, as she went on to tell how she and Charles had lived together for more than a fortnight until, one evening, he simply failed to return to the inn where they were hiding. He had abandoned her.

'There were days when I would not let myself believe it. I told myself all manner of falsehoods, that he had fallen ill somewhere, that he had been called off on secret, high state business. It was some time before I faced the fact of my ruin and called upon those who still, somehow, loved me.' Her father and brother, who had been frantically searching for her, came swiftly. They carried her home, where the matter was to have been entirely hushed up. But she was with child.

Her face, as she revisited these memories, had become increasingly drawn. The tears flowed freely now, but still she did not give way to sobbing but simply dashed them away with the heel of her hand and went on. It was as if the tale, once embarked upon, compelled her.

'I was desperate, and I was deranged,' she said. 'I violated my own body with a fire iron.'

I drew a ragged breath at this and hid my face in my hands. I could not bear to imagine such suffering, yet I could not prevent my mind from conjuring terrible images of it. I reached out a hand, blindly, and clasped hers once again.

'My father engaged the best physician, and so my life was saved. But not my womb, Anna, which they tell me is nothing now but a mass of scars. They gave me poppy at first for the pain, and then I think to keep me quiet. And I might very well still be wandering, lost in those empty dreams, if it were not for Michael.'

And so I learned that Michael Mompellion was not, as I had always thought, the scion of a distinguished clerical family. His father had been a cleric, it is true, but a curate merely. Michael, the eldest of three children, was but a small boy at the outbreak of the civil war. His father had been swept up in the turmoil, acquiring for himself powder and match, sword and halberd. Instead of leading people to their prayers, he had led them to war on behalf of the parliament. At first, his troop did well enough, but after the king escaped from the hands of the army, the second phase of the war went ill for him. The cavaliers routed the forces in his parish and plundered his own dwelling of all that was portable – brass, pewter, and cloth. Michael's father made off through the lines to save his own life. The next day, attempting to return home, he was mistaken by a party of his own men and mortally wounded.

As a result, the family was destitute, and Michael, as eldest, had to be sent from his home into a situation where he could be provided for. He had been placed into service with the steward of Elinor's family estate. So all his childhood learning had come at the elbow of the farrier and the cooper, the gamekeeper and the tenant farmers. He had grown up ploughing ground and bucking hay, breaking colts and shoeing mares, learning every detail of the estate's complexity.

'Before long, he was offering suggestions for its better management.' Her voice seemed to strengthen now, for in this part of the story she took pride. 'His intelligence caught the attention of my father, who undertook Michael's education. He went to the best of schools, where he excelled, and then on to Cambridge. When he came home, he found me, frail from my long illness. They would carry me out to the garden each day, and I would sit there, too lost in my own grief and remorse to get up out of my chair. Michael offered me his friendship, Anna. And, later, his love.'

She was smiling slightly now. 'He brought the brightness back into my dim world. He understood suffering, having felt it in his own life. He took me into the crofts of my family's tenants and taught me how to read people's lives. He showed me sorrows far worse than mine and pain far less deserved. He instructed me how futile it is to wallow in regret for that which cannot be changed and how atonement might be made for even the gravest sins. Even mine, Anna. Even mine.'

Gradually, with his encouragement, she regained some physical strength. Mental peace followed more slowly. 'At first, I borrowed his brightness and used it to see my way, and then gradually, from the habit of looking at the world as he illuminated it, the light in my own mind rekindled itself.' They were wed soon after he took Orders. 'To the world at large, it seemed that I stooped to marry him,' she said softly. 'But as you now see, the sacrifice in the match was all on the side of my dear Michael. More sacrifice than anyone could imagine.'

We sat for a while, staring into the fire, until a log suddenly shifted and sent a scatter of sparks onto the earth floor. Elinor stood up then, abruptly, and smoothed her long, white pinafore. 'And now, my dear Anna, now that you know everything, will you still work with me?'

I was too stunned by all I had heard to say anything, so I simply rose from my stool, grasped both her hands, and kissed them. How little we know, I thought, of the people we live amongst. It is not as if, had you asked me, I would have claimed to fathom the thoughts and sentiments of two whose station in life was so far distant from mine. But in my own unexamined way I had believed that, working in their house and seeing to their needs, watching their comings and goings and their dealings with others, I had come to know them. How little, how very little, that knowledge had really amounted to. Many things about the rector now seemed clearer to me – his physical strength, his easiness with all manner of trades and classes of people. So, too, did Elinor's kindness and her unwillingness to judge the faults in others.

Elinor embraced me, and I felt certain at that moment I would do anything for this woman, anything she asked of me. 'Good, then,' she said, drawing away, 'for there is much to do. Look, look at this.' She reached into the pocket of her pinafore and pulled out a folded parchment. 'I have made a list of all who have succumbed so far to the Plague and have laid it down upon a map of the dwellings in this place. From this I believe we can grasp how this pestilence spreads, and to whom.'

There it was, our Plague-scoured village, the names of all its three hundred and three score sorry souls pinned to the map like insect specimens on a board. Under the names of near fifty, Elinor had drawn a black line. I had not conceived that the sickness already had undone so many. The map showed it clearly: the way the contagion had spread out from my cottage, a starburst of death.

Elinor pulled on my sleeve, urgent. 'Look at the names of the victims. What is the first thing that you notice?' I stared at the map dumbly. 'Can you not see? The Plague does not distinguish between man and woman, for each are fairly represented in the dead roll. But it *does* make a distinction – it selects the very young over the very old. Almost half of the dead here have been not yet sixteen years of age. The rest are persons in their prime. None, as yet, have been silver-hairs. Why, Anna? Why? Here is what I think. I think the old in this village have lived long because they are good fighters of sickness; veterans, if you like, in the war against disease. So, what must we do? We must arm the children, make them stronger – give them weapons with which to fight. We have been trying, in vain, to cure the sick, and we have failed at it. Of all those who have got the Plague, only one – old Margaret Blackwell – has lasted more than a week with it.'

Margaret, the cooper Blackwell's wife, had sickened at the same time as the Sydells, and though she still ailed, it did seem as though she was destined to live through her ordeal. Because she had not died, some now doubted that she had Plague at all. But I had seen the swelling in her groin and tended her when it burst and spewed forth its pussy infection. Others claimed it was a boil or cyst merely. But I held it was a Plague sore, and so Margaret might be our first survivor.

'For most,' Elinor continued, 'the onset of the disease spells the end of life. What we must do, here in this sorry little cottage, is find all the herbs of a strength-giving virtue and combine them in a tonic to fortify the healthy.'

And so for the rest of that day, we pored through the books that Elinor had carried from the rectory, looking first for the names of plants said to be strengthening for any of the many body parts the Plague seemed to attack. It was tedious going, for the books were in Latin or Greek, which Elinor had to translate for me. Eventually, we discovered that the best of them was a volume by one Avicenna, a Musalman doctor who, many years since, had set down all his learning in a vast canon. When we had the names of the plants, we went through the herb bunches, trying, sometimes with great difficulty, to match the descriptions in the books with the drying leaves and roots before us. Outside, we searched the snow-blasted garden for any sturdy plants whose worts we could yet dig before the ground froze solid. By afternoon, we had assembled the weapons for our armoury. Nettle for the blood. Starwort and violet leaves for the lungs. Silverweed to cool a fever. Cress for the stomach. The worts of blow-ball for the liver, bat-weed for the glands, and vervain for the throat.

Elinor thought the last of these perhaps the most important. She called it the holy herb of Saint John and read out a prayer recommended to be said over the plant before we pulled up the roots.

'Hallowed be thou vervain, as thou growest on thy mound
For in the Mount of Calvary there thou was first found.
Thou healedest our saviour and stanched his bleeding wound.
In name of Father, Son, and Holy Ghost,
I take thee from the ground.'

We gathered all the bunches we could carry into a burlap to carry to the rectory kitchen. I was about to extinguish the fire in the grate when Elinor reached out and stayed my hand. 'What about these, Anna? What shall we do with them?' She held out the poppies. 'It is for you to decide.'

I felt the panic rise in me. 'But, surely, we need these for the succour of the many afflicted here,' I said, although my thoughts had sped immediately to my own needs rather than those of the dying.

'The Gowdies were sensible of the risk posed by this thing, Anna. They have only enough here to relieve a handful of grave cases. How should we choose who should suffer and who should be soothed?'

Without speaking, I reached for the bunch. I made to throw it on the fire, but found I did not have the will to open my hand. I ran a thumbnail across a still-green pod and watched the white sap ooze slowly from the incision. I wanted to lay my tongue on it, to lap the bitterness and feel its sweet sequel. Elinor stood silently, waiting. I tried to read her eyes, but she turned away from me.

How was I to face the days and nights to come? There would be no other relief for me; in my two hands I held my only chance of exit from our village and its agonies. But then I realized that this was not quite true. There was our work. I had seen that afternoon how it was possible to lose myself in it. And yet this loss of self was not selfish oblivion. From this study and its applications might come much good. But surely I could not attempt it without clarity of mind. I grasped the bunch then and flung it on the fire. The sap hissed for a moment, and then the pods burst, their showers of tiny seeds falling invisible among the ashes.

By the time we closed the stubborn door behind us, the wind had died and the air seemed milder. I would try to be the woman that Elinor wished me to be. And if I failed, I had learned enough from our work that day to know where to look for the pale green shoots of poppy, pushing through the soil of the Gowdies' garden, come the spring.

Among Those That
Go Down to the Pit

As we approached the rectory, we saw Michael Mompellion in the churchyard, his coat off, the wide sleeves of his white shirt rolled up past his forearms, his hair damp from his own sweat. He was digging graves. Three long holes lay open around him, and he was at work on the fourth.

Elinor hurried to him, reaching up to wipe his brow. He stepped back from her and waved away her hand. His face was grey with exhaustion and he leant upon the spud, heavily. She begged him to stop and rest, but he shook his head. 'I cannot stop. We need six graves this day, one of them for poor Jon Millstone.' Our aged sexton had died that morning. The rector had found him, sprawled half in, half out of the grave he had been digging. 'His heart gave out. He was too old for the labour that of late has been laid upon him.'

Looking at Mr. Mompellion, I worried that he, too, might drop. He looked worn to a nub. It seemed he had not slept the previous night but gone from one deathbed to the next. His pledge that none should die alone had become a heavy burden upon him. It was clear that he could not survive if now he attempted the sexton's work as well. I hurried to the kitchen, warmed a mug of purl for him, and carried it back out to where he stood, waist deep in the dirt.

'Sir, this is not seemly work for you,' I said. 'Let me fetch one of the men from the Miner's Tavern to do it.'

'And who will come, Anna?' He placed a hand to his back and winced as he straightened. 'The miners are ill set trying to pull ore enough from their claims to keep their mines from being nicked. The farmers are become too few to gather in the grain or milk their kine. How can I lay this melancholy work upon them? Those who are still in health to do it should not be asked to risk such proximity with the dead.'

And so he worked on, until the light failed. And then he sent word to the various houses that they might bring their dead for the burials. It was a sorry procession. No one was troubling with coffins now; there were no more planed timbers to be had nor time to fashion them. Families simply carried their loved ones to their graves, or, if they were not strong enough, dragged them thither with a blanket slung beneath the armpits of the corpse. Mr. Mompellion prayed over each one by candlelight and then helped in piling the soil back into the graves. While he toiled in the churchyard, pleas came from two more families that he attend them in their extremity. I would have kept the messages from him until morning, but Elinor said it would not be right to do so. When he came in, she carried the heated water for his toilet and fetched him fresh linens while I prepared a nourishing meal. He ate quickly and then put on his coat and rode off to keep his word.

'He cannot go on like this,' I said to Elinor as the sound of Anteros's hoofbeats faded.

'I know it,' she replied softly. 'His body is strong, but I fear that the strength of his will far exceeds it. It can drive him to do what any normal man cannot do. Believe me, I have seen this, for better and for worse.'

Among Those That Go Down to the Pit

The rector got little sleep that night, and the next day brought no respite. In the morning I went with him to the Merrill farm, where Jakob lay dying. Brand, who had lived with the Merrills since his return with Maggie Cantwell, had taken five-year-old Seth away to the sheepfold, to do some necessary chores but also to get the boy out of sight of his father's agony. Charity, exhausted by doing more labour, night and day, than should ever be meted out to a girl of ten, had fallen asleep on her pallet in the corner. As I patted out oatcakes for the children's supper, the rector spoke quietly with Jakob Merrill, asking him gently if there was aught he wished to say or have done before he might become too ill to think clearly.

Merrill's face was florid with fever and he got each breath by terrible effort. 'Rector Mompellion, I know it is unseemly to fear death, but I do fear it. I fear it, for I have sinned in my life. My wife, Maudie, who lies in her grave these last five years ... I have sinned against her, and I fear I will be punished for it ...' In his agitation, he had lifted himself up from his pallet, but the effort sent him into spasms of coughing. The rector reached out for him and raised him up, holding him close and letting him lean across his shoulder as Merrill tried to clear his rattling chest. The rector didn't even seem to notice the sputum and spittle that splattered his coat. When the spasm passed, he eased Jakob down again upon the bed. I handed the rector a mug of cool water, and he cradled Jakob's head as he held it up to the man's dry lips.

Jakob Merrill closed his eyes, wincing with pain. 'Rector, you did not know Maudie, for she died birthing Seth before you came to us. Maudie was a good woman, she was. But I never cared enough for her. I worked her to a ravelling, even when she was with child. I never gave her kind words or thought of her ease. Instead, I left her alone here to do all the toil while I took the pence her labour earned

161

and spent it buying ale for doxies who let me lie with them. And when God took Maudie from me, I felt it was His wrath on me for my neglect. And I knew I deserved it. But now, if He takes me, too, He punishes not me, but my children. I don't want Charity married off hastily as her mother was to me, married off to a lout too young to know what affection is, what duty is . . . And little Seth . . . I would not see him in the poor house, but who will care for him here? Charity is a capable girl, but a ten-year-old cannot be expected to raise a brother and run a farm . . .'

Mr. Mompellion laid his large hand tenderly upon Jakob Merrill's face. 'Hush now, for I hear your concerns.' His voice was low and even. 'And now I tell you this: do not dwell any more on things in the past that you cannot change. Who made man frail of the flesh? Who made our lusts, our low ways and our high? Did not God? Is not He the author of it all? The appetites we have all come from Him; they have been with us since Eden. If we slip and fall, He understands our weakness. Did not mighty King David lust, and was he not driven through his lust to do great wrong? And yet God loved David, and gave us, through him, the glory of the Psalms. So, too, does God love you, Jakob Merrill.'

Prone upon the pallet, Merrill gave a sigh and closed his eyes as the rector continued: 'When God took your wife to him, he punished you, it is true, but her He did not punish. No! He crowned Maude Merrill with a crown of righteousness. He freed her from all toil and tiredness. And, Jakob, He bathed her in boundless love, so much love that her need for the love that you withheld has been requited. Your wife's sufferings have been washed away long since, washed away and forgotten. And she has seen your remorse and knows your feelings to her now, so that when you meet in Heaven you may join hands in that perfect union that God means marriage to be. So think of this no more – or rather, think of it with joy.

'As for your children, why do you not commit them to the care of God, whose love for them is mightier and more constant than yours? Believe this, and then you will see that God has already made provision for your children. Did He not send young Brand to you, and did you not take him in to your home in his need? Do you not see God's hand at work there? I do, Jakob. For now, in *your* need, Brand is here for you: a good young man who has shown much character and has no place of his own in the world. Make him part of your family, Jakob, so that he might stay on here as he is, and so you will give to Charity and Seth an older brother to care for them.'

Jakob Merrill's hand tightened on the rector's, and his brow unknotted. He asked the rector then to help him make a last will to bind such an arrangement, and the rector pulled out the parchment he always carried upon his person, as he often was asked to write wills these days. It took much time, for Jakob Merrill was failing fast and having great difficulty both marshalling his thoughts and forcing his voice, but the rector's patience seemed limitless. While he had been talking to Jakob Merrill, the fluency of his speech and the clarity of his expression had belied the fact that he had been attending at deathbeds since dawn. The rector called me over to witness Jakob Merrill put his mark; where the rector's clear hand ended, Jakob struggled to inscribe a faint and wobbly cross. It was only when I took up the parchment to blot it and set it carefully away, that I saw the telltales of the rector's exhausted mind.

'In ye name of God, amen. I' – here Mr. Mompellion, in a moment of mental darkness, had written his own name instead of Jakob Merrill's and then had scored it out with a series of loops before inscribing the name of the farmer – 'Jakob Merrill in ye county of Derby, yeoman, on this' – here the rector's mind had failed him again, for he had left the date blank, probably because he wasn't able to recall it – 'being sick and weak but in good memory, do make this my last Will and Testament. First, I bequeath my soul into ye hands of God who made me, depending my salvation upon the account of Jesus Christ my redeemer. I give all my estate, house, land, goods, and chattels, moveable and unmoveable, quick and dead, that it has pleased God to endow me with, to my son Seth, my daughter Charity, and to Brand Rigney, formerly servant of Bradford Hall, whom I do assign as my heir equally with mine own natural children in the hope that he will dwell with them as a brother and be guardian over them.'

I did not say anything to the rector about the missing date, for it was not for me to be reading Jakob Merrill's private will, and I doubt that Mr. Mompellion would have given it to me if he had known that I could read at all. Indeed, I did not purpose to read the words; it was only that my eyes could not prevent me as I blotted the document and set it in the tin box that Merrill had pointed to. Charity was stirring in her corner then, so I warmed the child some caudle, instructed her how to complete the making of the stew I had begun, and set out with the rector.

Elinor met us, her face creased with concern. Two more bodies awaited their graves. Mr. Mompellion sighed and shrugged off his coat. He did not wait even for some nourishment but went straight to the churchyard.

I let go of my pride then, and took my courage into my hands instead. Without telling Elinor what I proposed, I trudged out to my father's croft, hoping that the day was young enough to find him sober still. Happily, Aphra and her children remained in health, although, as always, the little ones looked thin and ill fed, for my father and Aphra both liked better the act that led to the begetting of children than they did the providing for them.

I noticed that Steven, their eldest boy, had an angry welt across his cheek, and I did not need to ask how it had come there. I carried some of the herbs we had been preparing and showed Aphra how to make them up into the tonic that Elinor and I had devised. My father, who had not yet risen from his pallet, stirred himself as we talked. He rose, cursing his aching head and asking me if I had brought a draught for him as well. I held my tongue and forbore from saying that the cure for his malady was a little continence, for I wanted his help that day, and I would be hard pressed to get it if I angered him.

Speaking with a respectful deference that I did not feel, I explained the plight at the rectory, and, flattering him about his great strength and fortitude, beseeched his help. As I had expected, he cursed and said he had more than enough work to lay his hand to, and that it would do my 'prating priest' a power of good to get his white hands dirty. So I offered him his choice of my lambs for that Sunday's dinner and another at the new moon. These were generous terms, and though my father cursed and haggled and thumped the table till the platters rattled, he and I eventually came to an agreement. And so I bought Mr. Mompellion a respite from the graveyard. At least, I told myself, my father's clemmed children might get a portion of the meat.

T he weeks of that cold season wore me to a wraith. There were demands upon me every minute. You may note I do not say every waking minute, for sometimes I was wanted night and day, and I snatched at sleep as I could, at the bedside of the dying or upon a stool propped against a wall in the rectory kitchen. Yuletide passed and we barely marked it. At Shrovetide, I delivered Kate Talbot of a healthy baby girl and, as I put the babe into her arms, I hoped it might ease her grief over the loss of her husband. A week later, I midwifed Lottie Mowbray, a poor and simple woman who yet managed to deliver her baby with the least complaint or difficulty I had yet encountered. Every day we had occasion to bless the earl of Chatsworth. As he had pledged to do before we undertook the obligations of our oath, he continued to provision us. Every day, the carters came with their loads to the Boundary Stone, or to the little spring we had come to call Mompellion's Well. People like Kate Talbot, who had lived by her husband's skilled work, or Lottie and her husband, Tom, who struggled to eke an existence even in good times, would have starved without the earl's provisioning. But from the Bradfords, safe in their Oxfordshire haven, whom we might have expected to send some token of concern, we received neither alms of any sort nor even kindly word.

At the rectory, the kitchen had begun to look like an alchemist's den, swathed in fragrant steam. Chopped leaves bled green onto my well-scrubbed table, turning the bleached wood a grassy colour. I set my morning to the rhythmic thump of my own knife, and its tattoo became, to me, the hopeful music of healing. Elinor had some knowledge of this kind, and she wore her eyes red trying to glean more from diverse books upon the subject.

But chiefly we learned by doing, first trying one way and then another to extract a plant's virtues. Some leaves I seeped in slick and viscous oil, some into sharp-smelling spirit, some into plain, clear water. Then I waited to see which medium would yield the best results. Elinor worked beside me many mornings, her fine skin staining easily with plant tannins till sometimes it looked as if she were wearing pale brown gloves. With boiling water and our store of dried herbs, we made teas; when they were too bitter we dribbled thick spoons of honey to turn them into syrups. We evaporated some teas until they were potent decoctions, for we found that many people would take a little of a potion sooner than a lot. And then I chopped again, bundles of roots wrested out of the frosty ground. Some I packed in crocks and poured in oil enough to steep them. When I judged the plant had given up its virtue I plunged my hands into the silky pulp and kneaded in a piece of beeswax until I had a drawing salve to smooth on angry Plague sores. We saw our work as having two natures: the one, to ease the suffering of the afflicted, and the other, more important but far less certain in its outcome, to bolster up the defences of the well.

Elinor and I distributed our preparations and tried to show people how to find and recognize the new shoots of the wild leaves that they should eat to shore up their health. We learned much about how to ease common ailments and injuries, and though we were loath to turn aside from our main work, somehow we found ourselves sought out for the kinds of preparations the Gowdies once so readily supplied. After a little time, we began to learn some of what they had known: that a compound of mullein and rue, sweet cicely and mustard oil makes an excellent syrup for quieting a cough; that boiled willow bark eases aches and fevers; that betony, bruised for a green plaster, speeds mending of wounds and scrapes. There were some satisfactions in this work, bringing as it did comfort, ease, and the healings of small hurts.

But for what we most wished for, we had to wait. We knew it might be many weeks before we could hope to see, from our efforts, some abatement in the death roll. As the days lengthened, we spent much time at the Gowdies', trying to understand the layout of the physick garden and what was sown there, studying the small packets of saved seeds to determine which would yield what plant, readying the soil to assure the continued supply of our strengthening herbs.

Only on Sunday did we cease from the constant round of gathering and gardening, making and visiting. And of all days of the week, it was Sunday that I now dreaded. What had been my favourite day was now accursed to me, for it was on Sunday, in church, that our failure to arrest the Plague's ravages was apparent in the emptying pews and missing faces. There were also, I should say, some few new faces. For Mr. Stanley had commenced to attend Mr. Mompellion's services ever since the Sunday Oath, and in the weeks since, the Billings family and some others from among the nonconformists had begun to come as well. They did not join in all the hymns, nor did they follow the words of the Book of Common Prayer, but that they gathered with us at all was a wonder, and I was not the only one who seemed glad of it.

It was on the first Sunday in March that Michael Mompellion surrendered to the inevitable and closed the church. He stood in the pulpit that morning, his knuckles white on the oak, straining with the effort to support himself. Elinor had insisted that I move up and share her pew, since I was, she said, now a part of the rectory family. So I was close enough to see the exhausted tremor in his body and the lines etched in his face as he struggled to command his voice.

'My dear friends,' he said. 'God has tried us sorely these months. You have met His test with courage, and be sure you will be rewarded for it. I had dared to hope, we all had hoped, that the test would not be so long nor so hard as it has been, as it continues to be. But who can presume to read the mind of God? Who can understand the intricacy of His great design? For God is subtle; He does not point always at what He intends, but is more dark, and we must seek His face and entreat Him that He will, in His mercy, show it to us. Beloved, do not lose sight, during this our search, of God's great love and tenderness. For all of you who love your children know that affliction, too, can be a means of evidencing your care for them. Who but a negligent father allows his children to grow up unguided by sometime chastisements? And yet the good father does not knit his brow in rage at such times, but deals the necessary penances with love in his eyes, in hope of his children's betterment.'

He paused then and looked down, trying to gather his strength.

'My dear friends, soon God sets us a new test, perhaps the hardest we have yet faced. For soon the weather here will begin to warm, and this Plague – we know from the past accounts of those who have lived through it – this Plague thrives upon warmth. We can hope, we can pray, that it has spent its fury here, but we cannot count upon it. My beloved friends, we must gird ourselves now for the possibility of the worse times that may be coming to us. And we must make our dispositions accordingly.'

There were moans as he spoke, from the people scattered in the church. Someone started weeping. As he said he must close the church, Mr. Mompellion began weeping, too, his exhaustion making his tears invincible. 'Do not despair!' he said, struggling to smile. 'For a church is not a building, merely! We shall still have our church, but we will have it in the midst of God's own creation. We will meet and pray together under the ceiling of Heaven, in Cucklett Delf, where the birds shall be our choir, the stones our altar, the trees our spire! In the Delf, friends, we may stand at a safe distance from one another, so that the ill do not infect the well.'

Despite the tenor of his words, his face became more haggard as he came to the part of his message that would fall the hardest on our ears. 'Beloved, as well as our church, we must close our churchyard, for it has become impossible to bury our dead in a timely way, and with the coming of the warm weather, what is now unseemly will become unsafe. Beloved, we must shoulder the grim task of burying our own dead as soon as we may, in whatever near ground we can . . .'

There were howls now and terrified shouts of 'No!'

He raised his hands high, calling for quiet. 'Beloved, I know what you fear. Believe me, I know it. You fear that God will not find those who are laid down to rest outside of hallowed ground. You fear that your loved ones will be lost to you in eternity. But this day, I say to you, you have hallowed all the ground of this village! You have hallowed it by your sacrifice in this place! God *will* find you! He *will* gather you to Him! He is the Good Shepherd, and He will not abandon even the least of His flock!'

The strain was too much for him then. He lowered his hands to grasp the pulpit railing but missed his grip. There was no more strength left in him. He slid to the floor in a faint.

Elinor and I hastened forwards, as the congregation erupted in cries and weeping. I do not know what would have happened if Mr. Stanley had not stepped forward then and bellowed, with a voice that belied his age, 'Quiet!'

In the hush, he delivered himself of a sermon that recalled my childhood to me. It was a terse denunciation of superstition, railing against the unreformed Papistry lingering within our hearts. 'If your cow dies, and you do bury it in your field, do you plough it up again a year later because you forgot where you have laid it? No! No capable steward would make such a mistake. Well, then, if you do bury a beloved child, will you not hold in your mind every day of your life the memory of where it is that you laid him? Yes, you say, again. How could you forget? Then what foolishness leads you to think Almighty God will be in any great difficulty, in His infinite power and wisdom, to find these graves, these graves of His flock, these graves of His children, which we scatter now because we must.

'Cease your feeble weeping! Lift up your voices! Let us sing Psalm Eighty-eight and recall we are not the only ones that God has tested. And then go to your homes in peace and gather next Sunday in Cucklett Delf.'

Brand had rushed to Mr. Mompellion's aid, and now he supported the dazed rector down the steps of the pulpit as the grief-ravaged voices in the church began to sing that most desperate prayer for healing in sickness:

'O Lord, my God, I call for help by day;
I cry out in the night before thee . . .
I am reckoned among those that go down to the
    Pit . . .
Thou has caused my companions to shun me;
Thou hast made me a thing of horror to them.
I am shut in so that I cannot escape . . .'

The heavy church door thudded shut behind us, cutting off the doleful singing. But Michael Mompellion, staggering with Brand's help towards the rectory, continued the Psalm in his cracked, weary whisper:

'In the morning my prayer comes before thee.
O Lord, why dost thou cast me off?
Why dost thou hide thy face from me?'

Inside the house, we realized that we would not easily get him up the stairs, so Elinor and I ran up to the bedchamber and brought down some quilts to make a pallet in the parlour. As Brand helped him down upon it, he was still reciting:

'I suffer thy terrors; I am helpless.
Thy wrath has swept over me;
Thy dread assaults destroy me.'

And with that he rolled over and gave himself up, at last, to the sleep of the exhausted.

The next afternoon he roused himself to attend two deathbeds, but Elinor and I conspired to keep from him another piece of news that bore more nearly on the living. With so much death around us, it was hard to give any mind to the future, much less to those material matters that usually consume a person's waking hours. But there was one child's future that had been weighing very much on my thoughts, that of a nine-year-old girl named Merry Wickford.

George and Cleath Wickford, a young Quaker couple with three children, had settled in an abandoned croft on the outskirts of the village some five years earlier. They were lowlanders, but their queer faith had caused them to be driven off from their established tenant farm, and while they didn't get what you would say was a warm greeting here, at least they didn't have to fear their ricks being fired or their poultry poisoned, as I heard had happened to them where they'd been. They had lived very poor till one summer night almost a year since. George Wickford, up late and pacing because he could not sleep for worry about how to feed his family, saw a great burning drake streaking its white path across the heavens. The lore in these parts is that a burning drake in the night sky marks out the lie of a lead seam below, so George Wickford did not even wait till dawn to hie himself to where he thought the drake's path had passed across the moors. By morning he had dug out his cross in the turf to mark his claim, had cut his seven timbers for the stowe, and was whittling away at the wooden sprags to hold it upright. For a thousand years, so they say, the law has held that any man might claim himself a lead mine just so, no matter whose is the land it lies upon. He has nine weeks then to show the Barmester a dish of ore, and after, none may take his mine from him whilesoever he can keep it yielding, so long as he pays to the Crown that agreed portion of the ore known as the King's Dish.

Among Those That Go Down to the Pit

George Wickford and his Cleath and their three young ones had delved tirelessly at the claim they named Burning Drake. At first they had to scrabble at the earth with only a much-mended pitchfork and ploughshare. The other miners, though not men to scorn at sky-signs, laughed at young George Wickford then, for there was nothing in the lay of the land to give sign of lead beneath, and no one had ever laid a pick anywhere near his claim. But Wickford had the last laugh, for well within the Barmester's nine weeks he had his required dish of lead – and plenty more. What he had claimed turned out to be a pipe vein. These can be uncommonly rich, being as they are the mineral-lined caverns left behind from some long-ago underground stream. But they are hard to find, since they give no surface sign, and Wickford was considered a fellow blessed by fate.

That was before the Plague struck. George Wickford had been among the first felled by the disease. Then it took his eldest son, a well-grown lad of twelve years. Cleath and her two younger children had struggled on at the delvings, but then the boy sickened and the mother, between tending him and waning in her own strength, failed to pull the required dish of ore from her mine in three weeks. David Burton, a neighbouring miner, took his chance and placed the first nick upon the spindle of her stowe. There was much talk of the rights and wrongs of this in the village, with many censuring David and saying this was no time for such doing. Others defended him, arguing that the lead laws were the lead laws, and it wasn't the first time sad misfortune had put a claim at risk. I wondered if people would have felt it more nearly if the Wickfords had been members of our church. But to be fair, even I was not sure what to think on the matter, for I had expected nothing different than the loss of our mine when Sam died. And yet the current times did seem to ask us all for every kind of sacrifice, so why not the sacrifice of this tradition, too?

There was more talk at the end of the sixth week, when David

Burton placed his second nick on what happened to be the very day Cleath Wickford laid her other son into his grave. They said the shock of it hastened her own death, for the Plague took her faster than we had yet seen it dispatch any person. She buried her boy in the morning, seeming as well as anyone in that state of grief can be. By nightfall she was dead, her corpse covered in the rosy rings of Plague tokens. That left only the girl, the child whose name, Merry, now seemed like a cruel joke. She had been a jolly, kindly child, even when the family was counted with the town's poorest, and it hurt me to see her suffer so much loss. She was left, moreover, in dreadful circumstances, for George Wickford had to his name little but the mine. Wickford had been a prudent man; he had ploughed the monies from his first dishes of lead into better delving tools and he had bought decent food and clothing for the family that had so long had to do without. But the real wealth of the mine was in the ground yet, and young Merry seemed set to lose it in a sennight if someone did not bring out a dish of lead for her. As the days slipped by, I badgered every miner I knew well enough to approach, asking if one of them wouldn't do this kindness for an orphan. But the men, even the best of them, felt that their loyalty had to lie with David Burton, one of their own, rather than with a child whose family were neither Peakrill folk nor of their faith nor even long among the fraternity of miners. And so the weeks passed, and the child's chances waned, until the end of the ninth week drew closer and finally just one more day stood between her and a bleak future in a poorhouse.

I suppose I should have known better than to raise this case with Elinor. Or say, rather, that I should not have been surprised by the proposal that followed. 'You know about the mines, Anna. You and I together shall get this dish out for the child.'

In some ways, this suggestion landed on my ears even more unwelcome than her earlier proposal, that I midwife Mary Daniel. I had been afraid of the mines long before they claimed my Sam. I am not a creature for dim, slimy, airless places. I love what lives and grows on the surface of the Earth: I do not care to know the bowels of this hollow country. Though I am curious enough about most men's lives, I never asked Sam to take me down the mine. Not that I am sure he would have done so, for though he never denied me anything I asked of him, miners are superstitious men, and many believe that each mine holds an elf-sprite who is jealous of his miner and mislikes his womenfolk.

But Elinor had that look upon her face that I now recognized too well. It is hard to describe to one who has not seen it, how her delicate features could set themselves so. I have read that the Greeks could carve marble images so that the very stone seemed to breathe. The accounts I read said that the stone, in these likenesses, passed for tender flesh. When I try to imagine this, I think that perhaps Elinor's face, when she determined to do something she considered right, resembled one of these marbles. In any wise, I knew now we were headed to the Wickford mine whether I would or no.

We set off early, for the mine was a long walk from the village. I heard Elinor speaking to Mr. Mompellion in the library, telling him that we were going out in search of necessary herbs. As she came from the room, I noticed that her translucent skin was all flushed. She saw me gazing at her, and her hand fluttered to her blushing throat.

'Well, and so we shall, Anna, take satchels to gather likely plants on our way.' It was evident how much the slightest concealment or hint of falsehood cost her, even when the lie was fashioned only to preserve her husband's welfare. 'For you know very well,' she added, 'that if he winds our true enterprise this day, he will insist on trying to do the labour himself, which would likely be the finish of him in his exhaustion.'

We made our way first to the Wickford croft to tell the child Merry what we proposed. As we climbed up the muddy track to her croft, she flew out of her door, her little face lit with joy, and it struck me what an odd time we now lived in, that a child of such tender years should be left all alone in her dwelling. I had thought of bringing her back to bide with me, but had decided not to do so, for lonely and haphazard as her life now was, yet it seemed safer and more healthful for her out here, at some distance from the village, than to be brought into daily contact with Plague victims.

Somehow, she was managing to live, even thrive. She was a glowing child, even now, pink cheeked and dimpled, with a deep cleft in her chin and a tumble of dark curls that bounced as she skipped around us. Inside the croft, I saw the remains of that morning's breakfast: on the table was a pipkin of lard, the imprints of thin fingers on the slippery white surface betraying that she'd been eating it by the fistful. There was an eggshell, from which she'd sucked the contents raw, and an onion, with bites out of it, that she'd eaten like an apple. Uncouth, perhaps, but sustaining.

As we entered the tiny, earth-floored croft, she made haste to clear the table and asked us, most politely, to sit. I wondered at her self-possession and felt a stab that I had not made more of an effort to know her parents. They must have been fine people to impart such manners to their child.

Elinor's thoughts had been tending along a similar vein. 'Your mother would be very proud of you, Merry, to see how bravely and how well you are managing here.'

'Think thou so?' she said, her dark eyes earnest. 'I thank thee for saying it. I feel that Mother watches me still, and Father, and my brothers, too. It brings me comfort to believe that they do, and my life here feels less lonely for it. I thank thee both for thinking to visit me on this day, for it is hard for me to face the loss of my family's mine alone.'

'We intend that you will not have to face any such thing,' I blurted, suddenly glad that Elinor had convinced me to do this.

'At least,' Elinor added, 'we hope that you may not.'

Merry's gratitude turned to delight as we explained that we had not come to visit, merely, but to try to save her mine. Plucky little person, she then insisted on coming to do her share. 'You may help us, Merry,' I said, 'as you helped your parents. You shall have much to do in sorting the bouse we raise into ores and deads and buddling the ore in the wash to rid it of the toadstone. We will rely on you to send word down to us when we have achieved a dish. And mind, it must be a good dish, for David Burton thinks he owns Burning Drake already, and he will be quick to hold the Barmester to an exact measure.' Merry nodded, knowing well the dimensions of the Barmester's great dish. But Elinor looked puzzled, having never seen the thing, so I explained how it was sized to hold as much ore as an average man is capable to lift up off the ground.

The child looked troubled still, protesting that she had been down in the mine before and wished to guide us. Elinor seemed on the point of assenting, but I took her quickly to one side. To be down there with her father and mother, who knew every stone in the mine and had daily delved it, I whispered, was a different matter than being down in the dark with two such as we were, who knew just more than nothing of what we were about. 'I would help this child, Elinor, not bury her!' Elinor agreed then and gently told the girl that we needed her above, in case aught went awry and we did not return to the surface by afternoon. Then, and only then, Elinor cautioned, was she to run straight to the rectory and tell Mr. Mompellion what we were about.

When Sam died I had wrapped his tools in a piece of oiled cloth and set them away, meaning one day to give them to a needy miner. The Wickfords would have been the very ones to have gifted so, I realized with a pang, but my mind had been so much upon my own trials at the time they found their seam that I had forgot all about

Sam's idle kit and my intentions for it. Now, unwrapping the tools, I felt their heft in my hands. I thought of Sam's big, scarred fists and the hard muscles of his huge arms and wondered how I would wield these things. From amongst the tools I picked out the three essentials of the lead miner: straight pick, short hammer, and wedge.

Merry's family, in their thrift, had used a different style of tool: a curved piece whose single tine was balanced by a hammer end and used as either pick or sledge. This tool, lighter but less effective, would be what Elinor would work with. I asked Merry then to look out the leathers her father and brother had worn against the mine's wet. I did not have Sam's old breeches and jerkin, which would have been huge on me in any case, for they had been destroyed in his accident. I had had to pull the shreds of the hide out of his mashed flesh.

Elinor was slight enough to fit into the breeches and jerkin that the elder Wickford boy had worn. I found myself hoping there were no Plague seeds yet upon them. George Wickford had been a slight young man whom poverty had kept lean. I took his leathers and, with a pair of well-honed wool-shears, cut about a third of the length off the legs to fit my stature. Then I plunged a few holes in the waist and ran a rope through like a drawstring to keep the trews upon me. The jerkin flapped loose from my shoulders, but to that I paid no mind. We took the hats, also: sturdy leather hats with ample brims to hold the burning tallow candles that would light our way through the dark while leaving our hands free to work.

I looked at Elinor when she was attired in her miner's kit and wondered again about the strange turns this year was bringing us to. She seemed to catch my thought and laughed at herself. 'All those ancestors who stared at me from their portraits when I was a girl – all those silken ladies and beribboned men – I wonder what they'd say about their descendant if they could see her now?' I did not tell her that I knew quite well what my Sam would say: 'Happen ye mun be planet-struck, woman, to think on doing thus.' He would not, I knew, have been laughing.

But only Merry Wickford was there to see what we looked like, and to her at least we did not appear absurd. Her little face shone as she gazed at us and saw her only hope. And so we set off to the adit, with Merry leading the way. My feet felt like lead themselves as I trudged along, imagining the day ahead of us. I was breathing hard even at the thought of it; just the fear of being in an airless place made me gasp as if I were already down the mine rather than in the open, heather-scented air.

Wickford had made his shaft well – for all that people here disparaged Quakers for their peculiar beliefs, none could claim that they were not heedful craftsmen in all they did and made. Wickford had wedged great slabs of grey limestone carefully into the walls and hewn sturdy boughs to make sound stemples. But the shaft ran with damp, as most mines do, and mosses and ferns bloomed in the crevices. I could not see how deep the shaft sank before the turning off into the pipe vein, but I knew that the longer I lingered there, the harder it would be to plunge ahead, and so I slung myself over and felt for the first stemple.

As it happened, the shaft was about six fathoms deep, and there it veered off from the eye above. Wickford had prudently wrought out about six or seven yards sideways before the shaft sank downwards once again. That way, I saw, the bucket of bouse could be wound up in easier stages to reach daylight. But once away from the eye, the darkness was complete, so I stopped there to light my candle, dribbling tallow into the brim of my hat to make a base that would hold it fixed in place. The light leapt and trembled as I inched on and down. Merry had said I would find the cave mouth at the base of this second shaft, and so it was. I imagined for an instant how Wickford must have felt when he saw it: the gate to his fortune. By the bouncing light of my candle I could see where he had picked away at the rock to widen the passage, and I eased my way in without difficulty. The floor sloped sharply and was slick with mud, and in minutes I had lost my footing and landed hard, grazing my palm as I tried to break my fall. The air was already still and stale, just a few feet in from the shaft, and as I sat there in the muck I could feel the panic rise. Despite the cold, the fear-sweat broke out upon me, a thousand little needles prickling my skin. The dread seemed to spread upward through my body. I began to gasp in rapid, shallow breaths. But Elinor was behind me now and I felt her hand easing me up and onwards.

'It is all right, Anna,' she whispered. 'You *can* breathe. There *is* air. You must school your mind and not let your fears be your master.' As I struggled to my feet I felt a blackness closing in on me and, fearing I would faint, sat down again. Elinor kept speaking, gently but firmly, and made me match my breaths to the calm rhythm of her own. In a few moments my head cleared and I was able to go on. And so we inched and slithered, sometimes on two feet but stooped, other places, where the cavern narrowed, dropping to hands and knees, and sometimes, where the rock swooped down unwelcoming, skidding on our bellies.

The flickering tallow light showed walls that had been picked and cleft, and we followed the line of the delvings. These told the tale of the diminishing family, for at first the face was well-worked and clean of ore, and the places where George Wickford had plied his pick gleamed slick in the candlelight. Then, farther along, the pick-work became rough, shallower, and less thorough, as Cleath and her boy had carried on alone. When we got to the last pick-stroke, Elinor and I, kneeling side by side, unslung our tools and set to work hand-to-fist, and the effort of landing the blows drove my fears from the front of my mind. I have worked hard all my life, hauling water, chopping wood, and bucking hay. I can't count the number of times

I've chased a tup and caught him by his hind hoof, and last year I managed the whole shearing of my flock between sunup and the noon bell. But this labour – this tearing of rock from rock – was the hardest thing I had ever set my hand to. Within a half hour, my arms were trembling. For Elinor it must have been much worse. I could see how soon the strain of it began to cost her, as she paused longer and longer between each stroke. At one point, she struck her thumb with the hammer and cried out, and I could see the blood and the instantly blackening nail. She would not have me tend her, but waved me on with my work as she tied a bit of rag around the wound and went back to her toil. She swung slowly on, her face, mud-streaked and sweat-stained, set as hard as the stone. The sound of her ragged breathing was so terrible to me that I was glad for the clang of iron to mask the noise of it.

For myself, the greatest effort was to keep my panic banked. I tried to manage my terrors by concentrating only on the work and not on the walls of slimy darkness that seemed to advance and recede with every movement of my candle, neither on the choke-damp air that tasted as if all the good had long ago been sucked out of it, nor on the weight of the soil and rock piled thick and heavy above me. Each time the pick landed I felt the jarring all through the bones of my arms and up into my very teeth. It took me many, many blows to open a little crack, just sufficient to give the wedge a start. Once I had the wedge in, I had to raise the heavy hammer and let it fall with all the force I could, hoping thus to splatch off large pieces of rock. But more times than not my blow landed wide or else glanced off the wedge and sent the thing flying out of its crack and down into the cold mud, where I would have to grope blindly for it in order to start all over again. The mud made the wedge and my hands slippery. The cold cluzened my fingers so that instead of gaining skill with practice, my numb hands fumbled more and more. As the hours passed I felt like weeping with pain and frustration, for as hard as we plied the picks, the pile of bouse beside us grew only by inches.

It was Elinor who voiced it before I had heart to do so. For all her effort, she had managed to loose a pitiful few pieces of stone. She sat back on her heels and let the pick clang heavily on the rock beside her. 'At this rate, we will not draw a dish by day's end.' Her whisper fell dully in the cavern.

'I know it,' I said, flexing my numb fingers and rubbing at my aching arms. 'We were foolish to think we could learn skills in one day that strong men toil for years to master.'

'I cannot face the child,' Elinor said. 'I cannot bear to see the disappointment in her.'

For a long moment, I pondered what next to say. For while part of me was disappointed that we had not succeeded, a lesser part was mightily gladdened that Elinor was about to abandon this wretched quest. The worse part of me won. I said nothing and gathered my tools. Silently, we made our way back through the tunnel. My arms were so tired I could barely clutch the stemples, and as I gulped gratefully at the cool air, I told myself that in our already exhausted state, we would never have succeeded, even if I had confided to Elinor what more I knew.

It was Merry's face that undid me. Her look was so hopeful as we climbed out of the tunnel. And then, when she saw the miserable amount of bouse we brought up, her bright smile disappeared, and her lip trembled. And yet she did not cry, but schooled her small voice, and thanked us profusely for her efforts. My cowardice shamed me.

'There is one other way to get the ore out,' I blurted. 'Sam used it betimes, when his seam vanished into toadstone. But it was the doing of it cost him his life in the end.' I turned to Elinor then and told her all I had heard of the way fire and water, the power of opposites, could be harnessed to do the work of many miners' hands.

Elinor leant back against the stowes and brought her raw hands up to cover her eyes. She stayed so for a long moment. 'Anna, these days, all our lives hang by a thread. If we are spared today, we may well be felled by Plague on the morrow. I say we should take this risk, and try . . . but only if you are willing.'

Merry looked concerned. Miners' children are quick to learn what miners fear. And there are so many fears that go with fire-setting. The fumes from the smoke, added to the choke-damp, can steal the last breathable air out of the cavern. The cracking can free hidden water, letting in a torrent that floods the mine. Or, as happened with my Sam, the very bones and sinews of the Earth can break under the strain, and instead of freeing out a fother of ore, the entire weight of the ground above can come piling down to bury you. So dangerous is fire-setting, and so unpredictable in its effects, that its use is prohibited unless one gains the consent of all miners working in neighbouring parts. But there were no neighbours to this lonely mine, and so we had only our own counsel to take.

I gathered the greenwood as fast as I could. Dry tinder was more difficult to come by, since it had lately rained, and in the end Merry ran all the way back to her croft to fetch the seasoned kindling from her own hearth. When I climbed back down the shaft, Merry let down the cold stream water in a leather bucket. I spilled the first of it, crawling through the cavern, and had to waste precious time sending her for more. The second time, Elinor and I managed the bucket between us.

I ran my hands then along the rockface, feeling for cracks and working with the wedge to widen them. When I had a large enough line in the rock, I showed Elinor how we needed to stuff the greenwood boughs into every crevice, hammering each as hard as we could deep into the crack. Then, I laid the dried tinder for the fire all along the rockface. 'You must go back above now,' I said then to Elinor. 'I'll tug on the rope to summon you if we have any success.'

'Oh, no, Anna. I'll not leave you down here alone,' she said, and I could see the start of a long argument. It was going to take a desperate measure to move her, and so I spoke sharply.

'Elinor! We don't have time for this. Do you not have the wit to see that if this goes awry you'll do me more good outside, digging, than in here, smothering companionably?'

Even in the uncertain light I could see the bright glint as the easy tears of the exhausted sprang to her eyes. But my words did their work. Her head drooped. 'As you say,' she replied and began the long crawl out. As the sound of her scuffling subsided I was left then to silence broken only by the slow drip, drip of unseen water making its way through the stone. I worked quickly then, to light the wood before it became too damp to catch, but my hands on the flint and tinder shook and sobs caught in my throat.

I'd rather die bespotted from Plague venom, I thought, than end my life down here, buried alive in the dark. But then the fire flared, and it was dark no longer. The greenwood began to heat. The sap hissed, and then came the first sharp report as the expanding pressure cracked a rock. It was hard, so hard, to wait, as the smoke filled the air and choked me. I held a wet rag over my mouth and crouched, trembling, waiting and waiting, forcing myself not to make the next move before the time was ripe. We had only one chance, after all. Time was too short to try this again. If the rock was not sufficiently heated, the entire effort would be wasted, and our day's work entirely lost. Finally, as my chest began to feel as if it would explode from the breathing of the burnt air, I blindly reached for the bucket. I hurled icy water against hot rock. There was a sizzle, and steam, and a sound like a dozen muskets firing. And then the sheets of ore began to fall.

I slithered and stumbled to get out of the path of it, blinded by the smoke and coughing so that I thought my throat would tear. A sharp shard struck me on the shoulder and then a heavier slab landed hard on my back, slapping me facedown into the mud. I writhed to get out from under it, pushing myself up on forearms with muscles like jelly from the morning's delving.

'Stop now!' I prayed. 'Oh, please, stop now!' But the cracking did not stop, just continued, on and on, and with each crack came a new rain of rock. My arms flailed wildly, my fingers scrabbling on the hard stone. But the load pressed and pressed and pinned me still at last.

And so, I thought, it ends here after all. Dead in the dark like Sam. The crushing slabs pushed down upon me, heavier and heavier still. I felt the whole weight of the hillside shifting as rock slid against rock and earth oozed and sifted into every newly opened crevice. Wet mud pressed into my mouth like a disgusting kiss. I heard the beat of the blood in my ears – hammering, roaring – louder, finally, than the crash of rock.

And then an odd thing. The panic drained away from me, and my mind filled up with images of my boys. It had become hard for me to call up the exact details of their faces: the fall of Jamie's curls across his brow or Tom's sweet, serious frown at feedings. Now they were before me, vivid as in life. I stopped fighting for movement and exhaled the breath I had been hoarding. There was no air now to give me another. I relaxed my cheek into the rocks that would be my cairn and my tombstone.

It's all right, after all. I can bear this ending. A dark rim formed around the picture of my boys, and I willed it back. Not yet. Not yet. Let me see them a few moments more. But the blackness feathered inwards and their bright faces dimmed. With the darkness came blissful silence: a sudden stop to the beating of blood and the great roaring of rock.

I suppose that I would be dead, and no one left to make this accounting, if Elinor had abided by my instructions and gone back up the shaft as I had bidden her. And perhaps I might also be dead if Merry, too, had not disobeyed the both of us. Elinor had crouched by a column of rock just a hundred yards from where I did the fire-setting. Merry had lowered herself to the cave entrance just off the shaft. Both of them, when they heard the great crashing, had rushed to save me. I came to consciousness still buried to my neck but with my face freed by their frantic scrabbling.

The silence that had closed in upon me as I lost consciousness had been real: the roaring *had* stopped, and with it the rock fall. I had not, after all, brought the entire hillside down upon me. As the smoke slowly lessened, the three of us were able to see what had been done, in fact: my work had loosed a pile of the even-sided, gleaming cubes of ore that would give Merry Wickford her dish of lead today, and many more days if she needed. Elinor and Merry together heaved the rock off me, slab by slab, and then, with their help, I crawled painfully to the shaft and toiled my way slowly to the surface.

I do not know how I stumbled back down to the village. I ached all over, and each step brought a fresh spasm. But somehow we made our way with what haste we could, racing against the fading light. Elinor supported me with one arm and with the other held the end of the burlap on which she and Merry between them dragged the ore. We did not stop at the Wickford croft to retrieve our dress but went as we were straight to the cottage of the Barmester, Alun Houghton. Had I been able, I would have implored Elinor to spare herself the indignity of being stared at in such a state, but she hushed me when I muttered something about this. 'After all we've gone through to get justice for this child, Anna, I intend to be there to see that justice done.'

If old Alun was shocked by the sight of us – mud-bedaubed, rock-grazed, smoke-blackened, and sodden – he recovered himself quickly and executed his office, summoning David Burton and as many of the elected men of the Body of the Mine as could be gathered to the Miner's Tavern to bear witness. While the miners assembled, Elinor sent word to the rectory.

It was not very many moments before I heard the sound of Anteros's high-stepping hoofs. If I could, I would have slipped away into the yard rather than confront the rector. But Elinor had set me down before Alun Houghton's hearth and was bathing my grazes with warmed water. She had not troubled with her own toilet, and so when the rector entered the cottage, she rose to greet him just as she was. For an instant, I do not think he recognized her. She had lost her hat sometime during my rescue, and she stood now bareheaded, her fine hair all mud-caked and falling about her face in hard brown strands. The leathers, too, were daubed with soot and soil. She had a filthy, blood-soaked rag bound around her injured thumb.

The rector stood, arrested, just inside the doorway. There was silence from him for a long moment, and I feared he was struggling to contain his temper. Instead, he gave a great laugh and opened his arms to Elinor. I thought he would embrace her. But then, perhaps mindful of me and the child, or perhaps of his fine white jabot, he stepped back and simply clapped his hands together; when he asked for a full account of our day's work, his voice brimmed with pride.

The rector accompanied us to the Miner's Tavern, and I was relieved at it, for odd as the times were, I did not rightly know how Elinor Mompellion's reputation would weather this day's doings, falling as they did so far outside what is considered fit for a woman, much less a gentlewoman. But the men, scattered around the court-yard rather than packing the taproom as they would in former times, stood up from their benches as they saw us. 'A cheer for the new miners!' called a voice from the rear of the yard, and almost to a man they gave us their huzzahs. Only David Burton looked sour and was silent. The Barmester hung up his great brass measuring dish – as long as a tall man's leg and about as wide as a well-muscled thigh – and Merry came forward, struggling to drag the burlap laden with ore. The Barmester helped her up onto a tavern table, so that she could reach the dish. Carefully, her small face serious, she piled up the ore until the dish was full, and at that, the company cheered again.

'Friends,' said Alun Houghton, 'young Merry Wickford retains the rights over Burning Drake vein. It is hers until such time as her stowes be thrice nicked.' And then he stared round the room from under his impressive, bushy eyebrows. 'And while I'm saying nowt about his right to do it, I'd be a man thinking long and hard about cutting any nicks on this child's stowes any time in the near future, within our code tho' it may well be.'

I had to sleep that night lying on my grazed face, since my back was abloom with a great bruise where the rock slab had caught me. My arms and shoulders ached worse than my back, and it would be many days before I ceased to feel the weight of the pick each time I lifted so much as a fork. Still, I slept better that night than I had since the nights of the poppy dreams. There had been so much futile effort expended since the coming of the Plague, so many lives that could not be saved and hurts that could not be healed. For one time, at least, in that hard season, I had the satisfaction of having done a thing that had come out right.

The Body of the Mine

In the days that followed, I tasted what life would be like if I survived through this dying time to see my own old age. It is a great thing to be young and to live without pain. And yet it is a blessing few of us count until we lose it. For many days, my healing body ached at every move. To reach down a crock from a high shelf was a vast effort; to draw a pail of water an agony, and so I had to contrive new ways to go about the simplest of tasks. Sometimes, if she espied me struggling, Mary Hadfield would help me, but I was loath to add my needs to her already ample burdens.

So I was uncommonly glad, one morning as I went out to battle with the well bucket, to mark my father approaching, for I could not think he would grudge me a hand. He was staggering, which was not unusual, but not, this day, from drink. As he advanced, I saw that it was the weight of what he carried that unbalanced him – a large sack that clanked as he walked.

He was so bent by the load that I think he might have passed without marking me but when I gave him a good day, he raised his head and hailed me in turn. As he set down the sack, I heard the clang of metal plate.

'Eh, girl, and it *is* a good day, for Widow Brown has paid me in pewter for the graves of her man and boy. I suppose I should thank ye, for learning me the lesson that there's a profit in the hole-digging trade, these days.'

I did not know how to make an answer to that, and so I asked his help to draw water, which he did, though not without pausing to note that my face 'looked worse than a cow pat,' bruised and swollen as it was. When he hefted his sack and went on, I stood and stared after his retreating back, wondering what kind of ill thing my good intentions might have hatched.

All that week I began to notice that neighbours would break off their conversations when I drew near them, and gradually I became aware that they were speaking of my father, and sourly.

He had, as he had said, set himself up as grave-digger to the desperate. From those too ill or weak to bury their dead, he demanded a high fee. He would take whatever in the house or field had most value, be it the barrel of herring the children counted on for their winter nourishment, the gravid sow, or the precious brass candlestick passed father to son for generations. Sometimes he would take his trophies to the Miner's Tavern, set them upon the bar, and brag on his cleverness; when even his cronies began to remonstrate with him, he bought off their ill opinion by paying for their ale with the shillings of the dead. He would end every day there, drinking until he could barely stagger home. When I had suggested that he do this work, I had expected that he would take at least some pains about his person, so as not to expose Aphra and his children to the Plague seeds that he might carry from the corpses. But day by day I saw him come and go in the same earth-crusted breeches, and I wondered that even he could be so uncaring.

When I encountered Aphra at the Boundary Stone, I begged her to insist that he take more care in this, but she just laughed. 'You spend all your time at the Gowdies' studying weeds and teas,' she said. 'Happen 't would be better if you bethought what other knowledge those two held in their heads.' I pressed her to say more clearly what she meant, but it was no use. Aphra could be a stubborn soul, and the more I tried to reason with her on this, the more she withdrew, saying only that my father now was proving a good provider for the first time in his history, and she was not about to scold him over it.

One day not long after, I glimpsed my father, through the window of my cottage, swaggering down the street with a bale of finespun wool, taken from the weaver's cottage, slung over his shoulder. I rushed out into my garth, enraged. 'Father!' I called. 'You know that bale is a thieving price to charge Mrs. Martin for the hour's toil of burying her husband. How can you chouse the suffering so? You bring disgrace upon us by such conduct.' He made me no reply, just hawked and spat a glistening gob of green phlegm at my feet and continued on his way to the tavern.

Though Mr. Mompellion's strength had come back to him in some measure since his collapse in the church, he now knew he could not do the sexton's work as well as his own. So my father had no check on his increasing greed. On Sundays, we gathered now at Cucklett Delf as the rector had bidden us. When I stood in the sloping basin with the black boughs of the rowans arching above me, I saw the great wisdom in what the rector had wrought by moving us all there. For there we were not confronted by the memories of the past and haunted by the missing faces. We could stand where we would on that sward, although most of us kept to the old order, with the yeomen and the miners towards the front, then the artisans, then the crofters and the hands. We placed ourselves so that some three yards separated each family group, believing this to be sufficient distance to avoid the passing of infection. The rector had chosen for his pulpit a massive outcrop of limestone, weathered into the shape of an arch. From there, his voice filled the Delf. He tried to find sweet words to salve our sorrows, and their music mingled with the tinkling of the nearby brook.

My father did not come to the Delf, not the first Sunday nor any following. In normal times he would have been paraded to the village green and set in the stocks there for such behaviour. But none now had the strength or will to pursue such things, and the stocks had stood empty for many months. In consequence, as the weeks passed his wickedness only grew. He had become so fond of his afternoons at the alepot that he let it be known that he would not bury anyone past noon. In his callousness, he would knock upon the doors of the ailing, saying if they wanted a grave he would dig it then and there or not at all. And so a person who yet lived would lie in his sickbed and listen to the rise and fall of my father's spud. I think that his heartless behaviour hastened more than one person into the ground.

Mr. Mompellion sought him out at his croft, trying an appeal to any shred of good left deep within him. I went with him; I felt I should do so, though I dreaded such a visit. Although it was but early afternoon, my father was well soused, lying upon his pallet in a stained smock. He got up when we entered and pushed past the rector with a grunt. He barely stepped beyond the door to make his water, but just stood there shamelessly in full sight of both of us.

I had felt from setting out that the rector's effort would be wasted, and now I knew it with certainty. It was a long time since my father's coarse ways had put me to the blush: after I married Sam I had tried to school my feelings so that I would no longer hold myself account-able for what my father did or did not do. But it pained me to have the rector treated so.

'Sir,' I muttered, 'do not subject yourself to my father's loutish manners. Let us leave this place, for no good can be wrested from him in this state.'

The rector only looked down at me kindly and shook his head

with a slight smile. 'We are here Anna, and I will say what I came to say.'

His argument was eloquent and, upon my father, entirely wasted. Mr. Mompellion said that the whole village understood the value of the work he performed and the risk he was shouldering; that it was not marvellous that he should feel entitled to some reward for such labour, for even in the tales of the ancients, the ferryman who carried souls across the Styx had required his guerdon. 'But, Joss Bont, I beg you to be proportionate.'

'Pro-*poor*-tionate!' my father sneered. 'Aye, and poor is what you'd have me, you leech!' My father launched then into a long, self-pitying rant about how ill-used he'd been as a boy at sea, and how he'd never yet earned a fair day's pay as ploughman or woodcutter or in any of the other manner of labour he'd turned his hand to since.

'You bleed us dry, you do. Your kind, all of you, think nothing of breaking our backs for a pittance. And then you go on like we should lick your boots for the ha'penny you fling us.' Flecks of foam formed at the corners of his mouth as he raised his voice, and his spittle flew across the room. 'And when I finally find a way to make summat from me sweat, you come 'ere trying to tell me what I can and cannot be taking for me toil! Hah! You might have honey-tongued me daughter into emptying your pisspots, but Joss Bont won't be foxed by the likes of you! Bury the poxy dead yourself, if you feel so strong on't.' He turned his back on us then. 'Girl, get your priest out of here before I push 'im out,' he said.

'Save your strength for your spud, Joss Bont.' Michael Mompellion's face was quiet, but his voice was so cold I thought it would blast my father like an ice storm. 'Do not waste it upon ejecting me, and I will waste no more breath seeking the goodness in your heart, for I perceive you have none left in it.'

My father made no reply to this but simply flung himself again upon his pallet and, as I held open the door to the croft for the rector, rolled over and showed us his back. In the next few weeks, the rector did return to digging graves, somehow finding the strength to bury those so poor as to have nothing that my greedy father coveted. For myself, I was glad I no longer shared a name with him, as his became increasingly cursed in every croft and cottage.

And then he finally committed an act so vile that even our population, diminished and exhausted, was spurred at last to action. Christopher Unwin, the last surviving son of a family that had numbered twelve before the Plague claimed eleven of them, had lain nine days in his sickbed, much longer than most survive when once afflicted. I had visited him several times, as had Elinor and Michael Mompellion. We had begun to pray that he might be, like Margaret Blackwell, that one out of a hundred persons who gets the Plague and yet lives through it.

And then, one morning, just after I had carried in the brawn and oatcake for the Mompellions' breakfast, I found Randoll Daniel pacing in the kitchen garth. My first thought was that Mary or the babe had sickened, and my heart sank at it, for the little boy, the first babe I had delivered, was dear to me.

'No, by God's grace,' Randoll said, 'they are both well. No, it is my friend Christopher Unwin I am come about. Mary made a stew for my supper last night, and this morning I thought to bring him a portion. But he would not take any, and said he feels himself to be failing. He asked me to hasten here to fetch the rector.'

'Thank you, Randoll. I will tell Mr. Mompellion.'

The rector had scarce begun his meal, and so I thought to save the news until he had done with it. But Elinor had heard voices in the garth, and she summoned me to learn Randoll's business. I had no choice then but to tell it. The rector set down his fork, pushed his plate of uneaten food away, and rose wearily from the table. Elinor made to rise, too, but she looked even paler than usual that morning, so I quickly suggested that I go with Mr. Mompellion while she stayed behind to tend the kettles of our herbals.

We walked together to the Unwins' house, and as we went, the rector asked many questions regarding my work of the previous day, whom I had visited and how they fared, what tonics I had administered and which I deemed most useful. Somewhere in the passing weeks, I had lost my shyness in his presence, and now I found I could talk to him without reserve. He told me of those that he had seen, and then he gave a great sigh. 'How strange it is, Anna. Yesterday, I have filed in my mind as a good day, notwithstanding it was filled with mortal illness and the grieving of the recently bereft. Yet it is a good day, for the simple fact that no one died upon it. We are brought to a sorry state, that we measure what is good by such a shortened yardstick.'

The Unwin house stood west of the rectory, beside the village green. As we passed by the overgrown square, the rector inclined his head towards the stocks. A strand of ivy had grown up and through one of the ankle holds. Rust bloomed on the latches. 'That, I would say, could be counted also as a good thing brought by this grim season; that the stocks and the cucking stool and all such barbarous implements have fallen into disuse. I would I could persuade the people here to keep it so, even when this trial is past.'

We had reached the Unwin gate. The house stood back from the road, in what had been a handsome garden. The family had prospered from its lead seam for many years, and their house had grown, through well-built additions, into one of the finest in the village. Now, after so many deaths, the place had a mournful, neglected look. The rector, who had visited many times in the course of the family's trials, let himself in at the front door and called up to Christopher, where he lay alone in the room he had lately shared with his wife and infant son. The young man answered in a weak voice, but that he answered at all was a great relief.

While I fetched a mug from the dresser to pour some cordials for the sick man, the rector went on ahead of me to the upstairs bedchamber. When I entered a few moments later, the rector was standing at the window with his back to me, staring out into the Unwins' field. I noticed that his fists, at his sides, were working, as if what he saw was greatly discomposing him. When he turned, I saw that it was indeed so: his brow was knotted and his scowl fierce.

'How long has he been at this?' the rector demanded of Christopher, who was sitting propped against a bolster, looking less grave than I had expected.

'Since shortly after sunup. I awoke to the sound of his spud.'

I coloured then, in mortification and anger both. I walked to the window and saw, as I expected, my father standing waist-deep in the half-dug pit. I could imagine him, his greedy eye already counting the booty he would haul off from the Unwin house, for who would be left to gainsay his theft when Christopher followed his family into the ground? I felt sure then that it was simply the fact of my father's digging that had caused the young man to believe his state worsened, for he looked to me much improved. His expression was alert and his skin colour good, and I could see no signs of Plague upon him.

'I will go and speak with my father,' I said to the rector in a small voice. 'I shall send him away directly, for I do not think the young master will have need of such services, on this or any other approaching day.'

'No, Anna. You stay here and attend to Mr. Unwin. Leave me to deal with Josiah Bont.'

I did not protest, but felt much relieved. I was bathing Christopher Unwin's face with some lavender water and speaking to him encouragingly of the signs of his returning health when the sounds of raised voices came ringing up from the field. My father was cursing Michael Mompellion in the foulest language, unwilling to hear that the young man within was far from needing the grave he had dug. The rector, furthermore, was not standing mute, but answering my father in the kind of language I had never heard from him: coarse words that he did not learn from the great Divines at Cambridge.

My father bellowed that since he had laboured, he intended to be paid, 'Whether the crack of Unwin's arse feels the dirt this day or no.'

I went to the window then and saw him, his chest pushed out, almost touching the rector's chest, as they stood face to face at the lip of the grave. He made as if to head for the house – thinking, I expect, to claim his loot – but the rector put out a hand and seized him. My father tried to throw off the grip, and I saw the surprise register on his face when he found he wasn't able. His fist rose and I cringed, knowing the weight of it. Michael Mompellion stood stock-still. He doesn't realize that the man really means to hit him, I thought. But there I underestimated him. Mr. Mompellion waited just long enough for the whole force of my father's bulk to be committed to the punch, and at the very last instant stepped deftly to the side so that my father's own momentum caused him to stumble. As his head went down, the rector landed a swift blow to the back of his neck, and when he crumpled, he shoved him, hard. For an instant my father teetered at the grave's edge, his hands flailing wildly, his face almost comical in its rictus of astonishment. And then he toppled, landing with a wet slurp in the mud below. I saw the rector peering into the hole, probably assuring himself that my father wasn't badly hurt, although the streak of curse words coming from the pit testi-fied to his essential soundness. As the rector turned towards the house, I backed away from the window, for I suspected that he would not want to know that this scene had a witness.

I went to the kitchen then to make a meal for Christopher, for he said he felt the stirrings of some appetite. When I returned, he ate like the healthy young man he soon would be, while the rector jested with him on how the two of them that morning had choused more than the Reaper.

Later that day, I learned that my father had been thrown out of the Miner's Tavern, so violent had his temper become as he drank and pined over his lost booty and his muddy humiliation. I was glad at last that the innkeeper had begun to set some limits upon his depraved behaviour, but I worried for Aphra's children, in case he should vent his drunken rage upon them. I took my concerns to Elinor, who had the idea of sending for the children on the pretext of some employment in the Gowdies' physick garden. Certainly, there was much to do there that we hadn't yet managed, tilling and weeding and manuring for the large crop of plants we hoped to raise that season. I took the message, and worded it as tactfully as I could, so that Aphra might know there was a place for her also, if she wished to be out of her croft. But Aphra saw through my hint and laughed at me outright.

'Don't you worry about me, girl. I have my own ways of bridling that mule.'

And so I left her to do so if she could and resolved for my part to put the thoughts of my father from me, to let my shame over him subside again to just another nagging sadness – one more grim thought to ponder in my wakeful nights.

I rose just before dawn, ill rested, and went to the well to draw water. It was one of those rare days in early April when Nature lets us taste the sweet spring that is coming. It was so unexpectedly mild that I lingered in the garth, breathing the soft scents of the slowly warming earth. The sky was beautiful that morning. A tumble of fluffy, tufted clouds covered the whole from horizon to dome, as if a shearer had flung a new-shorn fleece high into the air. As I watched, the rays of the rising sun lit the edge of each cloud, turning it silver, until suddenly the fleece became instead a mesh of shining metal. Then, the light changed again, and the silvery grey turned deep rose-red. *Red sky at night, sailors' delight; red sky at morning, sailors take warning.* My father had taught me that verse. I thought absently about bringing the sheep into the fold before the gathering of the storm that this lovely sky foretold.

My reverie was broken by a bellowing. A figure from a nightmare hove into view. His skull was cleft across the crown, and his hair was matted into curtains of dried blood. He was covered in clods of dirt and smears of clay, naked save for the torn remnants of a winding sheet that trailed behind him. The figure cried out again, and I realized that the name he called was my father's. My first thought was that one of my father's shallow graves had spewed forth a ghostly sleeper awakened for revenge. Just as soon as the thought formed, I threw it off as impossible. And with that shred of sense came the knowledge that the figure in the torn shroud was Christopher Unwin.

My neighbours, those few gaunt survivors, had come out of their cottages in response to Christopher's cries. There was horror in their faces. I ran to him then and begged him to come inside where I could tend his hurts. 'Nay, Mistress, I will not, for what hurts me most is beyond your tending.' I tried to take his arm then, but he threw me off, steadying himself, instead, against the gritstone wall.

'Your father tried to kill me in my sleep this night. I woke in my bed to see his spud bearing down upon me. And then, when I woke again, I was in my grave! That spawn of Satan had laid me there, though I was yet quick as you are. Lucky for me, in his laziness and lust to be at my possessions, he scattered just a crust of earth to hide me and not enough to smother me entire. And lucky also that I am a miner and not affeard to lie my face into the ground.' The men nodded at this. Our miners have always had a tradition that if one of them is injured down the shafts, he will recover quicker if a sod of turf is lifted and he lies for a time facedown to the ground in the fresh-dug dirt. 'Still,' Christopher continued, 'I had to scramble like a mole to get free. I tell you, it's him that will eat dirt this day and never see the light of morn again!'

'Aye!' yelled a voice from the other side of the roadway. 'Aye! It's past time that villain was dealt with!' The crowd was thickening now as yarn gathers itself on a spindle. Someone had brought out a cloak to throw around Christopher. 'I thank you,' he said, his voice issuing from soil- and blood-caked lips. 'That swine not only tried to rob me of my life – he stole the very clothes I lay in.'

I felt like a piece of stone as I stood there and watched them, ten or twelve now, hurrying off in the direction of my father's croft. I stood there, and I didn't move to warn him, or to fetch Mr. Mompellion, or to do anything at all to save him. I stood there, and all I could think of was the sting of his fist and the stink of his breath. I stood there until the mob turned up the hill and out of my sight. And then I went inside and prepared for the labours of my day.

The storm that had threatened at morning blew in by early afternoon. It came from the northeast, in sheets of snow that marched across the far valley in separate leaves, like the pages of a letter whipped from someone's hands in a wind gust. It was a rare spectacle, and I stood on the hill in the apple orchard, transfixed by the slowing advancing columns of white outlined against the black clouds behind.

I was there when they came for me, a band of miners, marching up the hill through the trees as they had the night Sam died. This time, Alun Houghton led them. They wanted me, he said, to bear witness at the Barmote Court to what I had seen at the Unwin house. 'And to speak, if you will, in defence of your father.'

'I do not wish to go, Barmester.' After Alun Houghton's gravelly voice, my words seemed weightless, carried away by the wind. 'There is nothing that I wish to say. Anything I have seen, others have seen also. Please do not ask this of me.'

But Houghton pressed me and would not be satisfied. So, as the snowy fury descended upon us, I made my way with those men who would decide my father's fate in no less apt a place than the Miner's Tavern.

They gathered in the courtyard of the tavern, as they had on the night Merry Wickford brought her dish to the Barmester. They were, of course, fewer, for in the weeks between, the Plague had felled three of the twenty last sworn to the Body of the Mine. There were two long tavern tables in the courtyard itself, and a gallery ran all around, one floor above, from which inn guests, in other times, gained access to their rooms. Of course, there had been no travellers here since the Sunday Oath. The rooms had stood empty for half a year. Some of the miners were up on the gallery, whether to take better shelter from the snow there, or whether to keep a greater distance from their fellows, I cannot say. When the Barmester's party entered, some six or seven drew close to the railing and peered down at us. The men nearer to us, at the tavern tables, huddled each under his own blanket or cloak as the snow dropped its white flurries upon us. Every expression was grim. I looked around for Aphra but did not find her, and I wondered if she had been too cowed to come among these angry, sullen men.

The snowfall in the yard seemed to muffle everything, even the booming voice of Alun Houghton, who had taken his place at the end of the larger table.

'Josiah Bont!'

My father, his hands bound in front of him, stood at the far end of the table, held fast by two miners. When he made no response to the Barmester, Henry Swope, the larger of the two, brought his hand down hard on the back of my father's head.

'Ye'll answer "Present" to t' Barmester!'

'Present,' said my father in a surly murmur.

'Josiah Bont, thou well knowest the crimes that have brought you to this place. Thou art not a miner, and in normal times this court would have no dealings with such as thee. But we are all that is left of justice in this place, and justice we will do here. Ye all assembled here must also know that murder and attempted murder are beyond the scope of this Barmote Court. And so we do not bring Josiah Bont here to answer to these things. But the following we do ask him to answer:

'Ye first item, we set down, that on the third day of April in the Year of Our Lord 1666, thou art accused of entering the house of Christopher Unwin, miner, where thou did take from hence a silver ewer. What says thee?'

My father was again silent, his head sunk on his chest. Swope roughly pulled my father's head up and hissed at him, 'Look 'e at yon Barmester, Joss Bont, and pronounce 'e aye or nay before I thump 'e.'

My father's voice was barely audible. He must have felt the hatred coming from the men in that courtyard. And even his grog-addled brain must have calculated that to keep them standing in the cold would only enrage them all more and add to the fury in the punishment they finally meted out to him.

'Aye,' he said at last.

'Ye second item, we set down, that on the same day and from the same house thou art accused of taking a silver salt dish. What says thee?'

'Aye.'

'Ye third item, we set down, that on the same day from the same house thou didst take two brazen candlesticks, cunning wrought. What says thee?'

'Aye.'

'Ye fourth item, we set down, that on the same day and from the person of Christopher Unwin thou didst take one nightshirt of cambric. What says thee?'

Even my father seemed shamed by this last. His head dropped again, and his 'Aye' fell muffled into his breast.

'Josiah Bont, since you do own these crimes, we do find thee guilty. Does anyone wish to speak for this man before I proclaim his penalty?'

Every eye in the place turned to me then, where I stood by the wall to the right of Alun Houghton, trying to vanish into the shadows. Every eye, including my father's. His glare was hard at first, the prideful look of a cock o' the walk. But as I gazed back at him in silence, the look changed to one of surprise, and then confusion, and finally, as the realization that I would not speak came at last upon him, his whole face sagged. There was rage there, but also disappointment, and the slow dawning of a sad understanding. I had to look away then, for that hint of his grief was more than I could bear. Oh, I knew I would pay for my silence. But I could not speak for him. Or, rather, would not.

There was a shuffling and mumbling then, as the men perceived that I remained mute. When Alun Houghton was convinced I would say nothing, he raised a hand for silence, and when the men stilled, he spoke.

'Josiah Bont, thou should surely know that theft has ever been a sore matter to miners, who toil far off from their dwelling places and must betimes leave their hard-got ore in places lonely and unwatched. And so our code has penalty enough to deter greedy hands. Your hands have been uncommon greedy. And so the court does hereby impose upon you the age-old remedy: thou shalt be taken from here to the Unwin mine and impaled to its stowes by a knife through the hands.' Houghton looked down at his own large, hairy hands where they leant upon the table. He lifted them then slapped them down and shook his massive head. 'So there you have it,' he said, his voice no longer the formal boom of the Barmester but only that of a sad old man.

The light was fading as they led my father away. Later, I learned that he whimpered when he saw the blackened stowes rising from the snowy crust upon the moors. I learned that he begged in vain for mercy and howled like a trapped animal when the dagger cleft his flesh.

The tradition is that once the knife is placed, the convicted man is left, unguarded. It is understood that before very long someone from his kin will come to free him. I believed that Aphra would do it. It never occurred to me that she would not. For whatever I felt towards him, I would not have left my father to die in such a way.

That night, the snow turned to rain. By morning it was siling down with a force that peeled the soil from the hillsides and filled the streams until they broke brownly over their banks. All the next day, water landed on my windows slantwise, as if hurled from a bucket that never emptied. The very road became like a stream, the water pooling against the houses and running under the doorsills until every piece of spare cloth was too soaked to keep it from seeping inside. To open the door was to admit the deluge; to step outside was to be drenched. So no one went anywhere except of dire need.

I believe my father died waiting for Aphra, expecting her coming until his last instant. Otherwise he surely would have taken the wolf's choice: torn his own hands, letting the blade slice through palm flesh and finger sinew to buy his liberty, and his life. Perhaps he remained so disordered by drink that he did not realize the passing of time. Perhaps he fainted from the agony in his hands and so did not feel the seeping cold stealing over his body and slowing his heart until it stopped. I will never know exactly how it was that death claimed him. But I think of his body, needled by the lashing rain until his soaked flesh puckered. I see his mouth open like a cup, filling and filling till the water brimmed and spilled.

For Aphra did not come. She could not. At a single stroke, three of her four children had sickened with Plague that day. Her youngest, Faith, a girl of three years, was the only one not stricken. Had one of the elder boys been spared, she could have sent him to fetch help. But she had no one to send. And so she chose not to leave her children in that lonely croft while the rain soaked the thatch and the fire waned and they cried for comfort, not to make the long, soaking trek up to the moors to the man whom she blamed for bringing the infection upon them.

No one came near her all through that day or the next. I did not go, and for that I will forever reproach myself. Because out of our negligence and her loneliness came much rage. Much rage and some madness – and a surfeit of grief. For Aphra, and for all of us.

T he rain eased late on the second night, and by morning it had been replaced by a stiff wind that blew the water off the tree limbs and began the slow business of drying the saturated gritstones of our dwellings and the sodden earth of our fields.

Spring, 1665

And so my father was three days dead before I learned what had become of him. For Aphra appeared at my door that morning, earth clinging to her hands and falling in damp crumbs from her smock. Her cheeks were sunken, and her eyes had dropped into deep, mauve hollows. She was muddy up to her nethers, and she carried her little girl, Faith, clutched to her waist.

'Tell me he is here, Anna,' she said, and at first I had no idea what she was speaking about. The blank expression upon my face answered her question. She gave a great, animal-like wail and dropped to the floor, beating her fists on the hearth. Her hands were all blisters, which burst and splattered yellow fluid on the grey stone. 'He's still there then! The Devil take you, Anna! You left him there to die!' The child, terrified, began wailing as well. The noise brought Mary Hadfield to my door, and together the two of us grabbed hold of Aphra and soothed her as best we could. But she was wild under our hands as a weasel, thrashing to get free of us.

'Let me go! Let me go! Since I'm the only one who cares enough to tend to him!'

I was determined not to let go of her in that state, even though my bowels had turned to water at the implication of her words. In my heart, I hoped my father might have freed himself and just run off. It was the sort of thing he was capable of doing: oathbreaking – to Aphra, to the entire village, even to God – would mean little to him.

It was some time before I made enough sense out of her confused keenings to understand that her boys were all of them dead. She had buried them that morning. She had dug the grave big enough and laid them side by side, hand in hand. The ruin of her own hands had come not just from the blistering business of digging such a large hole in the water-sodden earth; as I picked the thorns from her wounds, she told me that she had covered the grave with brambles, plaited in threes, so that the power of the Holy Trinity would protect her sons from witches and demons. I thought, but did not say, that the only thing the brambles would protect them from was unearthing by rooting sows, who were about the village now, hungry and scavenging, like so much other livestock whose dead owners could no longer tend or confine them.

She winced as I salved her raw hands and bound them up with the softest cloths I could find. I thought that the last thing she need face after burying her boys was dealing with the matter of my father. If he were dead up there these three days, it would be a grisly business. But if he had run off, the discovery of his abandonment would be a grief to her. I said I would send Brand or another of the young men up to the Unwin mine, but this suggestion only set her keening afresh. 'They all hate him! I'll not have them near him! You hate him, too. You needn't pretend otherwise. Just let me go and give him his due.' In her anguished state, I could not subdue or gainsay her, so I resolved to go with her. But I made her leave the child with Mary Hadfield, so that the little one would be spared whatever we might find.

Alas, I didn't comprehend how great a horror, or perhaps I would have spared myself. Small mercy: the stiff wind rattled through the skeletons of winter-killed bracken and the bare legs of dead heather, so that the stench of shit and rot from my father's half-gnawed guts came to us only in the brief lulls between gusts. The wild creatures had had ample time to do their work, so what was left on the stowes was more like a clumsily butchered beef than the mortal remains of a man.

Approaching that ruined body was one of the hardest things I have done in my life. I checked when I saw it and thought to turn back and implore someone who was not kin to deal with it. But Aphra marched on. Her fit had passed now, or changed, at least. She had turned cold and calm, muttering and muttering under her breath. She walked straight up to the stowes and tugged at the dagger that held what was left of my father. It was driven hard into the wood and did not budge when she laid her bandaged hands upon it. Only when she planted a boot on the upright and threw her whole body's weight against it did the knife finally slide free, grating against bone. She looked at it for a long moment then began to wield it on my father's hair, shearing off large locks and plunging them into her pocket. Then she tore off a piece of my father's jerkin to wrap the blade and tucked the dagger into her girdle.

We had brought neither pick nor shovel with us, and the ground up there is so hard, even after such a soaking, that I would have been ill set in any wise to dig a decent hole. Still, I dreaded the thought of carrying this remnant of a corpse any distance. I feared that Aphra would want to bury him on her own ground, near her boys. But she said she would rather lay him right there, at the Unwin mine, so that Christopher Unwin would ever be reminded of the cost of his justice. So I spent the next hour gathering stones to raise a cairn. This, at least, was simply done, for the deads from the mine contained many large toadstones. When it was high enough, Aphra began searching for sticks, and then she shredded pieces from the hem of her placket to bind them. I thought she meant to form a cross for the grave, but when she was done I saw that she had fashioned, instead, a figure that looked like a manikin. This she laid atop the cairn. I commenced to say the Lord's Prayer, and I thought she was saying it with me in a low, deep-throated murmur. But when I said amen, her muttering continued, and the sign she made at the end of it did not resemble the sign of the cross.

The Press of Their Ghosts

That afternoon, I cried for my father. I had gone into the rectory kitchen to make a dish of vervain tea for Elinor, and as I stood there, waiting for the water to boil, the tears welled up and flowed, uncontrollably. The trouble with weeping was that once begun, it became almost impossible to stop. For I had not had sufficient space to mourn for my boys, or for the ruin of the life I had imagined for myself, mothering them both to an honourable manhood.

My face was all wet and my shoulders shaking, but I tried to make the tea anyway. I lifted the kettle from the hob and then stood there, frozen, unable to remember the simple sequence of actions that I needed next to do. I was standing there still when Elinor came. She took the kettle from my hand, sat me down, and stroked my hair and held me. Elinor said nothing at first, but as my sobs subsided, she began to whisper.

'Tell me,' said Elinor, and so I did, at last. The whole of it. All his brutalities; all the neglect and ill use of my lost and lonely child-hood. I told her then what I had learned of what lay behind his depravities, the same terrible stories he had poured into the unwilling ears of a frightened child who had not wished to hear them. How he had been buggered as a boy by the rough men of the fleet and learned to swill down the rum until he did not mind it. How he had gone under the lash of a boatswain's mate who had not troubled to comb the cat between each stroke, so that the tails landed all in one bloody tangle and left a rend in his back so deep that ever after he could not fully raise his left arm.

Elinor winced as I recounted all this, as I must have winced and tried to stop my ears when the tales had been laid upon me. But just as he would not relent from the telling, I found that neither could I. I heard my own voice, droning on and on with the litany of miseries: how he had seen his only friend ripped jowl to calf by barnacles in an unjust keel-hauling; how he had survived the term of his apprenticeship and got ashore at last, only to be picked up by a press gang and forced again to sea; how he had lived ever after in fear that he would somehow be pressed again, even far inland as we lived, and dragged back into his nightmares.

Somehow, the telling of all this rinsed my mind clean and left me able to think clearly once more. By gathering and sorting my own feelings so, I was finally able to fashion a scale on which I could weigh my father's nature and find a balance between my disgust for him and an understanding of him; my guilt in the matter of his death against the debt he owed me for the manner of my life. At the finish of it, I felt free of him, and I was able to think calmly once more.

Elinor sat quietly for a time. 'I always wondered,' she said at last, 'why one like your father bound himself here by the Sunday Oath. For it seemed to me that he was the very type of man who would flee and spare himself if he could. I suppose the fear he had of the press gangs would account for it.'

'Maybe so,' I said. 'But I think there was more to it. I do believe now that he felt himself protected.' I told her then of Aphra's strange behaviours during the making of my father's cairn and the laying of his corpse to rest. 'Aphra has ever been superstitious. I believe that she convinced my father that she had somehow obtained chants or charms or somesuch to preserve them from the Plague's infections.'

'Indeed,' she said. 'If that is so, Aphra and your father are not alone in embracing such beliefs.' She went to her whisket then and brought out a piece of stained, frayed cloth. She showed it to me and then let it flutter on to the hearth. She had made the tea for the two of us, and she sipped it absently as she watched the fabric burn. The marks on the cloth were clumsy, as if the hand that had made them was not used to forming letters. As best I could make it out before the flame tongued them black, the words were a nonsense foursome: AAB, ILLA, HYRS, GIBELLA.

'I had this from Margaret Livesedge, who lost her baby daughter yesterday. A "witch" gave it her. The ghost, as she said, of Anys Gowdie. The ghost told her the words were Chaldee – a powerful spell from sorcerers who worshipped Satan, naked and painted with snakes, at each full moon. She had her twine the cloth like a snake around the child's neck where the Plague sore was. As the moon waned, the Plague sore, too, was supposed to diminish.' Elinor shook her head sadly. 'Either Margaret has lost her reason and is having visions of women who are not there, or someone took a silver shilling off her for this wicked nonsense. Anna, I don't know what shocks me more in all this: that someone preys upon their desperate fellows, or that they besmirch the memory of Anys Gowdie in passing themselves off as her shade, or that people here are so desperate and credulous that they listen to these midnight whisperings and pay their last mite for these worthless amulets.'

I told her then of finding Kate Talbot's ABRACADABRA on that snowy day when we'd met each other unexpectedly at the Gowdie cottage. 'We must tell Mr. Mompellion of these things,' she said. 'He must preach against them and warn people not to fall into these superstitions.' The rector was out, writing a will for the miner Richard Sopes, but presently we heard Anteros blowing and snorting in the stableyard. Elinor went to greet him while I prepared some broth and oatcake, and when I carried it into the library, the two of them were deep in conference. Elinor turned to me.

'Mr. Mompellion, too, has come upon these talismans. It seems the madness is spreading as fast as the disease amongst us.'

'Indeed,' he said, 'I am come back here to fetch one of you to the Mowbray croft, for the infant there needs your herb-knowledge.' He had come in from the stableyard coatless, and he looked chilled, so I hurried to fetch him a jacket.

'Then it isn't Plague, Rector?' I asked, stretching up to assist him into the garment.

'No, no; it is not the Plague this time, or not as yet at least. But I found the babe's fool parents out in the Riley field, passing the poor naked child back and forth through the bramble hedge. By the time I got up to them his tender little body was all scratched and sliced, with the fools smiling and saying that they've protected him so from invasion by Plague seeds.' He tugged at his shirt sleeves and sighed. 'It took hard words and harsh looks from me to get it out of them, but finally they told me they'd had the instructions and the incantations from the ghost of Anys Gowdie, who'd visited them in the dark. I wrapped up the poor child in my cloak and made them carry him home, where I said I would send one of you directly with a salve for his scrapes.'

I told Elinor that I would go, since I needed some useful occupation to divert my mind. I made the salve as quickly as I could. The bramble leaf itself has that in it to soothe its own thorns' pricks, so I compounded some with silverweed and comfrey and a little cooling mint and bound the result with almond oil. It was a sweet-smelling ointment, and its scent lingered on my hands. But the stench as I neared the door of the Mowbray croft drove the fragrance from my nose.

As if the poor infant had not been enough imposed upon, Lottie Mowbray was holding the baby aloft and steering the thin stream of his piss into a cooking pot that had evidently just been lifted off the fire. I could not think why, but they clearly had been boiling this pot of piss for some time, for the stink of it filled the croft. She looked up blankly as I entered, and the last of the infant's pee dribbled onto her skirt.

'Lottie Mowbray, what new foolishness is this?' I demanded, gently lifting the whimpering infant from her hands. This was the boy I had midwifed just after Shrovetide and I had wondered, even then, how someone like Lottie, who was herself in many ways a child, would manage to care for him. The father, Tom, was little better than simple himself, scraping a poor living as ploughboy or mine-hand – whatever plain tasks his neighbours had need of him to do. But he was a gentle-seeming soul who was kind to Lottie and besotted by the babe. 'The witch told us we should boil the babe's hair in his piss and that this would keep off the Plague from both 'is innards and 'is outers,' Tom said. 'Since the rector was so vexed with us over the bramble charms, I thought to try this'n, in its stead.'

I had brought a lambskin from my cottage and I spread this before the fire. Tenderly as I could, I laid the little one down upon it and unwrapped the dirty cloths that Lottie had swaddled him in. He began to give a thin cry, for in places the cloth had stuck to the bleeding scratches.

'And how much,' I asked, trying to keep my voice calm so as not to alarm the infant, 'did the woman take from you for this advice?'

'Thruppence for the first, and tuppence the second,' Lottie replied. 'And I reckon it were a bargain, for she says that once the Plague be full upon a child, the charms for lifting it cost a lot more than them as holds it at bay.' I happened to know, because Tom Mowbray had sometimes worked for Sam, that even in good times five pence was his whole sennight's wage.

It was difficult to contain my anger. I did my best, for one could not blame simpletons like the Mowbrays for falling prey to such superstitions. But my wrists were limp with rage at this predatory woman, whomsoever she be. I tried to make my fingers light as butterflies upon the baby as I washed his scrapes and dressed them with my salve. When I was finished, I wrapped him in the piece of clean linen that Elinor had given me and tucked him up, with the lambskin, in the hollowed-out log the Mowbrays used for a cradle. Then I took the stinking piss pot to the door and flung its contents far out into the yard. Lottie cried out at this, so I took her by the shoulders and gave her a gentle shake. 'Here,' I said, holding out the salve. 'This costs you nothing. In the morning, if the room is warm enough, leave him bare awhile so the air can work upon his cuts. Then dress them, as you just saw me do it, with the salve. Feed him as well as you are able, and stay clear of any whom you know to be sick. That is all we can do against this Plague. That, and pray to God for deliverance, for it will not come from Satan, or for those who work in his shadow.' I sighed then, for her blank gaze told me I was wasting my breath.

'See that you scour that pot well before you cook in it again,' I said. 'Put water in it and boil it on the fire this night. Do you understand?' At that, she nodded dumbly. Potscrubbing, at least, was something she could grasp.

As I walked away from the croft, I caught my toe on a loose stone and stumbled, grazing the hand that I flung out to break my fall. My anger magnified this small hurt and I cursed. As I sucked at the injured place, a question began to press upon me. Why, I wondered, did we, all of us, both the rector in his pulpit and simple Lottie in her croft, seek to put the Plague in unseen hands? Why should this thing be either a test of faith sent by God, or the evil working of the Devil in the world? One of these beliefs we embraced, the other we scorned as superstition. But perhaps each was false, equally. Perhaps the Plague was neither of God nor the Devil, but simply a thing in Nature, as the stone on which we stub a toe.

I walked on, nursing my injured hand and probing my heart on these matters. Did I really believe that God put the rock in my path to trip me? Some would say certainly: the finger of God places every speck of dust. I did not see it so. Yet I would have inclined to believe God's hand at work if, as a result of the rock, I'd struck my head and lay now fatally injured. So where, exactly, in the design of the world, did I believe that matters' tilted the scale sufficient to garner God's notice? If I did not think He cared for the lie of a rock, why should I believe that He cared for a small life such as mine? It came to me then that we, all of us, spent a very great deal of time pondering these questions that, in the end, we could not answer. If we balanced the time we spent contemplating God, and why He afflicted us, with more thought as to how the Plague spread and poisoned our blood, then we might come nearer to saving our lives.

While these thoughts were vexing, they brought with them also a chink of light. For if we could be allowed to see the Plague as a thing in Nature merely, we did not have to trouble about some grand celestial design that had to be completed before the disease would abate. We could simply work upon it as a farmer might toil to rid his field of unwanted tare, knowing that when we found the tools and the method and the resolve, we would free ourselves, no matter if we were a village full of sinners or a host of saints.

We greeted our Maying with a mixture of hope and fear: the hope, I suppose, that comes naturally into the human heart at the end of any hard winter; the fear that the gentler weather would bring with it an increase in disease. The season eased in with an unaccustomed steadiness, as if the skies knew we could not cope, this year, with the sudden reversals that are more typical here – one day mild, encouraging the tender tips of grass shoots, the next bringing a biting frost to scorch all the new growth back to dun lifelessness. This year, the shoots opened and the buds swelled into bloom unblighted. Small, unseen creatures bustled through fields gilded by daffodils. The old apple trees burst into snowy blossom and cast their scent adrift on the warming breeze. Once, walking through the hazy mist of bluebells, I was pierced by a memory: 'This gladdened me once.' And for a moment, I stopped, and paused, and tried to grasp that sentiment. As I stood there, I thought of Jamie, still a babe, reaching up his tiny arms to try and clasp the moon. My effort was just as doomed. Then I had to walk on, towards the melancholy tasks awaiting me beside yet another deathbed.

In the fair weather my ewes lambed easily, which was a blessing given all else I had to do. Sometimes, the sight of those tiny creatures moved me, their clean fleeces so dazzling white against the lush new grass, springing on all fours in their joy to be alive. At other times, I would gaze at them and wonder if I would be yet living to see them grown, to clip their fleece or put them to tups to birth lambs of their own. At those times, I would feel a witless anger at their simple gambolling. 'Stupid beasts,' I would mutter, 'to be happy to be *here*, of all the accursed places in this world.' Those were the times when I had heard of yet another, and another, and another still, falling to the sickness.

For the warm weather brought death more than we had thought

possible. Even Cucklett Delf, beautiful as it was now, all decked with tumbles of hawthorn blossom lacier than our finest altar cloths, had become unable to conceal from us our diminishment. Every Sunday the spaces between us grew greater and the distance from the rector's rocky pulpit to the last row of worshippers grew less.

'We are become Golgotha – the place of skulls,' said Michael Mompellion, preaching to us in the Delf on the last Sunday in May. 'And yet we are also Gethsemane, the garden of waiting, and of prayer. Like our blessed Lord, we can only implore God: "Take this cup away from me." But then, like him, beloved friends, we must add the words, "Not my will, but Thine, be done."'

By the second Sunday of June we had reached a sorry marker: as many of us were now in the ground as walked above it. The passing of Margaret Livesedge meant that the dead roll now stood at one hundred fourscore souls. Sometimes, if I walked the main street of the village in the evening, I felt the press of their ghosts. I realized then that I had begun to step small and carry myself all hunched, keeping my arms at my sides and my elbows tucked, as if to leave room for them. I wondered then if others had these fell thoughts, or whether I was drifting slowly into madness. There had been fear here, since the very beginning, but where it had been veiled, now it had become naked. Those of us who were left feared each other and the hidden contagion we each might carry. People scurried, stealthy as mice, trying to go and come without meeting another soul.

It became impossible for me to look into the face of a neighbour and not imagine him dead. Then, I would find my mind turning over how we would manage without his skill at the plough or the loom or the cobbler's bench. We were sorely depleted already in trades of all kinds. Horses who threw a shoe went without since the death of the farrier. We were without malter and mason, carpenter and cloth-weaver, thatcher and tailor. Many fields lay covered in unbroken clods, neither harrowed nor sown. Whole houses stood empty; entire families gone from us, and names that had been known here for centuries gone with them.

Fear took each of us differently. Andrew Merrick, the malter, went off to live all alone, save for his cockerel, in a rude hut he built for himself near the summit of Sir William Hill. He would steal down to Mompellion's Well in the dark of night to leave word of his needs. Since he did not know his letters, he would simply leave a cup containing a sample of the thing he needed – a few grains of oats, the bones of a herring.

Some slaked their dread in drink and their loneliness in wanton caresses. Of these, the strangest case was Jane Martin, the strict young girl who had tended my babes. The poor wretch saw all of her family into their graves and then, though barely more than a child, became an alehouse haunter, seeking insensibility in the pot. Within a month, she had shrugged off her Sadd Colours and her tight-lipped ways, and it pained me when I overheard some of the young souses joking as to how she'd changed from being 'colder than a ley wall' into 'a bawdy jade who could scarce keep her legs closed.' One evening, when I came upon her weaving an uncertain way home in the dark, I took her into my cottage, thinking to get her warm and sober in a safe bed and speak some sense to her in the morning. I fed her some stew of mutton neck, but she quickly brought the whole of it up again and was still so wretchedly ill the next morning that I don't believe she heard much of anything I tried to say to her.

But it was John Gordon's fear that led him upon the queerest path. Gordon, who had beaten his wife the night of Anys Gowdie's murder, had ever been a solitary and difficult soul, so no one was much surprised when, in early spring, he and his wife stopped coming to Sunday services at Cucklett Delf. As they lived at the far edge of the village, I had not seen John for many weeks. Urith I had seen and had some short speech with, so I knew that their absence from the Delf was by choice and not caused by illness. Urith had ever been a woman of few words. She was kept so cowed by her husband that she crept here and there, timid and silent, afraid of conversation lest it somehow led her into conduct of which her husband did not approve. I had noticed that Urith looked thinner, more haggard and gaunt than usual, but as the same could be said for most of us, I did not think too much of it.

Yet John Gordon's altered appearance was another gate's business. I had gone late to the well one evening, on a day that had been filled with tending the sick, to fetch a sack of salt bespoke for the rectory kitchen. The light was fading, and it took me a long time before I recognized the stooped figure making a halting way up the steep track through the trees. Although the evening was chill, the man was naked to the waist, with only a piece of sacking bound around his loins. He was spare as a corpse, his bones like shiny knobs, pressing almost through his flesh. He carried a staff in his left hand, on which he leant heavily, for the effort of the walk was clearly costing him dear. In the gathering dusk I could not at first see what it was that his right hand held. But as I began to descend from the well and draw nearer to him, I finally made it out. It was a scourge of plaited leather, into the ends of which had been driven short nails. As John Gordon moved up the path, I perceived that he stopped, every five paces or so, straightened, and raised the scourge to strike himself. One of the spikes was bent crooked, like a fish-hook, so that where it connected with the skin it caught and tore away a tiny piece of flesh.

I dropped the salt sack and ran towards him then, crying out. Close to, I could see that he was a mass of scabs and bruises, with fresh blood trickling into the dried tracks of earlier injuries.

'Please,' I cried, 'cease this! Do not punish yourself so! Rather, come with me and let me lay a salve upon your wounds!'

Gordon only stared at me and went on murmuring. '*Te Deum laudamus, te judice . . . te Deum laudamus, te judice . . .*' He applied the lash to himself in rhythm with his prayer. The hooked nail caught in his flesh and raised up a little tent of skin. He gave a tug and skin tore. I flinched. His low voice never faltered.

He pushed past me then as if I were not there and went on, in the direction of the Edge. I picked up the salt and hurried on to the rectory. As unwilling as I was to lay any new burden on Mr. Mompellion, this was, as I thought, a situation only he could know how to address. He was in his library, working on a sermon. It was not my habit ever to disturb him there, but when I told Elinor what I had seen, she insisted that the news could not wait.

He stood up at once at our knock and looked at us with grave attention, knowing we would not interrupt him for a small matter. When I told him what I had witnessed, he pounded his fist upon the table.

'Flagellants! I feared it.'

'But how?' said Elinor. 'Far as we are from the cities, how should this thing arise here?'

He shrugged. 'Who can say? Gordon is a lettered man. It seems that dangerous ideas may spread on the very wind and seek us out near or far, as easily as the seeds of disease have done.'

I did not know what they were speaking about. Elinor, sensing my confusion, turned to me.

'They have ever been the spectre that stalks with the Plague, Anna,' she said. 'Flagellants walked the lanes of this land many hundreds of years ago, when disease and war were here. At the time of the Black Death, they gathered again, sometimes in very great numbers, passing from town to town, drawing the souls of the troubled to them. Their belief is that by grievous self-punishment they can allay God's wrath. They see Plague as His discipline for human sin. They are poor souls –'

'Poor souls, yet very dangerous,' Mr. Mompellion interjected. He was pacing now. 'Most often, the damage they do falls only on themselves, but there have been times when, in mobs, they have laid blame for the Plague on the sins of others – Jews, many times. I have read of how in foreign cities they put hundreds of such innocents to death by fire. We lost the Gowdies to a like madness. I will *not* lose another soul.'

He stopped his pacing then. 'Anna, kindly pack some oatcakes and some of your salves and tonics. For I believe we must visit the Gordons this night. I will not have this creed spread here.'

I filled a whisket as he bade me, adding in some sausage and the remains of a large custard I had made for that day's dinner. Outside, he handed me up onto Anteros, and we rode off for the Gordon farm. We had just made the turn from the main road when I noticed something white, writhing on a turf bank by the roadside. I would never have spoken had I realized what it was, but I took it for a person in distress – ill, as I believed – and cried out to the rector to stop. He halted Anteros with a quiet command and headed the horse in the direction I signed. He clearly read the true case quicker than I, for he checked Anteros after a moment, and I believe he meant to turn back to the road and leave the pair alone. But the girl had seen him, and she let out a wail, at which the man sprawled atop her jumped up, plucking at his breeches with one hand and trying to force his bare yard back inside the cloth with the other. Jane Martin lay sprawled on some turves, her dress pushed up to her head, too drunk even to cover her nakedness.

I slid off the horse and went to her, pulling down her skirt and searching in the grass for her missing undergarments. Albion Samweys, meanwhile, stood silent and shuffling before the rector, who had remained mounted. Samweys was a miner whose wife had died a month since. He had been a sometime tavern mate of my father's, although never as given to excess. The rector spoke to him quietly. His voice was oddly flat, sad, if anything, certainly not angry as I – and Albion – had expected.

'Albion Samweys, you have done wrong here this night. You do not need me to preach it to you. Get you to your home and do not dishonour yourself further.'

Samweys backed away, unsteadily, bowing and nodding at the rector until I thought he would overbalance himself. Then he turned and, weaving somewhat, made off at a good trot into the dark. The rector dismounted then and strode to where I sat with Jane, trying to steer her limp feet back into her boots.

'Jane Martin! Get you on your knees!' The voice was a roar. I started at the sound of it, and even Jane, in her stupor, shuddered.

'On your knees, sinner!' He took a step towards us, a looming black figure. His face, in the dark, was unreadable. I scrambled to my feet and stood between him and the crumpled girl, who was trying to raise herself but falling back, again and again, as her limbs refused to function.

'Rector!' I said. 'Surely you see that the girl is incapable of comprehending you at this time! I beg you, save your reproofs, if you must make them, until her wits are cleared.'

'You forget yourself.' His voice was quiet now but cold. 'This girl knows well what she does here this night. She is in command of the Scriptures as well as I. She has taken the pure vessel of her body and filled it with corruption. She has done this knowingly. She shall be punished –'

'Rector,' I interrupted. 'You know that she has been.'

There was silence then, broken only by the champing of Anteros's soft mouth, cropping the wet grass. My head was full of the pounding of my own blood. I could scarce believe I had spoken so. Then I heard a heaving behind me, and the stink on the still air told me that Jane Martin had spewed up the beery contents of her belly.

'Clean her, then hold the horse while I get her mounted,' he said. I wiped Jane's mouth with one of the cloths from my whisket. The rector lifted her into the saddle and signalled for me to mount behind her, to hold her on the horse as best I could as he led us back towards her cottage. We did not speak on the descent, nor as we lifted her down and helped her to her pallet, nor as we set off again on our original errand.

I was glad that it was dark, so that I did not have to meet the rector's eyes. I was mortified to have been the cause of his witnessing the coupling, and to have been witness, in turn, to his strange fit – so unlike anything I knew of him. We were passing the place where I had spied the pair when he gave a deep sigh. 'None of us is master of himself as we should be in these times. I would ask that you forget my outburst this night, and I will do the same regarding yours.' I muttered my assent into the darkness. Anteros had gone a few more paces when the rector spoke again.

'Especially,' he said quietly, 'I will be glad if no word of this business comes to my wife.'

'Very well, Rector,' I murmured. Of course, he would wish Elinor spared knowledge of our animal nature so coarsely displayed.

We rode on in silence. When we reached the Gordons' farm, Urith, at first, refused to open the door to us. 'My husband will not have me receive any man when he is not within,' she said in a voice that quavered.

'Do not be concerned, for Anna Frith is here with me. There can be no impropriety, surely, in receiving your minister and his servant? We have brought some victuals. Will you not break bread with us?' At that, the door opened a crack. Urith peered out, saw me and my whisket, and licked her lips hungrily. I moved forwards and threw back the cloth so that she could see the contents. Trembling, she opened the door. She was clad in a rough sort of blanket, belted with a rope at the waist. 'In truth,' she said, 'I am clemmed. For my husband has fasted me a fortnight on naught but a cup of broth and a heel of bread a day.'

I gasped when I entered the cottage, for all of its furnishings had been removed. Instead, the interior had been decked out in every corner with crosses of rough-hewn wood. Some were large, standing up against the wall; other, smaller ones made of sticks, hung from the rafters by strings. Urith saw me staring. 'This is how he does pass his time now, not in farming but fashioning crosses, one upon another.' The air inside the stone-walled cottage was colder than that out of doors, for it seemed that no cooking fire had burned in the hearth for some time. I laid out the oatcakes, the sausage, and the custard upon the cloths that I had wrapped them in, and Urith knelt on the floor and devoured them, even drinking the green tonic down to the dregs. Since there was no stool to sit upon, we stood and watched her eat. I clutched my arms about me and beat my hands against my sides to try to get warm.

When she had done she sat back on her heels and sighed deeply, sated for the first time in a fortnight. Then, scrambling to her feet, she looked at us with fear. 'I beg you not to tell my husband of this,' she said. 'He is already sorely aggrieved at me because I will not go about half naked as he does. It is the first time I have defied him in anything, and I have been sorely punished for it. If he knows I have disobeyed him as well in the matter of the fast . . .' Her words trailed off, but her meaning was plain enough. I gathered up the cloths and scanned the floor for crumbs so as not to betray her secret, while Mr. Mompellion questioned Urith gently about how she supposed her husband had come upon the teachings of the Flagellants.

'I am sure, I do not know how,' she said. 'But sometime in the midwinter he obtained a tract from London, studied it, and after became very strange. I pray you will not take offence, Rector, but he became most critical of your sermonizing. He said you do wrong in encouraging people to see the Plague as anything other than God's wrath made manifest. He said you should rather be leading us in public confessions of each and every sin that any one of us ever has committed, so as we might come upon the transgression that has brought down God's wrath and root it out from amongst us. It is not enough, he says, to search our soul, but we must scourge our flesh also. He began a fast, and it has become increasingly severe. Then he burned all our bedstraw and insisted we sleep on the bare stones.' She coloured a little and went on in a whisper, 'By no means were we to take any comfort of each other's bodies, but lie always chaste.'

Gordon had ceased to do any farmwork and railed at her when she left her place, beside him on her knees, to go herself and push the plough. 'Then, a sennight past, he hauled out the table and benches and burned them in a bonfire, throwing both his suits of clothes upon it.' He had ordered her to do likewise, but she had refused to doff her garments, saying his manner of dress was indecent.

'He cursed me then, declaring that I should be grateful to him for knowing how to stay the arrows of God's Plague from striking us.' Her whisper dropped till I could barely make out the words. 'He stripped me and burned my clothes.' He proclaimed that her weakness and her failure to make adequate penance would force them to mortify their flesh all the more severely. That is when he had made the leather strop and driven the nails into it. He beat her first and then himself. He had continued his scourgings every day since.

'You may try to talk to him, Rector, but I doubt he has ears to hear you.'

'Where do you think I might find him this night?'

'In truth, I do not know,' she said. 'But it has become his habit to deprive himself even of sleep, when he can. Sometimes, he does this by walking the moors until he drops exhausted. Other times he lies himself down on a rock outcrop upon the Edge, where he says the fear of falling if he gives way to sleep helps him stay wakeful until dawn-break.'

'He was heading towards the Edge when I saw him,' I murmured.

'Was he so?' said the rector. 'Well then, I must go that way also.'

Mr. Mompellion rose then and laid a hand gently on Urith's shoulder. 'Try to get some rest, and I will do my best to calm your husband's torments.'

'Thank you,' she whispered. And so we left her, in that bleak, bare cottage, I to go to my own warm hearth and the rector to his search. As to how Urith Gordon could find any rest lying down upon those bare gritstones, I did not rightly know.

M r. Mompellion did not find John Gordon that night, though he walked Anteros back and forth along the Edge until moon-set. Neither could any sign be found of the man on the following day, nor the one after. It was, indeed, a full week before Brand Rigney, out searching for a missing lamb from the Merrills' flock, spotted the corpse, lying splayed amongst the fallen rocks at the foot of the Edge's sheerest face. There was no way to retrieve the shattered body, or even to cover it, for to get near meant accessing a track that ran out of Stoney Middleton. That, in turn, meant passing through the town, which we were oathbound not to do. So John Gordon's flesh was mortified in death as in life, lying naked under the sky, left to the untender mercies of Nature.

The rector preached a memorial for John Gordon at the Delf the following Sunday. It was a sermon of love and understanding, saying that Gordon had sought to please God, even as he embraced conduct unpleasing to God. 'For, beloved friends, remember that God states in the Bible, "My yoke is easy and my burden is light." God does not love pain for its own sake. It is for Him to decide who shall suffer; He, and the vicars he appoints to give you penances. It is not for you to presume to do so.' Urith was there, dressed in clothing that other villagers had sent her when they learned of her plight. She looked a little better, despite her loss, for in the days since her husband's death she had been able to eat decently again. Villagers had sent her food and bedding.

But her respite was cruelly brief, for the Plague felled her the following week. While I wondered whether Plague seeds had been carried to her home with the good intentions of people who had gifted her bedstraw and clothing, others drew a different conclusion. Some muttered that perchance John Gordon had walked a true path, and so doing kept the Plague from his door. Whispers passed that Mr. Mompellion's sermon was mistaken. Most dismissed such talking. But fear, as I have said, was working strange changes in all of us, corroding our ability for clear thought. Within a sennight, Martin Miller had girt his family in sack cloth and fashioned himself a scourge. Randoll Daniel did likewise, though thankfully he did not ask it of his wife and babe. Together, Randoll and the Millers went about the village exhorting others to join them in their bloody self-chastisement.

At the rectory, Mr. Mompellion wavered between rage and self-reproach. When I would go to clean the library I would find many pages from his hand, close-written and scratched over and written again. Every week he seemed to find it more and more difficult to gather up words for sermons that would ease us and keep us all in heart. It was during this time that he began meeting with his old friend Mr. Holbroke, the rector of Hathersage. I say 'meeting,' but I do not use the word in any usual sense. He would walk up to the rise of land above Mompellion's Well and wait there for his colleague. Mr. Holbroke would draw as near as he dared and the two would converse, if you could call it that, shouting across the gulf between them. If Mr. Mompellion wanted to send a letter to the earl, or to his patron, Elinor's father, he would dictate it to Mr. Holbroke, so that the letter's recipient would not be alarmed by receiving a paper from a hand that had touched the hands of Plague victims.

Sometimes, Mr. Mompellion would return from these encounters a little lifted in spirits. On other occasions, the contact with the outside world seemed rather to press upon his mind, and as I came and went about my tasks, I would hear Elinor talking to him quietly, in her low, soothing voice, always reassuring him, always telling him that he was the author of great good for all of us, no matter how dark the present days might seem.

One such afternoon, I had stood outside the door with a tray of refreshment, heard their quiet voices – hers, most especially – and crept away so as not to disturb them. Returning a little later with the tray and hearing nothing, I had eased open the door and peeked inside. Elinor had fallen asleep, exhausted, in her chair. Michael Mompellion stood behind her, leaning over her a little. His hand hovered in the air, just above her head.

He will not chance her rest, even to caress her, I thought. I wondered if any couple had ever dealt so tenderly together. Thank you, God, I thought, for sparing them for each other. And then, as I stood there, spying greedily upon their intimacy, a baser feeling altogether swept over me. Why should they have each other, when I had no one?

I was jealous of both of them at once. Of him, because Elinor loved him, and I hungered for a greater share of her love than I could ever hope for. And yet I was jealous of her, too; jealous that she was loved by a man as a woman is meant to be loved. Why should I writhe on my cold and empty bed while she took comfort in his warm flesh? I crept away from the door, trying to still my shaking hands so that the rattling tray would not give me away. I entered the kitchen and walked to the wash trough. There, I set down the tray. From it, I lifted the delicate dishes, his first, then hers, and smashed them, one by one, against the unyielding stone.

A Great Burning

The first time I heard Elinor cough, I tried to will my ears into disbelieving it. It was one of those summer days as soft as the blow-ball fluff drifting on the honeysuckle breeze. We were walking back to the rectory in the bright evening, having visited, for once, the well rather than the ill. Elinor had wanted to call upon the six or eight elderly who had survived the Plague even as their vigorous sons and daughters had fallen to it. These widows and widowers were people with whom she had been much concerned before the Plague, but the exigencies of the dying had meant that the living, no matter they be needy, had been left to shift for themselves.

We had found all but one faring well. James Mallion, a toothless, bent old soul, we had found sitting in the dark, spare from lack of nourishment and most glum in spirits. Together we had lifted him out to take the warm air and fed him a good dinner, which I took the trouble to mash as fine as for an infant. As I spooned the soft food into his mouth and caught the dribbles from his chin, it reminded me of feeding my own babes, and a tear sprang unbidden to my eye. He had grabbed my arm then with his clawlike hand, and his rheumy eyes fixed on me. In a quavering voice, he had asked, 'Why should one like me, who is weary of his life and ready for the harvest, be spared, when all the young ones are plucked up unripe?'

I patted his hand and shook my head, unable to command my voice to reply to him.

Elinor and I spoke of this as we walked back to the rectory, for we still had come no nearer to fathoming why the Plague felled some and yet not others. Those few, like Andrew Merrick, who had taken themselves off to live away from others in caves or rude huts, certainly had escaped infection. So much we knew; proximity to the ill begat illness. But that we had ever known. What remained a puzzlement was why some lived who dwelt all together in one house, sharing with the ailing their food and bedding and even the very air they breathed. I said that Mr. Stanley, when he spoke to those who would hear from him, held that the choice seemed random to us because it rested entirely with God.

'I know it,' Elinor replied. As we walked, she plucked absently at the honeysuckle vines twining through the hedgerow. Once, I had shown her how to sip the nectar from the blossoms, and now, as we walked, she placed the flowers to her lips and drew out their sweetness as any lowly country lass might do. 'Mr. Stanley has ever believed that God bestows suffering on those whom He would spare from torments after death. It is not a view I can embrace, Anna. And yet, how can we know? Mr. Mompellion has ceased to speak on such matters in his sermons. He undertakes now only to uplift our spirits and strengthen our resolve.'

We fell silent then. I tried to rest my mind from such imponderables by keeping my thoughts only in the moment, watching the lazy wheeling of the kestrels and listening to the raw calls of the corncrakes. When Elinor coughed, I told myself it was a crake I had heard. I neither paused nor turned to look at her but kept on walking. A few minutes later, she coughed again, and this time there was no ignoring it. She stopped as the spasm racked her, pressing a piece of lace to her mouth. I immediately turned and placed an arm around her shoulders to support her. My face must have shown the depth of my feeling, for she looked at me and tried to smile through the coughing. When it subsided, she pushed me playfully away from her, saying, 'Now, Anna, don't bury me on the basis of a cough, merely!'

But I could not be laughed out of the terror that had seized me. I felt her face with my hand, but since the evening was warm and we had walked quite far, I could not tell whether the heat of her brow meant fever or no.

'Sit here,' I said, pointing to a large, flat stone under a rowan shade. 'Sit here, and I will run ahead and fetch Mr. Mompellion to you.'

'Anna!' she said, and her tone was peremptory. 'Stop this at once! You shall do no such thing!' She touched her brow and tossed her head, as if shaking off the heat she surely felt there. 'I perceive I am perhaps coming down with a slight cold, and I will not have you fuss and panic me so! I beg you will strive to command yourself. You are not a child, to quail at shadows, after all we have seen and done together. If I am truly ill, you will be the first person I shall confide in. Until then, do not you dare to trouble Mr. Mompellion with this.'

She walked on, briskly. I followed, caught up with her, and reached for her arm. She let me take it, and as we walked I tried to take note of every detail – the way her fingers lay across my wrist, the gentle sway of her body, the measure of her step. I could no longer see the bright buttercups or hear the birdsong. There was a roaring in my ears from my own pounding heart, and my eyes misted and over-flowed with tears that ran unchecked down my face.

Elinor stopped and looked at me, a slight smile upon her lips. She raised the hand that clutched her small lace handkin and was about to wipe my tears with it. But then she stopped in mid-gesture, crumpled the white square, and plunged it deep into her whisket.

That told me all. I wept then in earnest, standing right there in the middle of the field.

W hat shall I say of the next three days that has not been said already? Elinor's fever rose. She coughed and sneezed as others have coughed and sneezed, and Michael Mompellion and I tried to bring her comfort, as we had tried to bring comfort to so many others.

I was by her side as much as tact and duty would allow. For of course it was her Michael who had first call upon her last hours, and my role was to keep as much of his own work from him as I myself was capable to do. But some things I could not do, and from time to time he was called away to fulfil obligations at other deathbeds. And so I found myself alone with my Elinor. I bathed her hectic face with linens steeped in mint water and studied her delicate skin, waiting and dreading the moment when her general flush would blossom into the red-black petals of the Plague's roses. Her hair, so fine, clung damply to her forehead like silvery lace.

To me, she had become so many things. So many things a servant has no right or reason to imagine that the person they serve will be. Because of her, I had known the warmth of a motherly concern — the concern that my own mother had not lived to show me. Because of her, I had had a teacher and was not ignorant and unlettered still. Sometimes, when we worked together on our herbs in the rectory kitchen, I had forgotten she was my mistress; even, at times, I directed her in this or that knack I had mastered of identification or decoction. She never reminded me of my place. In my own heart, I could whisper it: she was my friend, and I loved her. Sometimes, late at night, when fatigue addled my thoughts, I blamed myself for her condition. I thought it was punishment for the sin of my presumption and my jealousy. In the daylight, when I was more lucid, I knew that her illness had no more nor less sense than any other person's suffering. But in the dark hours, I could not school my heart. Every time Michael Mompellion came to sit by her, the flame of jealousy flared up in me. I would leave her room seething over his greater claim to the place at her side. At first, when he dismissed me, I withdrew myself just outside her door and sat there, to be as close to her as possible. When Mr. Mompellion found me there, he helped me kindly to my feet but told me in clear terms that I was not to hover so, and that perhaps it would be better if I retired to my cottage until he sent for me.

It would have taken more than his word to keep me long away from her. The next day, as I placed the cooling cloths upon her brow, it was as if she read my thoughts. She sighed and gave a faint smile. 'That feels so good,' she whispered. Her hand fluttered weakly on mine. 'I am a fortunate woman, to have been loved so in my life . . . to have been given a husband such as Michael and a friend as dear as you, Anna.' She closed her eyes for a moment and then opened them and gazed at me. 'I wonder if you know how you have changed. It is the one good, perhaps, to come out of this terrible year. Oh, the spark was clear in you when first you came to me – but you covered your light as if you were afraid of what would happen if anybody saw it. You were like a flame blown by the wind until it is almost extinguished. All I had to do was put the glass round you. And now, how you shine!' She closed her eyes and squeezed my hand weakly.

After a time, her breathing slowed, so that I thought she had fallen into sleep. I rose as quietly as I could and crept towards the door, thinking to carry away the basin and the spent cloths. But she spoke again, her eyes still closed. 'I hope you will find it in your heart to be a friend to Mr. Mompellion, Anna . . . For my Michael will have need of a friend.' The sob trying to rise in my throat would not let me answer her. But she did not seem to need an answer, for she turned her face to the pillow then and fell truly into sleep.

I could not have been gone for more than ten minutes, but when I returned I could see at once that her condition had worsened. Her face was even more flushed – so livid that the blood vessels had burst into a fine spidery tracery on her cheeks. I lay the cool cloths upon her, but she tossed under my hand. She began speaking then, in a strange, high, girlish voice, and I understood that she was delirious.

'Charles!' she called. She was giggling, a light, lilting laughter that belied her grave state. Her breathing was fast, as if she were running or riding. I imagined her, a girl in a silken dress, at her leisure in the wide green park of her father's great estate. She quieted for a few moments, and I hoped she would slip back into sleep. But then her brow knit and her hands, on the counterpane, wrung themselves together. 'Charles?' She cried out the name in a pitch still high and childish, but distressed, agitated, keening.

I was glad it was I, and not the rector, who was witness to this. She was moaning now. I clasped her hand and called to her, but she was gone somewhere far beyond my reach. And then suddenly her face changed, and her voice became again her familiar adult voice, but speaking in a whisper so intimate it made me blush. 'Michael . . . Michael, how much longer? Please, my love? Please . . .'

He had opened the door and entered the room without my hearing him, and when he spoke I jumped. 'That will do, Anna,' he said, and his voice seemed strangely cold. 'I will call you if she needs anything.'

'Rector, she is much worsened. She is delirious . . .'

'I can see that for myself,' he snapped, distraught. 'You may go.'

Reluctantly, I rose and withdrew to the kitchen until he should call on me. Sitting, waiting, exhausted with worrying, I must have fallen asleep, for when I awoke it was to birdsong. Sunshine streamed through the high casements and fell in wide bands, like yellow Maypole ribands, across the kitchen floor. I crept upstairs in the buttery summer light and stood outside her bedchamber, listening for sounds from within.

All was silent. Gently, I eased open the door. Elinor lay sunken into her pillows, the vivid flush all gone from her face. She was pale as the counterpane and still as stone. Michael Mompellion lay sprawled across the foot of her bed, his hands outstretched towards where she lay, as if he reached to catch her fleeting soul.

The cry that I had been fighting back for three days escaped me then, a groan of grief and loneliness. Michael Mompellion did not stir, but Elinor opened her eyes and smiled at me.

'The fever is broken,' she whispered, 'and I have been lying here awake this hour, parched for a posset. I could not call for you because I did not want to bestir my poor, tired Michael.'

I flew down the stairs to make that posset. As I heated milk I felt like singing for the first time in nigh on a year. Elinor rose from her bed briefly that day. I sat her in a chair by the window with the shutters flung wide. As she looked out on her beloved garden, Mr. Mompellion gazed at her, as if he beheld a vision. I kept finding excuses to return to the room with foods and fresh linens and ewers of warm water, just so that I could be sure I had not dreamt that it was so.

The next day, she said she felt well enough to take a turn in the garden, and she mocked the rector and me as I refused to let her walk unsupported and he hovered, proffering unwanted shawls one moment and contriving unneeded shade the next.

Michael Mompellion seemed a man reborn that day and those that followed. To be convinced, as he had been, that Elinor was lost

to Plague, and then to find her recovered from an ordinary fever . . .
I did not have to imagine the wonder he felt, for I felt it also. His
face, which had been creased with worry, now lost the furrows about
the brow and gained back the laughing lines around the eyes. His
step was buoyant as a boy's, and he approached his grim duties with
a renewed energy.

Elinor was taking some air on a bench in the south corner of the
garden – a beautiful retreat she had created, all bowered over with
her favourite roses. I had brought her a cup of broth and she had
kept me by her, talking, as she had not done in an age, about pleasant
trivialities such as whether the iris clumps could do with dividing.

Mr. Mompellion saw us there and came striding swiftly from the
stableyard. He had ridden from the Gordon farm, where he had been
tending to matters left unresolved since Urith Gordon's death. Since
the Gordons were but tenant farmers, and since John Gordon, in his
fit, had destroyed all his chattel, there was little to trouble about in
terms of an estate. But neighbours had felt uneasy about all the crosses
Gordon had fashioned and had not known how to deal with them.
The rector had deemed that they should be burned, prayerfully and
with respect, and had gone himself to see to it. It was from this task
that he had returned.

The day was very warm, and as the rector settled himself beside
her on the garden bench, Elinor waved her hands before her face
playfully.

'Husband, you reek of woodsmoke and horse sweat! Let Anna
warm some water for your toilet!'

'Very well,' he said, jumping to his feet again and smiling. I turned
to do as she bade me. As I withdrew into the rectory, I heard him
speaking to Elinor in a most animated voice. Presently, when I carried
out a basin and some cloths, he was gesticulating broadly.

'I don't know why it did not come to me before this,' he said.

'But as I stood there, offering a prayer over those fiery crosses, I saw it so clearly, it was as if God Himself had placed the truth of it into my heart!'

'Let us pray that it is so,' said Elinor, her face ardent.

She rose then, and the two of them walked off along the path, side by side, leaving me standing there, forgotten. After a moment, I set the things down on the bench and went back inside to my tasks. Whatever engrossed them so, I thought, flinging a washclout into a pail, I would learn of it when they saw fit to tell me. But as I scrubbed hard upon the gritstones, there was a bitterness in my mouth, as if I'd chewed upon a fruit with sour pith.

T he next day was Sunday, and I learned along with everyone else in the village what it was that Michael Mompellion believed that God had shown him.

'To save our lives, my friends, I believe we must undertake here a great burning. We must shed ourselves of our worldly goods – all that we can of what our hands have touched and our bodies worn, all that we have breathed upon. Let us gather these things and bring them here, and then scour our houses as the Hebrews are commanded to do to mark the feast of their deliverance from Pharaoh. After, let us gather here this night and offer up our goods with our prayers to God for our own deliverance.'

I saw the faces frowning and the heads shaking around the Delf, for people had already lost so much that further sacrifice such as the rector proposed sat ill with them. For myself, I thought of young George Viccars rising himself from his deathbed and croaking 'Burn it all!' If I had done so, that very day, burned his workbox and all those half-sewn garments made from the cloth sent up here from

London, I wondered how many of us might have been spared.

This thought racked me so that I did not have the wit to concentrate on Mr. Mompellion's words, so I cannot recount how it was that he brought the villagers to a reluctant agreement. I know he spoke of Urith Gordon and how the Plague had struck her down after she had accepted those goods, offered in kindness, of clothing and effects from houses visited by Plague. I know he spoke about the cleansing power of fire and its use by men from the beginning of time as a symbol of rebirth. I know that he spoke, as always, with eloquence and force, and that he used his beautiful voice as an instrument fashioned by God for just such a purpose. Yet we were, all of us, weary of words. What had they brought us, after all?

As the afternoon wore on, the pile for the burning grew only slowly. The rector and Elinor, of course, set the example, carrying out many of their possessions. But even Elinor quailed when it came to the library, and she declared that she could not bring herself to burn the books, 'For though there may be Plague seeds within them, yet also may there be the knowledge to rid us of Plague, just that we have not yet got the wit to rightly read the way.'

As for me, there was one thing with which I could not part: the tiny jerkin I had made for Jamie in his first winter and had been saving for Tom when he grew big enough to wear it. This I hid away, embarrassed by my weakness, and gathered up my scant stuff to consign to the flames. It seemed odd, to be scrubbing and sweeping on the Lord's Day, but the rector had spoken with such conviction that even the ordinary business of cleaning house seemed somehow to have become sacramental. I boiled cauldron after cauldron, first at the rectory and then at my cottage, and scalded tables, chairs, every board and stone of those dwellings.

I was exhausted when we gathered at the Delf at dusk. I gazed at the sad pile of belongings – the sum of such meagre lives. For the first time in many months, I thought of the Bradfords and all their rich possessions locked up in the lonely hush of Bradford Hall. I supposed the Bradfords, safe in their Oxford sanctuary, were the only family from this village left whole. I imagined them, returning one day, sitting at their fine table with all their linens and silver. I saw the colonel's fat fingers drumming upon the table, impatient for his meal, while the ghost of Maggie Cantwell sobbed silently in the shadows. Perhaps, by then, we would be an entire village of ghosts and not even the Bradfords would dare to venture here, even for the sake of their big house and all its fine things.

We had been stripped bare indeed. At the base of the pyre stood the crib – hewn with such love and joyful expectation – that the Livesedge child had died in. There were hose lying limp that had held the muscled calves of strong young miners. There was much bedding, straw-filled pallets that once had provided sweet rest. All these humble things, waiting mute for the torch, spoke to me of the other losses that could not be piled up and regarded: the daily gestures of tenderness between man and wife; the peace in a mother's heart at the sight of her sleeping babe; the unique and private memories of all the many dead.

Michael Mompellion stood near the rock outcrop that was his pulpit. He held a flaming brand high in his right hand. The pile of belongings rose before him, and we stood below it, ranged yards apart from one another as always. 'Lord God Almighty,' he cried, his voice resonating through the Delf, 'as it once pleased You to accept burnt offerings from Your children in Israel, so may it please You to accept these things from us, Your suffering flock. Use this fire to cleanse our hearts as well as our homes, and deliver us at last from the wrath of the disease that assaults us.'

He plunged the brand into the straw spilling from a mattress, and the flames licked greedily upwards. It was a clear night, crisp and windless, a night such as are more common here in midwinter than high summer. The fire poured aloft in a twisting column of red and gold, hot sparks leaping wildly as if to join with the cold, white blaze of the stars. The heat seared my face, drying the tears on my cheeks. We sang then, against the roar of the burning, the Psalm that we had sung countless times since the Plague came:

> 'Thou shalt not be afraid of the terror by night,
>   nor for the arrow that flieth by day,
>   nor for the pestilence that walketh in darkness,
>   nor for the destruction that wasteth at noonday.
>   A thousand shall fall at thy side,
>   And ten thousand at thy right hand,
>   But it shall not come near thee . . .'

Once, we had sung these words with such conviction. I remembered how the music of our singing had soared in the church. Now, our voices were so many fewer, so tired and broken, dragging through the notes by rote. Because we stood so far apart from one another, not all could keep a common tempo, and some lost the pitch, so that our hymn became, verse by verse, more untidy and discordant.

As we sang, the objects in the heart of the blaze lost their singularity and became dark shapes merely, foils for the swirling brightness. For a moment, the black areas within the flames fell into a form that resembled the voids in a skull. The image alarmed me, and I blinked; when I looked again, it was gone.

Between the singing and the crackling of the fire, we did not hear the woman's cries until she was amongst us. There was a stir behind me, and I turned to see young Brand Rigney and the Merrills' nearest neighbour, Robert Snee, dragging a struggling figure between them up to the edge of the blaze. The woman was clad all in black, with a black veil tied around her head and falling down over her face. The singing stopped abruptly, as the two young men forced her forwards and flung her onto the ground in front of Michael Mompellion. Brand reached down then and pulled back the veil. It was Aphra.

'What is the meaning of this?' demanded the rector, as Elinor reached down to assist Aphra to her feet. Aphra pushed the black cloth back from her face and peered around wildly, as if she were searching for a bolt-hole through the crowd, but Brand lay a hand hard on her shoulder.

'Here is the "ghost" whose visitations have been chousing all of us!' Brand cried. 'I caught her, all clad as you see in these black weeds, hiding in the woods near the Boundary Stone, trying to frighten my sister, Charity, into parting with a shilling for a charm to fend the Plague away from young Seth.' He flung down a strip of fabric all awkwardly scrawled with foreign words, just such as Elinor had taken from the neck of Margaret Livesedge's dead baby. He held it up for a moment for all to see, and then dropped it, grinding it into the dirt with his boot.

'Shame!' yelled a woman's voice in the crowd. Looking around, I saw that it was Kate Talbot, her face awash with grief. 'Thief!' cried Tom Mowbray. The whole congregation erupted then, hurling insults at Aphra, who dropped to her knees and hid her face in her hands as the spittle and clods of earth began to fly.

'Dunk her!' someone called. 'To the stocks!' yelled another voice.

If the rector doesn't do something, and quickly, I thought, this crowd will become a mob, and unslakable. We were all of us like wounded animals, our hurts so raw and our fear so great that we would lash out at anyone, especially someone who had acted as evilly as Aphra. I was filled with disgust and anger and felt the urge myself to hurl spittle upon her. I looked round then, I do not know quite why, and saw at the edge of the crowd the tiny, tear-streaked figure of Aphra's daughter, Faith, her mouth open in a wail that no one could hear for all their own angry din. I turned my back then on the jeering faces and pointing fingers and ran to the child and gathered her into my arms. Whatever was going to happen at the Delf, I did not want that little girl, who was, after all, my half-sister and only surviving blood-kin, to witness it. The child was too shocked to struggle as I carried her away. We were halfway up the hill to the path, but the rector's voice, rising over the clamour of the crowd, carried clearly all across that basin-shaped dell.

'Silence! Do not you desecrate this sacred place – this, our church – with such unholy cursing!'

To my surprise, they all did fall silent then, and I turned to hear what next he would say.

'The charges against this woman are grave, indeed, and they will be heard, and she will answer them. But not here, not now. That is tomorrow's business. Go now to your homes, and pray to God to accept the offering we have made this night and to hear our prayer for His divine mercy.'

There was much muttering then, but the people, accustomed to obeying, did as he said. I took Faith home to my cottage, where the child tossed and whimpered all through the night, wandering in nightmare landscapes into which I could not follow her. For myself, I snatched at threads of sleep, and when I awoke, it was to the sour smell of smouldering ashes.

W ho am I to blame Michael Mompellion for what happened that night?

No one man, no matter how wise or well-intentioned, can ever judge perfectly in all matters. That night, he erred, and erred grievously, and grievously indeed did he pay for it. I believe it was because his opinion of young Brand was so high. He remembered Brand's brave loyalty to Maggie Cantwell in her calamity, and he had been proud of the way the youth had stepped into the role of brother to Charity and Seth, taking up the responsibilities of the Merrill farm after Jakob Merrill died.

Since Brand and Robert had uncovered Aphra's crime, the rector charged them with confining her until her hearing the next day. He did not think to tell them how she should be confined, nor to admonish them against taking her punishment into their own hands. But the young men's wrath was so hot that the idea, when it occurred to Robert, seemed to them in their bitterness an apt one.

Robert Snee kept pigs on his farm. He was a good farmer and had contrived many clever methods to raise his yields. One of his innovations was a way of turning swine shit quickly into useful manure. His practice was to muck out the slops and droppings of the pens together with the spent straw of the stableyard into a deep cavern in the limestone – a natural cistern set conveniently into the side of the hill. He had fashioned a gutter in the low side of the cavern from which he could spud the well-rotted manure into his barrow for spreading.

It was into this lightless, stinking pit that Brand and Robert threw Aphra. Later, when I saw the place, I could not imagine how she survived the night there. The stench was caustic, scouring the throat and chest. The muck lapped, brown and frothy and alive, high against the limestone – at least high enough, as I judged, that Aphra would have had to tilt her head to keep the slops from splashing into her mouth at the slightest movement. Yet since the manure on which she stood was only semi-solid, it was impossible to be still, for to keep from sinking deeper meant constantly scrambling for handholds in the slimy rock wall. While her muscles ached from the effort, and her chest burned from the rank air, Aphra must have used every shred of her will to keep her consciousness, for had she succumbed to a faint she would have smothered and drowned.

The woman they dragged out of that pit and brought to the village green the next morning was not Aphra but a gibbering, broken thing. The two young men had tried to clean her, pouring bucket after bucket of icy well water over her, so that she was wet through and shivering. But still she stank, giving off a reek that hit you halfway across the green. Her skin, where it had been immersed all night, was all broken out in blebs. She was too weak and exhausted to stand and so lay on the grass, all curled up on herself and whimpering like a newborn.

Elinor wept when she beheld her. Michael Mompellion balled his hand into a fist and advanced on Brand and Robert Snee, so that I thought he would strike them. Brand was pale as a ghost and ill with guilt at what he had done. Even Robert Snee, a harder sort of man, looked at the ground and would meet no one's eyes.

I had long disliked the spectacles that were enacted on this green, where our fellow villagers had been set in the stocks for swearing or scolding or ungodly behaviours. To be sure, our stocks were nothing so fearful as the Bakewell pillory. In that market town, where people came and went without deep ties one to another, to be pilloried was to be a target of rotten fruit or fish heads or any noisome thing the mob could lay a hand to. One woman, set up there for whoring, had lost an eye to some violent missile. In a small place such as this, one could not treat a neighbour so. But to be bound by the ankles in that splintery wood, under hot sun or chill drizzle, enduring hours of disapproving stares and the catcalls of unmannerly children – this, to me, was degradation more than most deserved. Even Reverend Stanley seldom called for sinners to be stocked, and Mr. Mompellion had actively discouraged it.

Some dozen had gathered to see to Aphra's punishment – a large enough number considering our depleted state. Margaret Livesedge's widower, David, was there, no doubt recalling his wife's great hopes from the 'Chaldee charm,' and how cruelly they had been dashed when their babe died still wearing it. There, too, was Kate Talbot, whose costly Abracadabra spell had not saved her husband. The Merrill children and the Mowbrays had come; simple folk seeking simple justice. There were some few others, also, but if they had been deceived out of their coppers by the so-called ghost, not all were of a mind to admit to it.

I think that these accusers had gathered ready to mete out a harsh punishment. But when Brand and Robert brought Aphra, so abject and miserable, they all of them seemed to lose the appetite for it, and one by one they melted away. The rector dropped into a crouch near to Aphra and bent his head close to hers. He spoke quietly to her, asking her to make restitution of the money she had choused, and gave her a penance. I could not tell whether she understood any part of what he said. The rector asked for a cart to carry her home, and Elinor and I rode with her. We had to hold her up, so weak was she. Because she cried out for the child Faith, we stopped at my cottage to fetch her. All the rest of the way, the child, wide-eyed and silent, cowered by her mother, clinging to her thigh.

Inside Aphra's croft we heated water and tried to bathe her, prising the manure from under her fingernails and salving her weeping sores. She submitted to our tending for a short while, but as her wits began to return to her, so, too, came her temper, and she began muttering fierce insults upon us, ordering us to go away and calling us all manner of ill things, which I'll not set down here.

I did not want to leave her so, nor leave the child Faith with her. 'Stepmother,' I said quietly, 'I pray you, let me take the child for a day or two until you are recovered in your strength.'

'Oh, no, you sly doxy!' she shrieked, clutching wildly at the frightened little girl. 'Pox take you and your schemes! You think I don't know?' She dropped her voice and stared at me. 'You think I can't see through you? You're not my stepdaughter now. Oh, no. You're too fine for the likes o' me. You're *her* creature,' she said, pointing a trembling finger at Elinor. 'That dry-snatched, barren scarecrow would steal my last babe, wouldn't she?' Elinor flinched. She had turned white, even beyond her natural pallor. She grasped at a chair-back as if she felt faint.

Aphra's voice was rising again, the words tumbling from her lips so fast I could barely make them out. 'That's what you're after, I know it. I know how it'll be. I'll not have you blacken me to m'own daughter. I'll not have your lies poured into her ears.'

It seemed clear to me that Aphra's agitation was only causing Faith further upset. I signalled to Elinor, and we went from there, although our attempts at a kind leave-taking did not stop the curses flying after us.

I worried all morning about the child. Although Faith was three years old, I had never heard her utter a word. If it hadn't been that she seemed to understand what was said to her, I would have taken her for deaf or simple. Instead, I had begun to believe that fear – of my father, while he lived, and of Aphra's oddity since – had blenched the will to speak away from her. In the afternoon I walked back out to the croft with a large whisket of food and more ointment for Aphra's sores. She refused to open the door to me and cursed me foully, until I finally left the food on the step and went away. It was a like story the next day, and the next. Each day, Faith would stand silently at the window, her eyes wide and grave, regarding me as her mother cursed in ways not fit for her to hear. But on the third day, as I stood in the garth, I did not see the child. And when I asked Aphra where Faith was, her only answer was a high-pitched, keening chant in words I could not fathom.

I went home then and called on my neighbour Mary Hadfield. I begged her to go to Aphra in my place, to see if someone less close to her could be of more use. Mary shook her head and looked doubtful.

'I mislike this request, Anna. I will not say I don't. That Aphra tried to pass herself off as the Devil's creature, and if she doesn't want the help her own stepdaughter offers, then I say let the Devil take her.'

I implored her not to feel so and begged her to think of the child, who was innocent and at risk. At this she reconsidered and agreed to do as I asked. But when she returned it was with no better success than I had had, for Aphra had once again refused to open the door and had unleashed a rant on poor Mary so fierce and vile that she vowed never to go near the croft again, child or no.

I found I could not rest for worrying about Faith. The next day, I again caught no sight of her, nor the next, so on the evening of that day I sat up late and made my way up to the croft in darkness. I do not know what I hoped to accomplish, other than that perhaps the surprise to Aphra of being woken from her sleep might give me a few moments when her guard was down, in which time I might gain some sense of how Faith fared.

But Aphra was not asleep. From far off I could see that the croft was lit from within by a goodly blaze at the hearth, which itself was odd as the night was so warm. When I drew closer, I could see darting, leaping shadows through the window, and as I came closer still I realized that Aphra was dancing, leaping before her fire and throwing her arms upward as lunatics do when seized by a fit. I had not meant to be stealthy, or to spy, but since the window was uncovered I stood in the shadow of a laurel bush to see if I could determine what it was that this odd behaviour might signify. She had sheared off her hair almost to her scalp and stood in a filthy shift that showed a starved, fleshless body beneath. She plunged and leapt, barking out a nonsense chant that rose in pitch to a piercing cry: 'Arataly, rataly, ataly, taly, aly, ly . . . eeeeeeeee!' She darted then towards the fire, seizing out the ends of andirons that had lain in the blaze, and placed them on the earthen floor so as to form an X. She prostrated herself four times, in each notch of the figure, and then reached up her arms as if in supplication. She seemed to draw something down to her from the rafters, but what it was I could not at first say. She held the dark thing in her two hands, but as her back was towards me I could not make it out, only that it seemed to move and be alive.

I will own it: I became afraid then. I do not believe in witchcraft nor spells, neither in incubus nor succubus nor familiar spirits. But I do believe in evil thoughts – and in madness. And as the snake slithered out of Aphra's hands and wound itself round her waist, my impulse was to run away as swiftly and as silently as I could.

And yet I did not run but stood rooted there, desperate to get Faith away from the lunatic that her mother had now become. I believe it was the dregs of my own mother-courage – the force within a woman that will drive her to do that for her babe that she would not dream was within her power to do – that impelled me to fling myself against that door so that it gave way and left me standing there, confronting Aphra and her snake.

She screamed when she saw me, and I might have screamed, too, had my breath not been stolen away by the stench, which was unspeakable. I knew without looking at the corpse that the child was long dead. In the corner, Aphra had Faith's body strung up like a puppet, suspended by the wrists and ankles from the rafters. The child's head tilted gracefully to the side, and a curtain of hair hid her ravaged face. Aphra had tried to mask the dead, black Plague flesh with some kind of chalky paste.

'For pity's sake, Aphra, cut her down from there and let her lie in peace!'

'Pity?' she shrieked. 'Who has pity? And where, pray tell me, may peace be found?' She hissed then and flew at me with the serpent in her hand. I am not, as a rule, afraid of snakes, but as the firelight blazed red in those two shining eyes and the forked tongue flicked at me, I will own that I quailed. There was nothing I could do for Faith, or for Aphra, so I gave way to my craven impulse and fled from that place as fast as my legs would propel me.

T he rector went to the croft that night, and again, with Elinor, the next morning. But Aphra had the door barred by then, and the window covered over. She no longer paused in her frenzied chanting to hurl abuse at them but simply danced on as if they were not there. The rector stood outside and said the customary prayers for the soul of Faith, as Aphra's unearthly voice rose, drowning out his words with chants in some heathenish, incomprehensible tongue. At the rectory, there was discussion of bringing a party of men to break the door and bring the child's body out, but the rector decided against doing so, for the risk to the men from Aphra in her distemper and the corpse in its decay he deemed too great.

'It is not as if we can do aught for the child but bury her,' he said. 'And that we can do in due time, when Aphra's frenzy has exhausted her.' There was another concern that he did not speak, but Elinor confided it to me. Michael Mompellion did not trust the men he might take to the croft to understand Aphra's behaviour as a lunatic malady, merely, and he did not want to unleash the kind of fear and rumour that encounters with a witch and her snake familiar might bring to the surface. I knew in my heart that he was wise, but the image of that child's tortured corpse was vivid to me. It robbed me of sleep for many nights – and does so still.

Deliverance

I did not go to Aphra's croft again. I told myself that with the child dead I had no useful business there. My heart whispered that I should not abandon Aphra to her madness, but I did not listen to it. For the truth is, I did not feel that my grip upon my own reason was strong enough to withstand the horrors of that house. And now, of course, when there is no way to know whether it would have made a jot of difference, I have had many days and nights in which to blame myself for my decision.

Within a very little time, I had schooled my mind to avoid the matter of Aphra entirely. I was helped in this by having much else to reflect upon. For during the fortnight that followed the great burning, something happened in the village. At first, none of us marked it. Then, when we began to do so, we none of us spoke of it. Superstition, hope, disbelief – all these made pact with our old friend, fear, and prevented us from doing so.

I said that something happened. But in truth what I began to take note of was the lack of certain happenings. For after the last Sunday in July, we heard no word of new coughs, or fevers, or Plague sores. For the first sennight I did not, as I said, mark this, for I was still concerned with a number who were already some days ill and approaching death. But by the next Sunday, when we gathered at the

Delf, I did my habitual count of persons and was surprised to find that all who had been there when last we gathered for worship were there again. For the first time in almost a year, there was not one newly missing face.

Michael Mompellion must have marked this, too, but he did not speak of it directly. Rather, he preached a sermon on the Resurrection. The rain had been siling down for much of the preceding week, and the bare, blackened circle where our goods had been consigned to the flames was hazed all over with a hopeful wash of new green. The rector drew all our eyes there.

'See, my friends? Life endures. And as fire cannot quench the living spark in a humble patch of grass, neither can our souls be quenched by death, nor our spirits by suffering.'

T he next morning, I went out to my yard to search for an egg and found a strange cock discomposing my hens. He was a bold fellow and did not budge when I shooed at him but stepped pluckily towards me, titling his fine red comb and regarding me with a sideways eye.

'Well, odd's fish! You're Andrew Merrick's cockerel, if I'm not much mistaken!' As I spoke, he fluttered up onto the well windlass and let forth a mighty peal to the morning. 'And what might you be doing back here, my feathery friend, when your master sits and bides on yonder lonely peak?' He made me no answer but flew off then, not, as I had thought, in the direction of the hermit-hut on Sir William Hill, but east rather, towards Merrick's long-abandoned cottage.

How did the bird know it was safe to return to his old roost? It will ever be a mystery. But later that day Andrew Merrick too came home, his beard grown long and bushy as an Old Testament prophet.

He came, he said, because he trusted in the judgment of his bird.

Shall I say we rejoiced as the conviction grew in man and beast that the Plague was truly gone from us? No, we did not rejoice. For the losses were too many and the damage to our spirits too profound. For every one of us who still walked upon the Earth, two of us lay under it. Everywhere we went, we passed by the sorry, makeshift graves of our friends and neighbours. We were all of us also exhausted, for each person who lived had, in the course of the year, taken up the duties and tasks of two or three of the dead. Some days, even the effort of thought seemed burdensome.

But that is not to say there was no lightening in even the heaviest heart, as one by one it came to us that at last our losses were stanched and that we ourselves were spared. For life is not nothing, even to the grieving. Surely humankind has been fashioned so, otherwise how would we go on?

A t the rectory, there arose a difference between Michael Mompellion and Elinor, the first I had ever marked. She believed he should hold a service of Thanksgiving for our deliverance; he held that the time was yet not ripe and that the risk of premature speaking outweighed any benefit that might be had in owning publicly what we all of us now in our hearts believed.

'For what will be the effect if I am wrong?' I overheard him say to her. I was passing through the hallway by the parlour and something in his tone arrested me, so that I stopped and listened, even as I knew I should not.

'If we have done anything at all here, we have succeeded in confining this agony amongst us. For there has been no case of Plague in all of Derbyshire that can be traced to our village. Why risk all we have sacrificed for in the haste of a sennight or two?'

'But, my love,' Elinor replied to him, her voice soft but insistent. 'There are people here – like the widows Hancock and Hadfield and the orphans such as Merry Wickford and Jane Martin and so many others – who have seen every member of their families into their graves. They have suffered enough. Why, when I know you do believe the Plague is gone, must you prolong it? They should not have to bide here, in their loneliness, for one day longer than needs be. They should be free to go on to their kin, or to have their kin seek them here, so that they may begin to find what love and comfort and new life that they can.'

'Do you not think that I consider them? I, who have considered nothing else these many wretched months?' His voice, as he said this last, had a bitter edge to it that I had never heard him use in their speech together. 'Despair is a cavern beneath our feet, and we teeter on its very brink. If I speak, and am mistaken, and the Plague is with us still, would you have me plunge these people into depths from which I cannot hope to fetch them back?'

I heard the rustle of her dress as she turned and moved towards the door. 'As you judge best, husband. But I implore you, do not make these people wait forever. Not everyone is made as firm of purpose as you.'

As she passed through the doorway, I withdrew into the library. She did not see me as she swept by, but I saw her, her lovely face twisted, struggling to hold back tears.

I do not know how it was finally decided, but only a matter of days after I overheard that conversation, Elinor whispered to me that the rector had fixed upon the second Sunday in August, provided no new cases blighted us beforehand. There wasn't any formal announcement, but word passed somehow, swiftly, through the village. When the nominated day arrived at last, we gathered in the Delf's stippled sunshine for what we fervently hoped would be the last time. People approached one another without fear and shook hands as they had not done, stood close, and chatted easily as they waited for the rector.

He came at last, wearing a white surplice edged in a lace so fine it seemed like foam. He had never yet worn such a thing – coming as he did into the pulpit vacated by a Puritan, he had chosen to bear himself plainly so as not to inflame passions on matters that he deemed insignificant to the manner of our worship. Elinor, by his side, was also clad in white: a simple gown of summer cotton embroidered delicately with white silk figures. Her arms were laden with blossoms that she'd gathered, all on a whim, from her garden and from the overgrown hedges along the path from the rectory. There were delicate pink mallow flowers and dark blue larkspur, deep-throated lilies, and sprays of fragrant roses. As the rector began to speak, she beamed at him, her face all lit, and in the dappled sunlight her bright, pale hair glowed around her face like a coronet. 'She looks like a bride,' I thought. But funerals, too, have flowers, and winding sheets are white.

'Let us give thanks –' That was all Michael Mompellion had time to say. The shriek that answered him was a raw, ragged thing, a piercing sound that rent the air and echoed around the high, curved walls of the Delf. Only after it stopped could I realize there were words, English words, embedded in the noise.

'For whaaaaat?' she shrieked again.

Mompellion's head had gone up sharply at the first cry, and now we all turned to look in the direction of his gaze.

Any one of us could have stopped Aphra. I could have done it.

The ravages of her madness had thinned her down to a wisp. To be sure, in her right hand she had a knife, and as she swept by me, waving it in wide, erratic curves, I recognized it as the large miner's knife she had pulled with such effort from the decaying sinews of my father's hand. Her other arm was occupied, clutching the maggoty remnant of her daughter's corpse, and so to come at her from the left should have been a simple matter. But instead of falling upon her, we all of us fell back, stumbling in our haste to put as much distance between ourselves and the horror of her as we could.

'Mom-pell-ion!' She screamed the word as a crake cries, from some deep place within her from which human voices are not usually drawn.

He, alone, did not back away, but answering to her call, stepped towards her, down from his rocky pediment, and steadily, calmly across the green sward that separated them. He walked towards her as one would walk to greet a lover. His arms, as he raised them, lifted the lace of his surplice in a wide arc. The breeze billowed the delicate stuff. It's a web and he'll catch her in it – so was the mad thought that fell into my mind. Aphra ran now, the knife raised above her head.

He stepped right into the path of it, his arms locking round her, gathering her to him as a father will sweep up a child grown wild with high spirits. His large hand circled her frail wrist, and though I could see the strain in her forearm, his strength was such that she had no chance of breaking his grip. Elinor ran towards both of them, dropping her armful of blossoms and opening her own arms wide. If it were not for the knife, you would have thought they were a family, meeting again after a long separation.

Mompellion was speaking to Aphra, his voice a low and soothing hum. I could not hear the words he said, but slowly the tension seemed to go out of her body, and as he eased his grip, I could see her shoulders heave with sobbing. Elinor was stroking Aphra's face with her left hand, while with her right she reached up to take the knife.

It might have been all right; it might have ended there. But the rector's arms, so tight upon Aphra, also encircled the remains of Faith's corpse. The pressure of that grip proved too much for the fragile bones. I heard the snap: a dry sound like a chicken's wishbone breaking. The little skull popped free of the spine and fell to the grass, where it rolled back and forth, the empty eyeholes staring.

I turned away in revulsion, and so I never saw exactly how it was that Aphra, wild in her new frenzy, landed her blows as she did. I know that it was an instant's work, merely. An instant's work, to take two lives and leave another ruined.

The wound on Elinor's neck was a wide, curved thing. For a second it was just a thin red line, upturned like a smile. But then the blood began spurting in bright bursts, streaking her white dress red. She crumpled to the ground, where the scattered flowers she had carried received her like a bier.

Aphra had turned the knife on herself and sunk it to the hilt, deep into her chest. Yet somehow she staggered, upright still, the uncanny strength of the lunatic keeping her on her feet. She lurched to where her baby's skull lay and then dropped to her knees, reached down, and with the most exquisite tenderness, gathered it up in her two hands and pressed it to her lips.

Leaf-Fall,
1666

Apple-picking Time

They buried Faith in the garth of my father's croft, beside the place where her brothers lay. I asked them, and then begged, to lay Aphra there as well. But the men would neither meet my eyes nor listen to my pleading. None wanted her body to lie within the precincts of the village. In the end, young Brand came to my aid. Together we took her corpse up to the moors and Brand toiled to dig her a grave in the rocky earth beside my father's cairn.

Elinor we buried in the churchyard. Since the Plague was past, there was no reason not to do so. Young Micha Milne, the son of our dead mason, graved the stone as best he could. But the boy had been but a beginner in the craft when the Plague took his father and was not much skilled. I had to show him where he had mistaken two letters in Elinor's name. He hacked out the error and patched it as best he could.

It was Mr. Stanley who prayed at the graveside, for Michael Mompellion was not capable to do it. He had expended the last of his strength in the Delf, fighting those who tried, finally, to lead him away from Elinor's body. He had clung to her till nightfall and nothing anyone could say would budge him from the spot. In the end, it was the old rector, Mr. Stanley, who commanded the men to remove him by force, so that Elinor's body could be decently tended.

That, I did. And afterwards, I continued to serve her as best I could, by following the wishes she had spoken when she lay sick with what we had all taken for the Plague. *Be a friend to . . . my Michael,* she had said. How could she have thought that he would let me be so? I did, instead, what was in my power to do. I served him. Most of the time, I might as well have been a shade, for all he noticed me. It was as if he commenced upon a journey at the moment of Elinor's death, and every day he moved farther and farther away, seeking for some refuge in the recesses of his own mind.

Attending upon Mr. Mompellion's grief, at least, gave me a way of managing my own. Walking each day where Elinor had walked and disciplining my mind to think, at every hour, what it was that she might do or say was an exercise that brought me a measure of mental peace. At the least, it cleared my mind of the burden of my own thoughts. As long as I could fill my days in emulation of Elinor, I did not have to closely consider my own state, or my own bleak-seeming future.

The day after her death he left the rectory, and I followed him, fearing that in his dark state he might mean to throw himself off the Edge. Instead, he walked up to the moors above Mompellion's Well, where his friend Mr. Holbroke was waiting, by what prior arrangement I do not know. There, he dictated the last of his letters of the Plague year. The first was to tell the earl that he believed the pestilence was fled at last and to beg that the roads to the village be reopened. The second was to Elinor's father, his patron, bearing the news of her death. Afterwards, he returned to the rectory, and he has not left it since.

The second morning, I arrived at the rectory not long after sunrise, hoping to be at my tasks before he arose so that he would not suffer the empty silence of that large house. Instead, I found him standing on the garden path, near a spot where Elinor had liked to cut flowers. I have no idea how long he had stood there, but later, when I carried fresh linens to his room, I found his bed unslept upon.

He did not move as I came up the path towards him, nor raise his eyes, nor greet me. As I could hardly push past him, I stood there, too, and gazed with him at the tumble of late-summer roses falling in bright cascades across the old bricks of the garden wall.

'She loved these, especially,' I said in a whisper. 'Sometimes I used to think it was because they were in her image, all pale and creamy, with just a hint of a blush.'

He turned to me sharply then and raised a hand towards my face, so swiftly that I flinched with the instinct of a child who has been struck too often. But of course he did not mean to hit me, only hush me. His fingers hovered near my lips. 'Do not speak, I beg you,' he said, and his voice grated, like a rasp. Then he turned and walked unsteadily towards the house, and it was I who was left on the pathway, fretting at my indiscretion.

It was a like story the next day. When I arrived for my work I did not find him in his room. Once again, there was no sign that anyone had slept there. I searched for him in the library and the parlour and then in the stable, hoping he had taken the horse out for some healthful exercise. But Anteros was there, strutting, frustrated in his unaccustomed confinement.

It was midmorning before I found him. This time, he was standing, still and silent, in Elinor's bedchamber, peering at the place where her head had rested, as if he could still discern some impression of its shape lingering there. He did not turn or move when I opened the door. His legs were trembling slightly, perhaps from the effort of standing so long immobile. There were beads of sweat upon his brow. I said nothing but came quietly to his side and took his elbow, and, with the slightest pressure, steered him away from the bed and back to his own room. He made no effort to resist me but let me lead him, saying nothing. He gave a great sigh as he sank into his chair. I fetched a ewer of steaming water and bathed his face. The scratching of bristles against the cloth brought sudden, sharp memories of Sam Frith, of how I had teased him when he came home all unshaven after long days underground and turned my face away from his kisses until he let me smooth his skin with the blade he kept for the purpose, honed to the keenest edge.

The rector had not shaved since the day of Elinor's death. Hesitantly, I asked if he would have me do it for him. He closed his eyes and made no answer. So I fetched the things and set to work. Such a different face from Sam's. Sam Frith had a face that was as open and blank as an unsown field. The rector's was all scored with expression lines and haggard now with exhaustion and grief. I stood behind his chair and bent over him, my fingertips, slippery in the creamy lather, sliding gently over his skin. I wiped my hands then, carefully, and set to work with the blade. I laid my left hand along his cheek, to hold the skin taut. My face was just inches from his. As I worked, a long strand of my hair came loose and fell from my cap. It brushed the side of his throat. He opened his eyes and returned my gaze. I drew back. The blade slipped from my hand and rang against the bowl. I felt the prickling of a blush steal over me, and I knew I could not continue. I handed him the blade and brought a glass so that he could finish the job, then I backed out of the room, saying something about fetching a dish of broth. It took me some time to become composed enough to bring it to him.

After that, he ceased to move around the house at all, keeping to his room day and night. I fetched Mr. Stanley at the end of the first sennight, hoping to do some good by it. The old man left the rector's room much agitated. As I brought him his hat, he seemed to be struggling with himself. Finally, he turned to me and, hesitatingly, began to probe me on the rector's mental state.

I was thrown into confusion by this. Not – as once would have been the case – because I thought my own opinions worthless. But rather because I did not feel it was my place to betray Mr. Mompellion's private behaviours, even to well-meaning Mr. Stanley.

'I am sure I cannot judge, sir.'

The old man muttered then, more to himself than to me: 'I think grief has undone him, yes; quite undone him. I don't think he comprehended any part of what I said to him. Why else would he laugh when I advised him to accept God's will?'

Mr. Stanley was so concerned that he returned the next day and the next, but Mr. Mompellion would not have me admit him. When he came the third time, I went up to bring the news to the rector. The lines about his mouth deepened with annoyance. He stirred from his chair and paced the length of his room.

'I would have you take a message to Mr. Stanley, if you are capable. Repeat this, please, Anna: *Falsus in uno, falsus in omnibus.*'

I repeated the Latin, and as I did so, it fell into my heart that I could grasp the meaning. Before I could school my tongue, I blurted it aloud: 'Untrue in one thing, untrue in everything.'

Mr. Mompellion turned sharply, his brows raised. '*How* can you possibly know that?'

'If you please, Rector, I have gathered a little Latin, a very little, from the great study we made here this past year . . . the medical books, you see, are mostly Latin, and we, that is . . .'

He stopped me then, not wanting me to speak her name. 'I see, I see. Then you may give Mr. Stanley the message and beg him to be so kind as to call upon me no more.'

It is one thing to know the meanings of words; it is another to grasp their intent. I had no idea what it was that Mr. Mompellion was trying to convey to the old man. But when I passed on the message, Mr. Stanley's face turned stern. He left directly – and did not come back.

I had much to do, outside my hours at the rectory. As well as caring for my sheep, the villagers looked to me still for tonics and small remedies, and for this work I had to keep the Gowdies' garden, cutting the summer's herbs and hanging them to dry whenever I had a spare moment to attend to it. I wondered if fate had marked me to be the next in the long line of women that Anys had once spoken of, who tended those plants and knew their virtues. The thought oppressed me, and I turned from it. The Gowdie garden would never again be a tranquil place for me. There were too many memories there: of Elinor, puzzling over a handful of wort and turning to me, her brow creased with a question; of old Mem, her skilled hands twisting twine around bunches of fresh-picked herbs; and of Anys, who should have been my friend . . . These memories themselves were no bad thing, but they led, always, to other recollections: the gargle of Mem's death rattle, the drunken baying of the murderers hauling on the rope that killed Anys, the still, pale body of Elinor, cold under my hands. The mind of a healer, I thought, should not brim so with images of death. And yet some memories cannot be rooted out like weeds, no matter how much one wills to do it.

The village itself reeled on in a stunned condition. It did not spring suddenly back to life with the opening of the roads. Some few fled the place as soon as they might, but most did not. They stayed, moving through their tasks in a weary daze. And hardly any persons from outside had the courage to make the reverse journey. At summer's end, some few relatives of the dead ventured here to claim their inheritances, but for most, the fear that the Plague might yet lurk within our village proved too great.

Mr. Holbroke, from Hathersage, was one of the first to come. I greeted him with gladness, hoping the presence of such an old friend would do something to ease Mr. Mompellion's melancholy. But the rector would not even see him and required me to send him off directly. Day after day, he sat in his chair, rising only to pace the floor. The weeks of his grieving turned to months, and finally, as summer faded into leaf-fall, a season.

For many weeks, I searched for ways to rouse him. I tried to bring scraps of good news. The handfasting of my widowed neighbour, Mary Hadfield, to a well-liked farrier in Stoney Middleton. The sisterly friendship that had begun to blossom between the optimistic little Quaker, Merry Wickford, and the grim and damaged Jane Martin, and how it seemed a healing thing for the spirits of both. But none of this touched him at all.

I begged him to think about his horse, fretting in his stall for want of exercise. I tried to work upon his sense of duty, suggesting that this person or that one might welcome a word from him, of counsel or of prayer. In truth, requests for the rector's attentions arrived seldom. At first I thought this was a natural reticence born of respect for his own great suffering. But then it came to me that many people in the village did not love him for what he had done here during the long months of our ordeal. Some went so far as to whisper blame upon him for their great losses. To others, he was simply the bitter emblem and embodiment of their darkest days. The unfairness of this pained me, and helped me, when I grew dispirited about my work, to deal with him tenderly. For I thought that perhaps he somehow sensed the feelings of the villagers and that this might feed his melancholy.

But despair I did, sometimes, despite my best efforts to be hopeful.

For no matter what I said, whether I couched my requests gently or firmly, he would answer with the same helpless shrug, as if to say he was powerless to do or to feel anything regarding these matters. All the strength that he had possessed, of mind and of person, seemed to be ebbing, steadily. And so we went on, each day as empty and quiet as the one before, until at last I believed that I was just biding my time, bound by Elinor's wishes, until Mr. Mompellion wasted away in his room with myself as the only witness.

A nd then, at apple-picking time, the Bradfords returned to the village. I have already set down how it was I encountered Elizabeth Bradford and how her demand that Mr. Mompellion attend her ailing mother rekindled all the rage he had felt when that family fled from here, abandoning their duty. I have set down, too, my botched attempt to bring him comfort and his flinging of the Bible to the floor.

I can tell you further that I was hard put to it not to run, after I closed the door to his room. There was a vivid red mark on my forearm where he had seized me, and I rubbed at it, angry myself, but also much confused. I left the rectory by the kitchen door and headed without thinking towards the stable.

Before he let fall the Bible, he had almost hissed the words of that beautiful Psalm:

> *Your wife will be like a fruitful vine*
> *Within your house;*
> *Your children will be like olive shoots*
> *Around your table . . .*

His wife had been hacked down in front of him. My olive shoots had been blighted. *Why?* His unasked question roared in my head. Just such a *why* had nagged at my unquiet mind through too many sleepless nights. But that he, too, should be asking it ... *Let her speak direct to God to ask forgiveness ... but I fear she may find Him a poor listener, as many of us here have done.* Could he really have come to believe that all our sacrifice, all our pain and misery, had been for nothing?

I needed solitude, but I couldn't bear the weight of my own confusion. I opened the door to Anteros's stall and slid inside, my back to the wall, holding myself as still as I could. The horse reared once, then stood, blowing and snorting, regarding me sidelong with one large, brown eye. We stayed that way for many minutes. When I judged that he meant me no harm, I eased myself slowly down upon the straw.

'Well, Anteros, I have come to tell you that he is lost, at last,' I said. 'His reason has left him entirely.' That was it, surely. He was mad. There could be no other explanation. The horse seemed to sense my distress, for he had ceased his restless strutting. Every now and then, he raised a hoof and dropped it, as an impatient person might drum his fingers upon a table.

'It's no good waiting for him anymore, my friend,' I said. 'You and I will have to accept that he has given himself up to his darkness. I know, I know; it is hard to credit, after all the strength he has shown us.' From my pocket I drew out a crumpled paper. It was the draft of the letter to Elinor's father that Mr. Mompellion had composed just after her murder. It was the last letter he would dictate so; the last before the roads were opened. I had stood with him that day – afraid to let him out of my sight, yes, but also I must own, afraid to be alone with my own grief. He had had trouble commanding even his powerful voice to call out the words of such a dispatch, and at the end he was piping with the cracked timbre of a boy. As he waved farewell to Mr. Holbroke and turned back towards the rectory, he had crumpled the draft and let it fall from his hand. I had run after and caught it, in case at some later time he desired a record of what he had written.

He had been in a dark mood that day – who would not be? – and yet his faith then had seemed unwavering. In the dim light of the stable, I read the paper again to reassure myself of it, although I made out the hasty scratchings with great difficulty:

> . . . Our dearest dear is gone to her eternal rest and is invested with a Crown of Glory and a garment of immortality that makes her shine like the sun in the firmament of Heaven . . . Dear Sir, let your dying Chaplain recommend this truth to you and your family. That no happiness or solid comfort can be found in this vale of tears, like living a pious life. And pray retain this rule: never do that thing upon which you dare not first ask a blessing of God, upon the success thereof . . .
>
> Sir, pardon the rude style of this paper, and if my head be discomposed you cannot wonder at me; however, be pleased to believe that I am, Dear Sir, your most obliged, most affectionate, and grateful servant . . .

Well, I thought, his head was not so discomposed then as it was now. For I doubt he would have dared to ask the blessing of God on his harsh dismissal of Elizabeth Bradford, or on his desecration of the Bible. If Elinor were here, she would be able to advise me what to do for him. But then if Elinor were here, he would not be in this state. I sat there, breathing the sweet rich scent of horse and hay. Anteros snorted then dropped his massive head to my neck and nuzzled me. Slowly, I lifted my hand and ran it down his long nose.

'Here we are, alive,' I said, 'and you and I will have to make of it what we can.'

He did not shy at my touch but pushed against my hand as if asking for more caresses. Then he raised his head, as if trying to catch the scent of the outside air. If a beast can be said to have an expression such as wistfulness, then that was how Anteros looked to me. 'Let's go then,' I whispered. 'Let's go and live, since we have no choice in it.' I stood up, slowly, and fetched the bridle from its hook. He did not flinch when he saw it. Only an ear twitched, as if to say, What's this? He lowered his head, and I slid it on, gentle as I could. I kept a good hold on him as I lifted the bar to the stable door, though I knew well enough that if he wanted to bolt I would have scant chance to keep him. He tossed his head, flaring his nostrils and breathing the longed-for scent of grass. But he did not strain or strive to throw off my hand. I lay my face against his neck. 'Good,' I said in a low voice. 'Steady for a minute more, and we'll go.'

Out in the courtyard, I mounted him bareback, as I had learned to ride as a child. Those horses had been old or spavined creatures, so the feel of Anteros unsaddled underneath me was a surprise. He was all muscle, gathered like a thunderhead. He could have thrown me sprawling in a second if he'd chosen to, and I was ready for anything, thinking that I'd cling on just as long as I was able. Instead, he danced a little as he felt my weight upon him but waited for my signal. When I clicked my tongue, we were off in a smooth surge. He leapt the wall as neatly as a cat. I barely felt the landing.

I turned his head for the moors and we galloped. The wind rushed by, blowing off my cap and freeing my hair so that it blew out like a banner behind me. The big hooves beat the ground as the blood throbbed in my head. *We live, we live, we live,* said the hoofbeats, and the drumming of my pulse answered them. I was alive, and I was young, and I would go on until I found some reason for it. As

273

I rode that morning, smelling the scent of the hoof-crushed heather, feeling the wind needle my face until it tingled, I understood that where Michael Mompellion had been broken by our shared ordeal, in equal measure I had been tempered and made strong.

I rode for the sake of the movement, not caring where. After a while I found myself in a wide meadow and realized that it was the field of the Boundary Stone. The path that had been so well-trodden throughout our Plague year was already all overgrown. The stone itself was invisible among the high grasses. Easily and easily I brought Anteros to a canter, then a walk, and paced him along the ridge of the spur until I found the stone, marked with its gouged holes. I slid from his back and while he stood, patiently, cropping the pasture, I knelt and pulled the grass away from around the stone. I laid my hands on it and then my cheek. In a score or so of years from now, I thought, someone like me will sit down to rest right here on this stone and her fingers will play idly in those holes, and no one will remember why they were hewn so or the great sacrifice that we made here.

I lifted my face, looked down the spur to Stoney Middleton, and recalled how I had longed to run down there and escape. Now there was no oath holding me. I gathered the reins and remounted Anteros, and we galloped at speed down the slope, barely slowing through the village, galloping fast again into the fields beyond. I am sure that the good citizens of Stoney Middleton did not know what to make of us. The sun was high before I turned Anteros's head for the climb back up to our village. As we neared the Boundary Stone we slowed, that powerful horse easing into a surprisingly soft, sweet trot. He was stepping as sedate as a phaeton pony when we reached the rectory yard.

Michael Mompellion strode out the door in his shirt sleeves, anger and incredulity upon his face. He ran towards us, grasping the horse's bridle. His grey eyes scanned me, and I suddenly became aware that

I was barely decent, riding astride with my skirt tugged up above my placket, my hair loose to my waist, my cap lost upon the moors, my cheeks flushed and misted with sweat.

'Have you,' he said, and his voice rang off the yard stones, 'taken entire leave of your senses?'

I looked down at him from the height of Anteros's broad back. For once, I did not flinch from his stare.

'Have *you?*' was my reply.

Anteros tossed his head, as if to shake Michael Mompellion's hand off his bridle. The rector stared up at me, his eyes now blank as slates. Abruptly, he looked away and let go of the horse, raising his hands to his face and pressing the heels of his palms into his eyes so hard I thought he might maim himself.

'Yes,' he said at last. 'Yes, truly, I think my senses have left me indeed.' At that, he dropped to his knees in that filthy courtyard. I swear, it was Elinor I thought of as I watched him collapse like that: how the sight of him, so utterly abject, would break her heart. Before I knew what I was about, I was off the horse and taking him in my arms, as Elinor surely would. He buried his head in my shoulder, and I held tight to him as one would cling to someone falling from a high place. I could feel the hard muscles of his back through the flimsy stuff of his shirt. I had not held a man so in more than two years. It happened then: a sharp pang of desire pierced me and I moaned. He drew back at that and looked at me. His fingers brushed my face and travelled into my wild hair. He buried his hands in the tangles. His grip tightened, and he drew my mouth to his.

And that is how we were when the stable boy found us. He had been cowering in the tackroom, fearing to be blamed for my wild ride. Now he stood, his eyes wide. We both jumped up and flew apart, putting Anteros's dark bulk between us. But he had seen what he had seen. Somehow I mastered my voice enough to speak.

'So there you are, Master Richard. Kindly see to Anteros. He will want water, and he is calm, I think, sufficient to tolerate a brushing after all this time. See that you do it thoroughly.' I cannot think how I kept my voice from trembling as I said all this. My hands were shaking as I handed him the reins and I walked towards the kitchen, not daring to look behind me. Presently I heard the door open and close and the tread of footsteps going up the stairs. I pressed my hands to my temples, trying to calm my breathing. Then I gathered my unruly hair and knotted it up behind as best I could. I was peering into the shiny surface of a hanging pan to see what kind of a job I'd made of it when I saw his reflection as he moved behind me.

'Anna.'

I had not heard him come back downstairs, but he stood now in the kitchen doorway. I stepped towards him but he put his hands out and grasped me by the wrists – gently, this time – and held me at bay. He spoke so softly I could barely hear him. 'I don't know how to explain my behaviour there in the courtyard. But I apologize to you for it –'

'No!' I interrupted, but he let go of one wrist and placed a finger on my lips.

'I am not myself. As you know, better than anyone. You have seen how I am, these last months. I don't know how to explain it, it is beyond any words that I have to describe. But it is as if there is a tempest in my mind, and I cannot see through the murk of it. I cannot think clearly – indeed, much of the time I cannot think at all. There is only a weight in my heart, a formless dread that shapes itself into pain. And then a greater dread of more pain . . .'

I barely heard his words. I know he did not want me to do what next I did. But desire was so strong within me that I did not care. I raised my hand to his hand, where it still lay on my lips, and then I opened my mouth and brushed my tongue lightly against the tip of his finger. He groaned, and as I sucked hard upon his finger he pulled me to him with the hand that was still upon my wrist. We fell together then, and nothing, I think, could have stopped us. We had each other, wild and hard, right there upon the gritstone floor, and the pain as the rough flags grazed my flesh seemed to match the pain that was in my heart. I do not know how we got upstairs, but later we lay together on the lavender-scented bed. We were tender then, and slow, taking exquisite care for each other. Afterwards, as rain rapped lightly on the windows, we rested there, speaking softly of all the things that we had loved in our lives before the ravages of the past year. Of the Plague year itself we did not speak.

In the late afternoon, when he seemed to have fallen into a light doze, I crept from the bed, dressed, and went to feed my sheep. The rain had stopped and a light wind whispered in the wet weeds. I was forking hay from the stook, when he approached me.

'Let me do that,' he said. He took the fork and then, pausing, reached down and dusted the straw from my dress, caressing me gently as he did so. He bucked the hay with the economical motion of a practised hand. At my direction, he hauled the load out into the field and up to where the flock grazed in the shelter of a copse of rowans. Together, we made short work of spreading it. The ewes regarded us with their sweet, blank faces and then went on with the serious business of eating. He broke open a dense clump of hay, releasing a sudden scent of white clover. He lifted it and breathed deeply. When he raised his face, it was lit with a smile the like of which I hadn't seen there in more than a year. 'It smells like the summers of my boyhood,' he said. 'I should have been a farmer, you know. Perhaps now I will be.' A rain-soaked bough trembled in a sudden gust of wind, showering both of us and letting fall a drift of slick, late-turning leaves. As I shivered, he reached down and lifted a single leaf from my hair, pressed it to his lips, and kissed it. We walked back down the hill in the low light, and as we neared my cottage, he took me by the hand.

'Anna, may I lie in your bed this night?'

I nodded, and we went in, he ducking his head to pass under the low lintel. I started to build up the fire, but he stopped me. 'Tonight, I mean to serve you,' he said. He led me to the chair and draped my shawl round my shoulders, tenderly, just as I had so often in the last month tucked a warming blanket round him. He bent to the hearth, and when he had the fire crackling, he knelt before me and eased off my boots and then my hose, laying his long hand gently against the pale flesh of my thigh. 'Your feet are cold,' he said, taking both into his broad palms. He fetched the kettle from the hob then and poured warm water into a basin. He washed my feet, kneading the soles with the pressure of his thumbs. At first, I was made all uneasy by this unaccustomed tenderness. My feet are unlovely, hard, and horny from poor boots and much walking. But as he went on, caressing my cracked heels, the knots of tension in me untangled, and I gave myself up to his touch, leaning my head back against the chair and closing my eyes and letting my own hands travel through the strands of his unbound hair. After a long time, his hands stilled. I opened my eyes and met his, gazing at me. He eased me down to him then, so that I sat astride his thighs. He pushed my skirt and placket up and went into me, gentle and slow. I wrapped my legs around him and held his face between my two hands. Our eyes fixed on each other's eyes, and it seemed that we did not even blink until the warm rush of our pleasure pierced us both.

Afterwards, he lifted me back into the chair and would not let me rise to bring food. He fumbled around in my crocks and pieced together a simple plate of cheese and apples, oatcake and ale. We ate it with our hands, off the same board. I think it was the most delicious meal I had ever had. We said little to each other as we watched the fire burn, but the quiet was a companionable one – not the usual empty silence that raked my nerves raw. When we finally climbed up to my bed, we lay for a long time just gazing at each other, our hands laced tightly and our dark hair mingling on the pillow. And sometime in the early hours of the morning I took him again, slowly at first, and then with passion. I threw myself on top of him. He held my wrists and cried out with pleasure. I could feel the straw shifting in my thin pallet and the old floorboards creaking in complaint. When we finally separated, I fell into an exhausted, dream-less sleep from which, for once, I did not waken until morning.

The room was sweet with the scent of straw that had tumbled from the burst seams of my pallet. Light spilled through the diamond panes of the casement window and fell onto his long, still body. I propped myself on an elbow and gazed at him, tracing the bright angles on his chest with a fingertip. He awoke then but did not move, only watched me, the crows' feet around his eyes crinkling with pleasure. As I looked at my hand on his chest, at its ruddied, work-rough skin, I thought of Elinor's fine, pale fingers and wondered if my coarser flesh was repellent to him.

He reached for my hand then and kissed it. I pulled it back, embar-rassed by its condition, and blurted out the thought that filled my mind.

'When you lie with me,' I whispered, 'do you think of Elinor? Are you lying with her in your memory?'

'No,' he said. 'I have no such memories.'

I thought he spoke thus to be kind to me. 'You needn't say that.'

'I say it only because it is true. I never lay with Elinor.'

I pushed myself up and stared at him. His grey eyes regarded me, inscrutable as pieces of smoky glass. I grasped a corner of the sheet to cover my nakedness. He smiled slightly, reached up and pulled the cloth away again, letting his fingertips brush my bare skin.

I seized his hand and held it still. 'How can you say such a thing? You – you were three years married. You loved each other . . .'

'Yes, I loved Elinor,' he said softly. 'And that is why I never lay with her.' He sighed loudly, and the truth of it flew into my mind: in all the time I had spent near them, I had never once seen a touch pass between them.

I dropped his hand and grabbed again for the sheet to cover me. He had barely moved, but lay there upon the pallet still, his body easy as if he spoke only of the most ordinary things. He did not look at me but stared up at low rafters. His tone was patient, the tone one would use to explain something to a child. 'Anna, understand: Elinor had greater needs than those of her body. Elinor had a troubled soul. She had need of expiation, and I had to help her. Elinor, as a girl, committed a great sin, of which you could not know –'

'But I do know,' I interrupted. 'She told me of it.'

'Did she so?' he said. He turned to look at me now, his brows creasing and the grey eyes darkening. 'It seems there was much between the two of you – much that I was unaware of. More, I should say perhaps, than was fitting.'

I thought, fleetingly, that he, lying naked upon my bed, was barely in a position to comment on the fitness of my friendship with his wife. But my mind was too much troubled to linger there.

'Elinor told me of her sin. But she repented. Surely –'

'Anna. There is a great difference between repentance and atonement.' He sat up at last, his back against the rough wood wall. We faced each other now upon the pallet. I had drawn my legs up under me and pulled the sheet all round my body. I was trembling.

He raised his large hands and held them open before him, like the dishes of a scale. 'Elinor's lust caused the loss of the life of her unborn child. How do you atone for a life? An eye for an eye, the Bible says. But what, in such a case as this? What could she give in atonement for the life that, because of her actions, never could be lived? Because lust caused the sin, I deemed that she should atone by living some part of her life with her lusts unrequited. The more I could make her love me, the more her penance might weigh in the balance to equal her sin.'

'But,' I stammered, 'but I heard you, at the deathbed of Jakob Merrill, consoling that man – telling him that as God made us lustful, so he understands and forgives . . . And when you caught Albion Samweys lying with Jane Martin, you chided yourself for your harsh words to that girl –'

'Anna,' he interrupted, and his voice was flinty now. He spoke to me as if his patience waned, as if the child he instructed did not properly attend to what was being said. 'When I spoke thus to Jakob Merrill, it was in the sure knowledge that he would be dead by twilight. So what good to speak of atonement? What atonement could his ravaged body make? As for Jane Martin, had I cared for her as I cared for my Elinor, I never would have relented, but punished her, punished her, body and mind, until her soul was cleansed. Do you not see? My Elinor I *had* to be assured was cleansed, or else risk the loss of her for eternity.'

'And you?' I said in a small, strangled voice.

'Me?' He laughed. 'For myself, I took a page from the Papists. Do you not know that women are the dregs of the Devil's dunghill? Do you know how the Papists teach their celibates to master their desire? When they want a woman, they school themselves to turn their thoughts to all the vile emissions of her body. I did not allow myself to look at Elinor and see her fair face or to breathe the fresh scent of her. No! I looked at that lovely creature and made myself think of her bile and her pus. I dwelt on the sticky wax deep in her ears and the green slime in her nose and the reek of the stuff in her nightjar . . .'

'Enough!' I cried, covering my ears. I felt ill.

His body is strong, but I fear that the strength of his will far exceeds it. It can drive him to do what any normal man cannot do, for better and for worse. Believe me, I have seen this. Elinor had said this to me, many months ago. Now I knew what had been in her mind.

He was kneeling now upon the bed, the light limning his body. His voice had gained the ringing timbre of the pulpit. 'Know you not that I, the husband, am the image of God in the kingdom of the home? Was it not I who drove the whore from Eden? I turned my lust into holy fire! I burned with passion for God!'

And then he laughed, a mirthless laugh, and fell back upon the pallet. He closed his eyes and a spasm racked his face, as if he suddenly felt a great pain. His voice dropped to a hoarse whisper. 'And now it seems that there is no God, and I was wrong. In what I asked of Elinor. In what I asked of myself. For of course I did love her and desired her, no matter how hard I turned the press down upon my own feelings. Wrong in doing that, and wrong, most shockingly wrong, in what I asked of this village. Because of me, many are dead who might have saved themselves. Who was I to lead them to their doom? I thought I spoke for God. Fool. My whole life, all I have done, all I have said, all I have felt, has been based upon a lie. Untrue in everything. So now,' he said, 'I have learned at last to do as I please!'

He reached for me then, but I was quicker. I slid away from under his hand and rolled off the pallet. Blindly, I grabbed what I could of my scattered garments and fled the room, shrugging my smock over my head as I stumbled down the stairs. My only thought was to get away.

I reeled blindly towards the churchyard. I wanted Elinor. I wanted to hold her and caress her and tell her that I was sorry he had used her so. My beautiful friend, full of affection, made for love. In lying with him, I had sought to bring her closer to me. I had tried to become her, in every way that I could. Instead, in taking my pleasure from his body, I had stolen from her – stolen what should have been hers, her wedding night. I went to her tombstone and lay down upon it. When my fingers found the place where the unpractised graver had botched her inscription, that tiny indignity undammed my grief, and the sobs racked my body until the stone was slick with tears.

I was lying there, prone on her gravestone, when I heard him calling me. I did not want to see him. The face that had moved me so, the body I had desired – suddenly his whole person was repulsive to me. I slid down off the stone and into a crouch, then edged on all fours to the giant cross, whose looming bulk might hide me. I leant against it, as I had been wont to do. But the carvings no longer felt alive under my hands. I no longer thought that its maker had anything to say to me. I could hear the crunch of boots on the churchyard pathway. I ran across the lumpy grass towards the church doorway. I had not been inside since the Sunday in March when the rector had closed it to all of us. I stepped up onto the stoop, letting my hand rest on the door. The wood felt warm after the chill of the stone. I pushed, and it opened. I slipped inside, easing it gently closed behind me. A flurry of wings declared that doves had taken up residence in the belfry. And why not? No one tolled the bells anymore; nothing would disturb their roosting.

The air inside seemed stale. On the brass candlesticks near the altar, green blooms flowered. As the birds cooed and settled, the silence seeped back. I slid forward, muffling my footfalls out of the habit of reverence so long ingrained in me. I ran my hands around the old stone font, remembering the two joyful mornings when I brought the babies to have their heads wet here. Sam, scrubbed to an unaccustomed shine, had beamed so that it seemed his face might split.

Simple Sam. Sometimes I had been ashamed of the plain feelings written on his face – the uncouth laughter at childish joys, the animal way he would fumble at my body and grunt his pleasure in our bed. How I had envied Elinor! The delicacy of her husband's manner, the subtlety of his mind. How could I have understood so little? And yet how could *anyone* understand such things: that delicacy masked a most unnatural coldness; that subtle thought had twisted itself into perversion.

Wax scents, damp stone, empty pews. I pictured the faces that had filled each one. We had sat here and listened to him, and believed in him, just as Elinor had done. Trusted him to tell us what was right and good to do. Now two-thirds of those faces were gone – buried in the ground outside or scattered in the shallow pits of our extremity. I stood there, willing a prayer to form for them. But nothing came. I tried the old, rote words on my tongue. They rang much more loudly than I'd intended, meaningless as the tumble of pebbles falling down a well. 'I believe in God, the Father Almighty, Creator of Heaven and Earth . . .' My echo whispered and died amidst the dry scratching of scurrying mice.

'Do you, Anna? Do you still believe in God?'

The voice came from the Bradford pew. Elizabeth Bradford rose from where she had been kneeling, hidden from my sight by the high oaken backrest. 'My mother does. She believes in the God of wrath and vengeance, who broke the pride of Pharaoh and laid waste to Sodom and rained down torment upon Job. It is on her request that I am come here, although I doubt it will do her much good. She has been in labour since late yesterday, a full month before her time, and the surgeon gives her up; he says a woman of her age flirts with death by getting with child, and that death will surely find her this day, as she absolutely cannot be delivered. And as soon as he had pronounced himself of this grim prognostic, he mounted his horse for home.'

She sank down then into the pew and her voice turned to a child-like whisper. 'The blood, Anna. Never have I seen so much blood.' She buried her face in her hands for a long moment, then I saw her back straighten. 'Well,' she said, gathering herself as I had seen her do the day before in the rectory kitchen, 'I have done as she begged me and said her prayers for her in this so-holy, so-sacred church, sanctified by all of you, the brave beloved of God. And now I must return and listen again to her screaming.'

'I will come with you,' I said. I had seen so much death that I would try to save a life if I could. 'I have had some small experience attending at childbirths; perhaps I can help her.'

For a second, something flickered in her face, an instant of hope-fulness. But then she recalled who I was, and who she was, and the face set again into its prideful sneer. She gave a snort and smiled superciliously. 'So the housemaid knows more than the London surgeon? I think not. But come if you like. She will die in any case. And it may gratify you to bring word to Mompellion of how thor-oughly God has fulfilled his prophecies regarding my family.'

I followed behind Elizabeth Bradford, trying to tamp down the anger rising within me. At the church door I paused, looking around for the rector. There was no sign of him, so I followed Miss Bradford to where her mare was tethered and clambered up behind her. We rode up the hill to the Hall in silence.

The building was a desolate sight. Towering thistles had pushed through the stones of the driveway. The carefully clipped topiaries that lined the drive had reverted to scraggly bushes, and weeds had claimed all the formal flower beds. Miss Bradford dismounted and handed me the reins, tacitly assuming that I would stable the mare for her. Without a word, I handed them back to her and turned towards the front door of the Hall. She made a sound that was half hiss, half sigh, and walked the mare towards the stables. Even from outside the vast door, I could hear the screams within the Hall. When Miss Bradford returned, we entered, passing by the hulking shapes of the shrouded furniture and mounting the stairs to her mother's chamber.

She had not exaggerated about the blood. The very floor was slick with it, and wads of linen and napkins, muck-wet, lay all about. The girl who tended Mrs. Bradford was a stranger to me. Her eyes were wide as chargers as she groped for a fresh towel to stanch the unabated flood. Quickly, I barked out a list of my needs. 'Bring me whatever you have of broth or jellies, a little good wine, and some warm toast to sop in it, for she is in dire need of strengthening, if she is to survive the loss of so much blood. Bring me also a kettle of boiling water and a basin and whatever you can find for grease.' The girl rushed from the room as if she could not quit it fast enough.

Mrs. Bradford did not make any protest as I approached her; perhaps because she was by now too weak to waste the effort, or perhaps because she welcomed any faint hope of help in her extremity. She had stopped her screaming as soon as we had entered, and I think that she had cried out not so much of the pain as of the fear of lying so long in her own gore. She reached out weakly for her daughter, and Elizabeth ran to her and kissed her tenderly. Whatever low opinion she had of my skills, she obviously wanted to calm her mother's terrors, for she spoke in a soothing voice of how she had heard high praise of my midwifery and how all would now be well. I looked at her across the body of her mother and gave a slight shake of my head, for I did not want to mislead anyone about how desperately the matter stood. Elizabeth held my eye and nodded, implying that she knew my meaning very well.

Once I had the scalding water, I washed my hands and drew away the saturated towel between Mrs. Bradford's legs. I did not need the butter the maid had fetched, for her passage was slippery enough with the fluids flooding from her. Despite her age, her flesh had a healthy soundness, and her body seemed well set for childbirth, for though her figure was slender, the bones of her hips were amply spaced. As soon as my hands were well inside, I could feel that the door of the womb stood fully open, and I easily introduced my fingers within. The bag of waters was not yet broken, and so I tore at it with my fingernails. Mrs. Bradford gave a weak cry at this and sank back in a near faint. I worked quickly then, not wanting to lose her before I saved the child. I let my hands search out the baby's lie and found it a simple breach. Why, I wondered, had the surgeon abandoned this case as hopeless? Had he persevered here he could easily have done what I was about to attempt. It came to me then that he must have arrived here under instruction to be negligent.

The baby, being before its time, was small, and I was able to turn it with very little difficulty. I urged Elizabeth Bradford to try to revive her mother so that she might push. The woman was too weak to do much, and for a while I feared we would fail because of it. But somehow, from some deep place, she summoned up just that small bit of strength we needed, and a perfect, precious little girl eased out, alive, into my hands.

I bent my head and breathed the fresh new scent of her. I looked into her deep blue eyes and saw reflected there the dawn of my own new life. This little girl seemed to me, at that moment, answer enough to all my questions. To have saved this small, singular one – this alone seemed reason enough that I lived. I knew then that this was how I was meant to go on: away from death and towards life, from birth to birth, from seed to blossom, living my life amongst wonders.

No sooner was the cord cut and tied than Mrs. Bradford's bleeding slowed to a trickle. The afterbirth came away without strain, and she was able to sip some broth. Silently, I cursed the surgeon for abandoning this woman. Had he delivered her hours since, she would not have lain here bleeding, and two lives would surely have been saved. Now Mrs. Bradford would need a miracle to survive the loss of such a prodigious amount of blood. Still, I meant to fight for her. I told Elizabeth Bradford to ride in haste to my cottage and instructed her where she might find a flask of nettle tonic, which I deemed might strengthen her mother.

'Nettle?' She pronounced the word as if it tasted ill inside her mouth. Even in such a crisis, the woman managed to sneer. 'I'm sure I cannot find such a thing.' She placed a hand gently upon her mother's pale brow, and her hard eyes softened as she looked at that exhausted face. 'I would she have what you deem her to need, but you must go yourself, for I fear to leave my mother lest she pass away while I am gone.'

I could see the reason in that, so I consented, instructing the maid how to clean the babe and settle her at her mother's breast as soon as may be. If Mrs. Bradford were to die, as seemed more likely than not, I wanted the babe to know at least a few precious minutes of comfort there. I was halfway to the stable when I realized I was chilled right to the bone. I was still wearing nothing but the thin serge smock I'd grabbed up that morning when I'd fled Michael Mompellion. I turned, thinking to borrow Elizabeth's cloak. The kitchen door was the one closest to me, so I made for it in haste and barged inside.

Elizabeth Bradford had her back to me, but it took just less than an instant for me to grasp what she was about. She had troubled to push her fine wool sleeves up past her elbows so as not to damage her dress. A bucket filled with water stood on the bench before her and her forearms were sunk into it, her muscles tensed with the slight effort of holding the baby under. I crossed the distance between us in a stride and pushed her aside with more force than I knew I possessed. She lost her grasp on the slippery babe and fell sideways. I plunged my arms into the bucket and drew that tiny little body out and hugged her to me. The bucket teetered and fell from the bench, splashing its contents over Elizabeth Bradford's skirt. The baby was cold from the water, so I rubbed her, hard, as I would rub the life into a new lamb born on a cold night. She sputtered, blinked, and let forth a cry of outrage. She was, thank God, unharmed.

Relief gave way to a rage that broke on me so strong that I grasped up a meat hook from where it lay on the deal table and lunged at Elizabeth Bradford with the child still clutched to my breast. She rolled sideways, saving herself, and scrambled to her feet with difficulty on the water-slicked stone. Horrified at my own action, I took a step backwards from her and dropped the hook. We stared at each other, wordless.

Finally, she spoke. 'It is a bastard, born of adultery. My father will not suffer it near him.'

'That may be, you murdering bitch, but you have no right to take her life from her!'

'Do not speak to me so!'

'I will speak to you howsoever I choose!'

We were screaming over each other now, like a pair of fishwives. She raised a hand to call a halt to it.

'Do you not see?' she said, and her voice was plaintive now. 'An end to this business is my mother's only chance for a new beginning. Her life is over, otherwise. Do you think I want to kill it? My mother's child, who shares my blood? I do it only to save my mother from my father's wrath.'

'Give the baby to me,' I said. 'Give her to me, and I will raise her with love.'

She stood there, pondering, and then she shook her head. 'No. It will not do. We cannot have our family's shame flaunted in this village for all to stare at and whisper over. Nor would it be any favour to this girl to grow up in the shadow of the Hall and yet be barred from it. For word would come to her of her true origins. It always does, in these cases.'

'Well, then,' I said, cooler now and as calculating as she. 'Give me the means, and I will take her far from here, and you will have my promise never to hear a word from either of us again. You and your mother may tell whatever story you like.'

Elizabeth Bradford raised her eyebrows at this and drew her lips tight together, considering. She was silent for a long moment, and my eyes searched her face for a trace of the compassion that she showed to her mother. But there was nothing like that there. Only cold reckoning. This matter, like all matters concerning the Bradfords, would be weighed on scales that could be raised or lowered only according to the heft of strict self-interest. I could not bear the sight of that hard, lipless face any longer, so I looked down, at the baby, and tried to form a prayer for her. A single word formed in my mind.

Please.

As hard as I willed it, I could not draw up anything to follow: no formal supplication, no Bible verse, no scrap of liturgy. All of the texts and Psalms and orisons I had by rote were gone from me, erased, as surely as hard-learned words written with painful effort onto a slate can be licked away with the lazy swipe of a dampened rag. After so many unanswered prayers, I had lost the means to pray.

'Yes,' Elizabeth Bradford said at last. 'Yes, that might do very well.'

I swaddled the baby warmly, and we sat then, at Maggie Cantwell's beloved old kitchen table, and haggled over the details. It did not take us long, for I was firm about my requirements, and Elizabeth Bradford was anxious to be rid of me. When we had agreed terms, I climbed the stairs to her mother's chamber. Her colour was surprisingly good. She had drunk the broth and managed a piece of sopped bread and lay back with her eyes closed, so that I thought she had fallen asleep. But her eyes opened as I stood there, and when she saw the baby, tears brightened her swollen, bloodshot eyes. 'She yet lives!' she quavered in an exhausted voice.

'So she does, and so she shall.' I told her then what Elizabeth and I had agreed upon. She struggled up from her pillows and grabbed my forearm with her limp fingers. I thought she was going to protest, but instead she kissed my hand. 'Oh, thank you! Thank you! Bless you.' But then her eyes widened and her whispering became urgent. 'You must go, quickly, this day, before my son or his father learn that the child lives.'

She pointed then towards a coffer at the foot of her bed. Inside, in a hidden drawer, an emerald ring and necklace gleamed against dark velvet. 'Take them. Use them for her if you have the need, or give them to her when she is grown. Tell her that her mother would have loved her, if she had been allowed . . .'

She had grown pale with the exertion of all this, and I knew she would remain agitated while ever I was there with the baby. So I hurried to fashion a warm sling from one of her fine woollen shawls and nestled the baby inside it, tight against my body. I knelt then beside her bed, took her white hand, and laid it on the child's silken head. 'Know, always, that she will be cherished.'

I descended the stairs and went outside to where Elizabeth Bradford waited with the horse. The three of us rode to my cottage, the baby's small coos turning to whimpers. Once there, I handed Elizabeth a flask of nettle tonic, with instructions on how best to dose her mother. In exchange, I took from her a purse containing more gold pieces than I had ever thought to see.

The cow eyed me reproachfully when I entered her byre with my bucket. 'I'm sorry I made you wait,' I said, 'but I've good use for your milk this day.' In the cottage, remembering my own milk, watery and bluish, I skimmed off the cow's rich cream and thinned what remained with a little water. I held the babe in the crook of my arm. Her mouth was wide now, uttering the weak cries of the newborn. I stroked her soft cheek until she turned towards my finger. It was a messy business and slow. I dribbled liquid down into her mouth for as long as she would take it. She stopped crying and presently became drowsy. I laid her then on some straw by the hearth and busied myself gathering the few possessions I would take with me. There was so little left. The winter jerkin I'd made for Jamie and saved from the great Burning; a medical book of Elinor's that she and I had pored over and studied until our eyes ached. These I took for the memories. A few phials of herbals useful for infant fevers and fluxes. I remembered, with a pang, the morning in Elinor's garden when she had tried to teach me the use of feverfew, and I had been determined not to hear her. How soon, how very soon after that day had I been forced to change my thinking.

And then I put the thoughts of the past year away from me and tried to think clearly of the future. I determined to give my land and cottage to the Quaker child, Merry Wickford, so that if she chose to stay in the village she would have a home more certain than a tenant's croft and something other than a lead vein on which to build her future. The flock I would give to Mary Hadfield in exchange for her older mule, which would do to convey us from the village – to where, I did not rightly know.

I still had the piece of slate on which Elinor had taught me my letters. I drew it out and was scratching down the directions for these dispositions when the door to the cottage opened. He had not knocked, and in the sudden glare, I could not make out his face. I jumped up from my stool and put the table between us.

'Anna, don't flinch from me. I am sorry for what passed between us, sorry for everything. More than you can know. But I have not come here for that, for I know that you cannot yet be ready to listen or to hear me on these matters. And you have every right. I am come now only to help you go from here.'

I must have looked surprised at that, for he rushed on. 'I know what happened this morning at Bradford Hall – *all* of what happened there.' He raised a hand as I was about to interrupt him. 'Mrs. Bradford lives, and gains in strength. I am just come from her. I have looked hard into my heart this day. You, Anna, have recalled to me what my duties are. I do not propose to go on as I have been, feeding on the gall of my own grief. For you grieve, and yet you live, and are useful, and bring life to others. One does not have to believe, after all, to bring comfort to those who yet do. I think you have saved more than two lives this day.' He took a step, as if he meant to come round to where I stood across the table. But the look upon my face stayed him.

'Anna, I am not come here to tell you these things, for I can well imagine that you might feel you have heard enough from me already on the subject of my sentiments. I am come because I do not know if you realize that you are in danger. For you are, Anna, and gravely so. Soon, it will occur to Elizabeth Bradford that you are the one person alive who can bear witness that she attempted a murder this day. Her father already wants the baby dead: it will be a small matter to such a man to add your life to the due-bill. I want you to take Anteros' – his eyes creased for a moment in the merest hint of amusement – 'for we both know you can handle him.'

I stuttered a few words of protest, saying that I planned to ask Mary for her mule, but once again he hushed me. 'You are in need of speed. By fortunate chance I am just met with Ralf Pulfer, an ore merchant from Bakewell. He leaves this day for Liverpool port with a load of lead pigs from the Peak mines. He has agreed that if you come to Bakewell before his departure, he will escort you to Elinor's father, my patron, whose estate lies close to the route that Pulfer will be taking. I have written a letter of introduction, setting down your situation. I think it is a good choice for you, Anna, for he is a fine man, and it is a large estate. Somewhere – in the village or the farms, if not in his household service – I am sure he will find a place for you. The Bradfords will not likely think to seek you there. They will look for you on the London Road rather. But you must go now.'

And so I left my home with barely the time for a last look at the rooms that had held the sum of my life's joys, and most of its grieving. The baby did not wake when I lifted the sling once again and secured her tight to me. There was a moment of awkwardness in the garth, when Michael Mompellion reached out an arm, meaning to help me up onto Anteros. I turned away from him and mounted unassisted, preferring an ungraceful scramble to the touch of his hand.

I was halfway down the road, and going at a canter, when I realized that I could not let it end so. I turned then in the saddle and saw him standing there, his grey eyes fixed upon me. I raised my hand to him. He lifted his in return. And then Anteros reached the bend that leads to the Bakewell road, and I had to turn away and give all my attention to the downhill gallop.

Epilogue

The Waves, Like Ridges
of Plough'd Land

O nce, a long time ago, Elinor Mompellion showed me a poem
that likened the sea to a pasture. I was thrilled by it, because
it was written by a woman, and at that time I had no notion that a
woman might do such a thing as making poems. In my excitement,
I memorized it and can recite it still:

> . . . The sea's like meadows seen
> Level; its saltness makes it look as green.
> When ships thereon a slow soft pace do walk;
> Then mariners, as shepherds, sing and talk . . .

I thought it very clever then, having never seen the ocean. But
now that I spend my days gazing at the sea, it is apparent to me that
Margaret Cavendish knew nothing at all about it.

I have my own room here, where I may study and do my work
in quiet, away from the endless chattering and children's noise in the
women's quarters. This house is large and very fine, set into the wall
of the citadel, high on the mount that rises sharply behind the wide
arc of the gulf. My room is circular, with a latticed window that over-
looks the garden, and then beyond to the hivelike roofs of the lower
town, and finally to the endless expanse of sun-spangled water. From

here, I can see the boats from Venice and Marseilles – and other, farther-distant ports – unloading their glass and tin wares and loomed tapestries and taking on their return freight of gold dust, ostrich feathers, ivory, and, sometimes, that saddest of all cargoes; the chained lines of tall Africans, destined to be slaves. I pity them their terrible journey, and wish them, at least, gentle winds.

For myself, I do not expect to travel anywhere ever again. But if I do, I am determined that it shall not be by sea. The waves that carried me away from England were not the even, furrowlike swells that Margaret Cavendish described in her poem. They were jagged crags from the landscape of a nightmare. Ravines one instant, soaring cliffs the next, not rooted in the earth but tossing and leaping and never still. For days and nights our ship plunged down their faces as a child's sledge skids wildly on an icy slope. As the timbers groaned and the mariners cursed at rending sails and fraying haulyards, I breathed the stink of tar and vomit and fully expected to die. Indeed, I was so ill that very often I wished to do so. It was only the thought of the child, and my determination to keep her alive, that gave me the will to continue.

But I do not mean to dwell on the great difficulties through which we are got hither. Only to say, in short, that Anteros carried me easily to Bakewell, where I hired a wet nurse for the baby and we left with Mr. Pulfer and his load of ore. But when we came to the turn that would have led us to Elinor's childhood home, I drew out Michael Mompellion's letter of introduction, tore it into a dozen small pieces, and watched the wind carry them away. I told Mr. Pulfer that I would not trouble him to escort us there after all but would carry on with him instead for the port. I do not rightly know, even now, what made me so headstrong in this, but it seemed good to me then to sever every tie that bound me to my old life. Suddenly, and very clearly, I knew that I did not want to walk each day in yet another place where

298

Elinor had walked. For I was not Elinor, after all, but Anna. It was time to seek a place where the child and I together might make something entirely new.

I bespoke a room at a portside inn, and in the following days, there were many times that I rued my rashness, for it proved no simple matter to decide what course to follow. I barely slept during that time. For our room was hard alongside the tower of a bell that tolled the hours, and every stroke only helped me keep count of the time I had lain wakeful and worrying about our future. Just before dawn, when I might have been exhausted enough for sleep, the gulls would awaken and scream in the sky as if the world were ending at sunrise.

In the end, I did not make the choice so much as have it made for me. The innkeeper, who seemed a decent man, came pounding on my door just as the seagulls had begun their clamouring chorus. He was in a great state of agitation, saying that a young gentleman had been asking my whereabouts all over the town. 'Don't be angry at this, now, but 'e's noising it all about that you've stolen jewels from 'is family – I didn't credit it, mind; as if you'd be 'ere wearin' your own name if you was a thief. And another odd thing: it was your baby he kept pounding on and on about. 'E seemed much keener on that than the matter of the jewels. I don't like to mind my guest's business, Mistress, but he's an unpleasant piece o' work, and if you known your'n, you'll be taking yer chances on the next ship, whatever it be and wherever it be bound.'

As it happened, and fittingly enough, I suppose, a carrack loaded with Peak-mines pigs was the only ship sailing on that morning's tide, bound for the great glassmakers of Venice. I knew nothing of that watery city, and the decrepit carrack looming alongside the dock looked scarcely seaworthy. But I had, as I have said, no choice. So I paid out some of the Bradfords' gold for a cuddy and more to quiet the wet nurse, who wailed that she had not bargained on a sea voyage. And thus I travelled away from my home atop a hold brimming with the very ore my feet had trodden over all my lifetime. I soon lost count of the days and nights as the babe and I rocked together in that gimballed bed, and I thought that our story would end there, with the glassy green water cracking through the timbers and carrying us down into the deep.

And then one morning I awoke to a smooth sea and warm air spiced with cardamom. I gathered up the baby and went on deck. I will never forget the dazzle of the sunlight, glinting off the white walls and the golden domes, or the way the city spilled down the mountain and embraced its wide blue harbour. I asked the captain what the place was, and he told me we were come to the port of Oran, home of the Andalus Arabs.

I had Elinor's book in my luggage, one of the few belongings I had brought with me. It was her precious final volume from Avicenna's *Canon of Medicine.* I had packed it, despite its weight, as a memory of her and the work we'd tried to accomplish together. One day, I thought, I will learn to read the Latin and memorize everything that great book contains. Elinor and I had marvelled that an infidel of long ago should have owned such a wonderful amount of knowledge. I thought then of all that the Musalman doctors might have discovered since it was written, and suddenly it seemed to me that I had been brought to this sunlit city so that I might learn more of the craft that had become my vocation. I paid off the nurse, providing for her return passage, reasoning that I could find another in so large a city.

The ship's captain tried to dissuade me from disembarking, talking of Barbary pirates and uncouth Spanish exiles. But when he saw I was fixed in my purpose, he kindly assisted me. The captain knew of Ahmed Bey, which was not strange, since his writings and his travels have made him the most famous doctor in Barbary. What was astonishing, to me at least, given my circumstances and condition, was the speed with which the Bey reached his decision to take me in. Later, when we knew each other better, he told me that he had just come from noon prayer, at which he had called on Allah to take pity on a tired old man and send him some assistance. Then, he had entered the women's quarters and found me, sipping coffee with his wives.

I am one of his wives now, in name if not in flesh. He said it was the only way he could bring me into his household that would win acceptance here. Since it was obvious that I was not a virgin, the mullah needed no male guardian to give consent for me, and so the rite was simply accomplished. We have spoken much since then about faith: the adamantine one by which the doctor measures every moment of his day, and that flimsy, tattered thing that is the remnant of my own belief. I see it like the faded threads of a banner on a battlement, shot-shredded, and if it once bore a device, none could now say what it might have been. I have told Ahmed Bey that I cannot say that I have faith anymore. Hope, perhaps. We have agreed that it will do, for now.

I think that the Bey is the wisest and kindest man I have ever known. Certainly he is the gentlest and the sweetest-spoken. He was flattering about the skills with which I came to him, but I have learnt so much from him in the years since that I now understand it was only the honey-tongued way of his people to say so. Ahmed Bey's medicine does not rely upon tearing at the body with sharp probes and blistering cups like the barber-surgeons at home. His way is to strengthen and nourish, all the time studying the workings of the well body and the nature of disease: how it spreads, and to whom, and how its course runs like or different in this person and in that.

I think that by the time I arrived here he had reached a point of despair, for the Musalmans' wives are so strictly kept that they quail at the sight of a strange man at their sickbeds, and he had anguished for many years over the numbers whose husbands would see them die rather than send for his assistance. And so I think he would have taken any woman of normal intelligence who was willing to learn from him. I have repaid his trust by bringing many safely through their labours and showing them ways to preserve their health and that of their children. As I continue to study and learn, I hope to accomplish a worthy life's work here. I am reading Avicenna now, or Ibn Sīnā, as I have correctly learned to call him. I am reading his writings not in Latin, as I had imagined, but in Arabic.

It has taken my eyes a long time to get used to the brightness of this place. For one who lived so long in a misty world, the vividness here can sear the sight. There are colours that I do not even know how to describe to one who has not seen them. Who can say what colour an orange is, who has not seen the thing itself? And the fruits called persimmons that hang on the branches beyond my window; sometimes, they glow so against the blue sky that I would say they are a colour like to new-beaten copper, flaring in sunlight. Other times their hue seems more of a golden pink, glowing faintly like the cheeks of Ahmed Bey's grandchildren when they run and tumble in the women's courtyard.

We have an abundance here of every vivid hue, except green. There is no grass, and the leaves of the palms are coated with a fine sand that covers them all in its dusty yellow mantle. I think it is green, perhaps, that I miss more than any other thing. One day, in Ahmed Bey's great library, I found a large book bound in fine-grained leather, dyed exactly to the colour of the summer pastures at home. I carried the book here to my room and propped it on my table, where my eyes could rest on it. I did not realize it was the Bey's sacred text, which unbelievers are not to lay a hand upon. It was the only time in these three years that he spoke harshly to me. He apologized for it, after I explained, and sent me a silken carpet figured all over with the great tree that the Arabs call *Anisa*, Tree of Life. Its twining leaves and branches glow greener than anything that even Elinor could grow, in that beautiful garden of our past.

Like my eyes, my ears, too, have had to learn the different way of being in this place. From fearing silence, I have learned to long for it. For it is noisy here, night and day. The streets teem with people, and the cries of the peddlers are incessant. It is sunset now, and the summons of prayer callers ring, urgent and soulful, from scores of high minarets. The hour after the sunset prayer is my favourite time to walk in the city, for the air has begun to cool and the pace becomes less hectic. Many of the women know me now and greet me as I go about the streets. As is the way of their culture, they know me by the name of my firstborn, and so here I am Anna Frith no longer, but *Umm Jam-ee* – mother of Jamie. It pleases me to have my little boy remembered so.

It took me a long time to name the Bradfords' baby. I did not call her anything during that terrible sea voyage, I think because I was sure we would not survive it. When we came here, Ahmed Bey suggested Aisha, which is his word for 'life.' Later, I learned that the women in the market also use it as their word for bread. It is an apt name, for she sustained me.

She is waiting for me in the women's courtyard, her white *haik* dragging in the dust as she skips towards me, straight through the small garden where Maryam, Ahmed Bey's eldest wife, cultivates herbs to flavour her tea. The air is suddenly tangy with the fragrance of crushed mint and lemon thyme. Maryam unleashes a torrent of scolding, but her tattooed face is crinkled with gentle amusement. I smile at the old woman and salaam, reaching for my own veil where it hangs, limp and ready, on a peg by the street door.

I look round then for the other one. She is hiding behind the blue-tiled fountain. Maryam inclines her head to show me where. I pretend I have not seen her and walk right past, calling her name. I turn swiftly and snatch her up into my arms. She gurgles with delight, her small soft hands patting my cheeks as she plants her wet kisses on my face.

I birthed her here, in the harem. Ahmed Bey helped in her delivery, but I did not need his assistance in her naming. When I toss the little *haik* over her head, she pulls it expertly into place so that all I can see are her wide grey eyes. She has her father's eyes.

We wave good-bye to Maryam and push open the heavy teak door. The warm air catches our veils and sends them billowing behind us. Aisha grabs one hand. Elinor clasps the other, and together we plunge into the jostling swarm of our city.

Afterword

This book is a work of fiction inspired by the true story of the villagers of Eyam, Derbyshire.

I first visited Eyam (pronounced 'eem') quite by chance in the summer of 1990. I was based in London then, working as Middle East correspondent for *The Wall Street Journal*. Between assignments in hot, troubled places like Gaza and Baghdad, I tried to find respite in the English countryside. It was on one of these hikes – or rambles, as the English euphoniously call them – that I came upon an intriguing finger post, pointing the way to the PLAGUE VILLAGE. There, I found the history of the villagers' ordeal, and their extraordinary decision, set out in a display in the parish church of Saint Lawrence.

The account was so touching and terrible that it took root in my imagination. For the next few years, as I reported the news of modern tragedies in places such as Bosnia and Somalia, my thoughts often returned to Eyam, and I began to realize that it was this story, above all others, I longed to tell. That feeling only became stronger when I went to live in a rural Virginia village about the same size as Eyam. There, the story of the quarantine and its costs grew even more vivid to me. What would it be like, I wondered, to make such a choice and to find that, in consequence, two-thirds of your neighbours were dead within a year? How would faith, relationships, and social order survive?

The summer before last, I returned to Eyam to do further historical research and refresh my memory of the Peak District's austere and beautiful landscape. I spent time with Eyam's local historian, John G. Clifford, author of the informative *Eyam Plague 1665–1666*. I visited the small but expertly curated village museum. William Styron once wrote that the historical novelist works best if fed on 'short rations' by the factual record. Much has been written about Eyam – books, plays, even an opera – yet facts remain scant. In Eyam, debate continues on issues such as what the village population was before the plague, how the infection got there, how many died. But at the same time, there is a wealth of anecdote handed down over the years, and from this I've borrowed heavily: the role of flea-ridden cloth as the possible plague vector; the greedy grave digger who buried a man alive; the prescient cockerel who knew when it was safe to come home.

For the rest, I delved into seventeenth-century medical texts, journals, sermons, and social histories. My library now includes tomes such as *A History of Lead Mining in the Pennines*, which is not a volume I ever expected to own. Anys Gowdie's 'confession' is adapted from the account of a Scottish witch trial included in Richard Zacks's lively collection of documents on sexuality, *History Laid Bare*. (The Gowdie confession differs from the many similar ones extracted under torture in that the accused woman claimed, most eloquently, to have enjoyed sex with the devil. The more standard line was that Satan was a lousy lover.)

While I have used some real names of Eyam villagers, I have done so only when my account does not press far beyond the known detail of their lives. Where I have invented, I have altered or created names to indicate this. Thus, Michael Mompellion reflects the true rector of Eyam, the heroic and saintly William Mompesson, only in the admirable aspects of his character and deeds. The darker side I have given his fictional counterpart is entirely imagined. William Mompesson had two children with his wife, Catherine, and sent them away from Eyam before the quarantine was agreed upon. Catherine chose to stay and help the sick, and died herself of plague. After her death, William Mompesson included a line in one of his letters: 'My maid continued in health; which was a blessing, for had she quailed, I should have been ill set. . . .' Trying to imagine who this woman could have been, how she may have lived, and what she might have felt provided the voice for my novel.

The book's title came as I tried to listen to words as Anna might have heard them, with all their attendant religious echoes. To a secular mind like mine, it always seemed incongruous that Dryden should have chosen the Latin phrase 'annus mirabilis' to describe that terrible year of 1666, marked by plague, the Great Fire, and the war with the Dutch. But Anna surely would have believed that 'God works in mysterious ways his wonders to perform.' She also would have been familiar with God's words to Moses: 'Thou shalt do my wonders' – which included calling down upon the Egyptians the first plague in recorded human history.

Like her seventeenth-century contemporaries, Anna didn't know what plague was or how it spread. *Yersinia pestis* – Bubonic plague, Black Death, pest – is an overwhelming infection by bacteria. The plague sores – buboes – are lymph nodes that have been turned into necrotic tissue. Within a day or two, vast numbers of bacteria find their way into the blood stream, resulting in fever, haemorrhage and thrombosis.

While rat death has been observed to accompany plague since ancient times, it wasn't until 1898 that a scientist named Simond discovered that fleas that had fed on infected rats were responsible for transmitting the disease to humans in 90% of cases. (Rarely, the bacillus enters the victim's lungs and is passed on to others in airborne droplets, or is contracted by direct infection of cuts while handling an infected rodent.) In 1666, the afflicted missed the mark, believing cats and dogs might be spreading the disease. The resulting slaughter of these animals eliminated rat predators and may have prolonged the pandemic.

Plague still exists: the World Health Organisation reports up to 3,000 cases a year. It is no longer a mass killer because of antibiotics.

Among the many books and individuals I have consulted for help, I would like especially to thank Amy Huberman for her diligent unearthing of seventeenth-century medical texts; Anne Ashley McCaig for advice on lambing and literature; Raymond Rush, for the fascinating farming lore in his *Countrywise* collection of articles; Amanda Levick and Lara Warner, whose help was invaluable; and Philip Benedict, for insight into the minds and libraries of seventeenth-century clergy. I would also like to thank my agent, the incomparable Kris Dahl. From early readers – Darleen Bungey, Caroline Davidson, Brian Hall, the Horwitz quartet of Elinor, Joshua, Norman and Tony, Bill Powers, Martha Sherrill, and Graham Thorburn – I received invaluable advice on everything from Restoration poetry to *Yersinia pestis*. For the precision of her blue pencil, I am indebted to Lisa R. Lester. For his insight, and his walking boots, I am grateful to my British editor Clive Priddle. To Susan Petersen Kennedy, who believed in the book, and Molly Stern, who helped shape it, I also owe a great debt. And to my mother, Gloria, a lifelong one. Thank you all.